PRAISE FOR MARK MORRIS
AND *THE IMMACULATE*!

"Skillfully constructed, with a mind-boggling twist."
—*The Times* (London)

"Easily Mark Morris's best novel so far. A real contribution to the literature of the ghostly."
—Ramsey Campbell

"Mark Morris is one of the finest horror writers at work today."
—Clive Barker

"Fast gaining a reputation as the most stunningly original dark fantasist working in Britain today."
—*Starburst Magazine*

IMPOSSIBLE

When Gail returned she found him sitting bolt upright, eyes squeezed tightly shut, hands clutching the edge of the table as if his life depended on it.

"Jack?" she said tentatively.

Without opening his eyes, he asked in a low, urgent voice, "Has he gone?"

"Has who gone?" Gail said, looking around.

"My father."

"What?" She looked confused.

"My father. Did you see him? He was standing out there, in the street. Looking at me."

Gail followed Jack's gaze. She was silent for a long moment. Eventually, in a guarded voice, she said, "What do you mean, Jack—he was standing out there?"

"He was there. In the street. Beneath that light."

Gail crouched beside him, took his face in her hands and turned him toward her. "Jack, I don't know what you're talking about. Don't say things like that."

"Like what?"

"About your father. You can't have seen him, can you? He's dead. You know that."

Jack stared back at her, his face and voice suddenly becoming calm. "Yes, I do. I do know he's dead. But I still saw him."

THE
IMMACULATE

MARK MORRIS

LEISURE BOOKS NEW YORK CITY

A LEISURE BOOK®

February 2006

Published by

Dorchester Publishing Co., Inc.
200 Madison Avenue
New York, NY 10016

ISBN 0-8439-5670-4

Visit us on the web at www.dorchesterpub.com.

THE
IMMACULATE

Prologue

1970

It was October 10th, still three weeks shy of Halloween, but to the people of Beckford it must have seemed that the ghouls had come early that year. The storm began as a mutter of wind in the treetops, a mischievous tugging of skirt hems, a tossing of litter through the grey streets. Above the Pennines the sky was the colour of dirty sheets, bestowing so little light that lamps burned in many houses throughout the day. By mid-afternoon the wind was stronger, rattling the windows of the local primary school where children sat huddled in the warmth, distracted by newspapers that wheeled about the playground in a mad game of chase. In the village itself, shoppers leaned into the wind, hair streaming behind them; the awning over the butcher's shop was flipped inside out, then torn from its metal framework. The Union Jack that flew above the village's only hotel, The Connaught, cracked like a whip, as though to cow the smaller buildings below.

In the home of Terry and Alice Stone the coming of the storm went largely unnoticed. Their house, built of the

rough local sandstone, was situated over two miles from
the centre of the village and some four hundred yards
from their nearest neighbours, the Butterworths of Daisy
Lane Farm. Daisy Lane was a bumpy track of hard-packed
earth that ran past the front of the house and was bordered by dry-stone walls and surrounded by fields and
clumps of encroaching woodland. Some parts of Daisy
Lane were so narrow that two cars could not pass; Terry
Stone had once witnessed a fist fight between two drivers,
each of whom had stubbornly refused to reverse. He
stood now in the kitchen of his home, rocking back and
forth on the creaky floorboard before the sink. His hands,
the fingernails dirt-encrusted, clutched the rim of the
sink, above which a window afforded a view from the
back of the house. Terry stared at the view without seeing
it, his gaze skating over the cobbled yard and the patch of
scrubland from which, some two hundred yards distant,
rose the dense mass of trees that marked the boundary of
Beckford Woods. The trees were creaking and swaying as
if in fury, the wind creating a tidal wave of sound as it
rushed through the leaves. But Terry was aware only of
the floorboard protesting rhythmically beneath his
weight. Beyond that, silence.

   He stopped rocking and looked up at the ceiling, as if
hoping his gaze would penetrate the plaster and then the
floorboards of the room above. He had not heard his wife
cry out for a while now. Perhaps, for the time being, her
contractions had eased. He looked at the clock on the
wall, of which the ticking was so much a part of his life
that he had to make a real effort to hear it, and saw that it
was inching toward six. Almost an hour before, Alice, her
belly huge, had ascended the wooden stairs to her bed,
goaded by her elder sister, Georgina, who had told her it
was the best place for her despite the obstacle of the
steps. Usually Georgina's brisk manner irritated Terry, but
just this once he was grateful for it. He had called Dr.

Travis' surgery only to be informed that the doctor was out making housecalls and asked if he could possibly take his wife to the hospital in Leeds fifteen miles away.

"Me wife's having her baby at home," Terry had told the nurse or the secretary or whoever it was. "The doctor said that'd be all right."

"In that case," said the woman, "I'll try to contact him for you. I'm sure he'll be there as soon as he can."

Terry had thanked her and put the phone down, then had wandered aimlessly from room to room on the ground floor, listening for sounds from upstairs. He had picked up objects, toyed with them a moment, then put them down again; he had sat in his armchair and stood up almost immediately; he had looked at the newspaper, on which there were so many meaningless black squiggles; he had poured himself a glass of milk and left it untouched on the kitchen table.

Finally he had settled, if settled was the word, on the creaky floorboard before the kitchen sink. The storm was making the day prematurely dark but he didn't notice it. The sound of the wind echoed his own raging thoughts but he didn't notice that, either.

The minutes ticked by and still nothing happened. At last Terry left his place by the sink and called the surgery once more. He was told that Dr. Travis had been informed of the situation and would be with the Stones as soon as possible. Terry was relieved, but when another twenty minutes passed and still the doctor had not arrived, he began to get agitated again. He considered calling an ambulance to take his wife to the hospital, but then decided against it. Alice had been adamant that she would have her baby at home, and at least Georgina was with her, who was more than capable in a crisis. Besides, Terry reasoned, his wife was not ill, was she? She was simply having a baby. It was a natural process, life-*giving*, not life-threatening. Women had babies all the time—in mud huts in the jungle, in tents in the desert, in fields and cars and barns—and most of them survived.

Most but not all, said a little voice inside his head, and Terry's stomach clenched as if he too was suffering birth pangs. It was no good. He couldn't stand here hour after hour worrying himself to death. He had to feel he was doing something, however bloody pointless it might be.

He stomped to the kitchen, snatched his old jacket from its peg on the back door, then made for the hallway, arms struggling to fill their tunnels of cloth. His hands emerged from the cuffs like funnel-web spiders and he yanked his collar straight. As he clodded along the narrow, dingy hallway toward the front door, there was a creak on the stairs to his left and the thumps of descending footsteps. Georgina's sleeves were rolled to her elbows and her face was red; she looked as though she'd been baking. "Where are you going?" she demanded as if Terry were a schoolboy sneaking out to play before he'd finished his homework.

He felt the familiar tightening in his throat and temples. "I'm off to see what's bloody going on. Me wife's having a baby and nobody seems to give a toss except me . . . and you, of course," he added grudgingly.

She gave a brusque nod and continued to descend. "Well, if that doctor doesn't come soon he's going to miss all the fun."

Terry stared at her. "It won't be that soon, will it?"

Her expression softened at the anxiety in his voice. "No, pet, I shouldn't think so. She's quiet at the moment. Could be hours yet." She rounded the post at the foot of the stairs, hand squeaking around the polished carved acorn on top of it. "Don't worry," she said, touching his arm with her other hand. "She'll be fine, you'll see."

Terry nodded, unconvinced. Georgina gave his arm a final squeeze, then pushed past him. "What have you been doing, sitting in the dark?" she exclaimed as she entered the kitchen. She glowered at the leaden sky and switched on the lights, instantly darkening the sky still further.

"I'll be off then," Terry said, trying to sound as if his intentions were not purposeless. He left Georgina filling a bowl with hot water and opened the front door.

The wind almost ripped it from his grasp. Terry flinched, screwing up his eyes, cursing as he struggled to close it again. He heard Georgina's voice, a wordless thread of annoyance in the twisting swathes of wind, and knew instinctively that she was exhorting him to close the door.

"What do you think I'm trying to do, you silly cow?" he muttered. His words were snatched from his lips and carried howlingly away. The wind sounded crazed and triumphant, as though celebrating its release from some asylum. Swirling autumn leaves speckled Terry's vision like ticker tape.

At last he won his battle with the door. He leaned against the heavy wood for a moment, breathless. When he exerted himself like this he could taste the accumulation of smoke at the back of his throat, could not help but imagine his lungs struggling to work beneath their coating of tar. Terry's father had died of lung cancer five years before, at the age of sixty, his grandfather of the same disease at the age of sixty-two. After his father's death Terry had tried to stop smoking, but had been only partially successful. He had not smoked yet today, which was a miracle considering how tense he felt, but he did not think his abstinence would last. He turned from the door to face Daisy Lane, and told himself, as always, that the law of averages would protect him. The likelihood of three successive lung cancer deaths in the same family must be pretty minute.

When he moved from the protection of the house the wind came at him again, almost bowling him over. "Bloody hell," he exclaimed, as if at a boisterous dog. The flowers in the small front garden that his wife had tended so lovingly were squashed flat. The grass on the hills ap-

peared to turn different shades of green as the wind ca-
vorted through it.

Terry kept his head down, and so at first thought the
dark smudge moving along Daisy Lane in his direction
was some article of clothing propelled by the wind. Then
a voice calling his name reached him, and he looked up to
see Martin Butterworth, eldest of the three Butterworth
sons, clumping towards him, hand raised. The Butterworths were all blond-haired, red-cheeked and built like
brick shithouses. The muscularity of their youth, however,
had a tendency to decline into obesity as the years progressed. Even so, old man Butterworth, with his four
chins and a belly larger than Alice's, still possessed fear-
some strength. Though Terry had never seen him do it,
Butterworth senior was reputed to be able to sling fully
grown cows across his shoulders and carry them on his
back with no trouble at all.

Terry raised his hand in response, though did not speak
until he and Martin were a few feet apart. "Hello, Martin,
how's it going?" he yelled then, hoping that his greeting
would not inspire one of Martin's interminable monologues,
for which he was renowned. Butterworth's frown, though,
suggested that he had more pressing matters on his mind.

"I was just comin' to see you," he said.

"Oh, yes?"

"There's a tree down up yonder. A big 'un, blockin' the
road. The doc's there. He says your wife's havin' a bairn."

"That's right."

"Aye, well, he's havin' to walk down. He says to tell you
he won't be long."

Terry grinned in relief. "Thanks, Martin. How long exactly, do you know?"

Martin considered, wide face childlike in its solemnity.
"I reckon the tree's about half a mile up the road. I ran all
the way 'ere, but the doc can only walk slowly on account
of his arthritis. He sent me on ahead 'cause he thought

you might be worried. He'll probably be . . . ten minutes or so."

"Thanks again, Martin," Terry said. He patted Butterworth's arm, which felt solid as a tree-branch. "Do you want to come back to the house? Have a cup of tea or something?"

"No, I'll be gettin' off. The beasts are restless. There's a bugger of a storm comin', I reckon."

"Okay. Well, I'll see you around."

"Aye. Good luck wi' the bairn."

Terry watched Martin stomp away, then turned and headed back to the house. The sky was now so dark that the building was almost in silhouette. The thrashing woods beyond it reminded Terry of westerns he had seen, the trees like the black flurry of Indians on the horizon. Terry's imagination had been largely stifled by his father, and when it occasionally resurfaced, such as now, he couldn't help but feel vaguely ashamed. He remembered the beating he had received at the age of nine or ten when his father had discovered his collection of comics, which he'd secreted under his bed. But worse than the weals left by the strap had been the sight of the comics being fed one by one into the fire, their fabulous, lurid images shrivelling to black ash. After the burning his father had sat Terry down and assured him that in the long run he would be thankful that his mind had been saved from poisoning. This sort of rubbish was written by dropouts and "poofters" and possibly even Nazis who had fled to America after the war.

As soon as Terry re-entered the house he knew that something was wrong. Five minutes ago Georgina had said that Alice was quiet, yet nevertheless there was something, some thrum of tension in the air, that convinced him otherwise. Hoping he was simply being overanxious, he strode to the foot of the stairs, hand sweaty on the banister rail. "Hello," he called. "Georgina, it's me. The doctor's on his way."

There was a moment of silence, then the shuffle of

movement and the sound of a door opening. Georgina's creaking footsteps were followed two seconds later by the woman herself. The expression on her face seemed to confirm Terry's fears; suddenly there was a large rock in his stomach, a smaller one in his throat. He stared up at her, unable to speak. She snapped, "How long will he be? Where is he now?"

Hesitantly Terry ascended two steps. His legs felt disturbingly weak. He tried to swallow his panic and croaked, "What's wrong?"

"Where's the doctor? I need him here now. I can't handle this by myself."

"Handle what?" Terry said, then when she looked impatient, "There's a tree down half a mile up the road. Travis is having to walk here. Shouldn't be no more than ten minutes." His feeble legs lifted him another step. "Georgina, what's wrong with Alice?"

Some of the anger left her face and was replaced by worry. "I don't know," she admitted. "The contractions started again suddenly. She's in a lot of pain and she's losing too much blood."

"Too much? What do you mean, too much?"

"Come up, Terry. She needs you. Maybe you can calm her."

He ascended like a marionette, feeling as if a cold fever were throbbing in his veins. Though desperately anxious, he felt strangely disembodied. When he was barely halfway up the stairs Georgina turned and clumped back to the bedroom he shared with his wife, the house creaking under her weight. He heard his sister-in-law making *shushing* noises, uttering soothing words. Beneath that was a series of tiny whimpers and gasps that terrified him; it sounded as if his wife had gone beyond normal pain, that her agony was now so acute it would not even allow her to scream. He did not realise he was biting his lip until he tasted blood in his mouth. Even then, though, he tried to tell himself that Georgina was exaggerating. The doctor would arrive and tell him everything was normal, that the blood and pain were just part of the process, that there was nothing to worry about.

He crossed the landing and entered the bedroom. Georgina had tried to clean up much of the blood, though its vividness on the sheets and on his wife's swollen body still seemed to shout at him. On the floor was a bowl that had previously contained warm water but which now contained blood. How many pints were there in the human body? Eight, wasn't it? A gallon? How much had his wife lost?

The woman on the bed did not look like Alice. Alice had rosy cheeks and sparkling blue eyes and thick chestnut hair. This woman had damp white flesh, lank colourless hair, tendrils of which adhered to her face, and watery eyes sunk in darkened sockets. When she turned her head towards him it seemed something invisible was trying to prevent her from doing so. Her lips, barely pink, struggled open and she whispered his name.

"Alice," Terry half-sobbed and staggered to the bed. He fell on his knees beside it, and groped for his wife's limp hand. When he squeezed she reciprocated feebly and tried to smile, but her expression was superseded by a grimace of pain. Her neck arched and she pushed her shoulders and heels into the mattress. Her clenched teeth parted to release a whimper, and Georgina moved forward to mop up more blood.

"Alice," Terry whispered again. "*Shhh*, it's all right. Everything will be fine." Though they appeared not to be doing so, Terry hoped his words were providing some comfort. They were all he had to offer his wife. He felt so desperate, so helpless. If he owned a car he could have driven down and fetched the doctor himself. He said to Georgina, "Isn't there something more I can do?"

"You're doing enough," she told him, picking up the

bowl. She moved from the room to empty it. Terry hoped it was only the first she'd emptied.

Alone with his wife he felt strangely uncomfortable, tongue-tied. He tried to smile but it was an effort. He did not think she was even looking at him. Her head was turned in his direction and her eyes were half-open, but they seemed to be focusing inward, perhaps concentrating on some small inner part of herself that was free from pain. Terry squeezed her hand again and felt the responding pressure of her fingers. He whispered, "Don't worry, Alice, the doctor will be here soon." Her only reply was a twitch of the lips, though he was not sure whether this was an attempted smile or another spasm of pain. His head jerked up as stones clattered against the window from outside. It took him a few moments to realise they were not stones but rain.

Within seconds it was falling in earnest. The sky was almost black with clouds, an army which had been gathering all day and had now been given the order to disgorge its artillery. The first flurry of drops was followed by the minutest pause, then a growl of thunder and lightning harsh as a flash bulb precipitated a far stronger and more sustained assault. Terry shivered, though only at the thought of being out there in the cold and not because he was cold himself. Every time lightning flashed, the lamp by his wife's bedside flickered as if in feeble imitation. He drew closer to Alice, struck by the melodrama of the scene despite his anxiety.

Georgina re-entered the room, the bowl now full of clear, steaming water. She glanced at the window, the glass of which seemed to be alive and ever-changing, then put the bowl down and drew the curtains closed. The screeching wind, the lashing rain, the rattling windows seemed impenetrable; Terry felt more isolated than ever before in his life. He pictured Dr. Travis hobbling along Daisy Lane, which this rain would reduce to a river of mud. Surely the old man was no match for these conditions. Terry imagined the wind picking him up like a scrap of litter and carrying him away.

His stomach clenched like a fist as Alice cried out again and more blood gleamed on her skin and spread across the sheets. Her legs trembled and jerked. The hand holding his tightened with painful suddenness; her nails dug into his flesh and raised tiny crescents of blood. "Alice," he said, "Alice," as if the sound of her name could stem the vivid flow from between her legs. Her lips were curled back, bubbles of spittle frothing up between her teeth. Her throat worked as whimpers of pain escaped her.

"Alice," he said again, "hang on, love, the doctor will be here soon." To himself he sounded like a broken record, offering the same meaningless platitudes over and over. He looked at Georgina. "Where the bloody hell is he?"

She glanced briefly at him and scowled, but said nothing. Terry shook his head. "Maybe I should go look for him. In this weather—"

"He'll be here," Georgina cut in firmly.

"But he's taking so long. Doesn't he realise—"

"*He'll be here,*" she almost hissed.

Terry glared at her, but lowered his gaze before she did. He lifted his wife's hand and kissed it gently. It was clammy as a fish. His knees were beginning to ache from kneeling; pins and needles tingled in his feet. "I'm just going to stand up a minute," he told Alice. "I'm not leaving the room. I'll be here if you need me."

Alice made no response, though Terry believed—or liked to believe—that she had heard him. He stood up and stamped his feet, wooden floorboards booming hollowly beneath the thin carpet. He crossed to the window, pulled the corner of the curtain back, stooped and peered out. This room was positioned at the front of the house, and afforded a view of the garden, Daisy Lane, and the fields beyond. At the moment, however, Terry could see little of this. The storm clouds had clotted so thickly that the sky was black as night. Rain, spattering the glass, streaming in rivulets down it, further fractured what little definition there may have been. Dry-stone walls were merely blurred black lines separating fields of dingy grey smog. Daisy Lane was like a crevasse filled with solid, unmoving darkness.

He pictured Travis again, trudging up the lane, head bowed grimly against the rain and wind. He had known the doctor all his life and took some comfort from the knowledge that he was blunt, pigheaded, determined. However, he was also physically frail; he could only walk slowly, sometimes needing the aid of a stick. And in these conditions . . . Terry allowed the curtain to fall back. This time he would not allow Georgina to intimidate him. He was going to look for the old man.

He braced himself to tell her this, but was saved from doing so by the sound of pounding from downstairs. "At last!" he exclaimed. He took the stairs two at a time and tugged the door open. The wind added its weight to the heavy wood once more, but this time he was ready for it and stood firm. The old man on the doorstep looked scoured, thrashed by the elements. Terry ushered him in, then wrestled the door closed.

"Doctor! Thank God you're here!" Terry exclaimed, though in truth the frail, slightly hunched figure did not inspire confidence. Travis' mouth hung open, his breath wheezing from it; his eyes were thinly slitted as though the rain had pressed his eyelids closed. His skin and hair and clothes were drenched; he dripped like a snowman before a raging fire. He put down what appeared to be a fat briefcase and with a hand that trembled alarmingly pulled a large blue handkerchief from his pocket and slowly wiped his face.

"Here, let me take that," Terry said, and relieved the unresisting doctor of the Gladstone bag he held in his other hand. Travis had had this bag for as long as Terry could remember. It was made of black leather, now so scuffed and old it was almost the consistency of cloth. It had probably once had a definite shape, but now it was lumpy and squashy as an old turnip.

Travis' lips struggled without success for a moment until finally he enquired, "Do you . . . have a towel I could use?"

"Yes, I . . . but please, doctor, my wife . . . she's very ill."

"A towel, if you don't mind, Terry. I'm no use to anyone in this state."

Flustered, Terry hurried to the kitchen, grabbed a towel from the rail by the sink and returned to the doctor, still carrying the sodden Gladstone bag. Travis peeled off his coat, revealing his familiar tight black suit with the shiny elbows, which made him look like an undertaker. The shoulders of the suit were wet. Travis towelled his hair and face, gasping like a cross-Channel swimmer. When he was done, he draped the towel over the banister rail and held out his hand for his bag. "Hideous weather," he growled, and nodded at the fat briefcase. "Could you carry that for me, please?"

Terry nodded perfunctorily, picked up the briefcase, then reached out, though he did not quite dare grasp the doctor's arm. "Please, Doctor," he said, "could we hurry? There's something wrong with Alice."

"Wrong?" repeated Travis as if the word offended him. "Whatever do you mean?"

Both men looked up as Georgina's bulk appeared at the top of the stairs, appearing to cast a shadow over them.

"Are you two going to stand there nattering all night?" she demanded. "There's a woman here that needs help—and quickly from the looks of her."

Both men began to ascend, Travis slowly, bony hand gripping the banister and hauling himself up one step at a time. Terry fluttered behind him, teeth clenched and forehead furrowed as if trying to propel the old man forward through sheer act of will.

"What's wrong with her?" Travis asked between gasps as he entered the bedroom.

Georgina tersely recounted the symptoms. She was sitting on a chair beside the bed and had enclosed Alice's left hand in both of hers and was stroking it tenderly.

Terry hung back as Travis moved forward to examine Alice. He probed her belly, making her moan and writhe. In the dim room he resembled a black spider hovering over something fat and helpless in its web. He snapped open his Gladstone bag, withdrew a stethoscope and listened to her tightly stretched stomach. Indicating the bowl of water, now stained pink once again, he said, "Could you fill that with hot clean water please, Georgina?"

She nodded curtly and did as he asked. Terry, hovering in the doorway, stepped into the room out of her path, studiously avoiding eye contact. Travis placed a palm on Alice's forehead, then half-turned and waved Terry forward, indicating his desire for the fat briefcase. Terry passed it to him. He watched as the doctor cleared the bedside table, placing the lamp on the floor. He put the briefcase on the table, opened it, and withdrew two squat cylinders, to each of which was affixed a length of tubing and a transparent plastic facemask. He said to Terry, "Why is it so bloody dark in here? Turn the light on, can't you?"

Terry did so, and immediately Alice groaned and screwed up her eyes. He did not realise how muted the colour of her blood had been in the dimness until the unflinching light made it spring up more vivid than ever. Georgina returned with the water and placed it, at Travis' request, on a chair that the doctor tugged from beneath the dressing table. As he scrubbed his hands with a brush and a cake of soap that had been wrapped in cloth in his Gladstone bag, he explained to Georgina about the cylinders, one of which would provide Alice with gas for her pain, the other of which would provide her with air.

It was when Travis reached down between his wife's

legs that Terry had to look away. Mumbling that he didn't feel well, he turned and stumbled to the door. Suddenly he thought he could smell blood in the room, something he hadn't previously detected. He felt lightheaded, the sensation like someone unscrewing the top of his skull as if it were a jar. The storm crashing against the house seemed to recede as if his ears were blocked. Outside the room he clung to the doorknob for a moment, certain he was going to faint.

Gradually his muffled senses cleared and returned to normal. Terry winced as he heard his wife cry out, and he tottered to the top of the stairs. He hadn't wanted to attend the birth or any of its preliminaries. He had known the blood and the mess and the pain would upset him too much. What he had envisaged was his wife going upstairs, the doctor arriving, and then, a couple of hours later, hearing the sound of a baby's cry. He'd imagined entering the bedroom to find his wife sitting up in bed, perhaps in a cloud-white nightgown, looking tired but beatific and serene. In her arms she would be holding a clean, pink, chubby baby, and she would look up at him and smile proudly. He would go to the bed and enclose the two of them in a protective embrace, and the child would blink its startling blue eyes and reach up for him with tiny, perfect hands. . . .

Alice cried out again, shattering the illusion. For a moment Terry felt almost resentful toward her. Why couldn't she just give birth like a normal woman? Why did there have to be all this palaver? He felt ashamed as he descended the stairs. He hadn't meant that. He was upset, that was all. His legs felt weak and he gripped the banister as tightly as Dr. Travis had done. He needed a cigarette. He deserved one. Just this once lung cancer could take a running jump.

He entered the sitting room and slumped into his armchair, which, after a decade of use, had moulded itself to his shape. The room was large, though its clutter of furniture and its lack of natural light made it seem cosy.

Terry was thirty-four, Alice two years younger. They had married in 1958, soon after he had come out of the army. At first things had been hard. They had lived in a cramped flat above the butcher's shop in Beckford. Terry had flitted from one casual labouring job to another, finding it more difficult than he had imagined to adapt to civilian life again. He had found himself increasingly irritated by the village mentality he encountered when he returned, scornful of the narrow-mindedness of community life. If it hadn't been for Alice, her inexhaustible sympathy and understanding, he would have pulled up his roots and made his way to Leeds, or even to London, in search of worth, direction, meaning. But gradually, backed by her love and support, he had rediscovered himself. He was offered, and was delighted to accept, a job as a mechanic at Joe Bates' garage in the village, thus utilising the trade he had been taught in the army. After his father's death in '65, he and Alice had moved from their cramped flat to the cottage and so had finally been able to discuss the prospect of starting a family. It had taken five long and uncomfortable years for Alice to conceive, but at last, in January, had come the news for which they'd been waiting. And tonight would see the culmination of all that heartache and uncertainty. Terry closed his eyes and tried to reproduce the mental image of Alice, angelic in a white nightgown, sitting up in bed holding their baby—but instead all he saw was her blood on the sheets and her white face contorted in pain.

He shuddered, opened his eyes and reached for his cigarettes, which were on the table by his armchair. He lit one and drew the smoke deep into his lungs. He stared at the fire, which was the only light in the room, a glow of orange coals behind a guard of fine wire mesh. Rain and wind battered the two small windows behind him, and Terry shuddered again, pulling in his legs like an animal preparing to hibernate. His armchair was to the left of the fire. Facing it was the settee, and to the right of that was a black and white television set. Behind the settee was a dining table and six chairs, and beyond that, against the far wall, a sideboard that had belonged to Terry's parents.

Alice's watercolours, mainly Yorkshire farming scenes, covered their walls despite her protestations that she didn't want them hung. Painting was a passion for her, though she ended up giving most of her pictures away to friends, and always felt terribly embarrassed when they insisted on paying her for them. Though he possessed his own creative tendencies, Terry had always stifled them. However, after the screening of *The Quatermass Experiment* on the BBC in 1953, when Terry was seventeen, those tendencies had almost emerged. Inspired by the series, he had begun to write his own science fiction story, but in the end the spectre of his father had been too much for him. One night he had fed his unfinished manuscript into the same fire that had devoured his comics a decade before. He had kept his literary exploits a secret from Alice, feeling as guilty and ashamed as if he'd been having an affair. A couple of times, mostly when he was drunk, he had almost told her of his aspirations, but in the end he had chickened out, and to this day she knew nothing of his suppressed dreams.

If she had known—if she *did* know—Terry was certain she would encourage him. "When the baby comes," he murmured, staring into the fire, "I'll tell her. And I'll start writing again. I'll write stories for her and my child." Only the storm answered his vow, and the coals, crackling gently. All at once Terry felt convinced someone was standing in the shadows at the back of the room. He turned, knowing he would see his father's scowling face.

But of course there was no one there.

He laughed humourlessly to himself and finished his cigarette. He waited five minutes, then lit another.

Time passed, though how quickly he was unsure. He smoked four cigarettes one after the other, stirring from his seat only to jab the embers into reluctant life when they began to fade. He looked up at the ceiling above the windows and saw the reflection of the rain there, a vague slithering of light and shadow. The storm drowned out whatever sounds may have been coming from upstairs, allowing Terry to indulge the belief that all was well in the house, that now that the doctor was here everything would be fine.

He did not remember falling asleep. It must have been the fire, the sinuous overlapping of flames, that stole his consciousness as stealthily as a pickpocket. He felt a hand on his shoulder shaking him, opened his eyes a crack, grimaced at the taste in his mouth, like the contents of an ashtray. He was cold. The fire had gone out. Rain still drummed at the windows, this sound laid over another almost constant sound, which was the hissing of rain in the undergrowth.

"Hmm, what?" he slurred.

"You'd better come," said Georgina in a sharp, tight voice.

"What time is it?"

But she had already turned away and did not answer his question.

Terry sighed and blinked himself awake. He looked at his watch and saw that it was quarter to one. He stared disbelievingly at the time for a moment as though his eyes might have been deceiving him. But no; he'd been asleep—what?—five, six hours?

He pushed himself up from the armchair and stumbled after Georgina. His legs ached as they ascended the stairs; he was halfway up when he heard a baby cry. He halted for a moment, his breath solidifying in his chest, feeling suddenly dizzy with wonder and excitement and more than a little fear. Then, grabbing the banister, he thrust himself forward, taking the stairs two and three at a time.

The baby was still crying when he entered the bedroom.

Georgina was rocking it in her arms. Dr. Travis was winding up his stethoscope. As he stuffed it into his Gladstone bag he looked askance at Terry.

"My baby . . ." he said, taking two hesitant steps forward.

"A son," Georgina said in a flat voice. "It was a breech birth, but he . . . he's fine now."

Something in her manner made him look at the bed. Only Alice's head and shoulders were visible above a clean white sheet. Her skin was almost the colour of the bedding. Her hair, by contrast, spread over the pillow, looked almost black.

"Alice?" Terry said. His excitement was draining away, the fear growing and intensifying.

"We did all we could for her," Travis answered in a burdened voice, "but I'm afraid it was a very difficult birth. In the end she just wasn't strong enough."

Terry swayed and blinked. Part of him wanted to believe he was still dreaming. "No," he mouthed, but the word failed to emerge. Grief suddenly flooded through him, hot tears spilling down his cheeks, sobs racking his body.

"No," he wailed, "no . . . no . . ." The denial, desperate, beseeching, was all he could manage.

As if it were consolation, Georgina said, "Your baby almost died, too, but we managed to save him. Come and hold him, Terry. He needs you now."

He looked at her and felt a sudden hatred seize him, so acute it was like pain. He jabbed a finger at the wriggling infant in her arms. "That thing killed my wife," he sobbed. "That bloody little thing took her away from me. I don't want it. It's not my son. I wish it had died instead."

He ran out of the room, down the stairs and dragged open the front door. The rain and wind welcomed him. Terry plunged into it, joining it in its rage.

PART ONE

PRIMAL MUSIC

1

STRANGE WORLDS

As soon as he turned from Shaftesbury Avenue on to Charing Cross Road, Jack saw the queue and his stomach began to flip. It was always the same: no matter how many public appearances he made or interviews he gave, the initial evidence of his popularity always came as a shock. He stood on the opposite pavement appraising the scene, telling himself to relax, that there was no need to be nervous. These people were here to praise, not to crucify him. He drew a deep breath, then clenched his fists and stuffed them into the pockets of his scuffed brown leather jacket.

He stood there for perhaps two minutes while the populace, a riot of cultures and creeds, flowed past him, while black cabs and red buses and the weaving motorbikes of couriers filled the air with noise and fumes. Only in London would his behaviour have been ignored. If he had stood stock-still on a busy street in any provincial town in Britain he would have attracted suspicious glances, veiled sniggers, perhaps even hostility. But London was tolerant of eccentricity, was even indifferent to it. Depending on his mood, this attitude either delighted Jack or dispirited him. Tolerance meant freedom, colour, a chance for creativity to flourish. Indifference, on the other hand, suggested selfishness, greed, a dearth of love. The city was a ruthless discriminator; it raised the successful high on its shoulders whilst grinding its boot-heel on the destitute. But Jack, who had felt the weight of its loathing, knew that there was a ladder to be climbed if only you could grasp the first rung. It had taken him fifteen years, but at last he was beginning to believe that his own personal summit was in sight. Events such as this were designed to bring that summit ever closer. Jack only hoped he had the strength to maintain his momentum.

His heart was not pounding quite so fiercely now, though he knew it would start hammering again as soon as he crossed the road and approached the shop and was recognised. Even as he watched, more people joined the end of the queue. Most were clutching books and magazines, though without his spectacles Jack could not see what they were from this distance. He unzipped his jacket halfway, reached inside, took his spectacles from their case and slipped them on. Now came clarity: Jack saw eager faces instead of blurs, saw the name above the shop, STRANGE WORLDS (red lettering enclosed within a yellow ringed planet), saw the right-hand window display, devoted exclusively to him.

As always, the sight of his own face exhibited so brazenly made him feel strangely uncomfortable, almost vulnerable. He read the blurb beneath the enlarged photograph: MEET THE AUTHOR, JACK STONE, WHO WILL BE HERE ON THURSDAY, 24TH FEBRUARY 2004 AT 1:30 P.M. TO SIGN COPIES OF HIS NEW NOVEL, SPLINTER KISS.

Bracing himself, Jack crossed the road, promising himself a cigarette over lunch once this was over.

He reached the opposite pavement without being recog-

nized, which was not entirely surprising, for in truth Jack
was unremarkable in appearance. He carried perhaps half
a stone too much weight for his five-nine frame, though
this was easily concealed beneath baggy clothes. He had
coffee-brown hair, slightly wavy, which he combed back
from his forehead and over his ears. His face was pleasant,
endowed—when he chose to display it—with a generous
smile and eyes every bit as blue as Paul Newman's. If Jack
had the chance to alter one aspect of his appearance it
would be his jaw, which he considered far too prominent.
At best he thought he looked like Desperate Dan, at worst
a chubby piranha fish. Sometimes he wore silver-framed
spectacles, and in his left ear was a silver ring, which he
had not removed for some half-dozen years.

On the photo in the Strange Worlds window Jack's hair
was longer than usual and he was not wearing his spectacles, so maybe he would be able to sneak in without anyone noticing. Sitting behind a table piled with books with
a pen in his hand would make him feel more confident.
What was it he had said to Gail, only half-jokingly, last
night? He had said that writing was the profession of disturbed people: obsessives, neurotics, schizophrenics, ego-
tists. "Which one are you?" she had asked him teasingly.
He had rolled his eyes, cackled, given her his most
crooked smile and hissed, "All of them."

He was a dozen yards from the shop's entrance when he
was spotted. He had his head down and his hands in his
pockets, but heard the shuffle of feet increase, the buzz of
voices raise a notch, and knew immediately what it signi-
fied. He raised his head in resignation, preparing to
smile. "Hiya, Jack." "Hello, Mr Stone." "I loved *Consummation.*" "When does *Splinter Kiss* come out in paperback?"

Jack did his best to reply to as many greetings and answer as many questions as possible; he hated the thought
that there were those in the queue who might feel

snubbed before the event had even begun. He reached the glass door and tapped on it to alert the muscle-man in the *Strange Worlds* T-shirt who was standing just inside, acting as security guard. In what he hoped was a loud voice he said to the crowd, "Please excuse me. Hopefully I'll get a chance to speak to you all inside."

It was obvious the muscle-man did not recognise Jack. He scowled and took his time strolling to the door, and once there kept his hands clasped behind him. Jack felt embarrassed and annoyed; he was aware that everyone in the queue was craning to look at him. Determined not to shout, he pointed very deliberately at the window display, then at himself, and then he mimed writing. The muscle-man's scowl softened to a frown as realisation began to dawn. The man at the front of the queue, who was around twenty with slicked-back hair and a hooded grey track suit jacket, said in an exaggeratedly dopey voice, "Duhh, my brain hurts." He helped out by holding up his rare first edition hardback of Jack's first novel, *Bleeding Hearts,* and pointing from the name on the cover to the man himself.

The muscle-man finally got the message. He twisted a key in the left half of the door and tugged it open. Jack slipped inside, thanking him curtly. "Uh . . . sorry, Mr. . . . uh . . . Stone," the muscle-man said in a voice that sounded as if it were being played at too slow a speed.

The owners of the shop, Pete and Barry, were far more enthusiastic. Pete rushed forward, flinging out his hand. When the handshake came it was a disappointment, the kind that Gail always referred to as a damp dishcloth. "We're *so* pleased to see you," Pete enthused. "It's going to be a super function. Well, you've seen for yourself, the hordes are massing outside."

Jack merely smiled and nodded vaguely, then turned to Barry, who was hovering at Pete's shoulder like a minder, and said, "Hi."

Barry murmured something inaudible, his gaze veering

shyly away from Jack's. They were a strange pair, these two, lovers by all accounts, though they were so different that the thought of them living together, sharing their lives on a day-to-day basis, made Jack's mind boggle. He always thought of Pete as a fox—tall, lean, with quick movements and sharp features. Barry, on the other hand, was a tortoise—short, dumpy, awkward and introverted.

"You'll be sitting here, if that's okay," Pete said, gesturing grandly at a spotlit table heaped with copies of Jack's new book. Cormorant, Jack's publisher, were really going to town on *Splinter Kiss,* his fourth novel.

"Fine," Jack said, hoping the combination of spotlights and nerves were not going to make him pour with sweat. Behind the table, on the wall, was a large poster depicting the cover of *Splinter Kiss*—a striking surrealistic portrait of a woman with moths hatching from her eye sockets— and beneath his name, in large white letters, a quote from *Starburst* magazine: "Jack Stone is fast gaining a reputation as the most stunningly original dark fantasist working in Britain today."

"I'll be sitting beside you, nearest the door," Pete was saying, "flogging the product, so to speak. We've also got plenty of paperbacks of the first three on the shelves if the cheapskates would rather buy those and have those signed instead."

"Great," said Jack, and glanced at his watch.

"Still five minutes to go," Pete said, as if apologising. "Well, six to be precise."

"I don't mind starting now," Jack said, "if that's okay with you."

Pete spread his hands. "Fine, fine. It'll reduce a bit of the two-thirty backlog, anyway."

Barry, who had been hovering on the periphery of the conversation, now edged forward and placed a copy of *Splinter Kiss* on the desk. "Would you . . . er . . . sign this for us first?" he mumbled.

"Sure," said Jack, producing his pen. "Might as well get a bit of practice in. To Pete and Barry?" Barry nodded. Jack did the honours and handed the book back with a smile. Barry muttered his thanks.

Pete said, "Would you be a dear, Barry, and make us all some coffee?"

Barry shuffled away. Pete flapped a hand at the muscle-man standing impassively by the door. "All right, Brian, up with the portcullis." Brian reached for the door handle but glanced back at Pete with a bewildered expression. "Well, open it then," Pete said, rolling his eyes.

As with all the signings he had done, Jack felt nervous and self-conscious at first, as if he had no right to be here, but after fifteen minutes or so he began to enjoy himself. The public—or "punters" as Pete referred to them—were chatty and friendly and often refreshingly weird, though from them all Jack detected a kind of reverence that he did not feel worthy of and that he did his best to break down. At ten minutes before two, Tamsin, the publicity manager from Cormorant who had set this up, arrived and asked Jack how it was going. Jack spread his hands and said, "Pretty well, as you can see."

"Have we sold many *Splinters* or is it mainly old stuff?" she asked.

Jack shrugged as he signed. "About half and half, I should think."

Pete did a brief calculation and said, "We've sold sixteen *Splinter Kiss*'s in"—he glanced at the clock—"twenty minutes. That's not bad. Almost one a minute. We'll get through fifty at this rate."

Tamsin nodded. She was petite with spiky ginger hair and an almost constantly smiling face. "Great," she said. "Well, I'll just hang around. Shout if you need anything."

Someone arrived with a proof copy of Jack's second novel, *Song of Flesh*. "Where did you get this?" he asked.

The girl looked a little alarmed, as if Jack had accused

her of stealing. "From a secondhand bookshop in Huddersfield," she said so quietly that he almost had to read her lips.

Someone else, who bought three copies of *Splinter Kiss* and wanted them inscribed "To Denise/Hilary/Sharon with big sloppy kisses, Jack Stone," (as the guy had forked out almost forty quid, Jack complied) asked, "Any chance of seeing *Consummation* or *Song of Flesh* as a film?"

Jack shrugged. "I think *Consummation* would be hard to realise on screen. *Bleeding Hearts* has been optioned, though, so it's fingers crossed for that one." When the guy screwed up his face as though he'd been eating a lemon, Jack said, "That doesn't appeal?"

"Nah. I thought *Bleeding Hearts* was a piece of shit. But it was only your first novel, so that's okay."

At twenty past two Tamsin moved to Jack's side, leaned over and said into his ear, "I think it would be best if we cut the queue off at the last person now. There's still quite a lot of fans outside. What do you think?"

Jack said, "Well, as long as everyone who's out there gets their books signed."

"They will, don't worry." She glanced at her watch. "I mean, we're going to overrun as it is."

He shrugged. "Okay, if you think it's best," but he didn't like the thought of people turning up at 2:25 and being turned away. Maybe some of them had left the office for lunch at two and had rushed across town to get here. The thought of being considered inaccessible or aloof dismayed him, but he was beginning to realise how some celebrities, particularly the more successful ones, could gain such a reputation.

"I'll tell the gorilla on the door," said Tamsin. "What's his name? Rambo?"

"Brian, believe it or not. Please make sure he doesn't start throwing his weight about, though, if people get tetchy. I don't want them to think he's associated with me."

"Relax," said Tamsin. "And start thinking about yourself. You're doing people a favour here, you know—meeting the public, signing their books."

"If they didn't buy the books I wouldn't be here in the first place," he replied.

He signed his final book at 2:45; Pete announced with obvious delight that they'd sold sixty-two hardbacks, then he and Tamsin went for lunch at Nafees, an Indian restaurant on Denmark Street where Jack had arranged to meet Gail.

She was not there when they arrived, though Jack had told her 2:40. He hoped she hadn't gone off in a huff because they were late; sometimes she had a very short fuse, and Jack knew she often felt second-best to his work. He'd told her he loved her and that there was no one in the entire world he'd rather be with. But he loved his work too: writing was an obsession with him, a necessity. Success was simply a wonderfully fortuitous consequence. Even if Jack was making no money at all, still collecting rejection slip after rejection slip like in the old days, he would continue to write.

The restaurant was colourful but tasteful: Indian fabrics and paintings on the wall, the suggestion of sitar music in the background. A soft-spoken waiter in a maroon suit and bow tie led them between affluent-looking city people to their table.

In the three years that Tamsin had been at Cormorant, Jack liked to think they had become friends. However, beyond their professional relationship, Jack realised he knew very little about her. She sometimes mentioned a boyfriend, though Jack had never heard her call him by name. She had also mentioned visiting her parents in Ipswich, but Jack did not know if she originated from there. Perhaps she was bubbly simply because she had to be. Maybe when she went home at night, to her boyfriend or whomever, she released all the vitriol she'd been storing up all day. Maybe tonight she would kick off her shoes, fling herself on the settee and say, "God, I had to take one of our authors, Jack Stone, out for lunch today. What a drag!"

Jack held the menu in front of his face to conceal his smile at the thought. Gail often accused him of being insecure and cynical and he hotly denied it every time. But it was true; he found it hard to trust people completely. He wondered whether this was a result of living in London or whether the roots were buried deeper, in the bitter soil of his childhood in Beckford.

"Are you ready to order?" Tamsin asked.

"I know what I want, but do you think we could wait for Gail? She should be here any minute."

"Sure. No problem. Shall we have some drinks while we're waiting?"

"Yeah, great. I'll have a Kingfisher if they serve it here."

When their drinks arrived, Tamsin said, "Do you mind if I smoke? Please say if you do."

"Not at all. In fact, I wouldn't mind one myself, though I'm trying to cut down."

"You do right," said Tamsin. "Disgusting habit." But she laughed easily to show that it was a habit she had no intention of stopping.

As Jack drew on the cigarette he felt the familiar twinge of emotion that was too slight to be termed fear or dread. His grandfather and great-grandfather had both died of lung cancer in their early sixties, though Jack consoled himself with the thought that as far as he knew his father was still going strong and he must be sixty-seven or sixty-eight by now. Tamsin began to speak enthusiastically about *Splinter Kiss* and asked him how the new one was coming.

"*The Laughter*? Very well, so far, though I never like to say too much about the novel I'm working on. I don't know why, it just makes me uncomfortable. Maybe because I'm so close to it, or perhaps it's just a superstition of mine that I don't even know about."

Tamsin nodded and Jack said, "God, that sounds pretentious, doesn't it?"

She laughed, flashing small white teeth. "No," she said, "not at all."

Out of the corner of his eye Jack saw the restaurant door open and he looked up. Gail had black hair cut as short as a choirboy's, large dark eyes, a dainty nose and lips that seemed to be pouting appealingly even when they weren't. Perhaps her most attractive feature, however, was her skin—lightly tanned, perfectly smooth, blemish-free. Jack's heart gave a joyous leap, as it always did when he saw her. Before he could raise his hand to wave, Tamsin said, "She's here, isn't she?"

Jack looked momentarily surprised, then broke into a wide, bashful grin. "Is it really that obvious?" he said.

2

SEAFOOD

He and Gail had met nine months earlier.

It had been May. May 16th, to be precise. A Friday. Two days after Jack had delivered the final proofs of *Splinter Kiss* to Cormorant and was subsequently in the process of taking what he'd thought would be a fully-deserved week off. To Jack the idea of a week off seemed blissful. It meant no toiling for hours over a word processor, no frying his brains as he searched his thesaurus for the exact word or phrase he was looking for (the one that normally he would pluck from his mental vocabulary with ease, but which today, because he needed it, had decided to play hide-and-seek), no feeling inadequate because he couldn't capture the atmosphere of a particular setting or the essence of a particular character, no feeling guilty because he was making tea, doing some housework, doing some "research," doing everything but starting writing.

A week off. Paradise. But it was only Friday and already he was getting itchy fingers. He'd already convinced himself that sitting at his word processor was okay so long as he didn't do any serious work. He could catch up with his correspondence, jot some notes for a short story, or even mull over some ideas for the next novel so long as he didn't actually start it. What he'd planned to do with the week was sleep late, grab some much-needed fresh air and exercise, leisurely scour the secondhand bookshops, read, socialise . . . but after only two days he found to his profound astonishment that this simply wasn't enough.

What's wrong with me? he thought. Why can't I relax? He told himself that writing was his relaxation, that words were his toys and he needed to play with them. Yet he knew this wasn't the answer. Sometimes, occasionally, the act of writing was exhilarating, but more often than not it was stressful, frustrating, tortuous. For Jack the joy came not in the process of building words, cementing one to the next, but in the final construction, the finished product. His old A-level English tutor, Mr. Wild, had once described novels as temples, and whilst Jack found this analogy a little pompous he also saw the sense in it. Certainly the words of his own books, taken by themselves, were simply the bricks, the framework. What was important was the emotion, the meaning, contained within.

So what did that make him? A literary masochist, flagellating himself with his own inadequacies? The thought depressed him. Perhaps if he could deflect some of his intensity into another area . . . a new girlfriend maybe? But no. Jack had always found relationships hard. He was far too secretive and selfish, far too protective of his space and his time, the domain of his life. He liked his life and he liked himself and he didn't want anyone intruding. After Carol the last thing he needed was someone telling him he had hang-ups just because they perceived him differently from the way he perceived himself.

On Friday, May 16th 2003, this was his state of mind. He got out of bed at 8:42 after promising himself he'd sleep in until at least nine. He made himself some breakfast—a bowl of muesli, wholewheat toast with honey and his obligatory cup of tea—and sat, unshaven and tousle-haired, watching breakfast TV on Channel 4.

The post arrived at 8:55. Jack put down his tea and scampered eagerly to the door. He wondered if all writers did this. Certainly the ones he knew did. He scooped up his mail—five letters, about average since he'd "become famous." There were times in the early days when he'd receive nothing of interest for weeks. He'd get to the stage where he'd think there was a countrywide conspiracy against him, when even a rejection slip would be welcome. On the board above his desk was a postcard a friend had sent him. On it was a cartoon of a seriously twitchy man, and below the cartoon the words: *I'm not paranoid—I know they're out to get me!*

His post bag was good this morning. It contained a fan letter from a forty-seven-year-old man in Chesterfield, a letter from his agent, a magazine he subscribed to, a letter from a contemporary who wanted to sell a werewolf anthology and wondered if he'd contribute, and a satisfyingly healthy bank statement. Jack read through it all as he finished his tea, then showered, shaved, dressed and congratulated himself on not having had a cigarette yet. He made his way to his study, sat behind his desk and switched his machine on before he even realised what he was doing.

"Relax, Stone, for God's sake. You're a bloody workaholic," he said out loud. He'd just have a quick dabble, just half an hour's tidying up and then he'd do something else. He picked up the phone on his desk and dialed Frank Dawson's number. Most of his friends were at work but Frank might be home.

After five rings Frank's answering machine cut in: "Tough shit, I'm out. You know what to do." Jack grinned. "Hi, Frank," he said, "this is Jack. I've just delivered a new book and I'm going stir-crazy trying to relax. Do you fancy lunch at Alfred's? If so, I'll meet you there at one. I'm off to haunt a few bookshops first. Bye."

He pushed his chair back, the castors making grooves in the rug he'd bought in Islamabad eleven years ago. He looked out of the window that was to the right of his desk. His top-floor flat in Crouch End was spacious and full of light. From his window he could see the houses across the street, the wide road, the roofs of cars. His street, indeed much of the area, was quiet, residential, relatively clean, at least by London standards.

It was a beautiful spring morning, the sky so blue that it made Jack's eyes ache to look at it. A few wispy clouds drifted past, the occasional one greying at the edges like sponges that still retained a little moisture. It was not a day for staying indoors when one didn't have to. Just twenty minutes, Jack thought, and then he'd go out.

Forty-five minutes later he looked at his watch and swore. He'd decided to do some light editing on an unsold short story and then maybe print it off to send some-where, but he'd become increasingly bogged down in the narrative. "Bugger you!" he growled at the screen, and de-cided to abandon what he'd thought would be a pleasant task, maybe to return to it later. He collected together the miscellany he always carried with him—credit card, phone, spectacles, cigarettes, notepad and pen, cash, a novel to read—and distributed them among the many pockets of his bulky brown leather jacket. Outside the house he patted his car, a red Mini Cooper, as if it were a pet. He left it where it was, though—driving was too much of a hassle during the day—and strolled to Arch-way, his nearest tube station.

At this time of year the underground was hot and crowded with tourists. It was irritating having to step over rucksacks and around suitcases, and Jack felt gloomy at the thought that it would become increasingly unbearable over the next three months. He found a seat and sat down and took out the book he was reading, James Ellroy's *The Black Dahlia*. Sometimes, when he told fans he didn't read horror and fantasy exclusively they seemed disappointed, as if he'd exhibited disloyalty to his genre. In truth, though, Jack found that most books were simply amalgams of separate genres—horror novels often contained elements of crime and romance, mainstream novels were often fantasy packaged as literature. Jack felt lucky that the "uniqueness and innovation" of his own work had been seen by the press, the fans and his publisher as a positive aspect from the word go. So many writers he knew complained that their publishers tried to pigeonhole them, balked at the proposal of even the slightest change in direction. For some of his colleagues writing a book had become almost a group project, a clinical exercise in producing the ultimate saleable commodity. Hallelujah for publishers like Cormorant, Jack thought. His editor there, Patricia Stephens, believed that a novel should be just what its name implied: something that was new and fresh and challenging.

By the time the tube arrived at Tottenham Court Road it was packed. Jack got off, scowling at people who stood there as if they had no idea why he was trying to push past them. The tube station smelled of stale breath and sour bodies. Everyone was hurrying as if London's entire population were late for appointments. Jack's clothes felt stuffed with damp warmth; he grasped the collar of his jacket in both hands and flapped it, trying to generate some air. At the bottom of the escalators, squatting on the floor, a man with sandals and a mop of dark hair was playing a didgeridoo. The sound was primitive and threatening and somehow delicious. Jack felt the hairs on the back of his neck stand up; he loved it when music did that to him. He fished in his pocket and was about to drop a fifty-pence piece into the shoebox by the man's right foot when he noticed that tucked into the shoebox's corner were half a dozen CDs, each with the same brown inlay card.

"Are these of you playing?" Jack asked.

The man glanced up, eyebrows becoming lost in his tangled fringe. Jack was sorry the music had to stop for the man to answer his question. A thread of spittle gleamed briefly between the mouthpiece of the instrument and the man's lips before snapping.

"Yes, friend," the man said, his voice soft and with no trace of an accent.

"How much are they?"

"Eight pounds."

Jack considered for only a second. "Go on then," he said, and pulled the money from his pocket. When he ascended the escalator, people looked at him as if he were mad. It had crossed Jack's mind that the CD might be blank, but then he thought that surely there were now too many people with Discmans for the didgeridoo player to risk such a swindle. Besides that, he wanted to believe that anyone who could coax such emotion from a musical instrument had to be possessed of integrity and nobility. The music began again behind him: an evocative, ancient sound. Jack shuddered and hurried up the steps into the sunshine and bustle of Oxford Street.

He lost the next two hours in the smell and sight and feel of books. Jack loved new books for their glossy covers and their smell of fresh ink, he loved old books for their sense of resilience and history, their musty lived-in odour, their browning pages, lovingly thumbed. His flat was full of books. They were crammed into every niche, into every available space. His study was simply four walls of books, multi-coloured spines towering to the ceiling. Even in the bathroom there were books, piled in the small alcove behind the toilet. The hallway in his flat, already narrow, had been narrowed even further by the installation of a long bookcase. There were small piles of books, still waiting to be sorted, in the most unlikely places: in the cupboard beneath the kitchen sink, on top of the TV, beside his shoes in the wardrobe.

Though Jack loved his books, his only regret at owning so many was that he would never have time to read them all. Someday, he often promised himself, I'll read all these. Yet Jack reckoned that for every three books he bought he probably read one. He glanced at his purchases for that day, which he'd assembled in a big yellow plastic Strange Worlds bag. Six new books, two of which were hardbacks, and eight secondhand; he dreaded to think how much money he'd spent. His love of books went back a long way, to a time when losing himself in fiction had been the only escape from his childhood.

As he travelled the two stops from Leicester Square, where his wanderings had taken him, to Green Park, Jack thought of his last girlfriend, Carol. She'd never understood his fascination with books. Every time he dragged her into a secondhand bookshop she would curl her face into a grimace and exclaim, "How can you buy these dirty old things? You don't know where they've been." Jack could not remember how he and Carol had ever got together. They had had nothing in common. He supposed the attraction must have been physical. He hadn't realised how much she was grinding down his spirit, expressing disapproval of every aspect of his lifestyle, until their relationship ended one terrible and glorious Monday morning. That was the closest Jack had ever come to hitting a woman. In the end he had hit the wall instead, denting it and bruising his knuckles. He had called her a "neurotic witch" (not exactly the most scathing put-down in the world, but it had made him feel good at the time), and she had simply consolidated her hatred of all that was Jack Stone: his appearance, his profession, his choice of friends and decor and restaurants and books and art and entertainment and music and politics. He was a worm, she said, a slimeball, a sick pervert who wrote and read what was nothing but pornography in disguise. That had got Jack mad, but the insult which had made him clench his fist and punch the wall was so obviously an attempt to goad him that he should have treated it with contempt. She told him he was crap in bed, that she'd always been repulsed by his sexual advances, that she had faked every orgasm she'd ever had with him and had wanted to wash herself each time he touched her skin.

Jack got off the tube and realised that his stomach was churning unpleasantly. Carol had really screwed him up. For months afterwards he had constantly felt on the edge of fever or neurosis, had suffered from headaches and sore throats and mouth ulcers. He had never seen her again, had not called her and she had not called him. It was almost fourteen months since they had finished, yet even now Jack would sometimes see a woman in the street or on the tube who, for a split-second, looked like Carol, and his heart would leap almost in panic, his mouth would go dry, he would begin to sweat.

Alfred's, where Jack had suggested Frank meet him for lunch, was a small pizzeria just round the corner from Berkeley Street. As with most of Jack's favourite restaurants, the decor was sparse, even shabby, but the food delicious. The clientele was mostly young and dressed casually. Many of them carried sports bags or folders or files, denoting their status as students. On the walls were framed black and white photographs of famous boxers. The chef, a stereotypical fat Italian with a heavy moustache, could be seen cooking in a large open-plan kitchen at the far end of the room, spinning pizza crusts with the panache of a circus performer.

The place was crowded when Jack arrived, but fortunately a couple stood up to leave just as he came in. He sat down, placing his bag of books on the floor by his chair. He was thankful to relieve himself of the weight; the biceps of both arms were aching as a result of swapping the bag from hand to hand. When the waitress arrived Jack ordered a mineral water and asked her to leave an extra menu. He called Frank at home and on his mobile and got his voice mail both times, and then, feeling guilty but telling himself he had no reason to, he took his cigarettes from his pocket and lit one. He'd been trying to cut down on booze, cigarettes, sugar, salt and animal fat since he'd turned thirty, nearly three years ago, but his intentions were stronger than his will power. Still, he didn't do too badly; this was his first cigarette of the day and he'd ordered mineral water instead of beer or wine to drink. He narrowed his eyes against the smoke that drifted in front of his face and watched the chef chopping a capsicum, his knife a silver blur.

"I'll just wait another five minutes," Jack said when the waitress came over for his order. "I kind of half-arranged to meet someone. They may not turn up, but . . . well . . . you know, they might." He forced a smile, admonishing himself silently for feeling he had to explain. He finished his cigarette, stubbed it out, and toyed with the condiments in the middle of the table. As well as pepper and salt there was a larger shaker containing dried chili seeds and a small bowl of parmesan cheese. He glanced up at the door each time it opened. It was twenty-three minutes past one.

When the waitress next came within earshot, Jack leaned forward and said, "I'll order now, please. I don't think my friend is going to turn up." She nodded, and reached for the pad and pen tucked into her belt. When she had left, Jack leaned over and rooted in his bag, pulling out four secondhand books. He had wanted to wait until he was home before looking properly at what he'd bought, but if Frank wasn't going to show he needed something to occupy his mind while he ate.

His first course arrived, mushrooms in garlic and

tomato sauce. Jack added pepper, chili and parmesan cheese and ate them slowly. Whilst he waited for his main course, chicken in cream and herbs with tagliatelle, he looked through the rest of his books. The two hardbacks were by genre contemporaries whose work he admired, the new paperbacks by writers he'd never read before. One was a collection of stories by a twenty-two-year-old science-fiction writer whom everyone was raving about. Jack was flicking through this, looking at the names of the stories, reading the first paragraphs of each, when a dark shape moved in front of him, blocking the light from the window.

He looked up, expecting to see Frank. A woman stood there. She was wearing a blue and orange skirt, a white T-shirt and a blue cardigan. She was looking at him quizzically, as if she knew him from somewhere but could not place where. On the rare occasions when Jack had been recognised he'd felt awkward and uncomfortable, but now he was willing the woman to say, "Excuse me, but aren't you Jack Stone, the writer?"

Not that he'd have anything interesting to say back. "Yes, I am," he'd admit modestly, and she'd maybe gush for twenty seconds or so about how she'd read all his books and thought they were brilliant. He would go pink and his smile would become fixed and he'd say, "Thanks very much. It's very nice of you to say so." Then maybe there'd be a pregnant pause and she would say, "Well . . . it's been good to meet you. I'll look out for the next one." And she would walk away, leaving Jack floundering frustratedly for witticisms that would come to him the instant she was out of earshot.

"Is anyone sitting here?" the woman said, pointing at the empty chair opposite him.

"Er . . . no," he said. "I was waiting for a friend, but it doesn't look as though he's coming."

"Would you mind if I joined you then? I'm not usually

so pushy, but it's the only free seat in the place and I've been on my feet all morning."

Jack half-stood and flapped at the seat as though scattering seeds. "Er . . . no. I mean, yes. I mean . . . oh, hell. Please sit down."

"Thanks," said the woman, and did so with a sigh of relief.

"Have you been shopping?" he asked, gesturing at the large canvas—obviously heavy—shoulder bag that she dumped on the floor by her side.

The woman ran a slim hand through her short black hair; Jack loved the way the glossy hair fell back into place in the wake of her raking fingers.

"No, I'm a relief teacher. I've been taking a class of nine year olds all morning in Kilburn. Absolute horrors. I dread to think why their normal teacher's off school. Probably knife wounds or head injuries or maybe they let her off lightly with a nervous breakdown."

"Oh dear," said Jack. "You don't have to go back this afternoon, do you?"

"No, thank God. I've been there every morning this week. Hopefully by Monday their usual teacher will be back."

He nodded and gave a sympathetic smile and tried to think of something else to say. He was saved from having to do so by the arrival of his main course. The waitress gave the woman a menu and took her order for a pineapple juice. Jack added pepper, chili seeds and parmesan to his food and began to eat.

Normally he relished this meal, but today he felt self-conscious. One errant strand of tagliatelle and his chin would be smeared in greasy sauce. Not that it really mattered. Half an hour from now he would leave the restaurant and never see the woman again. All the same he ate his meal slowly and carefully, taking pains to ensure that nothing slid from his fork at just the wrong moment.

"That looks good," the woman said. "I don't think I've ever had that before."

Jack looked up at her, swallowing quickly. "It is good," he said. "I usually have it when I come here. I always arrive determined to try something different, but this is so tasty that as soon as I see it on the menu I have to order it."

The woman laughed. Her tongue was small and pink, her teeth very straight and white; Jack wondered what it would be like to kiss her. "I'm just the same," she said. "I always go for the seafood pizza and side salad. Maybe we ought to swap meals just to be more adventurous."

Jack shook his head. "Thanks, but I couldn't. Not seafood."

"You don't like it?"

"I don't know how *anyone* can. All those tentacles and unidentifiable rubbery bits."

"You don't know what you're missing. Fried squid in garlic butter. Absolutely delicious!"

"I'll take your word for it."

"No, no, I'm serious. Look, if I order a seafood pizza will you promise to try a bit?"

Jack pulled a face. "No," he said apologetically. "I couldn't, honestly."

The woman looked at him with a half-smile on her face. She was very beautiful. Jack had to make a conscious effort not to gaze at her for too long. Her eyes were large and dark. She had little smile lines around her mouth. Jack would have loved to have been able to reach out and stroke her face just to feel whether her skin was as soft as it looked.

"Well, that's very narrow-minded of you if you don't mind me saying so," she said, but her tone was light, almost playful.

Jack shrugged. "I know. I'd love to try lots of different foods, but something in here"—he tapped his head—"won't let me."

"Perhaps you need a psychiatrist," she suggested teasingly.

"Ah, zo you sink my food phobias are buried deep in my subconscious?" he said, narrowing his eyes to complement his comic Freudian voice.

"Could be. Did your parents ever used to beat you around the head with baby octopuses?"

Jack tried to laugh, but her question, asked in fun, was too close to home and it emerged as a hard and hollow sound. He shrugged and sat up straight as though pulling back from the game. He twirled his fork in the tagliatelle and lifted it to his mouth.

"I'm sorry, did I say something wrong?" the woman asked.

Jack looked at her, re-establishing the eye contact he had broken abruptly when she'd mentioned his parents. She looked a little confused and genuinely concerned.

"No," he said with what he hoped was a convincing smile. "It's just . . . no, it's okay, forget it."

She was silent, as though uncertain whether to apologise or change the subject. The waitress arrived to take her order and the woman said, "I'll have what he's having. With a side salad." When the waitress left, she said, "See? I'm being adventurous."

Jack glanced up at her and saw she was grinning at him. He grinned back. The awkwardness between them passed.

"Have you ever tried sushi?" the woman asked, swirling the remains of the juice in her glass.

"An editor took me to a Japanese restaurant once," Jack replied. "It was a disaster. I hated everything."

"Jeez." She rolled her eyes. "You're a real fussy cater, aren't you?"

"No, I'm not," he said indignantly.

"Yes, you are. What do you mean, editor? Do you work in publishing?"

The abrupt change of subject threw Jack. He hadn't realised he'd said editor until she pointed it out to him. Shit, now he'd have to explain that he was a writer. People tended either to get all starry-eyed when he talked about his work or they treated him like a freak. Some of his friends still could not accept that writing was his job, that it was what he did for a living. Sometimes they would say, "Hey, Jack, I've got a day off on Thursday. Do you fancy a game of squash?" If he told them he had too much work to do, they would look puzzled for a moment and then say, "Work? Oh, you mean writing your stories. Yeah, but you can do that any time, can't you?"

"You don't have to tell me if you don't want to."

"Pardon?" said Jack.

"Whether you work in publishing. If it's a secret it doesn't matter."

"Oh . . . no. Sorry, I was miles away. I . . . sort of work in publishing." He leaned forward a little and subconsciously lowered his voice. "Actually, I'm a writer."

The woman looked at him a moment as though waiting for him to elaborate, then she replied, "You mean a working writer? You do it full-time?"

Jack nodded.

"That's great. What do you write?"

"Well . . . mainly horror, fantasy, science-fiction . . . that kind of stuff."

He expected her to recoil, to turn up her nose; it was the reaction he got from most people. However, she said again, "That's great. What name do you write under?"

He always hated this bit. He would say his name and she would give him a blank look and there would be embarrassment all round. "Jack Stone," he said quietly.

"You're joking! Oh my God, I read *Song of Flesh* earlier this year. I liked it so much I went out and bought *Bleeding Hearts* and read that, too. And now I can't wait for *Consummation* to come out in paperback. November, isn't it?"

"Yes," said Jack, surprised and delighted. "Beginning of November. I think Cormorant want to cash in on the Christmas market."

"Cormorant?"

"My publisher."

"Oh, yeah, right."

The woman beamed at him and Jack smiled back. He hoped she wasn't going to get all reverential. He lowered his eyes to his plate and scooped up a forkful of chicken and tagliatelle. The sauce was beginning to congeal a little. As he raised the fork to his mouth, the waitress arrived with the woman's food. Jack glanced up, and a sauce-laden gobbet of chicken slid off his fork and into his lap. "Oh, shit," he groaned. The creamy sauce left a white smeary trail on the crotch of his jeans. Opposite him he could hear the woman trying to stifle her giggles.

"Bloody hell," said Jack when the waitress had gone, "I knew that would happen." He wiped at his crotch as surreptitiously as he could with a wad of napkin.

"Never mind. What's a few stains between friends?" She raised a piece of chicken to her lips and began to chew it daintily. God, thought Jack, she's gorgeous.

"Not exactly cool though, is it?" he said ruefully.

"Thank goodness. People who think they're cool are normally utter prats."

Jack shrugged. Probing in what he thought was not an unsubtle way, he asked, "I'll bet I'm not quite what you expected, though, am I?"

The woman raised dark eyes to look at him. "How do you mean?"

Jack reddened a little. "Well . . . my books are . . . I mean, they've been *described* as . . . sort of . . . you know . . . nicely written, subtle, complex . . . evocative, sensual, all that kind of stuff. And yet look at me: a clumsy oaf who throws food all over himself."

The woman had stopped eating and was looking at Jack

half-smilingly, waving her fork in the air. "Are you fishing for sympathy or compliments?"

Jack felt his blush deepening. "Oh, Christ. See what I mean? Subtle as a house brick. I think I'll just crawl under this table until you've gone."

The woman put another forkful of food in her mouth. Chewing, she said, "I'll tell you what my mental image of you was, shall I?"

"Oh God, this'll depress me."

"No, it won't. Don't put yourself down so much."

Jack pushed his plate aside, folded his arms on the table and leaned forward. "Sorry," he said. "Go on then. I'm listening."

The woman smiled. "Okay." She looked thoughtful for a moment and then said, "I thought you'd be taller."

"Oh dear."

She ignored the interruption. "I thought you'd be . . . gangly, with short blond hair receding at the front, a thin face, little round glasses. I thought you'd dress more formally than you do. I thought you'd be . . . quietly confident, intellectual, very sensitive, very aloof. I even had a feeling you might be gay."

"Really?" said Jack, breaking into a grin. "Why?"

She thoughtfully drew back her lips and licked her upper teeth. Jack thought again how gorgeous she was. He could quite happily stay here all afternoon talking to this woman. He was beginning to feel very relaxed, very comfortable, in her presence.

"Because of the sensuality, the sensitivity, in your work. Despite some of the nasty stuff that happens, your good characters are very gentle, very caring. Through your work I imagined you having this shell around you, keeping publicity at arm's length, but inside I thought you'd be like your good characters—very tender, very, very gentle."

She'd cupped her hands while saying this and brought them up to her chest as though she was holding this inner core of gentleness in the form of a delicate flower. Jack felt strangely moved. He wanted to reach across the table and hug her.

"Sorry to shatter your illusions," he said, smiling to show he was only half-serious.

She raised her eyes heavenward. "There you go, putting yourself down again. You may not be how I imagined, but that doesn't mean I'm disappointed."

"Doesn't it?"

"Of course not. You're hunkier looking for a start, and you're much friendlier and more approachable than I thought you'd be."

Jack gave his soppiest grin. "Shucks, thanks."

"But don't take that as a chat-up line," she warned him. "I'm not some fame-hungry groupie, you know."

Jack laughed and she laughed along with him, causing a few people to turn and look at her. Jack hoped they thought she was his girlfriend or wife. He hoped they were envious.

"Hey," he said suddenly, "I don't even know your name."

"Gail," she said and held out her hand for him to shake. "Gail Reeves."

Jack took the hand. Her skin was smooth and as warm as it looked. He would have liked to have maintained this contact for a while, but he released the hand almost as soon as he had touched it, as if concerned his desire would somehow translate itself to her.

"Very pleased to meet you," he said with mock formality. "Would you care to join me in a cup of coffee?"

"Do you think there'll be room for both of us?"

"Oh God, I was hoping you wouldn't say that."

She laughed and apologised. Over coffee Gail asked Jack more questions about his work. She was intelligent and witty and genuinely interested without being over-awed, and he found after a while that he was actually enjoying talking about himself. He asked her about herself, too, and discovered she owned a flat in Tottenham, five minutes walk from Seven Sisters tube station. She was twenty-eight years old, had been a relief teacher for four years, was an avid cinema-goer, loved reading though was so busy she only managed one book a month (though she had read *Song of Flesh* in less than a week!), and ate out more than she could really afford to. Jack wondered if she had a boyfriend; she didn't mention one and the traditional engagement/wedding finger was ringless. He couldn't remember the last time he had hit it off with someone so quickly. Certainly after only an hour in this woman's company he'd established more of a rapport with her than he'd ever managed with Carol. Despite his intention to remain unattached, Jack found himself attempting to pluck up the courage to ask Gail for her address or phone number. He spent an agonizing twenty minutes trying to contrive a situation whereby he could do so before she conveniently provided him with one.

They had returned to the subject of his latest novel, *Consummation,* which had been published in hardback but would not be released in paperback for another six months. Gail had asked Jack to tell her what the book was about. "Whet my appetite," she'd said, "but don't give anything away."

"You don't want much, do you?" he said, smiling, and then had launched into a stumbling, long-winded explanation of the themes and ideas behind the book. Usually the question, "What's your book about?" made him want to run in the other direction. Jack thought all plots, especially of the books he wrote, sounded incredibly silly when summarised. It was how they were written that brought them alive, that made the outrageous credible.

"Pretty dumb, huh?" he said ruefully when he had finished.

But Gail's eyes were shining. "No," she said, "it sounds wonderful. Oh, wow, I can't wait to read it."

Jack saw the opening he had been waiting for suddenly appear, a great gash of light in his mind's eye, and he went for it before it could close up again. "Tell you what," he said, hoping his motives would not seem as transparent to Gail as they seemed to him, "as you're so enthusiastic, why don't I send you a copy of the hardback, then you won't have to wait another six months?"

She stared at him, dark eyes wide and breathtakingly appealing, and then slowly her lips spread into a stunning grin. Jack felt that light must be blazing from that grin, brightening the whole restaurant. She said, "Oh, wow, that would be lovely." Then a small frown appeared. "But I can't ask you to do that. You must think I'm incredibly pushy. I wasn't trying to drop hints, you know."

Jack shook his head, feeling a little guilty. "I never thought you were. Really, I'd love to send you a book. I've got loads at home. It's not as if you're depriving me of my only copy."

This wasn't strictly true. Of the dozen complimentary copies that Cormorant had sent him, Jack had only three left. But that's okay, he told himself. He'd be fine with one for people to look at and one to keep on the shelves in pristine condition, and it wasn't as if he couldn't get more if he needed them.

"Okay then," she said, "if you're sure. You'll need my address, won't you?"

"It would help," Jack said, "unless you want me to drop the package at some secret location?"

Gail rewarded him with another stunning smile and wrote her address in tiny neat letters in his notepad. Jack zipped the pad into the inner pocket of his leather jacket, and five minutes later he and Gail paid their bills, said their good-byes and went their separate ways.

Jack felt certain he would never see her again. When he arrived home the first thing he did was write a brief note to her that read, *"Dear Gail, Thank you for brightening up my lunchtime. Here's the book I promised you."* He held his pen poised hesitantly over the page for a moment before signing, *"Love, Jack."* Trying to make it look casual but as legible as possible, he then printed his address and telephone number in the top right-hand corner of the page. Only then did he listen to his answering machine, which contained a single message from Frank apologising for not turning up.

"That's okay, Frank," Jack said, looking out of the window at the bright blue sky and feeling very good inside. He took one of his three copies of *Consummation* down from the shelf. "That's very okay indeed."

He was disappointed, but not entirely surprised, when the following week passed without even an acknowledgement from Gail that she had received his book. Then on Friday evening, at twenty-five past six, the telephone rang. Jack was lying in the bath, snoozing. Beside him was a square wicker basket into which he dumped his dirty washing, and on top of the wicker basket was an empty mug that had contained tea, a half-eaten packet of digestive biscuits, a collection by Robert Aickman called *Powers of Darkness* (which was, in fact, one of the secondhand books that he had bought the previous Friday), and the telephone, the long lead of which snaked out into the hall. Jack came fully awake on the second ring. His arm and hand came out of the bath like a brontosaurus in miniature, water streaming from it. He quickly towelled the hand dry and snatched the phone up. "Hello," he said.

"Is that Jack Stone?"

"Yes, it is."

"Hello, Jack. This is Gail here. Gail Reeves. Remember, we met last week in the restaurant?"

As if he would forget! "Gail, hi. Of course I remember. How are you?"

"Very well, thank you. You?"

"Oh . . . fine. Listen, Gail, did you get the book?"

"Yes, I did. Thank you so much. I was so thrilled. Actually that's why I'm ringing. I'm sorry I didn't ring earlier, but I wanted to read it before I spoke to you again."

"Oh, right," Jack said. He felt a little surge in his heart. So she *had* intended to ring him right from the beginning! It wasn't just guilt or politeness that had prompted this call.

"I thought it was superb," she said. "I really did. Your best one yet. I actually cried when the little boy died."

"Great," said Jack, then laughed. "Sorry, I didn't mean it like that. I just meant it was great that you felt so emotionally attached to the characters."

"Oh, I did. The old woman, Florrie, was so lovely. And the wife, too—I liked her a lot. You really know how women think and feel, Jack. It's so refreshing to find a male writer who can write good female characters."

"Thanks," he said, flattered by her praise. "I don't really know where that . . . insight, if you want to call it that, comes from, though. I grew up without a mother and I never had any sisters. And I'm not particularly good at relationships."

He paused, surprised by his own openness; he had already revealed more of himself to Gail in those two sentences than he ever revealed to most people. "Anyway . . . ," he mumbled to cover his confusion "I . . . er . . . so . . . er . . . what are you up to this weekend?"

"Oh," she said, "nothing much. I might meet up with some friends for a drink tonight, but then again I might not. I may go see a film tomorrow—I think *Wild at Heart* is on at the NFT. I missed it the first time around."

"Do you like David Lynch?" Jack asked.

"Well . . . yes. I find his stuff incredibly powerful and

compelling, but the intensity is pretty unbearable sometimes. How about you?"

"Oh, yeah, he and Roeg and Cronenberg are my favourite directors. Pretty standard for someone working in my genre, I suppose. Did you see *Blue Velvet*? I think that may be my favourite film of all time."

"No, I think that's the only one of his I haven't seen."

"Oh, you must see it. It's excellent."

"I will," said Gail.

"In fact, I've got it on DVD. You'll have to come round and watch it sometime."

"Are you asking me for a date, Jack Stone?" Gail said, and he could almost hear the smile in her voice.

He blushed. "Well, I . . . I mean, if you want to, I . . ."

"It's okay, I know you were just being polite."

"No, I wasn't! I mean . . . Oh, Christ, look, I would love to see you again. I really would."

"Really?"

"Of course."

She was silent for a long moment. Jack was beginning to think she had put the phone down, or was about to. "Gail?" he said.

"Okay then," she said. "Why don't we?"

"What?"

"Why don't we . . . see each other?"

"Are you sure?"

"I wouldn't suggest it if I wasn't."

Jack felt a grin forming on his face. "In that case, why not come round tomorrow night? I could get *Wild at Heart* out as well and we could watch them both. I could get some beers and make some supper . . ." He tailed off, aware that his enthusiasm was running away with him. Clearing his throat, forcing himself to calm down, he said, "Or . . . I don't know, what do you think? Maybe it would be better if we met on neutral ground again first. I mean, you hardly know me, do you? Maybe we—"

"Jack?"

"Er . . . yeah?"

"I'd love to come round to your flat. But are you sure you really want me to? You haven't got anything else planned?"

"No, of course not. It'd be great if you came round. I really do want to see you again."

"Okay then. What time?"

"Seven-thirty? Eight?"

"I'll be there somewhere in between."

"Brilliant. I'll see you then."

"You certainly will. I'll look forward to it."

"Me too."

"Bye then, until tomorrow."

"Yeah, bye."

The next day Jack tidied and cleaned his flat thoroughly, and then spent a long time striding from room to room, trying to see the place with new, critical eyes. He really wanted Gail to like his flat. It was an extension of his personality and if she liked where he lived, if she felt comfortable here, then Jack felt they would get on well. Over the years he had accumulated a variety of paraphernalia, much of it bizarre, and he spent most of the afternoon wondering whether he should leave it all on show or whether he should hide much of it, let her get used to it in stages. Carol had never felt happy here, and that was something that had constantly set their relationship on edge. In the end, Jack decided to leave everything where it was. If this relationship was going to blossom, then it would be because Gail liked him for exactly who and what he was. He had compromised himself so much with Carol, had found it so disheartening, so soul-destroying, and in the end it still hadn't been enough. However much he wanted Gail to like him, Jack was damned if he was going to stumble into that trap again.

Despite his nerves, the evening was an unmitigated success. Gail did not just like his flat, she loved it; she spent a long time simply walking around exclaiming at things, picking objects up and examining them, asking him where he got this or that. The only time she grimaced was when she saw his bird-eating spider splayed out in its glass case on the wall with a pin through its abdomen. "I'm afraid I don't approve of killing things just to put them on display," she said.

"Neither do I," he said hastily. "I was given that by a friend. I would never have bought it myself."

When she asked about the skull propping up some paperbacks on one of the shelves, he told her it was a monkey's skull and that a friend of his called Nigel had brought it back from Borneo; when she asked him why he had an enormous framed photograph on his bathroom wall of a centipede emerging from a mound of earth he explained it was because he had a phobia about centipedes and was a strong believer in confronting one's fears.

She spent a long time perusing the bookshelves, pulling books out and looking at them, which he greatly approved of. He was enchanted when, at first, she hunkered down in front of the bookcase in the hall and, with an expression like a child in a sweetshop, asked, "May I?"

"Of course you may!" he replied effusively, and for the next hour he and Gail became embroiled in a passionate discussion about books. At one point they both crouched beside a bookcase, so close that their shoulders were touching. Jack could smell her perfume and the fresh scent of her hair, and he felt almost dizzy with happiness.

They watched the films and ate the food that Jack prepared, and Gail drank gin and tonic whilst he had beer. After the films had ended they talked about them over coffee, and then they talked about other films, and then books again, and then writing, and then London, and then just general stuff. Finally Jack drove Gail home in his Mini

Cooper. He dropped her outside her building, which looked white and modern and featureless in the darkness. She thanked him for a fabulous evening, and when she leaned across and kissed him on the cheek, Jack felt the breath hitch in his throat, a grin stretch his mouth for the hundredth time that evening. "Can I see you again?" he asked, aware of how corny it sounded.

She smiled as if she were the lucky one. "Yes, please," she murmured. "I'd like that very much."

When Jack arrived home it was 3:40 A.M., but he felt far too buoyant to be tired. He lay back on his sofa, lights turned low, the CD of didgeridoo music he had bought the week before playing on his stereo, and he thought of Gail until the memory of her face and her voice and her smell entwined with the ancient magic of the music and tugged him deliciously down into sleep.

3

THE OGRE

When Jack was in the tunnel he became almost overwhelmed by the knowledge that this was the only certainty in his life. It was awful, this knowledge, sickening.
It was like a poison seeping through his system, consist-
ing of dread and loneliness and a surging, terrible panic.
He could barely breathe; his clenched fists shook as
though the fingers were striving to burst open; his heartbeat felt like the cruel rhythmic squeezing of some tender
internal bruise. In his soul of souls Jack knew that this
place, this dark and dreadful place, was the single inevitable truth. The rest of it was a sham, a delusion of tin-
sel and glitter, which would fade little by little until he
was left dreamless.

He brought his shaking fists slowly up to his face and
pressed them against his forehead. No, he mustn't think
about that. Such a thought was enough to drive anyone
mad. While he could still dream he would try to return
there, he would cling with single-minded desperation to
the privilege. And he'd try to believe that there was mean-

ing to life, or at least obliteration at the end of it. For even obliteration had a kind of meaning. Far more, at least, than this sense of endlessness, this terror that was growing and growing, and which would continue to do so boundlessly, with no focus to contain it.

Concentrating as hard as he could on holding his thoughts together, Jack slowly spread his arms out to either side of him and touched the black walls with his fists. They were cold and dead, and they seemed to transmit their deadness to him. He felt a sense of despair, of defeat, that paradoxically was all the more acute because it was as murky and indistinct as undersea vision. He wanted to scream, to yell out his fury and defiance. He opened his mouth, but before the sound could emerge, a figure—grey and grainy, more like dust than shadow—emerged from the blackness and began to glide towards him.

He felt sharp, new fear, though now that there was a reason for it the emotion seemed almost welcome. He waited whilst the figure approached. It was so vague as to be sexless and faceless. When it was no more than a few yards away it reached out a hand, which Jack automatically took. The hand was neither warm nor cold; it was simply a pressure enclosing his fingers, offering to lead him. And Jack was quite prepared to let himself be led. It felt liberating to transfer the responsibility for his actions on to this shade, this phantom. The figure turned away, tugging at him gently. Jack tottered after it, feeling like a small child, his legs unsteady, his mind struggling with a situation too confusing to assimilate.

Obliquely, almost covertly, the tunnel first broadened and then changed into something else. He was unaware of this process; all he knew was that suddenly the ground was strewn thinly with undergrowth and stones and twigs, and that the black confining walls had become a wood or a forest, various perspectives of trees crammed into a dense wall of bark.

It was lighter than it had been, though the sky was still murky, as if the prelude to a storm was pressing itself on the land. Despite this the figure was no more detailed than in the tunnel. Jack found it almost impossible to focus upon, as if somehow it deflected his vision.

The woods were eerily still, depressingly colourless: leaves were more grey than green, trees more black than brown. Though Jack was beginning to feel he had a bond with this figure, that somehow he and it were the same thing, he nevertheless felt his dread mounting.

There was another strange spatial shift, and all at once Jack and the grey figure were standing in front of a house. As soon as Jack saw the building he tried to pull away, but he felt feeble and dumb; it was as if only his soul writhed, as if his body which contained it was mute, acquiescent. He felt himself walking through the gate and up the path towards the front door. The figure glided ahead of him, its hand clasped in his. The sky was yellow as curdled milk, the house enclosed within a watery haze, like a painting blurred in the rain. Jack knew this house, though why he knew it escaped his flinching mind. Though he did not know who or what waited inside, the thought of opening that front door and entering was so terrifying that he felt fragile as a glass that the sustained screech of his fear threatened to shatter.

And then he was inside the house, the dark blur of its walls, its thick smell, enveloping him. He had not opened the front door; it was as if the house had oozed around him, sucked him into its darkness. He was alone. The grey figure was gone. Though Jack's mind felt brittle, his flesh vague, there was a deep terrible sickness at the core of him. It felt like a shifting, dark tumour composed of all the badness—all the pain and fear and anguish—in his life. And this place, this house, was its home. This was the place where all the badness had originated.

Jack felt himself moving forward, though he had a

strong compulsion to flee. Perhaps it was the house that was moving, sliding over and around him, like some vast slow creature dragging him towards its ever-working, ever-hungry mouth. The smell was pungent and stomach-turning. It was ostensibly the smell of bad food and stale air, of grime and old sweat, though to Jack it smelled of cruelty and violence, of tears and dread. A staircase slid up and away on his right, doors passed by his shoulders. And then another doorway rose and gobbled him, and he was standing in a room.

It was a room he knew, though again the outlines were vague, sketchy, the details washed with a brown dingy murk that was like dust and shadow and muddy water. There were suggestions of furniture in the room, two small windows, a fireplace, perhaps even pictures on the walls. Jack's attention, however, was focused on a dining table and four chairs, two of which were occupied. For the moment, the occupants were blurred; Jack could not, or would not, look at them too closely. He could hear a clock in the room, a slow sonorous ticking. He pulled out one of the unoccupied chairs with a dull scrape and sat down.

As soon as he did so he realised that the table and chairs were much larger than they had appeared to be. The top of the table came to his chest, and though he stretched he could not quite touch the floor with his feet. He stared at his hands, not daring to look at his fellow diners. For, indeed, they *were* dining; Jack could hear the chewing and swallowing sounds they made, the smacking they made with their lips, the slurping and sucking and grunting that was more porcine than human.

And then one of them spoke to him, and Jack almost screamed with the shock of it. *Look at me,* the voice said. There was a threat in there, a dark undertone of menace. Jack did not want to look, but he knew that if he disobeyed, something very, very bad, something indescribably awful, would happen to him. He knew this because it had happened to him before . . . and would undoubtedly happen again.

And so he looked. He raised his head and he turned it in the direction of that terrible voice. The first thing he saw was the mouth—the slobbery lips, the blocky grey teeth and black gleaming tongue. There was food in the mouth, stringy and wet with juices. It was being mashed by the teeth; morsels of it, hanging over the lips like tiny eels, were sucked remorselessly into the maw. The face was huge and rubbery, misshapen as a caricature. Jack saw a prickly beard, a huge nose bulbous as a pear, a ridged slab of brow and wiry eyebrows. The eyes were mean and bulging, the irises completely black. The instant he looked into that face, Jack was hit by two sudden and shocking revelations.

This monster was his father.

His father was the ogre from his book.

Jack was astounded that he had never realised this before, though now that he had it made perfect and terrible sense. He looked down at his lap, upon which now rested the book in question. It was entitled *The Bumper Book of Fairy Tales,* and the cover depicted a princess in a ball gown and tiara kneeling beside a stream, apparently talking to a frog on a lily pad. Jack opened the book, turned the pages until he found the story he was looking for: *Jack and the Beanstalk.* He turned to the page that he knew had a picture of the ogre crouched malevolently over a pile of gold coins, but upon reaching that page he was shocked to discover there was only a black rectangular box instead of an illustration. Once again Jack looked up at the ogre, his father. He saw those black bulging eyes glaring down at him and knew he was in terrible, terrible trouble. The ogre's lips flapped and writhed. *Look at your mother,* it said. *Look what you've done to her, you little shit.* Jack turned his head to look at the table's other occupant.

He saw a woman with white-blue skin and black hair. This was his mother, the way Jack always thought of her. Her face was calm and still, her eyes closed. She wore a white gown that seemed to billow gently in some breeze that Jack could not feel. Her arms were held slightly out from her body, palms up; the image was somehow saintly. All that spoiled the aura of peace were the growing blood-stains on the bottom half of the robe, bloodstains that started as coins of red, and quickly expanded to the size of plates, and then coalesced into a single crimson mass, spreading and covering the white cloth.

Jack saw blood running down the smooth white flesh of his mother's legs and wondered how, if she was sitting behind a table, this could be so. Then he realised she was no longer sitting; she was rising like an angel into the air. She rose above the table and hovered there for a moment. Blood dripped from her robe; Jack heard the insignificant *pat . . . pat . . .* sound of it striking the wooden tabletop. Slowly, she opened her eyes, and Jack saw that the eye-balls were completely white—and even though they were white he felt himself squirming beneath their accusing gaze. A single tear of blood brimmed and then trickled down her cheek. She drifted closer to him. Slowly, her hands took the bloodied hem of her robe and began to raise it. Jack caught the barest glimpse of something slick and pulsing between her legs, something that seemed made of purplish-grey flesh. . . .

And then he woke, bathed in sweat, his choking cry teasing at his throat, puncturing the darkness.

He sat up in bed, panting, his heartbeat tight and violent in his chest. He had a sour taste in his mouth. The cold air quickly dried the sweat on him and started him shivering. He realised he was clenching handfuls of duvet, and relaxed his grip with an effort. He released a shudder of stale breath. Beside him Gail stirred.

"Jack?" she murmured dreamily. "Are you okay?"

He swallowed. "I had one of my dreams," he said hoarsely.

He heard the soft sound of her body on the sheets and knew that she was striving to wake, perhaps propping herself on an elbow. When she touched his arm he felt his skin flinch, shrivel into itself; a bristling wave of goosebumps coursed up his arm, across his shoulders and down his back. "Poor honey," she murmured. "What was this one about?"

Jack was getting cold again. He pulled the duvet up to his chin. "The usual," he said flatly.

"Beckford?"

"Yeah."

"Was it another childhood dream?"

This time he simply nodded.

She drew closer to him, began to stroke his hair with one hand and then gently to knead the bunched muscles in his neck and shoulders. "You're so tense," she said. She sat up, dragging herself from beneath the duvet, and then moved behind him and hugged him, her arms going over his shoulders and encircling his neck, her breasts pushing into his back, her legs straddling him from behind. She kissed his ear and cheek. His sweat was like the sediment of his dream, clinging and coppery. "It's okay," she whispered. "Everything's okay now. It's all over."

He was silent for a long, long moment. At last he said, "Why is this happening now?"

"What do you mean?" Gail said.

Jack shrugged, and again didn't reply immediately. He took one of her hands, meshed his fingers with hers.

Finally he said, "When I left Beckford I was pretty screwed up. I did not have a happy childhood." He snorted without humour. "That's an understatement. But . . . well . . . I'm over that now. I've been over it a long time. So why am I suddenly having these dreams? Why now, when everything's going so well?"

Gail kissed his ear gently, hugged him tighter. "Maybe you're not fully over it. Maybe it's been lying dormant inside you all these years and it's finally working its way out."

Jack thought of a friend of his who had had a car accident. It had taken two years for a shard of metal the size of a fingernail to work its way out of his leg.

"I don't know," he said, unconvinced.

"But you still don't like to talk about your childhood, do you?"

"No, but . . . I don't know. That's different."

"Why is it different? If you were over it you'd be able to talk about it. Whenever I ask you anything you just clam up, give me that dangerous look of yours. If I push it, you get angry."

Jack scowled, felt himself tensing. "No, I don't."

"Yes, you do. You're doing it now."

He was. He knew he was and he couldn't help it.

"Okay," he conceded grumpily, "but I still don't see why all this should choose now to emerge. I'm not unhappy. In fact I'm the happiest I've been for a long time. I've got you, and I've finally hit the bestseller lists. Everything's going really well."

"Well, maybe that's got something to do with it. Maybe, for the first time in your life, you've got something you're terrified of losing. Perhaps, subconsciously, you think the only threat to your happiness are the monsters of your childhood, the bad memories which are locked in here." She tapped his head.

Jack thought about it. At last he said, "No, I don't think so."

"Oh, you're impossible," Gail said in exasperation. "Tell me about your childhood then, get it all out in the open."

Jack felt his temper rising a little and tried to stifle it. "I will," he said.

"When?"

"I don't know . . . sometime."

"Why not now?"

Jack waved a hand at the clock. "Don't be stupid, it's . . . ," he squinted at the luminous hands "ten past three in the morning."

"So?"

"So it's bedtime."

"We're in bed."

"Okay then, sleep time."

Gail snorted. "Excuses."

Jack's breathing became quicker as his anger rose. "Don't hassle me, Gail," he snapped. "I'll tell you in my own time, okay?"

She hugged him hard, almost roughly. "I love you," she said. "I don't want us to have secrets from each other."

"We won't," Jack said.

"But we do."

"We won't," he repeated more firmly. "I'll tell you sometime, I promise."

"Soon?"

"Yeah, yeah."

"You mean it?"

"Yes," he snapped. "Now let's go to sleep."

She sighed, disentangled herself from him. They lay back, Jack grimacing at the clammy sheets.

There was silence for a time. Then Gail said, "Jack?"

"Mm?"

"Was your childhood really bad?"

He paused. "Yes," he said quietly, "it was."

"Oh. I'm sorry."

"It's not your fault."

"No, I know."

Silence enfolded them again. Jack closed his eyes and slept uneasily till dawn.

4

CROSS MY HEART

On Saturday, May 8th, Jack woke up feeling edgy, tense and irritable. Normally when he awoke, even without the aid of an alarm, Gail awoke too, as if their body clocks were perfectly attuned. Today, however, she slept on, perhaps because Jack's muscles had been so taut that his body had remained still even as his brain clicked on and his eyes fluttered open. He was glad that she had stayed asleep. He didn't know why he should be feeling this way and he wanted some time to ponder it. He stared up at the ceiling, aware of the rigidity in his back and shoulders and limbs, the nervous curling in his innards that Gail always referred to as a "twizzly tummy." He tried to smile at that, but it was a tight smile, hard to maintain. He felt as if his anxious thoughts were clenching their teeth and their fists, locking themselves into his head.

But why? He had no reason to be worried or uptight, had he? His new book was coming along nicely, his relationship with Gail was as close and loving as ever, his health, as far as he knew, was good, and his money worries minimal. His last nightmare, the one about the ogre, had been five days ago, and since then Gail had left the subject of his childhood alone. So why did he feel as if something bad was about to happen? Trying to create as little noise and disturbance as possible he slid out of bed.

He stood for a moment, naked, and listened to Gail's breathing; it remained unchanged. The sound of the heating, its soft, comforting *shhhh,* was like breathing, too. Jack could feel its benefit, its warmth permeating the flat, which meant it was sometime after 7 A.M. He crossed to the armchair, the seat on which he had tossed his clothes last night, and fished around in the folds for his watch. He unearthed it and looked at the time—7:15. Pale grey shadows, soft as felt, were laid over the room, muting its colours, though sunlight was pressing against the curtains in a butter-yellow block. Gail's clothes were neatly folded and draped over the back of the chair. Jack picked up her lilac sweatshirt and held it to his face. It was warmly imbued with the scent she wore, Magie Noire, and her own wonderful Gail-smell that to Jack was comforting and luxurious and arousing. Though he had just got out of bed he was not cold, and because of this, and because he didn't want to wake Gail by tugging out drawers to search for clean underwear, he padded naked out of the room.

He sat on the toilet, browsing through a book called *Magical Britain* that he had taken from the small alcove behind him. The pages of the book were corrugated from the steam of countless baths. Jack, however, was not really reading the book; he was merely giving his hands something to do whilst his mind chewed over some possible cause for his anxiety. He couldn't think of anything at all. To call the feeling presentiment or foreboding made it sound more mystical than it felt.

He went to the kitchen to make breakfast. The linoleum was cold on his bare feet. Sunshine streamed through the skylight and reflected in harsh spasms on the room's myriad gleaming surfaces. He poured muesli into two bowls, chopped half a banana into each, and then topped them with milk. He placed the bowls on a tray, to which he added a plate containing four crumpets with butter and jam, a pot of tea, a mug and a cup. Gail always only drank half a cup of weak tea in the morning; Jack drank at least two mugfuls, the stronger the better. He carried the tray into the bedroom and set it down on the floor next to Gail's side of the bed, having to first clear a pile of books that had been allowed to accumulate over the last couple of weeks.

Now was the time to wake Gail, now that he had brooded over the cause of his concern, without result. He leaned forward and kissed her cheek, which was flushed and hot because she had been lying on it. Her short dark hair was tousled, her brows slightly beetled as if she were concentrating hard on the dream she was having. When Jack kissed her she murmured unintelligibly, allowing him the minutest glimpse of her white teeth and pink tongue.

Seeing her like this, curled up and defenceless as she slept, made Jack ache with love for her. Sometimes he loved her so much that there were no words or actions to express the depth of his emotion. "I love you," or even "I love you so much," seemed woefully inadequate—to try and express through language what seemed limitless in his head and heart only served to diminish it. Hugs, too, kisses, even eye contact was not enough. Once, in Hyde Park, Jack had said, "How can I prove that I truly love you? What could I do that would make you realise just how much?"

It had been a cold day, a foreshadow of winter. Gail's nose and cheeks had been red, her eyes clear and sharp as the air. Lifting her chin from the fleecy swathes of her scarf she had asked, "Would you kill yourself for me?"

"If you like," said Jack. "Got a knife?"

"No, I'm serious. If you really had to . . . would you do it?"

Jack looked at her, and there was an earnestness in her face, an appeal, that both unsettled him and roused in him a love so acute it was like pain. He took her cold face in his gloved hands and pulled her gently to him so that their foreheads and noses touched. "Yes, I would," he said and kissed her warm lips. "I'd do anything for you."

She drew back from him. "Promise?"

Jack laughed. "Yes," he said, and drew two swift intersecting lines across his breastbone. "Cross my heart and hope to die."

He sat down on her side of the bed, making the springs creak and Gail murmur a little more. He reached out and touched her hair, tenderly running a finger along the points of her spiky fringe. "Come on, cutey pie, wake up," he said. "Brekky's ready."

Gail made a sound that seemed to suggest she was not impressed. Then she said very clearly, "Please don't disturb the herbs in my hair. I haven't got any more."

Jack laughed. Some of the stuff she came out with when she was half-asleep was priceless. "Don't worry," he said, "the herbs are safe. Will you wake up now."

"Mnn," she said, which could have meant either yes or no. Eyes still closed, she said, "Please, doctor, there must be something you can do. Alice can't die."

The anxiety inside Jack, vague and smouldering until now, suddenly flared, making his whole body jerk on the bed as if shocked from a dream. The movement woke Gail. Her eyes crinkled open into slits. She rolled onto her back and regarded him. "What are you doing?" she grumbled thickly.

"What were you dreaming about?" Jack said, aware that his voice sounded harsh, snappish.

At this moment, barely awake, the question was too taxing. "What?" she grunted.

"Just now. A minute ago. You were dreaming about something. What was it?"

Gail's eyes reluctantly opened a millimetre further. She looked at Jack as if he were a stranger accosting her in some language she did not understand. Then she yawned and said, "I can't remember. What time is it? Is there any grapefruit juice?"

He scowled at the irrelevancy. "No," he snapped. "Please, Gail, try and remember what it was you were dreaming about."

Even as he harried her, Jack knew this was quite definitely not the way to go about it. At the best of times Gail needed careful handling first thing in the morning. She was one of those people who woke up snarling and scowling, who would make even a bear with a sore head cower. Jack normally tried to ease her passage with loving words, soft kisses, a cuddle within the warmth of which she could groan slowly awake, allow her grumpiness to evaporate. At the moment, however, he was so wound up that whatever he said would come out sounding querulous, accusatory.

"I don't know what it was," she growled. "What does it matter, anyway?"

Jack reached out to stroke her face. She looked as if she were going to flinch away, then she capitulated, grudgingly consenting to his touch. Trying to modify his urgency, Jack said, "Please, Gail, just try and remember. It's important to me. Just try to remember and then I'll explain why."

"Muesli," she said sulkily.

"What?"

"Give me my muesli first."

Frustration twisting inside him, Jack reached down to the breakfast tray for Gail's bowl of muesli.

She chewed concentratedly and stared at him, a bead of milk quivering on her bottom lip before she flicked out her tongue to lick it off. Jack looked back at her; it reminded him of one of those staring games you played as a child—first one to blink is the loser. At last, in as calm a voice as possible, he said, "Well?"

"I'm trying to remember," she snapped. "Can't you see?"

"Grumpy pants."

"Grumpy pants yourself."

"Can you remember anything? Anything at all? Usually with dreams you either can or you can't."

Gail was simmering down a little now, finding her place in the waking world again. She yawned out more of her sleep and then said, "All I remember is . . . a kind of . . . impression. There was lots of green: woods, trees, plants and fields and stuff. It was quite wet and dismal. There was a smell of . . . I don't know . . . mulchy vegetation, earth, stagnant water." She frowned, fell silent, spooned more cereal into her mouth.

"Were there people in the dream?" Jack asked. There was a pulsing in his ears, his skin felt tight and cold. More than ever a feeling of dread was screwing itself tightly into the centre of his chest, making it hurt to breathe.

"Yes," Gail said, "but I can't remember who they were or what they were doing?"

"Was it a good dream or a bad dream?"

"It wasn't a good dream," she said at once. She paused, biting down gently on her lower lip as she tried to remember. "But I don't think it was a nightmare either. I think there was a sense of . . . urgency, maybe even panic, about it. I think I felt uptight, worried, scared for somebody, not for myself."

"Was there someone called Alice in the dream?"

She frowned at him, puzzled. "Alice? I don't know. Why?"

"That name doesn't mean anything to you?"

"No, I don't think so. Should it?"

Jack shrugged. "Just before you woke up you said something like, 'Please do something, doctor. Alice can't die.'"

"Did I?"

"Yes, you did. So none of that means anything? It doesn't jog any memories?"

Gail handed Jack her empty bowl and drew her knees up under the covers. She wrapped her arms around them and leaned forward, a thoughtful look on her face. Eventually she said, "Nope. Sorry. Jack, just what is this all about?"

He sighed, rubbing a hand slowly across his forehead as if to massage his thoughts, relax them. "I don't really know," he admitted. "This morning I woke up feeling . . . incredibly uptight, anxious, scared that something bad was going to happen. I still feel it now as a matter of fact. And then, just before you woke up you said that thing about Alice, and . . . oh, I'm probably being stupid, but it seemed . . . linked somehow, as if you were confirming that there was something to worry about." He snorted a half-laugh through his nose, lips curling stiffly into a smile.

"But who's Alice?" Gail asked. "I don't understand what that's got to do with anything."

"She's . . . she *was* my mother."

"Oh," said Gail, "I see." A small silence fell between them. Sunlight was seeping around the edges of the curtains, staining the walls like luminous paint. Gail reached out and touched Jack's bare shoulder. He shivered, though her hand was not cold.

"Don't you think you're probably reading too much into all this?" she said.

"What do you mean?"

"Well, Alice isn't an uncommon name, is it? Maybe I was dreaming about something I've seen on telly, or *Alice in Wonderland,* or even someone I know."

"*Do* you know someone called Alice?"

"Well . . . no," she admitted.

Jack pulled a face as if to say: *I don't like it but that proves my point, don't you think?*

"Maybe you told me your mother's name sometime and I kind of stored it in my subconscious."

"I don't think I've ever told you my mother's name."

"Yes, but you can't be sure, can you?"

"Pretty sure."

"But not one hundred percent sure?"

Jack looked unhappy. "Well . . . I suppose not," he said grudgingly.

"There, you see? Problem solved. You're just getting uptight about nothing."

"Am I?"

"Of course you are. Sometimes I wake up feeling anxious without knowing why. Everyone does. It's probably some minor physical thing. A surge of some chemical to the brain or something."

Jack looked unconvinced for a moment, then he shrugged and nodded. "Yeah, you're probably right. Probably just a touch of PMT."

She giggled. "What's that? Pathetic male tendencies?"

He grinned. "Putrid maggoty tentacles."

"Yuk, gross," she said, wrinkling her nose. "How about pink monkey tusks."

"Peripatetic metamorphic thespians," he responded immediately.

"Clever sod. Just 'cos you're a writer." She frowned hard, trying to come up with a suitable riposte, then her face brightened. "No," she said, "I know what it stands for."

"What?"

"It stands for Please May-I-have-my Toast?"

Jack laughed loudly, felt the tension easing inside him. "You're brilliant," he told her.

"True."

"Except that I haven't made toast today, I've made crumpets."

"Spoilsport," she said. Then she unexpectedly lunged for him, wrapping her arms around his neck from behind, her head darting forward, her small but very wet tongue invading his ear. Jack bellowed in mock-disgust and for twenty seconds or so the two of them wrestled on the bed, feet sliding on the duvet. Pillows plumped to the floor, one of them only just missing the breakfast tray. Gail was strong and sinewy; she wriggled out of Jack's grip like a snake, using her long fingers to dig into his waist and tickle, undermining his strength. At last she got on top of him, pinioning his arms to the mattress above his head with her hands. Jack lunged forward and licked her left breast as wetly as he could. Gail squealed, "You beast! You'll suffer for that."

"Ooh, yes please, mistress. Make me suffer," Jack wailed, rolling his eyes in exaggerated rapture.

Gail giggled and this time lowered her breasts to his face. Jack closed his mouth over her nipple.

Their lovemaking was unhurried and sensual. Afterwards, Jack's body tingled so much that he couldn't be touched without giggling. They snoozed in the warm afterglow for a while, Gail smiling as she drifted. At last Jack rolled over and murmured, "Gail?"

"Mmm?"

"The tea and crumpets have gone cold."

"Mmm," she said again, her eyes still closed, expression unaltered.

"You don't care, do you?" said Jack.

"Mmm."

"No, you don't. In fact you're not even listening to me, are you?"

"Mmm."

"No, you're not. I can tell. I think the time has come for you to be told that my real name is Spoof Blixen, and I'm from the planet Zeltoid Magnesium 3. I came to Earth in a spaceship shaped like a giant penguin, which I've cunningly managed to secrete behind the marmalade jar in the cupboard under the kitchen sink. My mission is to

make love to every Siberian hamster I can find, introduce
the word 'plaxicrolic' to the English language and wipe
out Mexico, thus undermining the world trade in som-
breros and enchiladas. What do you think of that?"

"Mmm."

"Oh, you're no fun. I'm going to have a bath."

As he lay back in the warm water, steam drifting about
him, blurring the mirror into grey marble, Jack was dismayed to find that his unease was returning again. It
seeped into his stomach, fluttered in his mind, like a fever
re-establishing itself after the temporary panacea of Gail's
soothing words and their lovemaking. Was there something he had to do, something vital he'd forgotten, some
appointment he was supposed to keep? Sitting up in the
bath, he scooped water into his face and over his hair as
though he could wash his anxiety away like dirt. He shook
his head angrily, creating a spinning halo of droplets that
fell in pinpricks on his shoulders. He lathered himself
roughly, grumpy at both his sour mood and himself for
harbouring it. When he was clean he yanked the plug
from the bath and stood up to towel himself dry. Water
swirled down the plughole with a sound like a giant sucking liquid through a straw.

He was nearly dry when the telephone rang. The fist in
his stomach spasmed so violently that he almost cried
out. Something told him he had to answer the phone, had
to get to it before Gail stirred from her snooze. He could
feel his heart pulsing strongly, felt beads of sweat spring
out on his forehead, his body turn clumsy with urgency.
He fumbled with the door handle, his hand like something he had to manipulate from afar with a delicate remote control.

"I'll get it!" he yelled, and wrenched the door open. The
air outside the bathroom now seemed freezing cold and
raised instant goose bumps on his damp flesh. Clutching
his towel to his stomach and groin, he ran into his study,

his thigh colliding painfully with the jutting edge of a bookcase. He snatched up the telephone receiver, juggled it for a moment in his sweating hand, and then gasped, "Hello?"

There was silence that reeked of surprise. Then a tentative, though imperious, old woman's voice said, "Is that you, Jack?"

"Er . . . yes," he said, thrown. He knew this voice, but couldn't place it. "Who . . . who is this?" he stammered.

He was not sure whether the person on the other end was amused or hurt by his question. "Can't you tell?"

Suddenly, as if his mind had taken pity on him, her name rose to his lips. "Aunt Georgina?"

"Of course it's me. It's been a long time, hasn't it, Jack? Too long—though you can hardly be blamed for that, I suppose."

Five minutes later, when he re-entered the bedroom, Gail was still snoozing. However, she came awake immediately as if she'd been jabbed with a sharp stick, took one look at him and said, "Jack, what's the matter?"

He stood in the doorway, face neutral, looking at her. "My father's dead," he said flatly.

There was a brief shocked silence, then Gail said, "Oh, Jack, I'm so sorry. What . . . what happened?"

He shrugged. "Heart attack, they think." He crossed the room and sat on the bed, facing away from her. Barking a mirthless laugh, he said, "At least it wasn't lung cancer."

"What do you mean?"

He shook his head. "Doesn't matter. Private joke."

"Who was that on the phone?"

"My Aunt Georgina. She looked after me for a while when I was a child. She's my mum's sister. I haven't spoken to her for about three years. She found my dad's body in his living room this morning."

Gail put her arms around him and hugged him. "Oh, Jack, I'm so sorry," she repeated.

"Thanks," he said vaguely. "And it's okay . . . about my father, I mean. We never got on. I haven't spoken to him for about twelve years. I haven't even sent him a Christmas card for about eight." He swivelled to face her and there was a pained look on his face. "It's just . . . she wants me to go back to Beckford . . . my Aunt Georgina, I mean. She says it's my duty to sort out my father's affairs."

Gail kissed his nose and said tenderly, "Well, I suppose it is really, isn't it?"

"Yeah, I suppose so, but . . ." His voice tailed off into a sigh, his shoulders slumped.

"What is it, Jack?" Gail said. "What's wrong?"

He sighed, pulled a face. "It's just . . . I don't want to go back there. It's a bad place. For me, I mean. A really bad place."

He disentangled himself from her embrace, stood up and walked across to the window. Tugging back the curtain, he peered out, sunshine sidling over him and into the room.

Tentatively, Gail said, "Do you want to talk about it?"

Jack let the curtain fall back into place, turned to face her. "Yeah," he said bleakly. "I think I'm ready now."

5

THE UNRAVELLING KNOT

"I'm not sure how old I was when I first began to realise that my father hated me. Maybe two or three. Or maybe I knew from the moment I was born."

Jack broke a piece of poppadum from the pile on the plate between them and crunched it. When he spoke it was in a flat, neutral voice, as if divorcing himself from his emotions would allow him to disown his memories.

"Anyway, I remember that my childhood was spent in a state of . . . well, I guess near-panic wouldn't be too strong a phrase. I seemed to be either trying to endure pain as best I could, or waiting for the next pain to happen, which in some ways was worse."

He broke off again to clear his throat and pour himself a glass of water. The jug wobbled in his hand, slopping water over the tablecloth.

"Shit," he muttered and half-heartedly began to mop the mess up with a paper napkin, aided by Gail. When he had done he said, "Look, are you sure you want to hear all this? It's not exactly cheerful stuff."

She reached across the table and took his hands in both of hers. "Listen, buster," she said firmly, "I love you like crazy and I want to be there for you at all times. I don't want us to have to pretend with each other. If you have a problem or you're feeling crappy, I want to know about it, and I hope that you feel the same about me. I want us to be soulmates, Jack. I want to share everything with you, good and bad." He must have looked dubious because she said, "I mean it. Honestly, I do. Whether you're a happy chappy or a glum bum, I want to be there."

Jack looked at her earnest face for a long moment, which seemed elfin in the reddish light of the restaurant. The flickering white image of a candle flame was reflected in the dark pupil of each of her eyes. Then he smiled and said, "I love you."

"Me too," she said. "So talk."

Jack picked a crumb of poppadum from the tablecloth and squeezed it between his thumb and forefinger like a bug. He sighed and looked up at the ceiling, resembling a nervous bridegroom who has left his speech in his other suit.

A waiter sidled up with their order. Jack looked glumly at the channa masala, pillau rice, mango chutney and naan that the waiter placed before him. Normally he relished this meal, but just now he didn't feel too hungry.

As though to make up for him, Gail made exaggerated yum-yum noises as her lobster-red tandoori chicken was brought to the table together with a small bowl of salad and an even smaller bowl of raita. Normally she and Jack shared a portion of rice, but from the looks of him she would be scoffing the lion's share this evening.

As they filled their plates from the various bowls, Gail prompted, "Why do you think your father hated you so much?"

Jack grimaced and shrugged, but muttered, "Because he blamed me for the death of my mother. I was a breech birth, you see, and apparently on the night I was born there was a terrible storm, so the doctor was unable to get to the cottage as early as he should have done. Because of the various complications, she died, and . . . well . . . I got the blame for it."

"But that's awful!" Gail exclaimed. "It wasn't your fault that your mother died."

Jack simply shrugged and spooned mango chutney onto his plate.

"Surely, though, when your father cooled down he must have realised how unreasonable he'd been?"

"He never did cool down. He ran out of the house into the storm and didn't come back. In the end, my Aunt Georgina had to call the police out to look for him. They found him in the woods, unconscious, lying in mud and soaked to the skin. He was suffering from exposure and concussion and a couple of broken bones. They reckon he must have slipped down a bank and knocked himself out. Aunty looked after me while he was in the hospital, which was about two or three months. He took a long time to come round from his concussion and a longer time for his bones to mend. Aunty always said that at that time she thinks he wanted to die, which is why he took so long to get better. Anyway, he was never the same man after that. He suffered from constant depression, and when he came out of the hospital he hit the bottle hard, which, mixed with the various pills he was taking, meant that he was only half-there most of the time. For the first few years of my life, I was shunted between my father and Aunty. My father was admitted to the hospital a lot, either with his depression or because he'd got drunk and hurt himself in some way."

He paused to scoop a small forkful of food into his mouth. Gail said, "You mean he hurt himself intentionally? He attempted suicide?"

Jack shrugged. "I don't know. Sometimes maybe. He

fell down a lot, broke bones, sprained things, stuff like that. Once I think he fell asleep with a cigarette in his hand and set fire to whatever he was sitting on. It wasn't that serious, but enough to put him in the hospital. I think most of the things he did were accidental. I mean, if he'd really wanted to kill himself he'd have taken pills or hung himself or something rather than throwing himself down stairs."

"If he was in such a bad way, I'm amazed that you were sent back to live with him so often."

Jack tore a piece of naan from the doughy mass, dipped it in his curry and popped it into his mouth. Chewing, he said, "Well, you've got to remember this was the mid-seventies. They weren't as socially aware back then as they are now, certainly not in Beckford. Aunty kept an eye on me, but I think she felt sorry for my father, and she desperately wanted the two of us—my father and I, that is—to make a go of it. Maybe she thought that in the long run I was the only thing that would pull him round. I was like the lifeline that kept the drowning man from going under for good."

"That's terrible," said Gail, "using you in that way."

"Oh, I don't think she meant to use me," Jack said hastily. "I don't think she saw it that way at all. I think she did everything out of love for me and my father, and maybe that made her a little blind to what was really going on. I think deep down she believed my father loved me, and by being persistent she thought that we would work our way through the bad times and become a real family again. Unfortunately, it never quite worked out that way. My father just kept on rolling further and further downhill. As time went on, the prospect of a reconciliation between us became less and less. As soon as I became aware of his hatred for me, I began to hate him in return—not openly, you understand, but secretly, with a deep, bright child's hatred that consisted of making myself as scarce as possible and discouraging any attempts at closeness, not that I remember there being any."

He stumbled to a halt and stirred his fork around in the brown mush on his plate.

Gail said, "You spoke about pain earlier. Did you mean physical or mental pain?"

Jack frowned. "Both. More mental than physical, though, I think. I remember my father threatening me a lot, saying he was going to give me a good hiding. I have an image of him unbuckling his belt and me running away with him roaring for me to come back. I think usually I hid somewhere for a while, often until it was dark. When I went back he was usually pissed out of his brain, dead to the world, and he would forget he'd been going to beat me until the next time.

"I vividly remember that once he grabbed me by the arm—I don't think I'd done anything wrong—and he leaned right into my face and told me that one night he was going to creep up to my bedroom with a big axe and kill me. I must have been about seven at the time. His eyes looked so small and crazy and he was unshaven and his breath stank, all hot and sour. It was at the dinner table and he was eating something. I can't remember what it was but I remember his lips being all greasy and I remember seeing bits of chewed-up food in his mouth, and I thought I was going to fall into that mouth and be crunched up like the food in there. Anyway, because I was seven I believed him, and I spent a long time after that sleeping under my bed, freezing cold, terrified every time I heard the house creak, which it did a lot. I slept on bare floorboards with no blankets, the reason being that I used my pillows and blankets to make it look as if I was sleeping in the bed under the covers. God, I really, really hated him. I prayed constantly that he would drop down dead. Quite often at school I was called out of my lesson to be told that my father had had another accident and had been taken to the hospital again. The teachers were always sympathetic and I knew I was meant to pretend I was sad and shocked, which I did. Inside, though, I always felt a great surge of happiness, knowing that I would be staying with my aunt again for a while. At least there I was fed properly and my clothes were cleaned and I could sleep without fear."

He paused to scoop a forkful of food into his mouth. He chewed unenthusiastically. When he swallowed, the spices seemed to churn hotly in his stomach.

"Oh, Jack," Gail said sadly, "it must have been awful for you."

He wanted to say something comforting, as if she was the one in need of it. He could think of nothing to say, though, and in the end he simply nodded.

Gail drained her glass. "Shall we have some more drinks?"

Jack looked at the bottle of Kingfisher by his right hand and was surprised to see it empty. "Yeah," he said. "Lots more."

They were ordered and brought to the table, the waiter eyeing their half-eaten food disapprovingly.

Though Jack had a glass he drank his beer straight from the bottle. He took a long swallow, grimaced, peered at the label as though to ensure the ingredients did not include paraquat, and then continued talking in a quiet, intense voice.

"I've made it sound as though I always escaped my father's beatings, but that wasn't the case. He hit me plenty—with his belt, with his hand, with the fire poker, once with a brick that had fallen down the chimney. There was always a reason for his beatings, I'd always been 'naughty,' " he said as he made quotation marks in the air with his fingers, "but often it was really trivial stuff: I wouldn't eat some vegetable that he'd under- or over-cooked, I'd left a book on the stairs, I'd left the top off the toothpaste tube. In those days people didn't really think anything of it if kids were hit by their parents, and it wasn't as though I went to school with black eyes and split lips. But I always ached somewhere due to his violence. My legs, my arse, my back, my arms; once he kicked me in the balls and I pissed blood for two days. I remember I occasionally went to Aunty's when my father hadn't been taken to the hospital, and I think that must have been when his violence got really bad, a cooling-down period, if you like. I'm not sure whether this is an actual memory or just a bunch of images that I've fixed in my own head as a kind of representation of what was going on at that time, but I remember sitting in a hot bath while Aunty bathed the bruises on my back, and then afterwards lying in bed and listening to her giving my father a real tongue-lashing."

Gail said, "Didn't you have anyone neutral you could turn to? A friend? A teacher at school?"

Jack smiled grimly. "I'm afraid school was another horror story. Now you know where I get my warped imagination from."

He took a sustained gulp of beer that emptied almost half the bottle, then wiped a hand across his face, groaning as if he were tired. He leaned back and then rocked forward in his chair, making it creak. The conversation from the other diners seemed distant, as though he and Gail were enclosed within a clear dome, shielded from the outside world.

"Because of my treatment by my father," he continued, "I was one of those grubby, undernourished, withdrawn kids at school. I didn't trust people, so I found it very hard to make friends. I was no good at games, and so was ostracised for that. My clothes were never very clean and neither was I; I probably smelled, though wasn't aware of it except that every time I went to stay with my aunt the first thing I was always made to do was take a bath. I read a lot, which was another reason I was picked on. I don't think even the teachers liked me very much; I was one of those kids that people probably feel sorry for, but still can't bring themselves to actually make friends with."

"How you've changed," Gail said.

"Yeah," said Jack heavily. "I've got it all now, haven't I? Success, adulation, wealth . . . a gorgeous chick."

Gail said pertly, "I'll allow you to call me a chick just this once, considering the circumstances. But any other time . . ." She narrowed her eyes dangerously and drew a finger swiftly across her throat, making a hissing sound.

Jack smiled, though only faintly. "You know," he mumbled, "I'm glad I'm telling you all this. It feels . . . cathartic."

"Good," said Gail. She reached across and squeezed his arm. "Do you want to tell me the rest of it?"

Jack nodded. "Yeah. I want to tell you about Patty Bates."

"Who was she? A girlfriend?"

Jack barked a sound that was a cold approximation of a laugh. "Patty," he said, "short for Patrick. He was the one mainly responsible for making my school days so awful."

He took a deep breath, as though bracing himself, and then said, "Everyone was scared of Patty Bates. He was big and mean and stupid. His grandfather, Joe, owned the garage where my father sometimes worked. Patty picked on a lot of people, but I was his favourite. He used to say the sight of me made him sick, and that was a good enough reason for beating me up. If he found me reading a book he would snatch it from me and tear it to pieces. Once he caught me on the way home from school and put a noose round my neck which he'd made from a length of rope and said he was going to hang me. He dragged me around for ages, looking for a suitable tree. I was terrified. Eventually an adult saw what he was doing and made him take the noose off. The worst time, though, was in the woods behind our house during the summer holidays." Abruptly Jack pushed aside his plate of rapidly congealing curry and said, "I don't think I can eat this."

"That's okay," said Gail, as if he were a child. "Shall we go home, finish this there?"

Jack gave a swift shake of his head. Doggedly, he continued, "It was a hot, dry day. I decided to go into the woods and lie on a grassy bank under the shelter of some trees somewhere and read the book I'd just borrowed from the library. I even remember what book it was: it was called *The Year's Best Science-Fiction Novels* and on the cover was a picture of a spaceship landing in a farmer's field. The farmer was in the foreground, sitting on his tractor. He was staring at the spaceship with his back to the reader, but even though you couldn't see his face you got the impression he was absolutely rigid with shock." Jack slowly clenched his right fist as though, just for a moment, he felt the weight of the book in his hand before it slipped away, a brief ephemeral happiness.

"Anyway, I found a place and started reading, but after a bit I began to get drowsy. So I put the book down and closed my eyes, and the next thing I knew there was an explosion of pain in my ribs. I woke up thinking a tree had fallen on me or something. But when I opened my eyes all I could see was this incredibly blue sky and one or two fluffy white clouds. I lay there wondering whether I'd dreamed the whole thing; you know how it is after you've been hurt—there's the initial pain, then nothing as all the endorphins or whatever rush to the area and douse it, then there's a dull throb which either fades off or gets worse depending on how badly you're hurt. Anyway, I was in the endorphin stage staring up at the sky when it's suddenly blotted out by this huge black moon of a head. I couldn't see any features at first, but then a voice said, 'Wake up, shitface,' and I knew straight away it was Patty Bates. My immediate thought was to jump up and make a run for it, but I was still pretty groggy from sleep and as soon as I tried it he booted me in the side of the thigh and gave me a dead leg.

"It hurt so much I was trying hard not to cry, and failing, which really disgusted Bates, not that he had the slightest ounce of respect for me anyway. I suppose I must have been about eleven at the time and Patty was a couple of years older and about twice the size. He grabbed the collar of my shirt and lifted me up like a doll. 'You're such a runt, shitface,' he said to me. 'I think you need building up so that you can stand up to big boys who push you around.' He thought this was hilariously funny, which just shows you what an incredibly witty person he was. 'Come on,' he said and started dragging me along through the woods. I got the feeling he had some sort of plan, which was terrifying because it implied I was in for more than just the usual kicking.

"That was an awful journey. I could hardly breathe because of his fist in my throat, and hardly walk because of the pain in my leg where he'd kicked it. I felt sick at the prospect of what lay ahead of me, and also I'd left my library book behind, which meant that if it was lost I'd have to ask my father for the money to replace it, which would automatically result in yet another hiding.

"Eventually Patty and I came to a clearing where there was a huge old oak tree. There were acorns scattered all over the ground and the roots of the oak snaked out of the earth in places and then plunged back in again like the tentacles of some creature which had died and ossified trying to break the surface of the soil. There were little spots of sunlight dappling the scene, and it smelt wonderful—verdant and tangy and alive. Normally in such places I would feel a flood of positive emotions. I would feel awestruck and peaceful and for a while at least my problems would seem insignificant. I would feel a sense of union with nature, I would pretend that I was the only human being alive in the world. I loved the woods because it was usually the only place where I didn't feel threatened, where I felt that nothing wanted to hurt me.

"But now Patty Bates had destroyed that. All I could think of as he dragged me towards the oak tree was how isolated we were. If he started to torture me, as I believed he might, it was unlikely that anyone would be near enough to hear my cries.

"When we got to the oak tree he banged me up against it and said, 'I'm going to let you go now, shitface, but don't try to run away because if you do I'll catch you, and I'll make sure you never fucking run again. Understand?' I nodded and he let me go. Immediately, I fell to my knees gasping and panting for breath. I could feel his presence above me, could feel his disgust and hostility curling around me like some stench that was thick and rotten and poisonous. I wanted to plead, to beg for him not to hurt me, but I knew that would only make things worse. So I said nothing; I even tried to swallow the tears that kept brimming up inside me. 'Get up, you fucking little poof,' he snarled, so I pushed myself up using the tree for support.

"'You're such a little shit, aren't you?' he said. I just looked at the ground and said nothing. I flinched, but I wasn't quick enough to dodge the hand that swung into my face. 'Aren't you?' he repeated. 'Answer me, shitface.'

"My nose and mouth were stinging from his blow and my eyes were watering, but somehow I managed to whisper, 'Yes.' He laughed, and said all sorts of degrading things about me which he made me repeat. I shouldn't have let it get to me, but by the time he'd finished I felt ashamed and worthless; I just wanted to curl up and die."

There was anger and frustration on Gail's face. "What a bastard," she said with feeling. "What an absolute fucking bastard!"

Jack nodded. He sounded weary and resigned. "Yeah," he agreed, "but kids are like that, aren't they?" He was silent for a moment then said, "So are a lot of adults, come to think of it."

"What's this Patty Bates doing now?" Gail asked.

Jack shrugged. "Don't know. His father took over the garage from his grandfather, so maybe Patty has taken over from him."

Gail shook her head. "People like that should be put down at birth," she said. "There should be some way of finding out what people are going to be like when they're older so that the bad ones can be drowned or something."

Jack smiled. "Do you want to hear the rest of this?" he said.

She took his hand and squeezed it tightly. "Of course I do. If you want to tell me."

Jack nodded abruptly and said, "When Patty Bates had finished abusing me he turned me around and pointed up into the branches of the tree. 'See that?' he said. 'I want you to climb up there and get the eggs out of it.'

"I could see immediately what he was talking about. There was a nest about twenty feet above the ground, sitting in the fork of a branch. I turned to him and said, 'Why?' which was a mistake. He hit me again. 'Don't ask fucking questions, just do it,' he said.

"I began to climb. There were a lot of branches, so normally it would have been easy, but I was hampered by my bruised ribs and numb leg and by my fear of Bates, which made me clumsy. However, eventually I reached the nest. I looked inside and there were three eggs in there, pale blue with black specks. I've no idea what kind of bird had laid them. From down below Bates shouted, 'Have you got them, shitface?'

" 'Yes,' I called back, feeling wretched. I'd always considered egg collecting a cruel hobby, but in my present situation I would have done anything for Bates if it meant there was a chance of avoiding a kicking.

" 'Bring them down then,' he said. 'But don't break them or I'll break you.'

"I wished I'd had the courage to drop them on him, to see them smash into his upturned face. But of course I hadn't. I made a sort of upside-down parachute out of my handkerchief, put the eggs inside, tied the corners of the hanky together, clamped it between my teeth, and made my descent.

" 'About bloody time, too,' Bates said when I reached ground level. 'Let's have a look at 'em then.' I placed the handkerchief carefully on the ground, untied the knotted corners and opened the hanky out, praying desperately that none of the eggs had been cracked on the way down.

"Fortunately they hadn't. Bates reached down and picked one of them up. Almost companionably he said, 'I like a nice egg for breakfast. Don't you, shitface?'

"I wasn't sure what to say. I never had eggs for breakfast, but I was eager to please so I nodded.

"I should have realised where all this was leading, but my fear of Bates had frozen my thoughts. He gave me a nasty grin and held out the egg he'd just picked up. 'Let's see you eat this one then,' he said.

"I stared at him. I couldn't believe he was serious. The grin disappeared from his face and he looked as mean, as sadistic, as I'd ever seen him. 'What's the matter, shitface? Not hungry?' he said.

" 'Not very,' I replied, hating the whine of my own voice.

" 'Tough,' he said, 'cause you're gonna eat it anyway. Now . . . open wide.'

"I shook my head. Just the thought of eating that thing, all raw and slimy, made me want to puke. Before I could move, Bates shot out his free arm and grabbed me round the throat. Immediately my breath choked off; I felt liquid come out of my eyes and trickle down my cheeks as if my head was a piece of citrus fruit that Bates was squeezing the juice out of. I tried to tell him to let go but my throat was paralysed. When he spoke his voice had a booming, fuzzy quality as if we were in a long concrete tunnel.

"'I said open wide. Whether you do it yourself or whether I make you, you're gonna eat this fucking thing.'

"There were black stars in my vision, spreading and linking together. I felt consciousness slipping away. Panic-stricken, I started to flail with my arms and legs but even that seemed feeble and distant.

"'Stop struggling, shitface, or I'll drop a turd on the ground and make you eat that for dessert,' he said. 'Now, you've got a choice. You can either eat this yourself without the shell or I can feed it to you, shell and all. What do you say?'

"I couldn't say anything. The whole world was going black; it sounded horribly echoing and distorted. I clearly remember thinking, 'I'm going to die and I can't do a thing about it.'

"And then Bates let go of my throat and air swooped into my lungs with such force and pain that it felt as though someone had put the nozzle of a flamethrower between my lips and turned it on."

Subconsciously Jack massaged his Adam's apple as he spoke, as if he could still taste the searing air burning its way into his lungs.

"My legs gave way beneath me and I sprawled on the ground on my back. I needed air desperately, and managed to gulp about two seconds' worth before Bates landed on my chest. I was crying now, all right. I really needed to breathe and this bastard wouldn't let me. He sat on my chest and pinioned my arms to the ground with his knees. All I could see through my tears was this big black mass of human being surrounded by wavy sunlit green: it was like being underwater. He grabbed my face in his hand and pressed hard into either side of my cheeks, trying to prise my jaw open. There was nothing I could do. They say the jaw can exert enormous pressure, but if I had bitten down I would have taken the inside of my cheeks off. I felt the egg being pushed into my mouth, all cold and rough like a stone. When it was inside, cramming my mouth, Bates released his fingers and slapped the underside of my jaw with his other hand. The egg broke."

Jack looked ill. He grabbed his bottle of Kingfisher, tilted back his head and took a gulp. The sound of his swallowing seemed exaggeratedly loud in the quiet restaurant.

"It seemed to swell up out of the broken egg and clog my throat. It was like sticky half-set jelly. It tasted horrible, all kind of . . . salty and brackish. And there were gooey lumps in it which slid around in my mouth like slugs. I would have spat it out but Bates clamped one hand over my mouth and started kneading my throat with the other, trying to make me swallow. I held out for as long as I could, but in the end I had no choice. I gulped it all down as quickly as possible. It was worse than anything I'd ever known before, worse than being beaten and kicked because it actually invaded the inside of me and the texture was so . . . so awful." Jack lowered his head and shuddered at the memory. He looked up at Gail and saw the revulsion on her face.

He swallowed more beer. For the first time ever the smell of Indian food was turning his stomach. But he hadn't told her the worst thing yet. He took a deep breath.

"He made me eat all three eggs," he said quietly. "In the last one there was a baby bird . . . a foetus. Bates was delighted. He said, 'You're in luck, shitface. Eggs for breakfast and chicken for dinner. Don't say I never give you anything.' He even made me eat this. It had a little black staring eye and you could see its tiny heart beating for a few seconds before it fluttered and stopped. . . ." Jack shook his head. "He made me *eat* it, Gail. What sort of person would do that?" He sucked in his cheeks, then blew out a short breath like a weight lifter preparing to lift. "I thought I felt it move as it went down . . . I thought I felt it struggling for life . . . I had nightmares for weeks afterwards. Its mother was this big black eagle shape, predatory, evil. And it was searching for its chick . . . getting closer and closer." He lowered his face into his hands, felt his throat closing up, his stomach turning over. Gail put a hand on his arm and Jack removed one hand from his face and placed it over hers. When he was able to speak, he said, "That's all there is. Let's go home."

She squeezed his arm and stood up. "You wait here," she said gently. "I'll pay the bill. My shout."

Jack heard the sound of her chair scudding back, her soft hurrying footsteps on the carpet. He felt scraped hollow, and tried to convince himself it was a positive feeling—the tumour of his past was being cut away; some pain was inevitable. He looked up, hoping he had not attracted the attention of the entire restaurant. Apparently not, unless both staff and clientele were being excessively discreet. He looked at the empty space where Gail had been sitting. Now he had an unobstructed view of the wide window that faced out onto the street. Below the window was a tray of pale blue gravel, the sort of stuff that looked like a cross between rat poison and bits of soap. In the tray, crammed leaf to fleshy leaf, was a row of Marantas, their general listlessness not quite hidden by sickly green lighting that played over them from below. The name of the restaurant—The Pride of Old Delhi— was painted backwards on the window in flaking gold letters so that it was readable from the street outside. The street itself looked like a set from a film noir, all sharp grim angles picked out by harsh white light and tar-black shadow. It was a quiet street; the only thing that moved, as far as Jack could see, was a battered cardboard box and its offspring of scuttering confectionery wrappers, given life by the wind. But hold on . . . wasn't that a figure, cowering within the shadow of that overhanging arch? As if Jack's thoughts were its cue, the figure stepped from its envelope of darkness and into the full white light of a streetlamp.

His breath curled on his tongue and changed to sour, dry fear that crawled back into his throat and jammed there. A piercing, hard-edged sound seemed to erupt beneath his skin, making his extremities tingle. His heart clenched, his muscles gathered and cramped; he wanted to tear himself away, to run in the opposite direction but couldn't move.

The figure standing on the empty street, staring in at him with cold grey eyes, was his father.

6

GOLD

Jack sat in his parked car smoking a cigarette and tried not to think about his last day in Beckford.

It was two days after the night at the restaurant with Gail. When she returned she had found him sitting bolt upright, eyes squeezed tightly shut, hands clutching the edge of the table as if his life depended on it.

"Jack?" she had said tentatively.

Without opening his eyes, he had asked in a low, urgent voice, "Has he gone?"

"Has who gone?" Gail said, looking around.

"My father."

"Yes," she said. "Yes, Jack, he's gone."

Jack opened his eyes and looked at her. "Did you see him?"

"What?" She looked confused.

"My father. Did you see him? He was standing out there, in the street. Looking at me."

Gail followed Jack's gaze. She was silent for a long moment. Eventually, in a guarded voice, she said, "What do you mean, Jack—he was standing out there?"

"He was there. In the street. Beneath that light."

Gail crouched beside him, took his face in her hands and turned him towards her. "Jack, I don't know what you're talking about. Don't say things like that."

"Like what?"

"About your father. You can't have seen him, can you? He's dead. You know that."

Jack stared back at her, his face and voice suddenly becoming calm. "Yes, I do. I do know he's dead. But I still saw him."

She shuddered. "You mean you *think* you saw him. It's possible, I suppose, after all that's happened today. I mean, you're bound to be a bit—"

"Unbalanced?"

She scowled. "No, not unbalanced. Confused. Overwrought. The mind can do pretty wacky things sometimes."

He shook his head slowly. "No, my mind was perfectly all right. I saw him standing out there, clear as I'm seeing you now."

Gail looked annoyed. A petulant edge to her voice, she said, "Jack, you can't have. You know you can't."

"Do I?"

"Of course you do!"

"Don't you believe in ghosts then?"

"No!" she said vehemently.

People sitting at nearby tables turned, attracted by her raised voice, by the prospect of anger in a public place. Gail, however, did not indulge them. She recovered her composure and sat down in her seat, facing Jack across the table like a police interviewer with a suspected felon. There was silence for a moment, as if each was wary of giving too much away. Then she sighed and raised a hand in a limp, hovering gesture that tended towards conciliation.

"I don't know," she said.

"Don't know what?"

"I don't know whether or not I believe in ghosts. But what I do believe is that you didn't really see your father."

"Oh? And how can you be so sure of that?"

Gail sighed. "It's this whole situation. This whole day. I mean, let's face it, Jack, if it *was* him his timing was pretty amazing, wasn't it? He made the perfect entrance."

Jack frowned. "What do you mean?"

"Well, he appeared just when you were at your most vulnerable, didn't he? Your most emotional. It was all too bloody neat."

"Well, if it wasn't really him," Jack said, scowling, "who do you think it was then? Do you think I was hallucinating?"

"Maybe. Or maybe it was just an old man peering in at the window, a tramp, something like that."

"Don't be stupid. Do you think I don't know my own father?"

"When did you last see him?" Gail asked.

"What's that got to do with it?"

"Just answer the question, Jack," she repeated calmly. "When did you last see him?"

"Fifteen years ago," he admitted glumly, as if it were a confession.

"Fifteen years," Gail repeated. She leaned across the table and took his hand again. "Fifteen years is a long time, Jack. People change, memories become muddled. Can you honestly remember what your father really looks like? I mean, you probably haven't even seen a photograph of him in all that time, have you?"

He stared at the table and said nothing.

"And besides, Jack, he's dead. You're talking about seeing a *ghost,* for God's sake."

Jack started to nod reluctantly, then looked up at her, startled by a new notion. "Maybe he isn't dead."

"*What?*"

"Maybe Aunt Georgina was lying. Maybe my father isn't dead. Maybe he's here in London."

"But . . . but why should she lie?"

"Because she's always wanted my father and I to be friends, to be a proper family. Perhaps he's decided to come and find me, to make amends."

Gail looked bewildered, lost for words. Finally, however, she shook her head. "No, I can't believe that. It doesn't make sense."

"Why not?"

"Because what possible reason would she have to ring you up and tell you he's dead?"

"She wanted to catch me off guard."

"But why bother? If your father had suddenly shown up out of the blue you would have been caught off guard anyway. If anything, your aunt has probably made you think about him more than you have in years."

Jack sighed and folded his arms grumpily. He did not offer any further argument.

Gail squeezed his shoulder and said, "Come on, let's go home."

Jack's Mini Cooper rocked a little as a black Porsche whipped past. He stared after it, muttering, "Arsehole. Driving like that on a country road. What's he trying to prove anyway?" If Gail were here he knew what she'd do. She'd cock her little finger like Julie Walters in Personal Services and say, "BCSD—big car, small dick."

He smiled. Thinking of the little things she said and did always made him smile. He wished she was here with him, that they could have seen this Beckford thing through together. But she hadn't had any work for a couple of weeks and now there was the opportunity of a month's teaching in Lewisham that she couldn't afford to pass up. She had promised to come to Beckford at the weekend if Jack was still there by then. He, however, hoped he wouldn't be. The funeral was on Thursday afternoon at 12:15 P.M., and his aim was to sort out his father's affairs quickly and head back to London either immediately after the funeral or first thing Friday morning.

He finished his cigarette and flicked it out the half-open window without thinking. It landed in a muddy puddle and sizzled out. Feeling guilty, Jack opened the car door and retrieved the sodden butt, which he squashed into the ashtray. Sweet wrappers unraveled and spilled over the rim like a feeble party popper. Jack sighed, crushing them all back in. Cleaning out the ashtray was just one of the little jobs he never got around to doing—like getting a new stylus for his turntable so he could play his old vinyl, taking the pile of clothes in his airing cupboard to the Oxfam shop, sticking down the edge of peeling wallpaper in the bathroom, writing to Aunt Georgina . . .

He smiled again, this time a little bitterly. Well, that was one thing he wouldn't have to worry about for a while after this visit. He had nothing against Aunt Georgina herself—in fact, quite the contrary: she had been the only person to inject his childhood with a little light, a little hope, a little love. He still associated her with Beckford, however, and for that reason could quite happily have shut her out completely from his life. He remembered the rare moments of security and contentment in his childhood so acutely, with such intensity and desperation, that it served only to exacerbate the pain.

He wound up the car window, shivering at the Northern cold. He had left London at nine that morning. It was now twelve-fifteen. He had turned off the M1 some five or six miles back and stopped in a layby for lunch, right after seeing the first sign for Beckford, which informed him he had sixteen miles to go. Actually seeing the name of the place written there, black on white, made him feel very strange indeed. He stared at the sign hard, as if unable to believe it was real, as if he had thought Beckford did not really exist except in his memories, which were themselves merely bad dreams. Christ, he was actually going back! Seeing the sign confirmed it, brought it home to him. He stopped the car, his stomach hollow, his mouth dry. He told himself he was being ridiculous even as he wiped his palm across his forehead and it came away shiny with sweat.

The sandwiches he'd prepared that morning—cheese and sweet pickle in slabs of wholewheat bread—tasted like cardboard, but Jack doggedly munched his way through them. He swilled it all down with semi-skimmed milk, a carton of which he'd bought at the last service station. Whenever he thought of Beckford, he thought of a dingy place, and once or twice he actually caught himself peering through the windshield into the distance, trying to discern some dark pall of smoke or fog that he felt sure would be hovering over the village. However, after undertaking most of his journey in the rain, the brooding clouds which he'd felt so appropriate had now all but dispersed. It seemed likely that sunshine and blue skies might actually accompany his homecoming.

He considered smoking a second cigarette before resuming his journey, but then decided against it. No, he was only putting off the inevitable. As he started the car he assured himself for the umpteenth time that day that there was nothing to be worried about. The horror of his childhood was long past; Beckford was only an empty stage, bare boards layered with thick dust. Even his father's house was no threat now that the ogre was dead.

He set off again, tapping his hands on the steering wheel in time to the Rolling Stones (the Strolling Bones, Gail called them), a gesture of defiant levity. As he drew nearer to Beckford the memory of his father grew larger, more solid, as though transmitted from the place itself.

Despite his best efforts, the events of that last day were coming back to him, pushing themselves to the forefront of his mind. Jack tried to defy them, but they forced themselves on him, an inexorable violation.

He remembered the date with ease: August 2nd, 1989, a Wednesday. The week had been hot and that day was no exception. By nine in the morning the sun was beating down remorselessly, bleaching the colour from the land. Daisy Lane was baked hard, cracked in places; stones jutted from its uneven surface like knobs of vertebrae. The surrounding fields looked parched. Cattle chewed their cud with glum indolence, indifferent even to the flies that swarmed around them, alighting on the rims of their eye sockets to drink. The air was muggy, slow and thick as molasses. Jack remembered it pressing down on him, on his eyelids and shoulders and the top of his head, licking him with its heat and leaving dampness behind.

He was eighteen years old and today was the most important day he could ever remember. For today he received his A level results, the outcome of which may well provide him with a key to unlock the trap of his life. Predictably, his father had been opposed to his taking the exams from the start. He had described Jack as a scrounger, had threatened on numerous occasions to throw him out unless he got a decent job and brought a bit of money into the house. Jack, however, had resisted the pressure from his father. Since he had turned sixteen the conflict and hostility between the two of them, whilst still present, had somehow become more distant. They were like a couple of belligerent hermit crabs, occasionally snapping their claws at each other, but on the whole keeping to their own territory. Certainly the physical violence had ceased; Jack was not sure whether this was because his father respected him now as an adult or simply because Jack was now big enough to hit back.

Much to his father's disgust, Jack wanted to go to University, somewhere far away like Kent or East Anglia, and to do so he needed at least two B's and a C on his exams. That morning, immediately after breakfast, whilst his father was still sleeping off last night's binge, Jack went outside and sat with his back against the gate, heels scuffing the dust of Daisy Lane, eyes straining for the glint of the postman's bicycle.

By his side, his tinny old tape recorder was belting out the first album by the Stone Roses, which Jack had been listening to almost constantly for the past few months. Two days before, he had been playing it in his bedroom when his father had burst in. "That's a fucking cacophony, that is," Terry had slurred, swaying from side to side like an undersea plant. "You turn that shit off. I'm not having it in my house."

Jack had propped himself up on his elbows, the familiar queasiness clamping his stomach. Though he defied his father more and more frequently these days, he was still scared of him. Indeed the only reason Jack *did* defy his father was because acquiescence didn't work; it simply made his father bolder, more querulous, more demanding. When he had spoken to Aunt Georgina about this she had said, "Your dad, Jack, is like a little boy with a stick. He'll tease and tease a dog until it bites him and only then will he leave it alone for a while."

Jack tried to remember this, tried to act on it, and for the most part it seemed to work. But still he was afraid. He couldn't help remembering the threat his father had made about the axe when he was little; for the more his father was forced to back down, the more infuriated he would become. What was to stop him snatching up the axe (or some equally lethal implement) in a drunken fit of pique, creeping up the stairs when Jack was asleep, and beating him to death with it?

For this reason Jack's throat felt thick, his voice fluttery, as he replied, "This is my room. I'll do what I like in here."

"This is my room," his father mimicked and took a lurching step forward. "Bollocks to your room. This is my fucking house and don't you forget it, you scrounging little git. What I say goes. And I say turn that fucking racket off now."

Jack swallowed. His temples were pounding. He felt vulnerable lying back on the bed so he swung his legs to the floor and sat up.

"No," he said, trying to make his voice sound cold and hard, stiffening the muscles in his face. "I'm listening to it. You mind your own business."

"Cheeky little bastard," Terry Stone snarled. Spittle flew from his mouth and drifted down through a shaft of sunlight in a fine spray. He took another step forward, and now Jack could smell him. It was a hateful smell, stale clothes ingrained with old tobacco, halitosis laced with alcohol.

Jack stood up as his father advanced. Terry Stone halted, rocking back and forth as though on the deck of a storm-lashed ship. He pointed a finger at the tape recorder where Ian Brown was proclaiming that he wanted to be adored. His lips and tongue writhed for a moment as though trying to fit around the shapes of the words in there.

"Either you switch that off," he said firmly, "or I'll throw the fucking thing out of the window."

"Just you try it," Jack said; his throat was so tight it hurt to speak. "If that goes out the window, you'll bloody well go after it."

Jack's father glared at him, eyes glazed and pink, teeth clenched like an animal. His bottom lip was wet and gleaming, his hair tousled. His skin was grey and slack except for his cheeks and nose, which were red flares of broken capillaries. His hands were like paws, stubby and grime-encrusted, powerful-looking.

Jack thought if it came down to it, if his father got

crazy or mad enough, he could still take Jack apart. He himself was no Adonis; he was as tall as his father but scrawny. He had been trying to remedy this with push-ups, but the results were not too impressive—not yet, at least. Jack, though, endeavoured to conceal his uncertainties behind the unyielding mask of his face. It must have worked, for his father suddenly swung around and stamped to the door.

He did not leave, however, without delivering a parting shot. His hand on the handle, as though to slam the door shut should Jack lunge for him, he sneered, "You think you're such a clever little bugger, don't you? You think you know it all? Well let me tell you something, shall I? It doesn't matter how many bloody exams you get 'cause you'll never get away from this place. Never." As soon as he pulled the door shut Jack began to tremble; for the rest of the day he brooded on what his father had meant by that last statement.

Staring at the same bend in the path, the vanishing point where all lines converged, had set Jack's mind wandering. Now, however, the lines were broken, snapping his mind back to the present, by a blue clad figure wavering precariously towards him, sunlight glinting and flashing from the spinning spokes of his bicycle.

Jack stood up. Suddenly he felt breathless. His heart began to thud, sweat broke out on his body. "Come on, come on," he urged. The postman seemed to be making interminably slow progress. "Pedal faster," Jack muttered, "pedal faster." The bike was crawling along at little more than walking pace. The postman glanced up and sunlight flashed on his spectacles as if his eyes were on fire.

When he came to within fifty yards of the house, Jack ran to meet him. He was a portly, laconic man, with hair like grey straw and squinty eyes that floated behind the thick lenses of his spectacles like small, dark fish. According to Aunt Georgina, he was always in the hospital for one operation or another. When Jack was little he used to be terrified of him, imagining his body all stitched up like Frankenstein's monster beneath his navy blue uniform. "Morning, Mr. Phillips," he shouted now, pounding to a halt.

Phillips peered at Jack—a little fearfully, Jack thought. Perhaps he was afraid of being robbed. Then he nodded and muttered, " 'Ow do." He dipped into his pocket and produced a vast handkerchief in bilious green tartan that he used to mop the sweat from his face.

"Have you got any letters for me this morning?" Jack asked impatiently. "I'm expecting my exam results. I need decent grades to get into University."

Phillips carefully folded up his damp handkerchief and replaced it in his pocket. Jack had to resist an urge to snatch his bag from him and rummage through its contents.

"Aye," Phillips said wearily. "Let's just 'ave a look." He tugged on the strap, pulling the bag open and delved into it. Eventually his chubby hand emerged clutching two letters. Jack saw that the top one was addressed to him, a brown envelope, his name and address computer-printed behind a transparent window. He wanted to grab the letter and tear it open there and then. He made himself accept it without snatching, made himself stand and smile politely whilst Phillips turned his bicycle round, mounted and weaved unsteadily away.

When he was gone, Jack held up the envelope and stared at it, his entire body seeming to pulse with anticipation. The envelope was smeared and wrinkled with the sweat from his hands. The other letter, addressed to his father, he stuffed into the back pocket of his jeans. "Please God," he said, then wriggled his finger beneath the loose corner of the flap and ripped the envelope open.

He pulled out the white slip of paper inside, almost dropping it in his haste. At first his mind raced, refusing to focus on the black print. "Come on, calm down," he urged and stared at the paper until he was able to take in its meaning. He saw the words:

ENGLISH LITERATURE: C

HISTORY: C

ART: D

"No," he breathed, not wanting to believe. "No, it can't be." He squeezed his eyes shut, thinking that maybe he had read the grades incorrectly, willing them to change before he opened his eyes again.

He opened his eyes.

The grades were the same.

"Aw, no," he moaned. He had a hollow feeling in the pit of his stomach; it was only now that Jack realised how completely he'd pinned his hopes on these grades being right, how he'd believed they would be, if only because he desired it so much. He felt desolate. He stared at the grades again, but still they hadn't changed. Despite the brightness of the sun beating down on him, he felt as if darkness were closing in, felt like a prisoner about to begin a sentence that would never end. He couldn't think straight. He turned, pushed open the gate and trudged up the path to the front door. He opened the door and stepped into the house. Its smell enveloped him, pungent and sour. It made him think of death. The death of his dreams.

He pulled his father's letter from his pocket and dropped it on the mat just inside the front door. He could hear his father in the kitchen banging blearily about. He tiptoed up the stairs, gritting his teeth at each creak; the prospect of a confrontation now was unbearable. He entered his room and threw himself face down on the bed, crumpling the letter in his hand. He felt like weeping, but didn't. He just lay there, not moving, eyes closed. However bad he felt, he had to be sensible about this, think it through, consider his options. He wouldn't give up; there *had* to be a way. But already he was wondering what sort of future there was for him around here, how he could bear to stay with his father much longer.

But of course he didn't have to stay with his father, did he? He was eighteen now, he could do as he liked. And he didn't have to stay in Beckford, either. Maybe he could move to Leeds and look for work there.

Even as he mulled over these possibilities, however, part of his mind rejected them. The fact was, he was scared. He'd spent his whole life scared, had grown up that way, had learned instinctively to be cautious, not to take risks, not to rock the boat. Moving away, finding a place of his own, getting a job—it all seemed like pie in the sky, a crevasse too wide to leap. Most kids who moved away still had their parents to cushion them against the blows of life, to guide them through the mine fields, to show up on their doorsteps when things got bad with a nice fat cheque and the reassuring words, "You can pay us back whenever. We're in no hurry." And those that didn't have such help ended up on the scrap heap. This, at least, was the way that eighteen-year-old Jack Stone saw the world. What he had been hoping was that he would be eased into the big bad world via University, which he saw as three years of independence without the crushing responsibilities of real life.

All his plans in ruins. What had he done to deserve this? He rolled onto his back, stared out across his room and hated everything he saw. All the things he had cherished and loved—his books and games and comics and posters and silly knickknacks—he now despised because it was all part of the trap. This stuff had comforted him, this place had been a haven, but now it felt burdensome, suffocating, intolerably heavy.

A thick cone of sunlight fell through the window and formed a glowing pool on the carpet. The sunlight oozed across his bookcase, touching the spines of books and making them flash like metal. Jack rolled off his bed, pulled himself into the sunlight and slumped down in front of the bookcase. He hooked his finger into the hollow spine of a large fat book and tugged. He shifted into a cross-legged position, back arched forward, cradling the book like a baby and smoothing a hand across its cool shiny cover. The book was entitled *The Bumper Book of Fairy Tales*. Jack opened it, anticipating the familiar soft creak of cardboard, the gentle rustle of paper. He began turning pages until he reached the story of *Dick Whittington and His Cat*. One illustration in that story showed the cat, standing upright and dressed in boots and gloves, gesturing to a thought bubble above his head that showed London as an opulent city, its streets paved in shimmering gold. Of course, Jack knew that London's streets were not really paved in gold, but that illustration had nevertheless captured his imagination as a child and had continued to inspire him as he grew older. Jack's plan had been to spend three years at a University within shouting distance of London, and then, when he had finished his studies, to move to London and find work there.

His father's words from two days before came back to him: *You'll never get away from this place. Never.*

"Fuck you!" Jack snarled, and hurled the book across the room. It flew like a heavy broken bird and crashed into the door. "You bastard," Jack muttered, "you bastard." He felt as though his father's outburst had somehow cursed him. "I'll fucking show you," he muttered, jumping to his feet and stomping to the window. He clenched his fist and drew it back as if to punch a hole in the glass. But after a few moments he lowered the fist to his side, still clenched.

Why would his father say something like that anyway? The number of times his father had threatened to throw him out of the house, Jack would have thought the old bastard would have been glad to get rid of him. He pressed his forehead to the warm glass. "It wasn't my fault she died," he muttered. "You killed her just as much as I did." He heard his father's heavy footsteps on the stairs and his heart sank. "Don't come in," he murmured, half-turning. "Not now."

The footsteps reached the top of the stairs and began to approach along the landing. "Go past," Jack murmured. "Don't come in." The footsteps stopped outside his door. Jack's heart was pounding; he felt suddenly afraid. But when his door handle turned and the door began to open, his fear was dispelled by a fierce black surge of outrage and anger.

"What do you want?" he snapped as his father entered the room. "Why can't you just leave me alone for once?"

For an instant Terry Stone looked taken aback, almost hurt by his son's venom, and Jack nearly felt sorry for him, nearly apologised. Then the rheumy eyes narrowed, the lips twisted into a snarl. "Don't you bloody talk to me like that, you little shit," he said.

Jack felt it all bubbling up, the years of resentment and anger, and it was like a power, like an irresistible energy inside him. He strode towards his father, feeling something wild, something primitive and dangerous, struggling for release inside his head. He screeched, "Don't you *dare* call me a shit, you fucking drunken waster! Look at you! You make me sick and ashamed! You're a nothing, a no-body! What fucking right have you got to call *me* names!"

He was three strides away from his father now. He halted, both hands squeezed into fists by his sides. Though he was the same height as his father, he suddenly felt two feet taller and twice as broad. His father's face was struggling for expression, so animated it was almost comic. Jack saw astonishment there, and fury, and—he believed—more than a little fear.

Eventually his father spluttered, "You . . . you little murdering bastard! How dare *you* talk to *me* like that!"

"Murderer," Jack sneered. "What a moron you are. Can't you get it into your thick skull that I never murdered anyone? I was a fucking baby, Dad. I didn't ask to be born, did I? If anything, you're the one who murdered Mum. You were the one who screwed her!"

With a howl, Terry launched himself at his son. Jack caught him by the sleeves, but could not prevent his father's weight from crashing into him. They fell to the floor, Terry on top. Jack felt his gorge rise at the stifling odours—unwashed flesh, stale urine, sour breath, smoke, alcohol—that settled over his face and seemed to cling there like a web.

"Get off me," Jack gasped, "get off me, you bastard!" He was still clutching his father's arms, which were thrashing like giant eels eager to bite. He brought his knee up hard and felt it make weighty contact with something—either his father's balls or the inside of his thigh. Whatever, it was enough to make his father grunt and suddenly weaken. Jack heaved off his weight and slid out from beneath him.

It was all so shocking and sudden. For a long time Jack had been expecting something like this, but he had also expected some warning, some ceremony, some preamble. The fact that he had goaded his father, that he had instigated this violence, did not make it any easier to accept that they were now rolling around the carpet, scrapping like dogs. Jack, off balance, tried to scramble to his feet, but felt a hand close around his ankle and yank back hard enough to make his knee pop. He's dislocated it, Jack thought in a flare of panic, but the pain, though excruciating, was momentary.

He felt hands climbing him, digging in, trying to reach his face. When involved in violence, Jack always found it confusing, a buzzing blur of movement and colour and pain. He punched down to where he thought his father's head would be and felt his knuckles make contact with something very hard, like a building brick encased in rubber. Through the tight radiance of pain that syringed up the bone in the centre of his arm he heard his father make a strange noise, a kind of giant gulp, as if he had been forced to swallow a cricket ball.

Again he felt his father's hands weaken, and threw them off him, scrambling backwards, out of his range. His spine cracked against the edge of the bed. Jack cried out, tears of pain springing to his eyes. Through the swimming film across his vision, he saw his father lying on his stomach, trying to push himself upright with arms that wouldn't quite respond. Did I really hit him that hard? Jack thought, and felt no glee, only fear. What if he had rattled his brain, given him a haemorrhage or something? He blinked his tears away and saw blood on his hand. He looked again at his father. Blood was gushing from a cut that bisected his eyebrow, running down his stubbly cheek, beneath his jaw and into the collar of his shirt.

"Are you all right, Dad?" Jack said. His voice was small, boyish.

His father paused, and then swung the top of his body round to face Jack, like a shark homing in on the vibrations of his voice.

"You're dead, boy, you're fucking dead," his father said. The words were spoken fuzzily, but with a certainty that made Jack squirm inside.

"No, Dad," Jack said. "Let's stop now. This has gone too far."

"*You've* gone too far," his father corrected him, still in that same quiet voice. "The first thing you ever did was to kill your mother, to ruin my life. I think it's time you paid for that."

"No, Dad," Jack moaned. "You don't know what you're saying. This is really stupid."

Terry Stone shook his head and immediately screwed

up his eyes in pain. "No," he mumbled, "this isn't stupid. Not stupid at all." He reached for a golf club that was propped against Jack's bookcase. It was a putter, the binding coming off the handle. Jack had bought it at a jumble sale once, intending to buy a whole set piece by piece and take up golf, but the fad had quickly died.

"Put that down, Dad," Jack said, his voice quavering badly. His anger had dissipated as suddenly as it had come. Now he felt only misery and a crushing depression, wanted only for this whole scene to end, for it never to have begun at all.

Terry Stone showed no intention of putting down the club. He dragged it to him, used it to prop himself up.

"Dad," Jack warned again, "you don't need that. Here, let me help you." He pushed himself to his feet, clutching his back, and took a step towards his father. Face twisting with hate, Terry grasped the club in both hands and swung it through the air towards his son.

Jack ducked, throwing up his arms to protect his head. He heard the club whistle through the air. He braced himself for the pain, but instead heard a crash and a curse. He opened his eyes and peeked out from beneath his armpit to see what had saved him.

Somehow his father had managed to snag the rumpled blanket of Jack's unmade bed with the head of the club. He had then tried to drag the club back too quickly whilst trying to free it and had succeeded only in knocking the lamp from the bedside table. He was up on his knees now, yanking the club from the debris, obviously in readiness for another try. "Dad!" Jack yelled. "Stop this! It's crazy!"

Terry Stone glanced at his son, and immediately Jack saw there was no reasoning with him. He made a bolt for the door, but just as his fingers touched the handle the golf club appeared beside him and smashed into the door, slamming it shut and denting it in the process. Jack went cold—that could have been his skull. He made a grab for the club but it was snatched away, the blunt head catching the ends of his fingers and making them sting. Jack was only grateful that the weapon was so cumbersome in the small room. He looked around frantically for a weapon of his own. All he could see was the big book of fairy tales lying open beside the door. He snatched it up.

He turned and flung up the book as a shield just in time. The head of the club slammed into it; a split-second later and it would have been his face. "Dad!" Jack screamed. "Dad, please stop!" As his father drew the club back and raised it to swing again, Jack ran at him, wailing in terror and desperation, and smashed the book as hard as he could into his face.

There was an awful crunching sound, and Jack thought he heard the air rushing from his father's body. Then Terry toppled backwards, his hands above his head, the golf club slipping from his grasp. There was blood on the back of the book; the centre of Terry's face was a crimson explosion. Because he had been kneeling, Terry's legs swung out from his collapsing body, slamming into Jack's legs and knocking him sideways. Jack fell into his bookcase, which rocked but remained upright. Books fell from the shelves, bouncing off his shoulders, slithering across the floor. For a moment after his fall, and after the books had stopped tumbling, there was complete silence in the room. Jack thought, *My father's dead! I've killed him!* Then his ears seemed to unblock and he heard the reedy sound of his breathing.

Jack got to his feet, trembling, nauseous. His body felt full of freezing air, making every organ shiver. His father was lying on his back, arms above his head, legs straight down, like a sacrifice. This is it, Jack thought. There's no way back from here. He didn't know what to do. He pushed himself back against the wall, looked down at his father's prone body and gnawed the fingernails on his right hand. His father gave a small groan and moved his head a little. Jack felt suddenly frantic. I can't be here when he wakes up, he thought. He'll kill me.

Moving slowly, gingerly, as though in a den of sleeping lions, Jack stepped over his father's body and picked up the golf club, which lay on the floor above the limp tobacco-stained hands. He looked around for a suitable hiding place, then, unable to find one, threw the club out of the window and watched it bounce and come to rest on the cobblestones below. Next, he dragged a black Adidas bag from beneath his bed and began to stuff things into it—clothes, wallet, cheque book and card, tape recorder, camera, the letter he'd received that morning. He worked quickly, urgently, terrified his father was going to wake up.

When he had all he wanted from his bedroom, he ran down the hall and skidded into the bathroom. He stuffed a towel into his bag, a toilet roll, his toothbrush. Soap and shampoo followed, deodorant, a comb. What else, what else? He thought he heard his father groan. He ran down the stairs and into the kitchen, grabbed a packet of biscuits from the cupboard, milk from the fridge. He ran back to the foot of the stairs. "Dad?" he shouted. "Dad, are you okay?" Silence. Was his father pretending or was he really still unconscious? Keeping his eye on the stairs, in case his father should appear, all bloody and snarling like a psycho in a film, Jack picked up the phone and dialed 999.

"Ambulance, please," he said when asked which service he required. He gave the address, then said, "The man you want will be upstairs," and replaced the receiver to stem any further questions.

Despite the heat, he took down his jacket from the row of hooks behind the front door and put it on. He took down his cagoul too, rolled it up into a tight ball and stuffed it into his bag. He glanced up the stairs again, then opened the front door, wincing at the creak it made, and stepped outside. Sweat was rolling off him; his skin was shining as if smothered in oil. He looked around, saw a slab of stone lying in the grass of the overgrown lawn, and used it to prop open the front door. Then he walked down the garden path and turned left outside the gate, heading up Daisy Lane in the direction of the Butterworths' farm.

He was almost at the top of the lane, where it joined the main road into Beckford, when he heard the wail of a siren. He tossed his bag over a dry-stone wall and vaulted after it, hoping a cowpat was not awaiting him on the other side. He crouched behind the wall until the ambulance had swept into the turning and begun its bumpy descent towards the house. At this rate his father would be in Beckford before him. He climbed over the wall, retrieved his bag, made his way to the top of Daisy Lane, then began to jog down the hill towards the village.

Ten minutes later he was at his Aunt Georgina's house. He rang the bell, hoping she was not shopping or at one of her WI meetings. He crossed from the front door to the small leaded window on the right and peered into the front room. He noticed a tea tray balanced on the pouffe before the floral-patterned settee; the pot was encased within a green hand-knitted tea cosy but its spout was exposed and steam was rising from it. At the back of the room, beside a small dining alcove, was another door, which led into the kitchen. This door now opened and his aunt appeared, wiping her hands on the apron round her waist. Jack waved but she didn't see him. As she crossed to the door the flawed glass seemed to tug at her, ballooning her head, swiping her features into a blur, fragmenting the outline of her hips.

When she opened the door she didn't look surprised to see him and immediately Jack thought, She knows what's happened. My father's told her. Or the hospital.

"Well," she said, "is it good news or bad?"

"What?" replied Jack.

"Your exam results. Wasn't it today you were getting them? Did you get the grades you wanted?"

"Oh," said Jack. He shrugged and shook his head. "No, I . . . I didn't." He saw her doughy face soften in sympathy and blurted, "Can I come in please, Aunty? I've got something to tell you."

"Of course." She stood aside to let him in. "What's the bag for? Going somewhere?"

He looked down at the bag in his hand and only now realised how much it was making his arm ache. He put it down at the foot of the stairs and flexed his hand. "Me and Dad have had a fight," he told her.

Aunt Georgina rolled her eyes. "Not another one. What was it about this time?"

Jack shrugged. He realised that when he had said "fight" his Aunt had automatically thought he meant argument.

"And I suppose you want to stay here for a while until things cool down," she said. "Am I right?"

Jack couldn't bring himself to look at her. He stared at the banister rail, ran his fingers across the smooth polished wood.

"Whatever happened to your hand?" Georgina asked.

The middle knuckle on Jack's right hand was now bruised and swollen. He tried to straighten the finger and immediately it felt as though broken glass were being forced into the joint and along the bone.

"You could do with a cold compress on that. Follow me into the kitchen and I'll fix you up."

She began to turn away. Jack held up a hand—his injured one—and said firmly, "Aunty."

She turned back, surprised. "Yes?"

"I . . ." His gaze skittered away from hers again. He had to force his words past an obstruction in his throat. He picked up his bag, took a deep breath. "I'm going away," he said.

She looked momentarily bemused, then Jack saw the familiar imperiousness begin to assert itself. She folded her arms, straightened her back and set her mouth in a terse line. Her eyes narrowed, and even appeared to harden, to change colour from azure-blue to a dull steel-grey. "Away?" she repeated, as if defying him to elaborate.

Jack swallowed. "Yes. Dad and I, we . . . it was . . . it was really serious this time. We came to blows. I can't stay here any more. . . ." He shrugged, grimaced. "So I'm going away. I'm leaving Beckford for good."

"I see," she said curtly, "and where do you think you'll go?"

An image immediately formed in Jack's mind of an opulent city, the streets paved in gold. "London," he said.

"London? Really? And what will you do when you get there?"

"I'll find work," he said defiantly.

"It'll be as easy as that, will it?"

Jack shrugged, feeling uncomfortable. "I don't know. But I'll be okay, don't worry."

"Where will you stay?"

"I'll find somewhere. I've got money."

"How much?"

"I don't know," Jack said irritably. "Enough."

In point of fact, he did know—approximately anyway—but he wasn't about to reveal that to his aunt. He had around thirty pounds in his wallet and perhaps two hundred in his bank account.

"Don't you think this is all rather silly?" his aunt said, smiling indulgently, belittling him with a twitch of the lips.

"No," Jack said, bridling, taking two steps towards the door. "I'm going and you can't stop me. Anything's better than being near him. I need to get away, Aunty, can't you see?"

She simply looked at him, her expression unchanging;

she had a knack for intimidating people without actually doing or saying anything.

"I'm old enough to make my own decisions. I'm eighteen." Jack became aware that he was babbling simply to fill the silence and made himself clam up.

Eventually his aunt sighed and nodded her head sagely, as if she'd always known that one day it would come to this.

"You're right," she said, "you're an adult now." Her voice was so neutral that Jack did not know whether she was making fun of him or not.

"I . . . I just came to say good-bye," he muttered. "And . . . and thanks. For all you've done for me, I mean."

Again she nodded, as if this was expected of him. "Will you at least have a cup of tea and a slice of cake before you go?"

The offer was tempting but Jack shook his head. If he paused to think about what he was doing his resolve might evaporate. Also, he didn't want to give his aunt the chance to dissuade him from leaving.

"No," he said, looking at the floor, "I'd better go."

She did not immediately respond, and Jack thought she was never going to. He did not feel he could make the break until she said something; perhaps this was her way of keeping him here, prolonging this moment forever. He was relieved when she finally sighed. It seemed like a signal that time was no longer suspended, that it had been allowed to move on. She said, "All right. But wait here a moment. I want you to have something." She turned and huffed her way upstairs. It would have been easy to have fled while her back was turned, but he loved and respected her too much for that.

She returned a few minutes later clutching an envelope. "This is for you," she said. Jack took the envelope. It was unmarked and unsealed, the flap simply folded inside.

Jack looked at his Aunt quizzically, but her expression gave nothing away.

"Can I open it now?" Jack asked.

"If you like."

He did so. Inside were two slips of paper. When he extracted and unfolded them he saw that one was a cheque for £500 made out to him and the other was a name—Molly Haynes—and an address in Wimbledon.

"What's this?" he said.

"Isn't it obvious?"

"Yes, but . . . ," Jack waved the cheque in the air, "I can't accept this."

"Why not?"

"Because I can't. You can't afford to give me this sort of money."

"Who says?"

"I just . . . It's too much, Aunty. I don't want handouts. I'm not a charity case."

Georgina rolled her eyes. "Oh, stop being so pious," she said. "I'm giving you that for my own peace of mind. I'd never sleep if I knew you were down there with no money and nowhere to live. If you don't like it you can pay me back when you've earned something."

"But . . . five hundred pounds," said Jack. He shook his head. "I have got my own money, you know."

"Not very much, though."

"How do you know?" he said indignantly.

"I'm not daft, Jack. Your father never gives you any, and working weekends at the co-op hasn't made you a millionaire, has it?"

Jack shrugged, knowing he was conceding defeat. He brandished the other piece of paper. "What's this then?"

"What does it look like?"

"An address," he said, annoyed at how stupid she made him feel sometimes.

She smiled and raised her eyebrows. "It's the address of

an old friend of mine," she said. "Molly was born in Brad-ford but moved to London just after the war. She's a the-atre designer. You'll like her. I'll ring her and let her know you're coming."

Jack felt his stomach tightening; even in this, his break-ing away, his ultimate statement, his independence was being taken from him. He braced himself to protest, but his pride could not quite supersede the relief he felt at knowing he had a solid base to aim for. He put the two slips of paper back into the envelope, folded it and placed it carefully in the inside pocket of his jacket. On impulse he stepped forward and kissed his aunt; she smelled of fresh bread. There were tears in his eyes when he stepped back. "Thanks, Aunty," he said in a stuffy voice, trying to conceal them.

"Come here, you great daft thing," she said gently, and held out her plump arms. Jack moved forward into her embrace. It was tight and warm and comforting. "You look after yourself now," she said as she released him.

Were there tears in her eyes, too? Jack could not tell for his own were still swimming. He nodded and said, "I will. Bye. Thanks again." He picked up his bag and walked quickly to the door.

He turned back once, mouthed "Bye" again, then stepped outside, closing the door firmly. The sun was a sheet of brilliant light on his face, blinding him. He shud-dered despite the heat and began to stride away from the house, in the direction of Beckford's tiny station. From there he would catch a local two-carriage train to Leeds, and then change to one of the sleek never-ending Inter Cities. Jack had never been to London before; he felt as apprehensive as he had felt on his first day at secondary school when he'd been eleven. But he felt a squirmy kind of excitement, too, and a sense of unreality at the prospect of walking down streets whose names he knew from films or the news or through playing Monopoly with his Aunt.

Oxford Street, Carnaby Street, Trafalgar Square, King's Cross. When he boarded the train for Leeds half an hour later, his heart was sprinting, his stomach churning, his mouth dry, but he was determined, too. Whatever happened, there would be no chickening out, no running back home with his tail between his legs.

Sitting in his Mini Cooper, thirty-three-year-old Jack Stone allowed himself a faint smile. He now found it inconceivable that he and that naive eighteen-year-old boy were the same person, and yet the events of that day and the many years that had preceded it still affected him deeply. It was the most intrinsic part of his makeup, that other life, it was the foundation—indeed, the driving force—behind all he had achieved. Even now his throat was dry, his hands clenched too tightly on the steering wheel. He felt his memories sinking, a solid dull mass like a floating tumour. As if his thoughts had conjured it, a signpost rose from the grass verge as he swept over the brow of a hill. Its ominous message was: BECKFORD 6. Jack followed its pointing finger to the right.

As he neared Beckford and landmarks started to appear, Jack began to feel a vague, almost detached sense of apprehension, as if the water tower looming on his right, the black ruin of a castle, like a jagged stump of tooth, on the hill to his left, were images from a recurring dream. He cleared his throat, which felt lined with sand. The steering wheel felt either slippery with sweat or tacky as flypaper depending on where he put his hands. At each mile a signpost appeared as if some sinister countdown were under way. As his apprehension grew, Jack began to feel as if Beckford were drawing him in. If he tried to turn the wheel now, to head back to London, he felt sure it would not respond; the car would keep moving unerringly forward. So convinced was he of this that he sat rigid in his seat, reluctant to test his theory even by easing the wheel a little to the left or right.

Farmhouses began to appear more frequently in the fields on both sides, squared-off masses of dark stone like the roughly sculpted bodies of vast insects whose legs were the dry-stone walls that separated one crop from the next. Jack crested a hill and suddenly there was Beckford. The most prominent landmark was the slate blade of the church spire jutting from a prickly mass of stone interlaced with the grey threads of streets. Jack could see two areas of green within the grey, like irregularly shaped postage stamps: the park and the allotments that bordered the Stanmores. He saw the railway station, its track stretching away on both sides like a stitched-up scar, and some new houses whose roofs were as red as raw steak. He strained his eyes to see his father's house on the far side, but the dense green mass of woods that rose up beyond the village swallowed the track, concealing the buildings beyond.

"Home sweet home," he murmured and tried to laugh. He didn't much like the sound he made. All at once he re-alised that he had stopped the car, that he was holding it on the foot brake in the middle of the road just beyond the brow of the hill. "Not clever," he told himself, put the car in neutral and released the brake, allowing himself to roll. The panoramic view of Beckford sank behind the first of its buildings. When he reached the flat ground, Jack put the car into second and touched the accelerator.

Driving through the centre of the village was like a dream, like finding himself in one of his memories; it was amazing how little had changed. The Union Jack still flapped above the Connaught like a stubborn reminder of the past, and even many of the storefronts seemed the same. Jack was almost relieved when he passed the glass and plastic facade of a video store, and then a little further on a Chinese takeaway with a garish yellow sign that bore the proud legend, TOP WOK. He almost expected people to turn and stare at him as he drove past, but nobody seemed to pay him the slightest attention.

He felt nervous all over again when he drew near to his aunt's house, and almost drove straight past it until he realised it was hiding behind a mask of ivy. She must have planted that soon after he had left. He remembered her door—now white—being blue, but the leaded window was the same.

He pulled up at the kerb outside, obscurely glad that the house looked different; it seemed somehow to prove that time had moved on, that things had changed, significantly and irrevocably. He removed his spectacles, got out of the car and turned to close and lock the door. When he turned back, the front door of the house was open and a woman was standing on the front step, arms folded, watching him. She was thin, grey-haired, sombre-faced. Jack smiled at her uncertainly, wondering whether he had got the wrong house after all.

It was only when she smiled back that Jack realised with a shock that the woman was his Aunt Georgina. But she was so thin and old! Her flesh was wrinkled and sagging, as if the aunt he had known had been partially deflated and her hair scattered with dust. He felt a lump rise to his throat—he'd been vaguely aware, of course, that she was now in her mid-seventies, but he hadn't expected this. Last time he had seen her his eyes had filled with tears, and now, for different reasons, the same thing was happening.

"Hello, Jack," she said, and he was relieved to find her voice was strong and imperious as ever. "How are you?"

"I'm . . . I'm fine, Aunt. . . . Very well," he struggled to say.

"You've put on weight."

He laughed. "You've lost some."

She laughed, too, and immediately Jack felt a surge of love, the intensity of which surprised him. He pushed open the gate, marched up the path and flung his arms around her. "I've missed you," he told her. "It really is good to see you again. . . ." He wanted to say more but emotion choked his words.

She patted him on the back, turned her head and planted a kiss on his cheek.

"Welcome home, Jack," she said.

INTERLUDE ONE

1983

The tabby cat that the boys had just stoned to death belonged to Mrs. Akhurst, Carl Priestley's next door neighbour. Mrs. Akhurst was in her seventies and arthritic, and she doted on her little Georgie.

Sometimes Carl heard her talking to the cat in the backyard as she hung up her washing; because of her hands, hanging up washing was a long and tortuous procedure for the old lady. Some of the things she said made him want to either puke or laugh or both: "How's my little Georgie Porgy Pudding n' Pie?" "Does Georgie want Mummy to get him his dinnums?" "What has my little Georgie been doing today? I hope he hasn't been chasing those nice little birdies again."

But despite his contempt for the way she spoke to the animal, Carl felt bad about actually killing it. Even the fact that it had not been his idea didn't make him feel any better. As usual, it had been Patty who'd initiated events. It was always Patty who led the lads one step further than most of them were really prepared to go. They were now standing in the bumpy dogshit-covered field that backed the houses along Carl's street, Patty nudging the pathetic little corpse with his foot. The rest of the lads—Guy, Wally, Ossie and himself, were joking around. Carl believed that he was not the only one hiding a sense of shame beneath an outward exhibition of raucous good humour.

The thing was, Mrs. Akhurst was old and lonely and Georgie was—had been—her only friend. And just because Patty was bored, just because Patty was feeling mean (when *wasn't* he feeling mean?) . . . Carl's stomach felt hollow. Shame was too feeble a word for the way he felt.

They were skiving off school as usual. They had decided to come to Carl's house because his parents were out, and because Carl had an awesome collection of dirty books. Carl's father owned Priestley's Newsagent's on Bridgewater Road. Kids were always nicking sweets and magazines, and it was easy for Carl to add to his collection without the slightest suspicion ever falling on him.

They had been sitting at the edge of the field, drinking Coke and goggling at the latest *Penthouse* when the cat slunk into view. Without even thinking about it, simply because it was part of his makeup, Patty picked up a chunk of dark-grey slate that was lying close at hand and flung it in the cat's general direction.

That might have been the end of it if the slate had not struck the cat's hindquarters. Its yowl of pain was music to Patty's ears. Thrusting the *Penthouse* into Ossie's eager hands, he stood up, eyes gleaming in a way that always made Carl feel both scared and excited.

"Fucking bull's eye!" he cried. "Did you see that? What a fucking shot!"

Quickly he began to range about, looking for more missiles. Wally, who was not exactly renowned for his intelligence, said, "What you doin', Patty?"

"What's it fucking look like, arsehole? We're gonna have a competition. It's called Splattering the Cat's Brains."

Wally sniggered. The battalion of yellow-tipped spots that had claimed his face as its territory did not make him the most attractive fifteen-year-old in Beckford, but he looked even uglier when he laughed.

Ossie was holding the *Penthouse* up close to his face, as if believing he could somehow slip through the glossy two-dimensional barrier and wallow in the soft, scented reality of naked female flesh. Guy, a squat, broad-shouldered troll of a boy, was picking his nose and secretly flicking the boogers at the back of Wally's head.

Carl recognised the cat at once. Amused as he was by the way it had yowled and leaped into the air, he didn't really want things to go much further.

"Aw, that's boring," he said. "Let's go to the rec and play football."

"We will," said Patty. "After we've done this. Come on, you lot, help us look for some more bricks."

The boys did as Patty asked, Carl half-heartedly. He wished the stupid cat would just piss off, but it was frolicking about in the long grass, amusing itself, its recent pain forgotten.

A few minutes later the boys had accrued a fair pile of missiles. This field had been intended as a play area for the local children, but it was so full of shit and glass and stones and rubbish that no one ever played on it; it was safer kicking a ball about on the street.

Patty picked up a scarred chunk of house-brick. "Right," he said, "I'll go first."

"What's the rules?" asked Wally.

Patty gave him a pitying look. "To hit the fucking thing," he said sarcastically.

"Why?" asked Ossie. He had tossed the *Penthouse* into the long grass and was hoping Carl would forget about it. He wanted to come back for it later.

Patty rolled his eyes. " 'Cos it's a laugh," he said. "Fucking hell. Talk about brain dead." He drew back his

arm and lobbed the brick. It missed the cat by a good
three feet. Georgie's head snapped up, ears pricked and
alert. Carl urged the cat to flee, but it had been molly-
coddled all its life and seemed not to recognise the
prospect of danger. After a few seconds it began prowl-
ing through the grass again, hunting or playing or whatever it was up to.

For the next ten minutes or so, the boys hurled missiles
without success, Carl throwing deliberately wide each
time. As the pile of missiles sank lower and lower, Patty
became more and more irate.

Finally, Guy said, "This is a fucking waste of time.
Come on, Patty, let's play darts instead."

The boys had their own special version of darts. They
would catch an insect, normally either a spider or a crane
fly, sellotape it by its legs to the dart board, and then try to
impale it.

"Fuck off," Patty snarled. "I'm gonna get that fucking
cat if it's the last thing I do."

"What's the point?" said Ossie. A moment later he was
blinking in pained surprise, as Patty whirled and shoved
him so forcefully that he sat down hard on the grass.

Patty turned back and pointed at something in the long
grass. "Here, Guy," he said, "give us that."

Grinning at Ossie, who was scowling and rubbing his
chest, Guy picked up the object and passed it to Patty.

Patty hefted the object in his hand, nodded in satisfaction. It was a rusty length of car exhaust. "Stay here," he
said and began to creep towards the cat. He moved carefully, slowly, half hunched over, reminding Carl of the abo-
riginal hunter in a film he'd seen about two kids in the
desert. He couldn't remember all that much about the film,
except that the girl had swum naked in a lake and he'd
been able to see her pubic hair.

Not that Patty needed to tread carefully, Carl thought.
Georgie the cat was so trusting that if Patty had marched

up playing a trumpet the stupid animal would probably have just curled itself around his legs, demanding to be stroked. When Patty was right over the cat, he grinned savagely back at the boys, then raised the length of rusty metal above his head. Carl wanted to shout for him to stop but he bit his lip. When the blow fell, Carl closed his eyes. He couldn't close his ears, though. His stomach lurched at the cat's screech of pain.

"That should slow it down a bit," Patty said, lolloping back toward them. It did. It slowed Georgie down to crawling pace. A couple of minutes later the cat's wails of agony were silenced for good.

"Hey, lads," Patty called now from across the field, "come and have a look at this. You can see its intestines."

Wally looked as though he didn't know what intestines were, but he ambled dutifully over to join his leader. Guy went, too. Ossie and Carl stayed where they were.

"What shall we do with it?" Carl heard Guy say as the three boys stood over the motionless heap of fur.

"Why don't we smash its head open and have a look at its brains," suggested Wally.

"Yeah, maybe you could borrow some," Patty said, and he and Guy cackled.

"What's the definition of loneliness?" Guy said, and then answered himself quickly before anyone could spoil his punchline: "Wally's brain cell."

"Fuck off," said Wally, and threw a slow, meaty punch at Guy, which the smaller boy dodged easily.

"Hey, I know," said Patty. "Let's leave it on the doorstep of that silly old cow what owns it. We could put a sign on it saying, 'You're Next' or something."

Guy laughed. "Yeah. Or we could hang it on her washing line."

He and Patty roared with laughter. Wally grinned vacantly along with them.

Carl wandered over, hands in pockets, trying to appear

casual, trying not to look at the mangled animal. He'd heard their entire conversation and was horrified at what they were suggesting.

"Hey," he said in an attempt to deflect their attention, "are we going to play footy or what?"

"Nah," said Patty. "Footy's boring." He began to gather up the missiles that lay scattered around the area. "Let's find some more things to bung rocks at."

"Yeah," said Guy. "We could go down to the woods. There'll be loads of birds and rabbits and stuff down there."

"Yeah, good idea," said Carl eagerly, stooping to pick up rocks himself. "I'm sick of hanging around here. It's boring."

Ten minutes later the boys were on the move, heading in a meandering fashion towards the woods. To Carl's relief they had left the cat where it had died. With any luck he could go back later and bury it before anyone else found it. Maybe then the blow for Mrs. Akhurst would be softened. She would just think Georgie had run away, could imagine him living a long and happy life somewhere else.

The boys followed a circuitous route, avoiding the school and the main streets of the village. That was the trouble with living here. There was always the danger of meeting someone you knew, and who knew you should be in school.

Their journey took them close to Cleckheaton Road just outside the village, which was where Patty's dad's garage was. It was a run-down place—cracked windows, peeling paint, patched roof, forecourt black and tacky with oil—but it was profitable. Bates's Garage was the only one in Beckford, and in Patty's dad's opinion, appearances were unimportant when you had a monopoly. Patty's dad had inherited the garage from his dad before him, and as far as he was concerned it was simply a money machine. Everyone expected Patty to take over the garage when his father died, but Patty had other ideas.

"I just wanna call in at dad's place," Patty said, "get some fags."

This was one of the things for which the other boys envied Patty. Patty's dad didn't care whether or not Patty went to school; neither did he care whether Patty smoked or drank. He occasionally grumbled when Patty got into trouble with the police, but not much, only when it caused him inconvenience. Carl had heard it said that Patty was a "chip off the old block," though he had never heard the phrase used in a complimentary way.

There were three people at the garage when they arrived. Patty's dad was not one of them. He didn't actually *work* at the garage that often. Usually he was away "doing deals," though exactly what was meant by that none of the boys, not even Patty, had any idea. Joe Bates was six feet three inches tall and weighed eighteen stone. He smoked cigars, wore a lot of gold jewelry and was forever stuffing five and ten pound notes into people's breast pockets. Once, when the boys had been sitting around on the garage forecourt, swinging a length of chain around and threatening any kids who happened to walk past, Joe Bates had driven up in his Alfa Romeo. He had squeezed his bulk from behind the wheel, strolled up to the boys and growled good-humouredly, "What're you layabouts hanging around here for? Chasing off me customers, are you?" He had then produced a crocodile skin wallet, opened it and thrust a tenner towards his son. "Here," he said, "buy you and your mates some fish and chips." It was a gesture that had impressed Carl deeply at the time and which he had never forgotten. He wished his own dad could be like that. In Carl's opinion, Joe Bates had class.

But Joe Bates was nowhere to be seen that day. Patty explained to the boys that he was in Leeds, "doing a bit of business." Linda Beesley, the girl with the pneumatic tits, was there though, sitting behind the counter in the office. Linda was eighteen and Patty had told the lads that he had slipped it to her loads of times, but no one really believed him. Not that anyone would dare call him a liar to his face.

Linda looked up as the boys passed the big office window, but returned to her Danielle Steele novel without acknowledging their leers and crude remarks. From around the back, the boys could hear the sound of metal striking metal, the intermittent rumble of conversation. They wandered round there, pockets still sagging with the rocks they had used to stone Georgie.

Patty was first round the corner. Seeing what was there, he turned back, motioning the lads to silence, ushering them back behind the cover of the wall.

"What's up?" said Wally, too loudly.

Patty backhanded him across the face. It was not hard but it made Wally flinch, and left a red mark. The other boys stifled their giggles.

"Take a look," said Patty, moving away from the corner to let the others see.

The gang craned their necks to peer around the corner. Carl was puzzled and unimpressed.

A battered red Ford Capri had been jacked up and from underneath protruded a pair of legs clad in oily blue overalls. These legs, the boys surmised, belonged to David Rookham, who had worked at the garage since leaving school at sixteen. Rookham was Joe Bates' best friend's son, but he was also a good mechanic.

Standing beside the car, leaning forward, hands on knees, was Terry Stone. He had his back to the boys and he too was wearing blue overalls. Terry Stone was the father of Jack Stone, the school weed. Patty couldn't understand why his father employed Terry Stone; half the time he didn't turn up for work, and when he did he was usually half-cut. When he had asked his dad about it, he had been told, "I've got a big heart, Patty. Terry and I go back a long way."

Guy pulled back from the corner and looked at Patty, face expressing the bewilderment they all felt. "Stone and Rookham," he said. "So what?"

Patty grinned and pulled a rock from his pocket. "I thought Stone's arse would make a good target."

The boys sniggered and again tried to stifle it. It was true. The way Stone was standing, his scrawny arse was sticking right up in the air. For fuck's sake, he was virtually offering himself. He was like a guy in a cartoon, bending over to sniff flowers as a bull on the other side of the field paws the ground, snorts steam, and lowers its head ready to charge.

"Yeah," said Guy. "Baggsy I have first shot."

"Bollocks," replied Patty, "I saw him. I'm gonna have first shot."

"Why don't we all throw at the same time?" suggested Carl. "I mean, once the bricks start coming in, he's not gonna stand in that position until one of us hits the target, is he?"

Patty frowned. It was obvious he had not thought of that. "Yeah," he said, "okay. But on my word, all right?"

The boys nodded.

"Right then. Come on. And be quiet."

The gang tiptoed round the corner and lined up, pulling missiles from their pockets. Just like the Magnificent Seven, thought Carl. Except that there were only five of them.

Patty looked along the line, grinning. The boys grinned back. Terry Stone was still bent over, talking to Rookham's legs. Very deliberately, Patty mouthed, "One. Two. Three." Then he yelled, "Now!" and hurled his rock.

Terry Stone had already begun to straighten up, startled by the cry, when Patty's rock hit him just above the kidneys. Four more missiles followed in quick succession.

Two hit the Ford Capri, causing sizeable dents in the bodywork, one—Wally's—flew high and wide, and the other—Ossie's—struck Stone on his right shoulder.

Stone fell forwards against the car as if a truck had hit him, crying out in pain. The car rocked as his hands and body slapped against it, and for one horrible moment Carl thought the jack would give way, causing two tons of metal to crash down on top of David Rookham.

Fortunately, however, the jack held. The boys heard a shrill, strangled curse from beneath the car, and the next instant Rookham catapulted out, face very white beneath its smudges of oil, hair awry, eyes and mouth wide open. "What the hell's going on?" he screamed, voice high-pitched, almost girlish. He looked at Stone, who was rubbing his back and shoulders, face puckered with pain. Then he looked at the boys and repeated, "What's going on?"

Patty, Guy and Wally were laughing. Ossie looked a little pale, a little scared, and Carl thought that maybe he did, too. Patty waved a hand in a gesture of dismissal. Still grinning hugely he said, "Aw, c'mon, Dave, it was a joke, that's all."

"You call trying to squash me to a pulp a joke?"

Patty rolled his eyes. "It wasn't our fault that old bony fell over the car, was it?"

Terry Stone turned slowly, still rubbing the places where the rocks had hit him, but now Carl saw that his face was puckered not with pain but anger. His expression deepened quickly, became more than anger; it became rage, fury, dementia.

"You . . . ," he said in a strange, strangled voice. He picked up one of the rocks that had struck him, looked at it disbelievingly. "You . . . you *fucking little shits!*"

Carl stepped back, as did Ossie and Wally. He wouldn't have admitted it, but he was more than a little scared of Terry Stone. It was generally regarded in Beckford that the man had a few screws loose. He drank a lot, and it was rumoured that he beat up his son.

He looked pretty crazed now, right enough. His face was red, his eyes bulged and froth was collecting at the corners of his mouth. The boys began to break rank as he strode towards them, still clutching the rock in his hand. Even Guy, Patty's unofficial second-in-command, backed away. Only Patty himself stood his ground.

"What do you think you were doing?" Terry screeched. Froth sprayed from his lips as if he had a mouthful of washing up liquid.

He came to a quivering halt, no more than six feet away from Patty. Patty raised himself to his full height, arching his neck, drawing back his shoulders, pushing out his chest. Patty was big for a fifteen-year-old, but he was still an inch or two shorter than Terry Stone. However, he made up for that in bulk. Stone was skinny, haggard-looking. Patty probably weighed fifteen or twenty pounds more than the older man.

"Keep your fucking hair on, Bony," Patty said. There was no humour in his voice now. His eyes had a flat, predatory sheen, his voice was belligerent, goading. Carl knew he was spoiling for a fight, and usually when Patty wanted a fight he got one.

"You could have split my head open with this! You could have killed David! What the fuck did you throw it for?" Stone yelled into Patty's face.

Carl realised exactly what it was about Terry Stone that made him uneasy. The man always seemed full of rage, so much so that no amount of screaming and ranting would ever get rid of it. Even when Carl had seen Terry sober, as he was now, even when he'd seen him having a laugh in the pub or chewing the fat with the locals, that rage seemed to cling to him, seemed to swirl beneath the still blue surface of his eyes, biding its time. Carl thought of guys who, one day, for no good reason, took a gun to the local supermarket and killed as many people as possible, coldly and indiscriminately, usually before blowing their own brains out. Whatever it was that made people do that, Carl thought that Terry Stone possessed it. He was a time bomb on a slow-burning fuse, a touchpaper waiting for the flame.

"I didn't throw that one. I threw that one over there," Patty said in a tone of hostile sarcasm.

Even as the boys were sniggering, Terry said, "Well, you can have this one back," and he whirled his arm around, bowling the rock underarm at Patty's midriff.

The distance between Patty and Terry, and the suddenness of the movement, meant that Patty had no chance to dodge out of the way. The rock hit him hard in the stomach, doubling him over. Before anyone could react, Terry kicked Patty in the face, then kicked him again and again and again. He became a dervish of flying feet and fists. Carl was chilled to see that on Stone's face was an expression of cold, calm madness, like frozen, contained rage moulded into a mask. Carl wondered whether Patty could have beaten Terry Stone if Stone had not had the element of surprise, if Patty had not been winded. In this mood, he wasn't so sure.

The boys stood round in a rough semicircle, as always happened when there was a fight. This fight, however, was different from usual. Normally it was Patty who was standing up, doing the kicking. Now, though, he was curled into a ball on the dusty ground, not moving, not making a sound. Carl could see blood around his face and head, glimpsed flashes of it, startlingly red through the blurred screen of Terry Stone's boots. Carl wanted Terry to stop, wanted to scream at him to do so. Even Patty would have stopped by now.

But Terry looked as if he would never stop. He would kick Patty until he was dead, until his head was an unrecognisable mess. And the boys would simply stand there and watch it happen, too terrified to intervene, afraid Stone would turn his rage on them. Carl looked desperately at his friends. They were transfixed, as horrified as he was—even Guy. Carl's mouth was so dry that his tongue seemed to have glued itself to the roof of his mouth. His throat felt like gravel.

It was David Rookham who stopped the fight. He plunged in beneath Terry's whirling limbs, locked his arms around his chest and dragged him away. For an instant Terry resisted, even snarled like an animal and tried to bite Rookham. Then he seemed to realise what he was doing and became limp, acquiescent.

Only when Rookham had pulled Terry away from the scene did the boys move in. Guy was the first to react. He hurried forward, grabbed Patty's arm and tried to haul him to his feet.

"Hey, Patty, you all right?" he said.

Carl felt a scream of laughter, hard and painful, like a bubble of indigestion, working its way up from his hollowed-out stomach. "Does he *look* all right?" he said to Guy, and his voice was strange—tight and high and scratchy, a hint of hysteria running through it like a fine gold thread. Guy looked at Carl. Normally he would have taken the piss out of him for speaking in such a puffy voice, but today he simply shook his head.

The boys shuffled over and looked down at Patty, not sure what to do, not sure whether to pull him to his feet or simply wait for him to recover in his own time. At least they knew that Patty was alive. He was making horrible gasping, gagging noises as if about to throw up. At last, he began to move his limbs, floundering like a beached fish. White-faced, Ossie said, "Come on, let's get him up." He tentatively took Patty's left arm, Guy took his right, and together they hauled Patty to his feet.

His face was a mess, all cuts and bruises. His eyes and

top lip were horribly swollen. He was bleeding so freely that it was hard to tell exactly how bad his injuries were. His breath was rattling liquidly in his throat. A stream of saliva mixed with blood drooled out of his mouth. He tried to spit, but the stuff slid down his chin and spattered on his T-shirt. His legs were all over the place, like a boxer who'd been KO'd. Through the swollen slits of his eyelids, the boys could see that the whites of Patty's eyeballs had turned pink; Carl wondered fearfully whether this meant Patty had internal bleeding in his head. He saw Patty's lips moving, heard a rumble of sound dribbling from between them.

"Hey, lads," Carl said, "I think he's trying to say something."

The boys pushed their heads in to listen. At first it seemed that Patty was just mumbling nonsense. "Killim . . . ," he slurred, ". . . killim . . ."

"What's he saying?" asked Wally, blinking in his slow, almost sleepy way.

"Shut up, cretin," hissed Guy, "and listen."

The boys crowded in again. Patty cleared his throat, dribbled more blood, wiped a shaky hand across his mouth.

"He's dead," they heard Patty say. "He's fucking dead. I'm gonna kill the bastard."

Carl had heard Patty make such threats before, but this time he shuddered. Despite being only semiconscious, Patty sounded as if he really meant it.

PART TWO

LAID TO REST

7

FIRE AND LONELINESS

"I expect you'll be wanting to get off to the house, get yourself settled in," Aunt Georgina said.

Jack brushed his hands together, ridding them of cake crumbs. "Actually," he replied, "I thought I'd stay at the Connaught."

For the first time since he'd set off that morning, he was beginning to feel almost relaxed. His aunt's lounge was cosy as ever, and even though arthritis had seized her joints, gnarling her hands into claws, he quickly discovered she had lost none of her culinary skills. Despite her comment about his weight, she had insisted on fetching him a bowl of soup that she had made from parsnips and apples, and a sizeable hunk of fresh-baked bread. Jack made a feeble objection, but his aunt waved it away. "I'll not hear any arguments," she said. "I knew you'd be hungry when you got here, so I made it especially."

While she was in the kitchen Jack allowed himself a wry smile; she had lost none of her forcefulness. Mentally apologising to the God of Weight Loss, to whom he had made a solemn vow, he had begun, at first reluctantly, to eat the soup, and then had found to his shame that it was so delicious he simply could not refuse a second helping.

He salved his conscience by insisting on only a small slice of her equally delicious fruit cake and by promising himself that tomorrow, before breakfast, he would spend half an hour pounding the country roads. He sipped his tea and said, "Actually, I'd better give them a ring. This has all happened so quickly that I never thought about booking a room."

Aunt Georgina looked surprised and a little disapproving. "What's the point of spending good money on a hotel when you've got a big empty house all to yourself?"

Jack pulled a face. "Well, that's just it. It's big and it's empty, and . . . to be honest, the memories that fill it are not exactly pleasant ones."

He expected Georgina to admonish him for his extravagance, but she simply nodded, albeit half-heartedly, and said, "Hmm, I do see your point. Well, look sharp. You give the Connaught a ring while I fetch my coat."

"You're coming with me?" Jack said.

"Of course. I haven't seen my nephew in fifteen years. I'm not about to let him out of my clutches now." She pushed herself from her chair with obvious discomfort. "You know," she said when she was on her feet, "I'd offer you accommodation here, but I've only got one bedroom and a piddling little settee. The neighbours would talk. They'd think I'd got myself a toy boy."

He laughed, both at the phrase, which sounded odd on her lips, and the mischievous glint in her eye.

She hobbled through to the kitchen, rubbing her knee with a clawed hand and muttering what a wreck she was. Whenever Jack thought of her kitchen, he pictured work surfaces piled with chopped vegetables, her solid wooden table scattered with flour in readiness for the pastry that would be scrolled around the rolling pin. She used to love cooking, for neighbours and friends as well as herself. She baked cakes aplenty for church fetes and WI picnics and God knew how many other causes. Jack always remembered her as an active, energetic woman, but it was only now, with the advantage of hindsight, that he realised just how active and energetic she had been. Apart from her involvement with the WI and the Church committee, Jack remembered her attending meetings of the Beckford Art Society, the Amateur Dramatics Society, the Horticulturalists Society and the Knitting Club (it probably had a grander title than that but Jack didn't know what it was). And on top of all this she used to make frequent visits to the elderly for some charity or other, she helped out with some part-time nursing at Dr. Travis' surgery when the pace became too hot for the old man, and didn't she also used to sing in some sort of choir? He suspected that was something to do with the church as well.

"That's my aunt," he muttered, picking up the phone, shaking his head in admiration. And then, all at once, Jack realised *why* she had been involved in so many village activities. It was a revelation that felt as if it had been waiting for years to emerge.

Aunt Georgina, he realised, had been—and still was—a very lonely woman.

He stood for a moment with the phone in his hand, staring into space, and all at once felt a wave of sadness sweep over him. He felt an urge to rush into the kitchen and hug his aunt, to apologise for all the years he had neglected her. It had never occurred to him, when he was younger, that his aunt had problems and anxieties just like everyone else. She had always seemed like a rock, so steadfast, so uncomplicated, so . . . so . . . the word that came to him was *pure.* It seemed a strange phrase, yet apt. She had seemed so certain of her own emotions, so open and honest and thoroughly without deceit. Jack's sudden realisation had thrown him off-kilter, perhaps more than it should have.

"What did they say?" Georgina asked, emerging from the kitchen, struggling into her coat.

"Er . . ." Jack replaced the receiver clumsily and noisily and snatched up the telephone book. "I haven't actually rung them yet. I'm still looking for the number."

"Honestly," Georgina sighed, "how have you managed all these years? Here, let me." She took the book from him before Jack could protest.

She found the number in seconds and read it out clearly, as though to an imbecile, while Jack dialed. After two rings an oily voice enquired, "Connaught Hotel. How may I help you?"

"Oh, hello. My name's Jack Stone. I was wondering whether it would be possible to book a room?"

"Certainly, Mr. Stone," said Oily-voice. "When would you like the room for?"

"Tonight, if possible. And I'll be staying for three or four days."

"Ah," said Oily-voice pointedly.

"Is there a problem?" asked Jack.

"Yes, Mr. Stone, I'm afraid there is. You see, we're fully booked until Friday. There's a marketing convention in Leeds and we have a group of forty staying here from the Midlands."

"Leeds," said Jack as if the man had made a mistake, "but that's fifteen miles away."

Oily-voice's tone became a little less accommodating. "That's true, Mr. Stone, but our setting is far more picturesque, I'm sure you'll agree. The drive to Leeds is relatively free of traffic congestion, and we have a very reliable train service. We do like to encourage this sort of custom."

Jack felt his temper rising at the man's insinuations, but tried to repress it. "Is there no chance of a room before the weekend?" he asked.

"None at all, Mr. Stone," said Oily-voice with obvious satisfaction. "Very sorry. Good-bye."

" 'Bye," said Jack, but he was already speaking to a dead line. He turned to his Aunt Georgina, whose face was set in a sympathetic expression.

"No luck, I take it?"

"No. Is there anywhere else I can try?"

She narrowed her eyes, considering. "The Dog and Gun used to have a couple of rooms, but since Shelagh had her baby I think they've stopped all that. . . ." She made a ticking sound with her mouth as though flipping through a mental index file. Eventually she said, "I'm sorry, Jack, but I don't think there *is* anywhere else in Beckford. You could try one of the other villages."

Jack thought about it, then shook his head, trying to dislodge the feeling that there was a kind of ominous inevitability to all this. "No," he said, "that would be silly, wouldn't it? As you said before, why spend good money on a hotel when I've got a big empty house all to myself?"

Georgina smiled, rubbed his upper arm briskly as if he'd banged it. "That's the spirit," she said. "I'm sure you'll be fine there. What's past is past, there's no bringing it back. It might even help you lay a few ghosts."

Jack looked at his aunt, a little startled. *Lay a few ghosts*—that was exactly the phrase that Gail had used yesterday. "Yeah," he said, "that's what Gail reckons."

"Gail?" said Georgina. She tilted her head coquettishly. "And who might she be?"

Jack sighed inwardly and reminded himself that it would take his aunt a while to adjust to the fact that he was now a grown man. "She's a girl—a woman—I'm seeing," he explained.

"Oh, courting, are we? You've kept that one quiet."

Jack felt embarrassed in spite of himself. "Not really. We . . . er . . . we haven't known each other that long." He hoped his aunt wouldn't ask *how* long because it would emphasise his recent lack of communication with her.

"Well, what's she like? What does she do? Is she from

London?" His aunt's tone seemed to suggest there was something slightly disreputable in that.

Jack laughed, flattered by her interest but also a little uncomfortable, a reminder of how cagey he was, how he valued his privacy. "Still as nosy as ever," he said, grinning to show he was joking. "Come on, I'll tell you all about her in the car."

As far as Jack was concerned, the only drawback to living in London was being unable to get to the countryside easily, and if he'd been anywhere else he would have found the drive to his father's house exhilarating. The spring sunshine seemed clean and fresh, making the earth appear newborn. Trees seemed to stretch out their leaves to capture its light, fields to bristle, verdant, as though soaking up its goodness. The closer they came to the house, however, the more Jack's trepidation grew. He scorned himself silently for the groundlessness of his emotion. When he changed gear to scale the cobbled hill that led to Daisy Lane, he turned to his aunt and in an attempt at levity said, "It's just like a Hovis advert." However, the look of disapproval she gave him made him feel ashamed; it was the comment of a patronising townie.

She looked childlike in the passenger seat, the seat belt slanting across her chest. Looking at her, Jack again felt sad, though he guessed she would have been appalled had she known. He saw the opening ahead on the left, the faded sign, half-concealed by foliage, reading DAISY LANE. He breathed deeply, as though bracing himself for some ordeal, then changed down to second and swung the car into the narrow opening.

Here was the dry-stone wall over which he had leaped to avoid the ambulance. Fifteen years did not seem to have changed it; if stones had crumbled and been replaced in that time, Jack did not notice. What did seem thicker were the trees, which craned over the track in a natural arch, the tips of their branches probing the car's roof. Sunlight dripped through the trees and winked softly on the road ahead. Fifty yards further the trees petered out abruptly; Jack screwed up his eyes as the sun pounced brilliantly from a glittering field on his left.

Daisy Lane twisted and turned for three-quarters of a mile before it reached Jack's father's house. Georgina had been fairly silent for most of the short journey—she had not even asked anything more about Gail—but now, as the Mini Cooper jounced and crawled along the uneven road, she said, "Tell me, Jack, do you *really* like London?"

He smirked, but turned away so she would not think him supercilious; there was so much in that one simple question. She was asking, "How can you really like such a noisy, smelly, busy place?" and "Isn't it simply pride that keeps you there? Now that your father's dead, wouldn't you rather come home?"

Jack knew that if his reply was at all half-hearted, his aunt would continue to probe at his uncertainty, subtly undermining his lifestyle. In order to paper over that particular crack before she could widen it any further, he replied with gusto, "Oh, I *love* it. It's such an exciting place to live—there's so much to do, so much to see. I've got a lovely flat and all my friends are there, and Gail, and my work. . . . I don't think I could live anywhere else now."

His aunt merely grunted. Jack glanced at her and saw she was scowling; he wondered if that was because she realised he'd guessed her intention. Pretending not to notice, he said, "Look, why don't you come and visit me when I get back? It's only a few hours on the train. You could meet Gail. I'm sure you'd have a nice time."

She pulled a face. "No," she said a little sourly. "I don't think I'd like it. It's not for me." She raised a bony hand and swept it at the windshield. "This is where I'm comfortable. I don't know how you put up with all those cars and people, all that pollution."

"Oh, it's not half as bad as they make out."

"Huh," she muttered disparagingly and relapsed into silence.

They were getting close now. Jack could see the Butterworths' farm in a fold of land ahead. A wisp of smoke rose from the chimney like a thread of frayed wool. Cows speckled the field beyond the farmyard; Jack could hear them lowing as though playing at ghosts. He felt an urge to chat to allay his nervousness. "Do you ever speak to Molly Haynes nowadays?" he asked.

His aunt gave him a look that Jack could not quite read; it was somewhere between disappointment and exasperation. "Molly died last year," she said flatly. "I'm surprised you didn't know."

He felt like sinking into a hole in the earth. Knowing his face was reddening, he stammered, "Oh . . . n-no, I didn't know. What happened? I mean . . . what happened to her?"

"She had cancer," Georgina said curtly. "In the throat."

"Oh no," Jack said again, but could think of nothing else to add. The last time something like this had happened had been early in his relationship with Gail. She'd been pestering him about his childhood again, and he'd got annoyed and said, "Well, you never talk about *your* parents. What's the matter? Are you ashamed of them or something?" Gail had glared at him, angry and hurt, had told him curtly that her father had died when she was four years old, her mother just a couple of years ago.

Jack became aware that his aunt was talking and adjusted his concentration. "I believe it was quite quick," she was saying, "but I *am* surprised you didn't know."

"Well . . . I . . . er . . . I lost touch with Molly a year or two ago," Jack said. It was actually more like five, but he wasn't going to let his aunt know that. Immediately that thought was overlaid by another: perhaps she already *did* know and was testing him, in which case he would sound like a complete heel. "Or perhaps," he blundered on, "it was longer than that. I can't really remember. I'm so busy nowadays time just seems to fly by."

He resented his aunt for making him feel guilty like this. He had his own life to lead, didn't he? He couldn't be expected to stay in touch with everybody he'd ever known. Besides, communication was a two-way system. However, he knew that since he'd met Gail he'd happily become part of what he'd always despised: a couple. That was not a couple as in two individuals, but a couple as in an insular, self-contained unit. He'd lost or was losing touch with many of his pre-Gail friends. Even his best mate, Frank Dawson, was becoming a stranger now. They still went out occasionally, but it wasn't like the old times. They didn't seem to have that much in common now, and sometimes, in moments of piquant and usually drunken objectivity, Jack would hear himself talking and realise he was turning into a Gail-bore.

They passed the Butterworths' farm. Jack glanced at it, solid and rugged as though it had become part of the land itself, then he fixed his gaze on the road ahead. He knew that if he looked up he would see his father's house and he felt an almost superstitious desire to delay that moment as long as possible. Nevertheless, a block of shadow seemed to snatch at the edge of his vision; Jack knew it was the dark stone of the house contrasted against the sparkling sky.

"Do you remember the Butterworths, Jack?" asked Georgina.

Jack opened his mouth to reply and was surprised to find it dry and tacky. His tongue flickered between his gums and his lips, lubricating, unpeeling the two surfaces from one another.

He cleared his throat and said, "Oh, yes. There was the old man, wasn't there, and three sons? Martin, Edward and . . . what was the other one?"

"Gerard."

"Gerard—that's right. They were big and blond-haired, and—"

"Jack, we're here," his aunt said softly.

He stamped on the brake as if an animal had run in front of the car. He was aware of his tires sliding a little on the bumpy road, a billow of dust that quickly dispersed, his aunt lurching forward, then snapping back as the seat belt locked. A tingle of reaction scuttered up his legs, up his back, across his shoulders and down his arms. It settled in the palms of his hands, itching as if his skin had gone from cold to hot too quickly. The pores in his body seemed to gape and ooze sweat. "Sorry about that. Are you all right?" he said.

His aunt was frowning in pain, her eyes half-closed, kneading her breastbone with the tips of her fingers. "Why did you do that?" she said, grumpily but weakly. "Whatever were you thinking of?"

"I'm sorry," he said again. "I don't know. I was day-dreaming. . . . I'm sorry."

"Were you trying to see me off as well?"

Jack knew she was joking, but bad-temperedly. "No," he said, and added again, "I'm sorry."

She glared at him a moment, then her expression softened. "Ah, well," she said, "no real harm done." She pointed over Jack's right shoulder. "What do you reckon of the old place then?"

For a moment, he actually felt reluctant to turn round. He smiled at his aunt and said, "Give me a chance," before swivelling slowly.

And there was the house. At first Jack thought it was stirring, its roof splitting into a pattern of interconnected spines that were waving like tendrils. Then the light shifted, perspective imposed itself, and he saw that the tendrils were simply the peaks of the tallest trees in the woods behind the house. The house itself was as he remembered it, louring and inhospitable. There was no colour about the place, no flowers in the garden, no brightly painted door. Even the curtains at the windows appeared grey, like thick swathes of dust or cobweb. By contrast, the sky seemed almost impossibly blue—the colour of the sea on a holiday brochure. There were some alterations to the place, though, since the last time he had been here: a new wrought-iron gate to replace the rickety wooden one, the front lawn mowed stubble-close, revealing the dull mounds of intermittent molehills.

"Welcome to your luxurious holiday home," he murmured. "Guaranteed to make your stay a happy one."

"I've cleaned and aired the place for you," his aunt said. "Well, with some help from young Tracey, the landlord's daughter from the Seven Stars. She was telling me she'd read all your books. I think you might have a fan there."

Jack gave a vague smile.

"Shall we go inside?" said his aunt.

Jack took off his spectacles, slipped them into the inside pocket of his jacket, and got out of the car slowly. He turned to lever the front seat down and grab his suitcase from the back.

"Is there anything I can carry?" Georgina wanted to know, but Jack shook his head.

"No, there's just my laptop in the boot, but that can wait until later."

Despite the gate being new, it still creaked; true to form, Jack thought wryly. As though this walk up the path to the front door meant nothing to him, he asked his aunt, "Will it be okay to park my car on the verge over there?"

"Oh, yes, I should think so," she said, and took a key-ring containing two keys from her pocket. It was the same heavy wooden door, but with an extra lock. Thinking of her arthritis, Jack put down his suitcase and said, "Here, let me," but she had already pushed the door open.

The smell that enveloped them when they stepped into the gloomy hall took him by surprise. The odour of to-

bacco and alcohol and of something sour and organic, like
rank sweat and rotting vegetables, had been eradicated by
the chemical tang of furniture polish, disinfectant and
lemon-scented air freshener. It was certainly a far prefer-
able smell to the one Jack had expected, though it nevertheless made him uncomfortable, for it seemed to suggest
it was covering up something bad. His "dark and quirky
imagination," as *The Daily Mail* had once put it, began to
shift into overdrive. Had he been told everything about
his father's death or had his aunt left out a vital detail?
Such as the fact that his father's dead body had remained
undiscovered for some considerable time?

As if guessing his thoughts, Georgina said, "It's a bit
stuffy, isn't it? I'll open a few windows."

Jack smiled vaguely at her, put down his case and
looked around. Being here made him feel very strange indeed. There was a weight in his stomach, as if his memories of childhood had congealed there.

The hall was exactly as he remembered it, so familiar
that it could have been only a week or a month since he
was last here; it seemed inconceivable that fifteen years
had passed. The wide staircase was immediately in front
of him, clinging to the right-hand wall; the corridor which
slipped down the left side of it led to the vast kitchen and
the dimly lit sitting room. At the bottom of the stairs was
the wooden telephone table, scratched and battered. A
red telephone—it looked like the exact same one that he'd
used to call the ambulance for his father in 1989—sat
atop a local telephone directory and Yellow Pages that
seemed barely to have been touched. Curiously, Jack
picked up the receiver and put it to his ear. He was oddly
relieved to hear the familiar hum of the dial tone. The
mouthpiece smelt of stale breath; his stomach turned
slowly as he realised whose breath it must be. Behind the
door were a row of coat hooks, none of which were
presently occupied. There were four of them, ornate

pieces of brass set on a wooden plate. Jack remembered his father always used to moan about having to traipse through to the kitchen every time he wanted his coat; eventually he'd remedied that by purchasing these hooks and putting them on the wall.

The wooden floor and stairs were uncarpeted, though Jack always recalled them being scuffed and muddied, not gleaming as they were now. Even without his spectacles he could see how the polish really brought out the deep red of the wood, the intricate whorls of the grain, the minute distortions in the floor's surface. He reached out his hand and cupped it around the carved wooden acorn atop the post at the foot of the stairs. He would always reach out instinctively for this when he was about to ascend and would use it to swing himself onto the second or third step. The memory of this little thing, which he used to do a dozen times a day and not even think about, was so sharp he could almost taste it. He felt his heartbeat snagging his breath, making him pant slightly, because just for a moment the passage of the last fifteen years seemed so quick and ephemeral and insignificant that it frightened him.

The wallpaper was the same—white with a squiggly blue pattern endlessly repeated—though it was more faded than Jack remembered it. However, it was cleaner, too: perhaps Aunt Georgina and her helper, Tracey, had even gone so far as to swab down the walls. At the top of the stairs early afternoon light spilled in through a window, saffron at the edges, misty white in the centre. All at once Jack shuddered and looked away. The place gave him the creeps. As if some presence . . .

"Mcmories," he said out loud to quash the thought. "Bad memories, that's all."

Georgina appeared at the end of the corridor and hobbled towards him. "That's better," she said. "Nothing like a bit of fresh air to blow the cobwebs away." She stopped some yards away and regarded him quizzically. "What's the matter, Jack? You look a little queer."

Normally he would have found her choice of words amusing, but just now he didn't feel like making anything of it. "It's just this place," he said. "Coming back . . . You know?"

She nodded, not unsympathetically. "It's been a long time, hasn't it?"

He nodded and smiled. He wanted to make some comment, to say something appropriate, but he couldn't think of anything and the moment passed.

"I expect it'll just take a bit of getting used to, that's all," she said. "How about a nice cup of tea to get you settled in?"

Jack shrugged. "Okay."

"Lovely. I'll put the kettle on if you'll make up a fire in the living room. It's a bit chilly in there. It doesn't get much light."

She disappeared into the kitchen. Jack sighed and walked toward the sitting room. His recent dream came back to him, the house as some hostile, living entity, swallowing him whole, but he forced it to the back of his mind.

The sitting room was a little smaller than he remembered it, but apart from that it looked much the same. The carpet was brown—to absorb alcohol stains, thought Jack—and had obviously been recently cleaned. He couldn't recall what the old three-piece suite had been like, so was unsure whether this was the same one. It certainly looked old enough to have been. The fabric was faded and a little threadbare, the cushions shapeless as boulders. The dining table and chairs were in the same place as he remembered them, with the sideboard flush against the wall behind them. Again his dream came back to him: his father as the ogre in his book, his mother in her white gown, rising into the air as she gave birth to some twisted, nightmarish thing.

He shivered a little, jiggling his shoulders as though shucking off the memory like a coating of snow. He looked around again, working out how to best impose his personality on the place. He was pleased to see his father had replaced the decrepit black-and-white TV with a colour one; pity there wasn't a DVD player, too. He would set up his laptop on the dining table, together with his various other writing accoutrements, and would plug in his CD player to fill the place with music and noise.

He circled the settee, knelt in front of the soot-blackened grate and began to build a fire. He was surprised by how quickly he recollected the process; he hadn't done this in fifteen years, yet his movements were swift and automatic. When his aunt entered with a tea tray he was carefully laying coal on top of his construction. He lit a match and touched it to the paper underneath. He felt absurdly proud when the fire quickly began to blaze.

"Soon be warm now," Georgina said, pouring the tea. Jack sat beside her on the settee, facing the fire, and she handed him a cup. The china service looked delicate, a little cracked and stained, but despite its obvious age Jack didn't recognise it. Probably packed away when his mother died, he thought, and felt a twinge of sadness. Just like his father's love had been packed away and left to wither and turn bad.

The fire danced for him, flames weaving sinuously as though in a desperate attempt to sustain its meagre life. Occasionally it popped and crackled, black sparks fleeing up the chimney like inverted fireworks. Like the sea, Jack had always found fire awesome and beautiful. He still felt tense, but gradually the heat of the flames seeped into his skin, lapping at his muscles, relaxing his body. He was aware that at some stage he and his aunt would have to talk about his father. How about now? He shifted on the settee, turning to face her. "Aunt," he said tentatively, "how was my father . . . I mean, how had he been since I . . . since I left?"

Georgina put down her cup, which rattled in its saucer, and leaned back with a sigh. She looked not at Jack but into the fire. Flames flickered in her eyes, making them oddly feral.

"How was he after you left?" she repeated, and pulled a face as if the question was too large for her to answer. She was silent a few moments longer, then said, "You never used to want me to talk about him when we spoke on the telephone."

"I know, I know," Jack said, feeling guilty in spite of himself. "But I do now. Now that he's . . . no longer here, now that I'm back in Beckford. . . ." He scowled, confused. "I don't know . . . I feel an urge, a need, to fill in the gaps."

His aunt didn't question this. Instead, after a slight pause, she said, "When he came out of the hospital after the two of you had had your fight, he wouldn't speak to anyone. Even I couldn't get through to him. He just stared into space and grunted when I tried to make conversation. Even when I became angry he failed to respond, and that frightened me because it seemed as if he didn't care any more. He was very subdued, very listless. He sat around the house all day, which admittedly was nothing unusual, but he wasn't even drinking or smoking very much; it was as if even that was too much of an effort. He . . . ," she screwed up her face, searching for the right expression, "I don't know. It seemed like all his spirit, bitter though it was, had gone right out of him."

"There was no one left to hate any more," said Jack.

She shook her head. "No, I don't think that was it. I remember once, I came here unannounced to see how he was, and I found him crying. He tried to cover it up at first, said he had a cold, but I kept on at him, asking him what was the matter. I felt as though he desperately wanted someone to talk to, although he wouldn't have admitted it. That was the closest your father ever came to pouring his heart out. He said to me, 'I've messed it all up, Georgina, haven't I?' 'Messed what up, Terry?' I asked him. 'Everything,' he said. 'My whole life. Everything I ever wanted has just gone down the drain and I've done nothing to stop it. I've lost everything in this world that I've ever loved and it serves me bloody well right.' 'Do you mean Jack?' I asked him, but he wouldn't say any more. He jumped up, suddenly angry, and said, 'I don't want to talk about it, I'm going out.' I tried to stop him, but there wasn't much I could do. I tried to get him to discuss it on a few occasions after that, but he just clammed up or got angry and stormed out. When he died he was a virtual recluse. He just used to sit around the house all day, brooding."

She shook her head sadly; Jack heard the slight strain in her voice as she tried to contain her emotion. "Such a waste," she said, "such a waste of a life. He wasn't a bad man, Jack. I think he wanted to love you, but the poison just built up in him and he couldn't ever get rid of it. When he died I felt almost relieved for him because I knew he was finally at peace. . . ." Her voice had become a whisper and now it tailed off completely. Jack had been staring into the fire, a lump in his throat, a knot in his belly. He looked at his aunt and saw she was wiping tears from her wrinkled face with a tissue. "I'm sorry," she said. "Just ignore me. I'll be all right in a minute."

Jack didn't know what to think. Despite the obvious tragedy of his father's life he couldn't reconcile the tortured, lovelorn image his aunt had portrayed with the drunken, vindictive slob he had known. He felt sympathy for his father's circumstances but not for the man himself. He supposed, as usual, that his aunt was looking at the situation through rose-tinted spectacles; it was not that she didn't recognise Terry Stone's considerable faults, but simply that she had so badly wanted Jack and his father to be friends that she had something of a blind spot where Terry's treatment of him was concerned. Oh, she had berated Terry about Jack's cuts and bruises, but she had always allowed him to go back to his father, hadn't she? Jack thought he had a right to hate her a little bit for that but he didn't; he knew her intentions, though misguided, had been well-meaning.

"Look . . . don't cry," he said awkwardly. "You did all you could for him. Nobody could have done any more. He didn't have to live like that, did he? He didn't have to grieve and hate all his life."

His aunt blew her nose. "I know," she said, "but I don't think he could help it. It just took him over. I don't think there was anything he could do."

Bollocks, Jack wanted to say, but didn't. He wanted to point out to his aunt that plenty of other people get the same bum deal from life, but they don't all crumble as his father did. And they certainly don't take it out on their kids. Jack felt that if the same thing happened to him, he would give his child twice as much love, would work doubly hard to create a bond that would never be broken.

He voiced none of this. It felt too much like speaking ill of the dead. Instead he leaned forward and placed his hand on the pot to ensure it was still warm, then he poured his Aunt another cup of tea.

"Here," he said, "drink this." Georgina took the cup, sipped it once, then put it aside.

"He was very proud of you, you know," she told Jack.

"Proud," he repeated, unable to keep the scorn from his voice.

"He was proud of your success. It was the only time after you left that he showed any sort of enthusiasm. He used to tell people about his famous son."

Jack snorted. The disclosure made him angry but he wasn't sure why. Perhaps because of his father's strange duality: he had hated Jack to his face, boasted about him behind his back.

Abruptly his aunt pushed herself up from the settee, tottering for a moment before stabilising. "Well, I'd better be off," she said. "Leave you to get settled in."

"You're going already?" he said, surprised. The prospect of being left alone here was not appealing. He tried to make light of it. "Was it something I said?"

"No, of course not," said Georgina, patting his arm. She looked momentarily uncomfortable, as if she wanted to tell him something but was not sure how to go about it. Eventually she said, "To be truthful, the house upsets me a little bit, seeing all his things and knowing he won't ever be coming back. And seeing you again, it's all been a bit too much for me. . . ." Her voice choked off and tears sparkled in her eyes once more. Embarrassed, she waved a hand. "I've told you before, just ignore me. I'm nothing but a silly old woman."

Jack stood up, slipped his arm around her back and gave her a brief hug. "You're not silly at all," he said. "I think you're brilliant. Come on, I'll take you home."

She insisted on walking, and although Jack thought at first she was either joking or simply being polite, she stuck to her guns until finally he had to concede.

"You may think I'm on my last legs, Jack," she said defiantly, "but I've walked two miles a day ever since I can remember and I don't intend to stop now. It's what keeps me alive and breathing. It may take me a while to get from A to B but I always get there in the end. Besides, it's too lovely a day to be stuck in a car. You'd be doing yourself a favour by getting some fresh air into your own lungs instead of all that London muck." She struggled into her coat. "Now, the pantry's well-stocked and you know where I am if you need anything. Perhaps if you're not too busy tomorrow you can pop down for lunch."

Jack said he would certainly do that. He walked his aunt to the door and kissed her good-bye.

"Now, are you sure you're going to be all right here?" she asked.

"I'll be fine," he said, "don't worry. I'll see you tomorrow."

They said good-bye again and she left. When Jack closed the door he couldn't help thinking he was sealing himself in. Immediately, he began to hum to allay the silence that pressed in around him. He took out his mobile to ring Gail, but there was no signal, not a single bar. "Typical," he said, and picked up the telephone receiver in the hall. He dialed Gail's mobile number, but her phone rang several times and then cut the connection with a trio of beeps without diverting him to her voice mail. Irritated, he dialed her home number. He knew she'd be out, but at least he could leave her a message. However, her phone rang fifteen, twenty times without reply. "What is this, a fucking conspiracy?" he muttered before reluctantly replacing the receiver. The fading *ching* of the phone was gulped by the silence. He glanced up the stairs, where the light through the window seemed to be curling like smoke, trying to find form. "No way, Jose," he said loudly and stomped back to the sitting room. He whistled as he jabbed at the fire with a poker, but it seemed a thin, somehow lonely sound, and quickly became lost in the stillness of the house.

8

THE SEVEN STARS

He spent the next two hours "settling in." The first thing he did was to open the front door again as an invitation to the light; the second was to fish his CD player from his suitcase and set it up in the sitting room. He was soon singing along to The Clash's "London Calling," aggressively, raucously, to counter the stillness of his surroundings. He fetched his laptop from the car and then parked the car on the grass verge, still singing.

He put off the moment of going upstairs for as long as possible. Despite himself, he kept stealing glances at the afternoon light angling in through the landing window. It did not seem so strong now, for which he felt curiously grateful. It zigzagged partway down the stairs, clarifying the roughness of the grain beneath its layer of polish. Jack took his time setting up his writing space on the dining table. Notepads, reference books, his Filofax, a mug shaped like a skull containing pens and pencils—all these were arranged and rearranged around his keyboard as though their positioning were an intrinsic part of the cre-

ative process. When the music finished, he switched on
the television and found only children's programmes—
Blue Peter was still on? The format seemed the same as
ever, but he didn't recognise any of the presenters. He
looked around; was there anything more he could do
down here? Perhaps a cup of tea? He stood up, suddenly
decisive. No, it was time to lay a few ghosts. Nevertheless,
he felt nervous as he ascended the stairs. His suitcase
bumped against the back of his knee like a cumbersome
weapon he was dragging in his wake.

He stepped into the shaft of sunlight, squinting, the
topmost stairs creaking as he put his weight on them. The
view from the landing window was of undulating hills
separated by the hard black lines of dry-stone walls. The
Butterworths' farm sat in the midst of this, a chunk of
grey stone beside the salmon-coloured thread that was
Daisy Lane. On the horizon trees were clumped darkly, as
if the boundaries of a dry-stone wall had blurred and
seeped into the exquisite blue sky. Jack stared at all this,
thinking it should be making him feel restful, not isolated.
He sighed and turned back to face the landing. After the
brightness outside the window, the shadows in the house
seemed darker than ever, as if they had been gathering behind him.

He blinked to rid his eyes of the swarming brightness of
the sunlight, and eventually the landing's muted tones
rose up through the murk: the wooden doors, the white
wallpaper whose blue pattern had faded almost to grey,
the beige landing carpet, the landscapes on the walls like
smears of green and khaki. There were four doors on this
landing—two to his right, one at the far end, and one to
his left just beyond the stairwell. The door nearest to him,
on his right, was his old bedroom, with a view of the cobbled backyard and the woods beyond. Next to that was a
bathroom, whose most abiding memory for Jack was the
brown scummy ring in the bath, his father's slimy hairs in

GET UP TO 4 FREE BOOKS!

You can have the best fiction delivered to your door for less than what you'd pay in a bookstore or online—only $4.25 a book! Sign up for our book clubs today, and we'll send you **FREE* BOOKS** just for trying it out...**with no obligation to buy, ever!**

LEISURE HORROR BOOK CLUB

With more award-winning horror authors than any other publisher, it's easy to see why CNN.com says "Leisure Books has been leading the way in paperback horror novels." Your shipments will include authors such as RICHARD LAYMON, DOUGLAS CLEGG, JACK KETCHUM, MARY ANN MITCHELL, and many more.

LEISURE THRILLER BOOK CLUB

If you love fast-paced page-turners, you won't want to miss any of the books in Leisure's thriller line. Filled with gripping tension and edge-of-your-seat excitement, these titles feature everything from psychological suspense to legal thrillers to police procedurals and more!

As a book club member you also receive the following special benefits:

- **30% OFF all orders through our website & telecenter!**
- **Exclusive access to special discounts!**
- **Convenient home delivery and 10 days to return any books you don't want to keep.**

There is no minimum number of books to buy, and you may cancel membership at any time. See back to sign up!

*Please include $2.00 for shipping and handling.

YES! ☐

Sign me up for the Leisure Horror Book Club and send my TWO FREE BOOKS! If I choose to stay in the club, I will pay only $8.50* each month, a savings of $5.48!

YES! ☐

Sign me up for the Leisure Thriller Book Club and send my TWO FREE BOOKS! If I choose to stay in the club, I will pay only $8.50* each month, a savings of $5.48!

NAME: _____

ADDRESS: _____

_____

TELEPHONE: _____

E-MAIL: _____

☐ I WANT TO PAY BY CREDIT CARD.

☐ VISA ☐ MasterCard ☐ DISCOVER

ACCOUNT #: _____

EXPIRATION DATE: _____

SIGNATURE: _____

Send this card along with $2.00 shipping & handling for each club you wish to join, to:

Horror/Thriller Book Clubs
20 Academy Street
Norwalk, CT 06850-4032

Or fax (must include credit card information!) to: 610.995.9274. You can also sign up online at www.dorchesterpub.com.

*Plus $2.00 for shipping. Offer open to residents of the U.S. and Canada only. Canadian residents please call 1.800.481.9191 for pricing information.

If under 18, a parent or guardian must sign. Terms, prices and conditions subject to change. Subscription subject to acceptance. Dorchester Publishing reserves the right to reject any order or cancel any subscription.

JOIN NOW!

the plugholes. The door at the far end, which overlooked the front lawn, was his father's bedroom; Jack wondered whether Aunt Georgina had had to fumigate it after his death. And the fourth door, the one on the left, was simply a storeroom. That was where all his mother's things had been put after she died. Jack remembered the smell that drifted over him whenever he opened that door as a child; a dry fragrance, like parchment imbued with lavender. It was a smell that never failed to both soothe and sadden him. He used to open that door purely for the smell itself, closing his eyes and breathing deeply like the cartoon kids in the Bisto advert.

His memories were filling him like caffeine, causing his heart to thump, his breath to quicken. He walked to the door of his old room and placed his hand on the handle. The last time he'd seen it his father had been sprawled unconscious on the floor with a broken nose; books had been strewn across the carpet. Some emotion he couldn't define seemed to be rising to a crescendo inside him. He shoved the door open and strode in with a sense of defiance, though exactly what he was defying he was not sure.

For a heart-quickening instant he saw himself as a skinny, downtrodden eighteen-year-old standing by the bed, then the image faded as he realised the startled eyes he was staring into were set in an older, chubbier face. A mirror, full-length, stood upright against the wall. Jack's reflection was captured in it perfectly, all jowls and pale skin and casually expensive clothes. He set down his suitcase and ran both hands through his hair. Glancing at himself in the mirror again, he thought how incongruous he looked in these surroundings.

He'd half-expected the room to be as he had left it, full of his possessions, posters on the walls, the bed unmade. The furniture was the same as he remembered it, but it seemed skeletal, somehow forlorn in its denudation, as though the room's flesh had been stripped from its bones. Though the floor was carpeted his footsteps boomed hollowly as he crossed to the window and drew back the curtains. He pushed the window open, thrusting his face at the wind, taking a deep breath.

His aunt and her helper must have cleaned this room, too, but Jack felt a sneeze building at the back of his nose. He groped for his handkerchief in his pocket and caught the sneeze just in time. It was followed by another, and then another, before the urge subsided. Maybe it wasn't dust at all but hay fever; maybe living in London had lowered his immunity to grass seeds and pollen and stuff. He blew his nose, mopped his streaming eyes, and looked up in time to see a figure step out of the woods two hundred yards away.

Who was that? One of the Butterworths? A nosy local? Jack screwed up his eyes but myopia reduced the figure to a blur. He could see dark clothes and a pink blob of a head. He took his spectacle case from his pocket, withdrew his glasses, fumbled the bows apart and put them on.

The cobbled yard, the scrub land and the trees sprang into sharp focus. Jack had only looked away for a few seconds, but the figure was now nowhere to be seen. Whoever it was must have stepped back into the trees, realising he or she was being observed. Jack scanned the collage of trunks for any flicker of telltale movement but saw none.

"Nosy bugger," he muttered and turned back to his room. He would sleep here despite the dust. Perhaps he ought to clean up a bit first, push a vacuum around, but almost as soon as the thought formed he discarded it. No, this wasn't house dust, it was the stubborn and accumulated dust that came from years of disuse. Jack wondered what his father had done with all his stuff; probably gave it to Oxfam or burned it. The latter option seemed the most likely; it was just the kind of thing—wanton, vindictive, somehow cowardly—that he would have done. Jack felt the back of his throat tightening in anger. How dare he? How dare he destroy all those books? Fucking barbarian.

There appeared to be no bedding, merely a white sheet stretched over the mattress. Jack placed his hand on it, sniffed it; it seemed fresh enough. He swung his now partly depleted suitcase on to the bed and unzipped it. He'd brought four books with him (more than he'd ever get through in three days, but overcompensating when it came to reading material was a weakness of his) and he placed them on the top shelf of his four-shelf bookcase. They looked lonely stuck up in the corner, as if cowering from all that emptiness. Jack fished around in his suitcase and found his *Skoob Directory of Secondhand Book-shops,* which he carried everywhere with him. If he had time, he intended to tootle around in the car, looking up a few of these places. He added his *Skoob* to the other four books, and decided that he ought to make it his aim to fill at least one shelf of this bookcase before he left.

He unpacked the rest of his stuff and spread it around the room, hoping it would give the place a lived-in quality, a sense of homeyness. It didn't. It looked like a bare, underused room with a few bits and pieces scattered about. He sighed. Ah, well, he'd done his best. He shoved his empty suitcase into the wardrobe, glanced once more out of the window but saw nothing, and went in search of bedding.

He found it in the bathroom airing cupboard, freshly laundered. The bathroom itself was as clean as Jack had ever seen it, lots of gleaming porcelain and a strong smell of pine disinfectant. He also opened the storeroom door, but was disappointed to find it empty and smelling only of staleness. The house seemed so uncluttered that Jack wondered whether his aunt had spent much of the weekend stripping it of his dead parents' personal effects, perhaps in the belief it would lessen the trauma of his homecoming. If so, he was touched by the gesture. It must have been hard for her, overcoming her grief in that way.

"The ogre's lair," Jack murmured, looking at the door of his father's room. It was the only one in the house he had not poked his head into. He felt both attracted and repelled by the thought of entering. The closest he'd previously come to this emotion was when he'd been seven or eight years old and Aunt Georgina had taken him to the nearby seaside town of Starmouth for the day (if he remembered correctly it had been during one of his father's frequent sojourns in the hospital). That had been the best day of Jack's young life. They had sat on the beach, walked up and down the promenade, eaten ice cream and fish and chips and more ice cream. And then in the afternoon his aunt had taken him to the fairground.

Jack had loved the fairground—still did, in fact. He had plans to go there with Gail someday soon, maybe this summer. His previous girlfriend, Carol, would never entertain the idea of a day in Starmouth, or any other seaside resort. She had once scornfully described such places as the "naffest on Earth," and Jack as the naffest person for wanting to go there.

Jack's favourite place on the fairground was the Ghost Train. He remembered it now only as an impression—the front of it had been painted to look like a huge amorphous green mass, populated with staple horror images: a gigantic leering skeleton, a hooded figure holding a blood-stained axe, a screaming man whose left eye was an empty, seeping socket, a vampire with a stake through his heart.

Standing in front of it for the first time Jack had felt much as he did now. He wanted so desperately to go inside, but at the same time felt reluctant to do so. In the end he had queued up with the rest, sweaty hand clutching his money, heart thumping, mouth dry. The worst (and best) part of the ride was right at the beginning when his car—a little black train painted with shaky silver cobwebs—had suddenly lurched forward along the track, bumped open a pair of black double doors and plunged him into darkness.

He licked his lips, still tasting the candy floss of that day, the thrill of it all. But there was no thrill now. The way he felt standing at the door of his father's room was similar to the way he'd felt outside the Ghost Train, but not the same. The difference now was that there was no fun, no excitement, no delicious childlike fear. Coupled with his curiosity was a sense of unwillingness, of directionless trepidation. Before he could think about it any more he walked to the door and opened it.

The room beyond was grey, silent, unimpressive. It contained an old double bed with a chipped, scratched headboard, stripped down to a single sheet; off-white curtains partly closed; a bedside table with a lamp on it; grey-blue carpet; a cream rug; a wardrobe; and a wicker chair with a high rounded back like the throne of some South Sea island prince.

Jack took all this in with a single sweep of his head. There was no atmosphere of any kind in the room, no suggestion of any presence. It was empty. With a capital E.

He pulled the door closed. Strangely he felt sad and dissatisfied rather than relieved. On his way back along the landing he glanced up at the dark square set into the white ceiling. This was the entrance to the attic, a place Jack had never seen. His father had always forbidden him from going up there, though in truth Jack had never felt much inclination to do so anyway. He didn't think there was an attic room as such; more likely just a poky storage space full of spiders and dirt. He considered having a quick shufti now, just to see if there was anything interesting up there, but the idea was only a half-hearted one and quickly discarded. Nah, too much trouble. He'd have to fetch the steps from the walk-in pantry in the kitchen and hump them all the way upstairs. And for what? Probably just a head full of dust and an arse full of splinters.

He went back downstairs and smoked a cigarette while he watched the news. Then he went into the kitchen to make himself something to eat. His aunt had certainly stocked the pantry and fridge, but there was a lot of processed stuff and meat products, the kinds of things he didn't eat any more. He made himself some scrambled eggs on toast, and washed himself an apple from the bowl on the counter. He carried his plate through to the sitting room and watched TV as he ate.

By the time he finished, it was getting dark. Through the two small windows set side by side, Jack saw the dry-stone walls, the trees and fields merging into a felt-blackness beneath a denim-blue sky. He crossed the room and yanked the curtains closed, averting his gaze from outside. His mind drifted back to the other night in the restaurant, to the memory of his father's colourless face staring in at him through the window. He'd half-managed to convince himself that Gail's explanation of that incident was most likely—that the figure had been an old tramp to which Jack's imagination had affixed the image of his father. Nevertheless, if he saw a figure out there now, a dark silhouette watching the house, he didn't know what he'd do. There were no bright lights and bustling crowds to escape into here. He had only himself to depend on.

There were two lamps in the room whose frilly shades had most likely been provided by his aunt; Jack turned both of these on. The fire was collapsing into a cluster of glowing coals, like lumps of orange candy. Only the occasional flame still flickered. Jack dragged the fire-guard across and imprisoned the dying embers.

He straightened up, aware that he was listening carefully . . . for what? Smiling at his own misgivings, he crossed the room and switched the television off, then stomped out into the hall. He lifted his brown leather jacket from one of the four hooks behind the front door and shrugged it on. He straightened the collar of his shirt, zipped the jacket, then snatched up the door keys from where his aunt had left them on the telephone table. He decided to go for a drive, find a pub, have a drink and a smoke, maybe do a bit of writing.

Daisy Lane seemed bumpier at night, as if the shadows shifting and looming in the ruts were solid mounds or squatting animals. One invisible and particularly deep pothole jolted Jack a couple of inches out of his seat. "Good-bye suspension," he muttered, scowling and leaning forward over his wheel. He rooted among his CDs and eventually found what he was looking for. Within seconds James Brown was proclaiming, "I *feeeeeel* good." Jack whooped in defiant agreement.

When the trees at the top of Daisy Lane closed around the car like the entrance to a cave, Jack found he was hunching up his shoulders as though bracing himself. The stealthy scratching on the car's roof were only the tips of branches; the crooked black shapes keeping pace with him were merely tree trunks, the shifting emphasis of their shadows and perspective.

Less than two minutes later he was out of the trees, and four minutes after that he was turning into the entrance of a pub lot. The pub was called the Seven Stars, which sounded familiar; then he realised why. It was where his "fan," Tracey, lived, the girl who had helped his aunt clean his father's house. She was the landlord's daughter.

"She was only the landlord's daughter," he warbled, and wondered whether what he was singing was a real song; if so, he didn't know any more of the words. His neck and shoulders felt stiff with tension and too much driving. Sometimes, when his back and neck hurt from writing all day, or he was just feeling uptight, he and Gail would climb into a hot foamy bath and she would massage his aching muscles. He groaned longingly at the recollection. What he wouldn't give for that to be happening right now. Thinking about Gail reminded him that she should definitely be home by now. He took out his mobile and swore. *Still no fucking signal!* Did these people not live in the twenty-first century? Oh well, if the pub had a phone he could ring her on that.

Eager to hear her voice, he parked quickly and got out. The lot was only a quarter full. Along the wall of the pub Jack noticed a row of motorbikes, six in all, huge powerful machines, black, gleaming, ominous. He approached the door beside them, labeled LOUNGE, pushed it open and went inside. A flow of chatter rose to meet him, buoyed by cigarette smoke and the warmth of an imitation log fire. His eyes were soothed by familiar pub colours— plush red, rusty orange, the harsh yellow gleam of brass, the rich cherry-brown of the bar. The place was fuller than the number of cars outside had suggested, but by no means packed. One or two people glanced at Jack as he entered and then returned to their conversations. He wondered who the motorbikes belonged to; no one here seemed to fit the bill.

He made his way to the bar and was served at once by a bubbly, overweight girl with crimped blonde hair and trowelled-on makeup. "Do you have a phone?" Jack asked as she dropped change into his cupped hand. She leaned forward a little to point and he was instantly smothered by her powdery scent.

"Yes," she said, "there's one just over there. You see by the door that says 'Public Bar?'"

Jack thanked her and hurried across, clutching his pint of Carlsberg in one hand, sifting his change around with his thumb in the other. He only had two twenty-pence pieces. He would have to give Gail the number of the pub and get her to ring him back. From behind the door marked PUBLIC BAR Jack could hear the bludgeoning mayhem of a thrash metal song and the sound of raised voices. He stopped and peered through the pane of clear glass above the frosted lettering. The first thing he saw was the green baize of a pool table that dominated the centre of a functional, carpetless room; the second thing were the pool players—all long hair and studded black leather.

He had found his bikers. Predictably, there were six of them, the four non-pool players sitting around a table in the corner. They were showering their two compatriots with either derision or admiration, depending on the shots they played. In return, the pool players were responding to their audience, bowing exaggeratedly or punching the air when receiving adulation, fielding insults and firing them back with equal vigour. It looked very much a closed community, a clique. Jack was glad he hadn't walked in among them. Not that he was worried about violence, or even hostility. He would simply have felt awkward—it would have been like invading a Women's Institute meeting or entering a train carriage full of nuns.

He stepped back from the door and picked up the telephone receiver. Placing his beer on the shelf below the phone, he fed a twenty-pence piece into the slot and dialed Gail's number. Once again it rang and rang without reply. "What's wrong with the answering machine all of a sudden?" he murmured and replaced the receiver with a sigh. He waited for his unused money to drop through, then tried her mobile, with the same result as before. Frustrated, he used his last twenty pence to dial his own number. Perhaps she would be there. She'd promised to call in and check his post if she got the chance. He listened to the thin trilling and thought, My phone in London is ringing at this very moment. I wish I was there to answer it.

He was, in a sense; or at least, his voice on the answering machine was. "Hi, this is Jack Stone. I'm afraid I'm dismembering a body in the kitchen and can't come to the phone right now, but if you'd like to leave a message, I'll call you back as soon as I've cleaned up the mess."

He waited for the beep and said, "Gail, hi, it's Jack. I've been trying to call you, but haven't been able to get through. I know I only saw you twelve hours ago, but I'm missing you already. I'll call you at home about eleven tonight. If you're not there I'll want to know why." That was supposed to sound flippant, but it came out stern and possessive. "Oops, that wasn't supposed to come across like it did. Er . . . I love you, Gail, and . . . I'll speak to you later. Bye." He put the phone down, feeling hollow and dissatisfied.

He sat down in a bay beneath a sweep of orange curtain and sipped his drink. The pub was beginning to fill up a little more. He took out the notepad and pen that he always kept in his jacket pocket. He had done no work for three days and was starting to feel restless. It was a familiar emotion, and one he found hard to shake, even on holiday, even when he was supposed to be relaxing. Gail was hugely supportive of his work, but even she got pissed off occasionally. Sometimes they would arrange to go out in the evening, but if he'd had an unproductive day he'd ring up and say, "Look, do you mind if we cancel tonight? I really want to get this chapter finished." Invariably they would have an argument and she'd slam the phone down, and then he'd feel too unsettled to work anyway. And so he'd stomp around behaving like a temperamental artist or he'd drive round to her flat in Tottenham and try to make it up to her.

The book he was writing at the moment was called *The Laughter* and centred around two clowns, one good, one evil. The good clown was called Cyril and the bad clown Popsy. Popsy was the leader of the Secret Society of Comedians, whose aim was to capture the world's laughter and imprison it. Although Jack wrote mostly on computer, he preferred to write longhand in public places. Taking a laptop into a pub or restaurant always struck him as horribly pretentious. He opened his notepad now, read the brief notes he'd made, and then wrote: *It was never the lion's intention to eat Raoul.* He squinted at the sentence, sat back, swallowed a mouthful of beer, placed the glass back on the coaster and leaned forward. The next sentence was already forming, poised to spring from brain to paper, when a voice said, "You're Jack Stone, aren't you?"

He tried to grab the shattered pieces of the sentence as they slipped through the mesh of his mind, but surprise made him clumsy and he lost them. He looked up, frowning his annoyance. The sight of beauty quashed his anger. The girl was perhaps seventeen, with stylishly tousled reddish-blonde hair, huge blue eyes and very full, very red lips. Her skin glowed with the kind of pure, vibrant health that made other faces seem haggard and grey even when they weren't. Her bone structure was a mathematician's dream, the angles were so perfect. She had a long neck, delicate fingers tipped with red fingernails and long coltish legs poured into the tightest of jeans. Her upper body was clothed in a white collarless blouse and a well-worn biker's jacket. She smelled . . . *exciting*—the faint tang of black leather, a subtle soap or perfume, and some underlying secret scent that was muskier, spicier, like paprika and marijuana combined.

Jack breathed in her smell and tried not to be too obvious about it. "Er . . . yes, I am," he replied in answer to her question.

She nodded, not shyly but with confidence, self-satisfaction. "Knew it," she muttered, dragged a stool from beneath the table and sat down. She leaned forward on her elbows, long hair tumbling forward (Wow, that smell!), and without asking, spun Jack's notepad round and began reading it. "What's this?" she said. "New book?"

He felt immediately defensive, vulnerable, as if she were scanning his innermost thoughts. "Er, yes," he said. His hand reached out and he said, "Do you mind?" before snatching the notepad from beneath her gaze.

She squinted at him, managing to look both innocent and arrogant. "What's it about?" she asked.

Argh, the dreaded question. Avoiding it, Jack said, "Look, I don't even know who you are."

"Tracey Bates," she said. "My dad's the landlord here. I've read all your books. I helped your aunt clean the house this weekend."

Of course. Tracey. The landlord's daughter. He was aware that something she had said just then had rankled him, as though a discord had been struck. But the girl was talking again now, giving him no time to backtrack.

"Some of your stuff is really weird," she said. "Brilliant, but weird. Where do you get your ideas from? I reckon you must do drugs to get ideas like that."

Jack felt uncomfortable, but tried not to show it. "No," he said, "I don't take drugs, apart from a little alcohol and tobacco. If I took drugs I'd never be able to write at all. You don't take them, do you?"

She shrugged, picked up a coaster, tapped it twice on the table and then put it down again. Raising her fabulous blue eyes to him she asked, "Are you married?"

Jack felt both amused and, despite himself, a little alarmed. Was that a chat-up line? Was this . . . this sex kitten trying to seduce him? Clearing his throat he said, "No, I'm not married."

"But you have a girlfriend." She stated the fact as though she knew.

"Yes," said Jack.

"What's her name?"

"What do you want to know for?" Jack wished he could shake off his feeling of edginess.

The girl rolled her eyes as though he were being unreasonably obtuse. "I just wondered," she said. "Just making conversation, that's all."

Jack looked down at his beer, ran a finger through the condensation on the glass. "Her name's Gail."

Tracey pulled a face as if to say: Not much of a name, is it? "What's she like?"

"What do you mean?"

"Is she pretty?"

"Yes, she's very pretty. I think so, anyway."

The girl smiled slyly. "Prettier than me?"

Jack felt his face becoming hot. He forced a smile, tried to keep his voice light. "Look," he said, "why are you asking me all these questions?"

Tracey made a face. "I've told you," she said, "just making conversation." There was a silence between them for a moment, then she said, "You can ask me questions if you want. I'm not bothered."

Jack shrugged, snorted a laugh. "Look," he said, "I'm sorry. I'm a bit touchy just now. It's been a bit difficult these past few days."

"Yeah, I know, your dad died. Your aunt told me. But you haven't seen your dad for years, have you? You never came back here after you went off to London."

Was she accusing him of neglect or merely stating a fact? Her tone was neutral; her face revealed nothing.

"You'd make a great social worker," Jack told her, smiling.

She scowled as if he'd said something tiresome and irrelevant. "What are you on about?"

Jack sighed inwardly. "Nothing," he said. "Forget it. Just my feeble attempt at humour."

She tossed her head, unimpressed, and her fabulous smell washed over him again. "So, what's this new book called?"

"*The Laughter.*" Before she could respond he tried to grab the initiative. "You haven't told me what you do?"

"No."

"So . . . what *do* you do?"

She shrugged. "I'm a student. A levels."

"Oh, yeah. What subjects?"

"English lit, art and history." She reeled these off with a sigh as if it were a question she had been asked a million times before and of which she was now heartily sick.

"Hey," Jack said. "Same subjects that I did."

"Really," she said, unimpressed. "Whoopi-doo."

Jack was beginning to feel annoyed now. He wished this girl would go away. She was being as offhand with him as if he were a creep pestering her at the bar, but it had been she who had approached him for God's sake! If she was a fan, then maybe she found Jack Stone in person disappointing, or perhaps her rudeness was a way of covering up her true, more vulnerable emotions. But Jack was not really that interested in excuses. The fact was, the girl was arrogant, and he was getting fed up with her. "Was there something you wanted to see me about specifically?" he asked and immediately thought, Christ, I sound like a headmaster.

She shrugged again, and pouted. "Not really," she said. "I just saw you in here so I thought I'd come across and say hi."

"Oh, right," said Jack, and almost added: Well, now you've said it. He smiled at her and picked up his glass. As he swallowed a mouthful of beer he heard a bellow of laughter from the bar and glanced in that direction.

What he saw almost made him choke. At the same instant he realised what it was that Tracey had said earlier. Leaning against the bar, chatting to a couple of his regulars, was the landlord, Tracey's father. He was fatter, older and balder than Jack remembered him, but his identity was unmistakable.

The landlord of the Seven Stars was Patty Bates.

9

WASPS

For an instant after seeing his old adversary, Jack was reduced to a state of almost schoolboyish alarm. A thought flared in his mind: I've got to get out of here. Then the adult barged in, pushing the child aside, speaking in a calm, reasonable voice. Don't be silly, Jack, you're a grown man now. Bates is a responsible citizen, a publican. He's hardly likely to start beating up his customers, is he?

Jack relaxed—a little. He picked up his glass and took another gulp from it, peering at Bates over the rim. His old enemy looked older than his thirty-six years. His florid complexion and expansive gut were evidence of his love for his own beer. He had always had thick hair, but now he was balding rapidly, and what hair he did have was cropped close to his scalp. And yet strangely, for all this, Jack thought that Bates hadn't really changed that much. He was wearing a grey Adidas sweatshirt and ill-fitting jeans, the kind that had a knee-level crotch and were low-slung at the back to reveal a bulging, hairy expanse of bum cleavage.

Tracey, sitting across from Jack, said, "Seen something interesting?"

In the last few moments he had almost forgotten she was there. Now he turned his attention back to her and thought he saw a gleam in the girl's eyes that unsettled him. It was so fleeting he was not even sure he *had* seen it, and yet he couldn't shake off the feeling that she had been gazing at him with an expression of . . . triumph? Eagerness? As if she had been relishing his shock. He considered telling her the truth, making a joke of it, but unease prevented him from doing so. He also considered, albeit briefly, wandering over to Patty Bates and saying, "Remember me?"

In the end, however, he simply shook his head and smiled. "No," he said, "just looking around."

She raised her eyebrows and her face slipped back into its expression of sullen arrogance, which she wore like a symbol of her youth.

Jack sighed. All at once he felt tired, impatient. He had had a lot to cope with today, and felt a need to speak to Gail, or, failing that, to be on his own. He looked at his watch, drained his glass. "Look, it's been nice meeting you," he said, "but I've got to go."

She shrugged, striking the pose of the nihilistic teenager. "Okay," she said as if she couldn't care less. "See you."

Jack felt an urge to blurt out scornful laughter at her attitude, or to shake her angrily and tell her how artificial she was, how transparent. But she would probably only have glared at him and curled her lip and sneered that he was too old to understand. Each successive generation reinvented rebellion and claimed it as their own. Jack had been there himself, fifteen years ago, during the heady, vibrant days of the Madchester scene. He'd believed then that the music of bands like The Smiths and the Happy Mondays and The Stone Roses could change the world, that a night of noise and sweat and energy was an earth-shattering event. It all seemed so fatuous now, so insignificant. The thought depressed him: had he really become so *adult,* so *mature?* He hadn't even noticed it happening. Time was like a pickpocket, sneaking up behind you, stealing away your youth. You didn't realise it was gone until it was too late.

He left the pub without looking over at Patty Bates and his cronies, and so did not know, nor did he have any desire to know, whether he was noticed and recognised. When he stepped into the parking lot the cold air punched into him, making him catch his breath. He wondered how a Neanderthal like Bates could have fathered such a stunning daughter. Tracey must have inherited her looks from her mother's side of the family. He got into his car, grimacing at the coldness of the seat, and started up the engine. He pulled out of the lot and turned right on a whim, deciding to take a spin around the village before heading home.

There was nothing much to see. Beckford's nightlife seemed to revolve around its six or seven pubs. There was no theatre for miles around, and the cinema that had been there when Jack was a boy had now been converted into a shabby furniture showroom. He passed the Top Wok; a group of kids were hanging around outside, drinking beer from cans. They looked bored and mean. Jack felt depressed. Some, if not most, of these kids would spend their whole lives here, lacking the ambition or the curiosity to go elsewhere. Though Jack knew he had no right to judge them, he nevertheless hated them for it; to him it was like opting out of life, being satisfied with second best. One of the lads, goaded by the others, mooned at two girls who came out of the Top Wok clutching a brown paper bag. Jack turned the car around and drove back the way he had come, heading for his father's house.

The trees at the top of Daisy Lane sucked him into the

void and spat him out the other end. The wind hushed him constantly, as if the sound of his car annoyed it. Now and then the moon peeked from a murk of cloud, scattering slivers of light, like broken glass, across the land. Jack was leaning so far forward that his head almost touched the windshield.

He put on a CD, *Elephant* by the White Stripes, and began to beat out a rhythm on the steering wheel. Almost immediately he became aware of a whine that rapidly changed to a buzz, underlying the music. It made him think of a swarm of wasps. "Shit," he muttered, deciding that there must be something wrong with the CD player. He hit the STOP button, but when the music ceased the buzzing didn't. Indeed, if anything it increased in volume. "What the . . . ," Jack muttered, looking around for the source of the noise. He glanced into his mirror and saw a moving mass of darkness behind him: the buzzing was the sound it made. At first he was puzzled, but then he realised with shock that the noise was the combined racket of half a dozen motorbike engines.

He saw me, Jack thought immediately. Patty Bates saw me. And now he's sent his storm troopers to do me in. He looked quickly left and right as if in the hope that some escape route might suddenly appear. It didn't occur to him that he might be wrong; the appearance of the bikers here, in this remote spot, was too much of a coincidence. Regardless of the road surface, he floored the accelerator, felt the car scream and slew a moment before picking up speed. He tried to keep calm, to concentrate on the road ahead, but his thoughts were in danger of being overwhelmed by his combined emotions of fear and anger. He felt like a rat chased into a dead end by a bunch of slavering cats. He was also furious, outraged. What had he done to them? His only hope was to reach the house before them, call the police before they broke in or cut the wires.

But how long would it take the police to reach him—ten, fifteen minutes? He tried not to think about that.

Despite his efforts, the bikers were gaining on him, fanning out behind him in a pincer formation. What meagre light there was glinted on their machines and leather jackets. Their faces were blurred whitish ovals beneath their helmets; Jack imagined each of them slashed with a savage red predator's grin. The car hit a bump and something crunched; Jack's seat belt locked across his body, cutting into the soft flesh beneath his ribs. "Fuck!" he shouted when he had his breath back. Though he knew they couldn't possibly hear, he yelled, "Fuck off, you bastards. Leave me alone!"

The bikes were right on top of him now, their headlamps like the luminous eyes of some gigantic insect. They were bathing him with light, pinpointing their prey. In his rearview mirror he caught glimpses of black leather etched with zips like battle scars. The bikes were bellowing their hunger; Jack's adrenaline was cranking his heart up to such a rate that he could barely breathe. Behind him the left and right headlamps detached from the rest, like eyes on stalks, and began to crawl up the sides of his car.

Later, Jack realised there was a great deal he could have done to disable his pursuers if he'd had his wits about him. He could have slammed on his brakes to take out the four bikes behind him, and then slewed left and right, using the car as a giant fly swatter, to take out the other two. Of course the car would have been damaged, if not written-off, but when his life was at stake what the fuck did that matter? However, what he could have done was immaterial; he was so scared he could think of nothing but headlong flight.

The bikes continued to overhaul him until their headlamps were level with his wing mirrors. Jack was now going so fast that the road no longer seemed uneven; it had become a colourless blur. The bikers seemed unfazed by the speed they were going, or by how narrow the gap was between Jack's Mini Cooper and the dry-stone walls. All it would take would be the slightest contact on either side, and biker and machine would become a spectacular Catherine wheel of metal, leather and flesh. Jack glanced out of his right-hand window; the biker was so close that Jack could see the dirt beneath his fingernails, the skull ring he wore, the swastika tattooed on the back of his hand. The bike began to pull round in front of him, and now Jack saw that two people were riding it. The one at the back, though jacketed and helmeted, was undoubtedly a woman. Her legs, encased in tight jeans, were long and shapely; her blonde hair blew out behind her, beneath the rim of her crash helmet.

Though Jack hadn't liked Tracey Bates very much, it still disheartened him to know that she was in on this. Had her father put her up to it or was she doing this off her own bat? Both of the lead bikes were pulling round in front of him now, and the two bikes on the outside behind were peeling off, presumably to overtake him as their companions had. Jack saw Tracey half-turn towards him and make a sweeping motion with her arm. He ducked as something thumped against the windshield. For an instant he lost control of the car, heard the tires screech, glimpsed a black blur of wall veering crazily towards him on the left. His foot stamped instinctively on the brake at the same time his hands regained the wheel and twisted it to the right. For a long moment the world became a screech of tortured, high-pitched noise, a spinning confusion of blackness and glaring light. It slowed minutely, then abruptly stopped. Jack closed his eyes, shaking all over, and listened to the fading sound of wasps. His throat felt like torn paper and his ears were humming; he realised he must have been screaming. When he finally raised his head into the silence he saw that he was alone. The bikes were intermittent pricks of light far, far ahead.

He felt exhausted, cold, shocked, horrified, angry. What in God's name had he done to deserve that? The car was dead, though Jack hoped that it had only stalled. It was skewed a little to the right, pointing in roughly the direction he wanted to go. His mind ground into gear again, anger his most dominant emotion. What had those morons hoped to achieve by their actions? Had they wanted to kill him or simply scare him? Christ, they had almost killed themselves! When Tracey had thrown that thing at the windshield, he could so easily have ploughed into one or more of them. At that speed there would have been little left but a mangled mess.

It was only when he reached for the ignition key that he realised how badly his hand was trembling. He formed a tight fist, but the sensation slid up his arm, into his bones, and seconds later his belly was juddering, his teeth chattering uncontrollably. He knew it was the shock of the accident, and that he ought to get back to the house, drink something hot, keep himself warm. Driving did not seem a good idea, but he couldn't just leave the car in the middle of the road, especially in the dark.

"Thank you, God," he muttered when the engine started first time. He scanned the road ahead once more, half-fearful that the bikers may be coming back, and only then did he notice the object that Tracey had thrown at the windshield. Miraculously it was still there, having slithered down to rest on his wiper. It was small and pale and pulpy, and had left a glutinous trail like a slug. Jack's face creased in disgust. It was a used condom. He stabbed at a button and twin jets of screenwash sprayed over the glass. He prayed that the condom would not become caught in his wipers as he turned them on, forcing him to extricate it with his fingers. Fortunately it didn't; the

wipers swept it and its slither of semen disdainfully away.
Jack put the car into first and tentatively eased it forward,
as if in the belief that such careful treatment would neu-
tralise any damage that had been done. The car responded
immediately, seeming to have suffered no ill effects from
its misuse. Still shaking, Jack crawled back to the house at
fifteen miles per hour.

He parked carefully and got out of the car. At once, the
wind seemed to slice straight through to his core, making
his flesh writhe, his teeth chatter violently. He hurried
through the gate and up the path to the front door. The
key rattled in the lock like an echo of his teeth. He turned
and slammed the door quickly after switching on the
light, and then hugged himself, taking one long breath after another. He walked through to the kitchen and made
himself a pot of tea. The window was a black mirror, re-
flecting his pale face, his wild hair. He yanked down the
blind, wishing he could get warm. He felt confused, depressed, angry, thought longingly of Gail, his flat in London. He felt as though his flayed emotions were almost
down to the bone; he could feel their coldness, their hard
sharp points.

He waited until the tea was almost stewed, then poured
himself a mug and laced it generously with honey. His
stomach muscles cramped momentarily against the hot
sweet liquid, then seemed to settle, allowing the warmth
to flood them like a panacea. He sat down in the kitchen
and savoured the tea, cupping his hands around the mug,
enjoying the sensation of steam rising into his face like a
mask of soft warm kisses. As soon as he finished the tea,
he poured himself another and stood up, intending to
carry it through to the hall and ring Gail. He reached
across the table for the teaspoon . . . and heard the unmistakable creak of footsteps above his head.

He looked up, mouth slightly open, as if afraid the ceiling was about to fall in. Footsteps. An intruder. "Oh,

shit," he breathed. He couldn't believe he now had this to contend with. Hadn't he been through enough for one night? He felt exhausted, but looked around for a weapon. When he left the kitchen he was holding a carving knife in his right hand, a rolling pin in his left.

He stood for a moment in the hall, listening to the sounds from upstairs. Obviously whoever was up there saw no need to be cautious. This could mean one of two things: either they didn't know Jack was in the house or they didn't care. Jack felt both angry and scared, though strangely detached. It suddenly occurred to him to just get out of the house, get into his car and drive away. There was nothing much to steal up there anyway. A few clothes, a few books, and that was it.

Yes, that was what he would do. He would call the police and then get the fuck out of there. He sneaked along the hallway to the foot of the stairs, jamming his tongue between his teeth to stop them from chattering. He reached the telephone table, put the rolling pin down on it, and picked up the receiver. The dial tone filled his head as he brought the receiver to his ear. But before he could punch in the first number the dial tone abruptly cut out and from the hissing silence that replaced it a male voice said, "Jack."

He dropped the receiver and leaped back from it as if it had turned into a snake. That had been his father's voice. It had spoken only one word, one syllable, but he was certain it had been his father's voice. Panic suddenly overwhelmed him and he spun round, bouncing off the wall, and plunged towards the front door. With his free hand he scrabbled at the handle and managed to yank the door open.

He ran out of the house, almost stumbling on the path. He came to the gate, pulled it open so violently that he cracked his shin with it. Tears of pain sprang to his eyes. Muttering curses he limped into Daisy Lane. He began to hobble towards his car, patting his pocket for keys. Then he stopped.

There was a dark, humped shape beside the car. At first he thought it was a bush or the stump of a tree, but then it began to unfurl, to straighten up, and he realised it was a man. The man had his back to Jack but was already beginning, painstakingly slowly, to turn. As he did so, moonlight spilled across his face, turning his skin into a ghastly blue-white clown's mask. Deep black wrinkles were etched into his cheeks; his eyes were sunken pits of shadow. Jack began to back away as the figure raised its white hands towards him in an almost supplicatory gesture. When his father began lurching in his direction, face expressionless as a death mask, Jack ran.

10

THE GRAND DESIGN

He didn't get very far. His left foot hit a patch of mud and slid from under him. Jack cried out at the wrenching pain in his leg, and then his whole body was going down, arms flailing for balance. Impact with the ground knocked the wind out of him. For a moment he could only lie gasping, trying to blink away the fuzzy bursts of light that had arrived with the pain. His mind was racing. He had seen his father. This time he had really seen him, there was no mistake. Did that mean his father was still alive, that Jack had been tricked into coming here? He couldn't believe his aunt would deceive him, but that would leave only one alternative.

His father was a ghost.

Jack's vision began to clear, the lights fizzling out, as his breath came back and his pain subsided. He was staring into a black sky, across which the tattered remnants of grey cloud occasionally drifted. He needed to know where his father was now, he needed to lift his head and see. When he did so it was like raising a boulder using only his neck muscles. Bits of muddy gravel pattered from his hair onto his shoulders.

There was no one standing by his car. He looked around; he was completely alone. Painfully, he stood up, his fear pounding dully in his skull like a headache. He patted dirt from his clothes and hands. Light was pouring from the open front door of his father's house. Jack remembered the sounds he'd heard, what he had thought was an intruder. Could there really be an intruder in there or was it all part of the . . . the (he felt reluctant to even think it) . . . the haunting?

For a few moments he simply stood, not knowing what to do. He did not want to go back into the house alone, but what was the alternative? Drive to his aunt's and ask to stay there? Find a B and B in one of the nearby villages? What he really wanted to do was go back to London and stuff this whole fucking business. He sighed and rubbed a hand across his temple as if it might help soothe his thoughts.

He looked at his watch and was amazed to discover it was not yet ten o'clock; it felt like the early hours of the morning. The moon slithered from behind a bank of spongy cloud, bathing the land in light once again. Four hundred yards away the cluster of buildings that comprised the Butterworths' farm resembled gigantic blocks of ice. Suddenly decisive, Jack hobbled toward his car.

He got in, started the engine, executed a shaky three-point turn, and drove back along Daisy Lane. He cruised to a halt in front of the Butterworths' farm, got out of the car and pushed open a metal three-barred gate. This led into a yard with worn cobbles that peeped above a layer of mud like the slick grey heads of frogs. Jack began to tiptoe through the mud toward the farmhouse, muttering, "Wonderful," when it oozed up over his black suede shoes. Soft light glowed from behind orange curtains, making him think of Halloween. His knock was followed by surprised voices from inside, the scrape of furniture. The door opened and a plump dark-haired woman said, "Yes?"

"Er . . ." Jack was thrown; he hadn't expected a woman. He tried to remember the name of one of the Butterworth brothers. He had reeled them off to his aunt in the car that afternoon, two of them at least; he could never remember what the youngest was called.

The woman's eyes were narrowing suspiciously. "Is . . . er . . ." Jack thought he was going to have to admit defeat—then suddenly he remembered. "Is Martin in?" he blurted. "Martin Butterworth? Or one of the other brothers?"

The woman's expression became more, rather than less, suspicious. "Who wants them?" she asked curtly. Then a hand with the thickest, reddest fingers Jack had ever seen appeared above the plump woman's head, curled around the door and pulled it all the way open.

Jack felt like a character in a cartoon, rocking back on his heels and gaping up with awe at the man-mountain who had just appeared. The guy was vast, at least six foot eight, and he must have weighed all of twenty-five stone. His pale blue and black lumberjack shirt stretched over a belly that looked as though it were pregnant with quints. The sleeves of the shirt were rolled up, revealing arms covered with a fine downy blond hair that any adult male gorilla would have been proud of. Despite the awesome bulk, however, the man's face—smooth and red and topped with a straw-blond thatch—held an expression of inquisitive geniality. "'Ello, Mister," he said, nodding. "What can we do for you then?"

"He asked for Martin," the plump woman said before Jack could reply.

The man-mountain appeared to consider this sombrely for a moment and then said, "Our Martin don't live 'ere any more. Hasn't done now for about ten year. 'E's got a place over in Mirfield. If you want to come in a minute or two, Mister, I can write y'out some directions."

He began to turn away, but Jack said, "No," a little more sharply than he intended. The man-mountain's eyebrows raised a notch in surprise. "It wasn't Martin specifically that I wanted," Jack explained. "You'll do fine. What I mean is, my name's Jack Stone. I'm staying in the house just up the road. I'm Terry Stone's son. I've come from London for his funeral. I used to live here in Beckford."

The man-mountain blinked rapidly a few times as though digesting the information, then a wide and delighted grin seeped across his face. "I remember you," he said. "You went off an' become a writer. You're pretty famous, aren't yer? Yer dad always used t' tell us how you was doin'."

"Did he?" said Jack, surprised. Then: "Yes, that's right."

"Come in, old son," exclaimed the man-mountain effusively. "Barbara, put t' kettle on. We've got a celebrity come t' visit."

Barbara ducked under her husband's arm to do as she'd been asked, but Jack held up a hand. "No, please," he said. "To tell you the truth, I didn't come over just to say hello. I . . . er . . . I've got a bit of a problem. I wondered whether you could help me out."

The man-mountain's face creased in concern and he bowed his head as if to impart or receive secrets. "Oh, aye?" he said. "What's up?"

Jack told him about coming back from the pub and hearing noises upstairs; he omitted the part about the bikers and the phone call, and about seeing his father standing by his car. "I wondered whether you and your brothers could pop back to the house with me and check it out," he said lamely. "I mean, I wasn't sure how many intruders there might be. I didn't think it would be a good idea to try and handle it myself."

Butterworth (Jack was still not sure which of the brothers this was) nodded sagely and said he'd be glad to. "There's only me 'ere now, though," he said. "Well, me an' t' missis. Our Ed's got a place in Sheffield and, like I said, our Martin's in Mirfield. Me old dad died about six year ago. 'Ad an 'eart attack in t' pigsty." He seemed about to say more on this subject, then shrugged. Instead he said, "But I'll come back wi' yer if yer think the two of us can 'andle it?"

"Oh, yes," said Jack. "I don't think there were many of them, two at the most. They'll probably be long gone anyway by the time we get back."

Butterworth called his wife from the kitchen and told her what was going on. In the course of the conversation she called him by name—Gerard—and immediately Jack realised this was the youngest of the Butterworths. Nevertheless, he must have been ten years older than Jack, which would put him in his early forties. It was only when Jack led him out to the car that he realised the Mini Cooper and the big man were not exactly compatible. Butterworth somehow managed to squeeze inside, though. Jack half-expected the seat to groan and collapse, the bodywork to bulge, rivets to spring from their sockets. Butterworth looked both comical and uncomfortable, like Desperate Dan in a kiddie-car. Suppressing a smile, Jack clambered into the driver's seat.

When they reached the house, Gerard commented on the open front door, from which light blazed. Jack muttered that he mustn't have closed it properly. Gerard surmised that perhaps it was the intruders who'd left it open after their departure. Jack said nothing. Because he hadn't told Gerard about his father's voice on the telephone, the admission that he'd left the door open after fleeing the house would seem like an overreaction.

They got out of the car, Gerard with difficulty, and approached the house. Butterworth showed no trepidation whatsoever. Followed by Jack, he marched into the hallway, checked both kitchen and lounge, and then retraced his steps to the foot of the stairs. There were no sounds now, and indeed the house proved to be empty. Gerard paused outside each door for a couple of seconds to listen before ramming them open and leaping inside, but all he disturbed was air.

"Nothin' 'ere now," he said unnecessarily when he and Jack were standing in the hallway again.

"No," said Jack with a shrug. "Thanks a lot, Gerard. I'm sorry to have interrupted your evening."

The big man seemed embarrassed by the apology. "No problem," he murmured. "No problem at all. Always glad to 'elp." He clumped to the door and stepped outside. Before walking away he turned back and shyly offered Jack a few words of advice. "I'd 'ave a wander about if I were you an' see if there's anythin' missin', then you'd be best callin' the police and lettin' 'em know someone's been 'ere. It's probably nowt, just kids who'd heard about the old . . . yer dad, and thought the 'ouse'd be empty. But it's always best to let the police know. We're a bit isolated out 'ere." He raised an arm and began to walk away. "Aye, well, it's been nice seein' yer. You'll pop round again before yer go back, I 'ope."

"Yes," said Jack, doubting that he would. "Good night, Gerard. And thanks again. I really appreciate your help."

He waited until Gerard was a vast lumbering silhouette before he closed the door. Too late, he thought about asking the big man for his phone number, and pulled the door open again, but Gerard had been swallowed by the darkness. Sighing, Jack pushed the door closed and, after a moment's hesitation, locked it. He stood for a moment in the hallway, listening, but apart from the distant moan of the wind the house was silent.

He picked up the telephone receiver and tentatively placed it to his ear. All he heard was the idiot *burr* of the dial tone. He dialed Gail's number and waited, half-expecting the connection to be broken at any moment, his father's rasping voice to reach for him across the emptiness. But the phone simply trilled softly like before, on and on. No answering machine. No reply.

Where was she? She'd said she was going to be in tonight. He hoped she was okay. He made more tea and carried it through to the sitting room. If he didn't feel so on edge, if this house didn't have such bad associations for him, this room would have been cosy, despite the death of the fire. Jack wondered whether to build another, but decided to leave it for the moment. There was enough residual warmth in the room, and besides, he was feeling pretty beat—hardly surprising after all that had happened. He put the telly on, turned up the volume, then flopped onto the settee. He sat there for a long time, drinking tea and staring at the telly, watching whatever was on. The loudest programmes were the best—a quick-moving comedy with canned laughter, a debate about the social service's handling of child abuse cases—for they allowed no other sounds to breach their voluble defences. So reluctant was Jack to move that he ignored the urge to pee for as long as possible. At last, though, heart beating quickly, he ventured upstairs, locking the bathroom door as he emptied his bladder. Downstairs again, he built himself a fire and stretched out on the settee to watch a late film starring Harrison Ford. Somewhere in the middle his eyes began to close. When he opened them again it was morning.

He felt cold, stiff and disoriented. Dawn was bleeding the curtains of colour, diluting the hard yellow glow of the table lamps with its own insipid light. Last night, despite his tiredness, he wouldn't have thought he could have slept, or at least not deeply. However, the fact that he had managed a solid six hours seemed to have done him little good. He felt groggy and ponderous, his head ached, his limbs were sluggish. Sleep was a vampire that continued to cling to him and wouldn't let go. He felt enervated rather than refreshed by it.

At least the daylight took the edge off his fear. The house was bearable with sunshine pouring through the window, especially if he filled the silence with music. Jack realised his hair was still matted with dried mud; there were flakes of it all over the settee. He dragged himself into the bathroom and ran himself a hot bath. He stripped off and sank into the steaming water, groaning at the sheer pleasure of it.

Almost immediately, his eyelids drooped closed. When he next woke the water was still warm, but only just. As though moving in slow motion, he leaned across and twisted the hot water tap. The water was cold at first; he tugged out the plug with his feet, allowing some of it to drain away. When he found his optimum temperature he washed his hair, then soaped himself slowly. After his bath he went into his bedroom and changed into fresh clothes, then went back downstairs. Despite his efforts to wake he still felt muffled, inert, as though trying to shake off the effects of an anaesthetic. He built a fire, smoked a cigarette in front of it as he listened to the birds. Anywhere else, he thought again, and this would be idyllic—the dawn light sharpening and brightening as it filtered through the window; the land awakening; the start of a new day, full of promise.

For breakfast he ate cornflakes, toast with honey, and drank two cups of tea. He remembered the vow he'd made yesterday to go for a run this morning. The way he felt now, it seemed like a bad joke. Nevertheless, the breaking of his promise to himself niggled him. He decided to compromise; he'd go for a stroll, acquaint himself with nature. After last night it was just what he needed. He pulled on his leather jacket and let himself out of the house at 7:45 A.M. He thought of everything he had to do before the end of the day—solicitor, registrar, undertaker. Even without last night's events he needed a few lungfuls of fresh air before dealing with that little lot.

The air was more than fresh, it was fragrant. The sky was so clear that he was filled with a delicious sense of insignificance, of his problems receding into its vastness. He breathed deeply, filling his lungs. He smiled; already he could feel his fear melting away.

He turned right outside the gate, towards the woods where he had played as a child. Patty Bates had soured the sanctity of this place for him, yet Jack could now sense its innate benevolence, its recuperative qualities. It was only the black souls of human beings that stained this place, and then only temporarily—their actions were petty and quickly consumed. When Jack turned off Daisy Lane into the woods, about a mile further on, he was immediately embraced by its calmness, the smell of its life, its verdancy.

The ground was lush, springy beneath his feet. Sunlight slanted through gaps in the trees, dappling the ground. Jack wondered how he would describe such an effect, how such beauty could be captured by the written word. Like interchanging coins of shimmering gold, he thought, and then shook his head; no, too clichéd. The textures were richer, more vibrant, the light was tenuous and yet, simultaneously, almost palpable, like honey. It was as though the trees had somehow distilled the light, drawn its essence down through their leaves in strands that pooled on the grass. Words, images, crowded Jack's mind, all of which sold their subject woefully short. How, he wondered, do you describe the immaculate? There were no words, or combinations of words, that would suffice.

Walking, he felt a part of all this, part of the grand design. It was how he had always felt as a child, the only place where he felt he slotted in. Thankfully, that feeling was commonplace to him now. In London he felt he was a central piece in a jigsaw. The components of his life—his flat, his work, his relationships, London itself—fit snugly around him, forming a neatly interlinked pattern, a perfect self-contained circle. It was only Beckford and his memories of it that impinged on this circle, that scraped at the edges of it and occasionally drew blood. It was only his past that prevented him being truly happy.

He sat on a grassy bank beneath the languid trees, the winking sun, and told himself that this was the ideal opportunity to pluck the thorn from his flesh. So far he'd been backpedalling, had allowed his fear of this place to come at him. What he had to do was attack, to laugh in his father's dead face and Patty Bates' live one, to "lay a few ghosts" as both Gail and his aunt had termed it.

It was easy sitting here planning all this. The difficult part would be to defy the voice on the phone at the dead of night, to storm from room to room, throwing open doors, at the sound of footsteps. Now, in the daylight, he wondered again whether he really had seen his father. Though he'd always regarded the supernatural with an open mind, even with sympathy, he found it hard to accept the existence of a real M. R. James/Algernon Blackwood-type ghost. He actually smiled at the idea, as though it were somehow quaint. Already he felt better, equipped to face whatever challenges the day held. He stood up, brushed grass seeds from his jeans, and began to stroll back the way he had come.

Later that morning he visited the solicitor, who explained that his father had died intestate and his affairs would probably take two to three months to sort out. Jack made a note of all the documents the solicitor required and promised he'd do his best to find them. Next, he went to register his father's death, and watched as the registrar, a hunched gnome-like man with sparse stringy hair, scribbled down the details.

Jack found it scary and sad that what a life amounted to, in official terms, was simply three pieces of paper documenting details of birth, marriage and death. It all seemed so final and pointless, so unfeelingly efficient. It was a sharp reminder, if one was needed, that life was short and that there were no happy endings.

He was pleased to see Georgina at lunchtime, though she commented immediately on how tired he looked. Jack admitted that he hadn't slept well, and simply grunted noncommittally when she remarked that she too always found it difficult to sleep in a strange bed for the first time. He told her about his morning, relayed as succinctly as he could what the solicitor and registrar had said. She nodded airily, as though it was all routine, but Jack suspected she was relieved he was dealing with the legalities.

For lunch she made gammon steaks, roasted potatoes, green beans, carrots and gravy. Jack couldn't remember the last time he had eaten red meat; nowadays he found it heavy and salty. Nevertheless, he was touched by the trouble she had gone to and ate with gusto, murmuring sounds of appreciation. By the time she produced an enormous rhubarb crumble and a vat of custard, he was sated, but forced himself to exclaim, "Oh, wonderful!"

Over tea, he steered the conversation toward Tracey Bates. "I met her last night," he said, "when I popped in to the Seven Stars for a drink."

"Oh, yes? And what did you think of her?"

"She's . . . ," Jack dithered an instant between adjectives, "very headstrong, isn't she?"

Georgina laughed, as if Jack had made the understatement of the year. "Yes," she agreed, "she is headstrong. Wild, some would say. I expect you'll have found out who her dad is then?"

"Patty Bates," said Jack, grimacing.

Georgina nodded. "He used to bully you at school, didn't he?"

"Yeah." Jack ran a finger around the rim of his teacup.

"I guess he must have changed now, though? I mean, he's grown up, hasn't he? He's got responsibilities."

"Oh, he hasn't changed that much," said Georgina. "He's still an oaf and a bully. I'll say this for him, though—he dotes on that daughter of his. She wants for nothing, that one, can twist her father round her little finger like a piece of string."

"And what about Mrs. Bates?" Immediately an image came to Jack's mind of Norman's mother in *Psycho,* a mummified husk in the fruit cellar.

"Oh, she was a real beauty," Georgina said. "She came from York, I think. Goodness knows how the two of them started courting. Whenever I saw her, even just shopping in the village, she'd be dressed up to the nines and plastered with makeup as if she had something to prove. From what I hear she and Patrick didn't get along very well—I don't expect they had very much in common. There were all sorts of stories: screaming matches in public, physical violence, even talk of her having had an affair with some businessman from Leeds. I never actually spoke to the woman, but from all accounts she was very high and mighty. She hated being referred to as a pub landlady, and she regarded Beckford as a horrible little backwater and the villagers as nothing but peasants. I think she wanted Patrick to pull up his roots and move back to York with her, and when he refused she left him."

"When was this?" Jack asked.

"Let's see—Tracey was about . . . ten then, and she's seventeen now. I'd say around ninety-seven, give or take a year."

"And Patty got custody of the child?"

"Yes. You see, the pub was in Patrick's name and Mrs. Bates didn't work expect for behind the bar. Besides, this is where Tracey was born and bred. She was at school here, she had all her friends here, and it was not as if Mrs. Bates could provide Tracey with a stable environment. I think she went back to live with her parents. I don't know what became of her after that."

"Tracey never talks about her?"

"I don't know her that well. She only got in touch and offered to help with the house because she heard that you were coming back to Beckford and she'd read all your books."

Jack nodded, a little troubled. He couldn't make Tracey out. From what he had seen of her, her behaviour was erratic, and dangerously so. His aunt made it sound as if she was simply a harmless fan, all eager and starry-eyed, but in the pub last night she'd been offhand, even arrogant. Such behaviour could perhaps have been seen as a defence against shyness if it hadn't been for the incident later that evening. Had he upset her in some way to make her act like that? Or had she been trying to prove something? Maybe the business with the condom was intended to be some kind of clumsy sexual advance. If so, her seductive methods left a great deal to be desired. He thought briefly of John Lennon, of fans so obsessed that they would kill the people they adored so their names would become inextricably linked with their hero's. If the thought wasn't so alarming it would have been hilarious. Him, Jack Stone, the idol of a deranged sex kitten? Come off it!

"I expect her parents' break up was hard for her," Jack said.

Georgina nodded. "I expect so. But it's becoming the norm, isn't it? These days people treat marriage far too lightly. I don't want to sound like an old duffer, Jack, but when I was younger, you only married someone if you were certain you wanted to spend your life with them. Divorce was a dirty word back then; there was a stigma attached to it. These days anything goes. I don't know what the world's coming to." She shook her head, then released a croaky laugh. "Listen to me. I *do* sound like an old duffer."

Jack laughed too. "Never," he said. "As far as I'm concerned, you'll always be fab and groovy."

Their conversation drifted away from the topic of Tracey and Patty Bates. Jack reminisced about people he'd known and Georgina brought him up to date with potted histories and the occasional caustic comment. Beckford was not exactly *Twin Peaks,* nor even *Coronation Street;* the general trend seemed to be for a stodgy continuity that Jack found stifling. Not that he was opposed to community life—far from it—but the place seemed drained of all colour, all innovation. It had become so introverted that it had, in Jack's opinion, disappeared up its own backside. People had got older, got ill, got married, had children, died, but none of them had actually *done* anything. No one had gone on a safari to Africa, become an Olympic athlete, had a sex change operation, robbed a bank. In Beckford, such movers and shakers were not encouraged, and indeed Jack felt as though his own achievements were generally frowned upon. He was an impudent upstart who had drawn unwelcome attention, albeit minimal, to the village in which he had been born. And now he was back like the prodigal son, come to weep crocodile tears at the graveside of a father he had never loved.

Jack wondered how much of this was in his imagination and how much was true. He looked at his watch and was surprised to find it was almost two-twenty. "I'd better get going," he said. "I've got to see the undertaker this afternoon, make all the final arrangements."

"I'll come with you if you don't mind," Georgina said, pushing herself up from her chair as if Jack were already leaving. "I wanted to see your father again before Thursday."

She made it sound like a social call. "Of course I don't mind," he said, though in truth he was reluctant for his aunt to accompany him. She had always been such a rock in his eyes that he hated the prospect of seeing her grieve.

It would be like seeing her naked, totally vulnerable, and what would make it worse would be his own inability to share her tears.

Locking the front door behind her, she asked, "Will you be wanting to see your father, Jack?"

It was a question he had asked himself. If he did see his father, it would not be to say good-bye, but merely to confirm that he was dead, and somehow that seemed like the wrong reason. "I don't know," he replied.

"Well, it's your choice," Georgina said neutrally. "Don't feel as though you have to."

They drove to the funeral home in tense and contemplative silence, Georgina squeezing a handkerchief in her right hand as if in readiness. The undertaker, Jeremy Coombs, had clear blue eyes and a snow-white beard; Jack wondered whether he hired himself out as Father Christmas at children's parties. When he spoke it was softly, leaning forward so you could smell the Listerine on his breath. Perhaps, thought Jack, he was afraid that if he raised his voice it might rouse the dear departed from their slumber. He and Jack discussed the financial arrangements as Georgina sat mutely by. She had already chosen the wood for the coffin and the music for the ceremony. Jack concurred with her choice in a library-soft murmur. Final details were ironed out—flowers, cars— and then Coombs placed his hands together and asked if they now wished to view the deceased.

Jack hesitated, staring at Coombs. Then he became aware that his aunt was nodding her head and, almost grudgingly, followed her lead. Coombs led the two of them along a wood-panelled corridor, opened a door and ushered them inside. They found themselves in a tiny room that was simply furnished, austere even. A table supported two white candles and an arrangement of artificial flowers. The candlelight was supplemented by the light of a fluorescent strip along the far wall, which was itself muted by a wooden pelmet so as not to dazzle tear-spangled eyes. The coffin stood at waist height on a velvet-draped platform in the middle of the room. Jack approached it.

So this was it: death, the great unknown. He was staring down into its face for the first time and he was feeling . . . what? He wasn't sure; there was a little sadness, a little fear, there was even relief. In a way, however, he felt detached, perhaps numbed by the unreality of the situation, anaesthetized by anticlimax. He was half-aware of a studiedly detached train of thought which ran: *It doesn't look so bad. It's peaceful, it's dignified, it's painless.* And yet beneath these thoughts could other darker, more primal thoughts be simmering?

Perhaps the most surprising thing was that he felt no hatred towards his father. The old man did not look as bad as Jack had anticipated. He was a little older, a little slimmer, but Jack had half-expected something haggard and shrivelled, clawed hands drawn up, cheeks sunken, flesh ghastly pale. His earlier suspicion that his father's body had lain undiscovered for some time appeared mercifully unfounded. He became aware of his aunt standing close beside him and automatically draped an arm across her thin shoulders.

There was nothing to be learned here, no revelation to be had. Certainly seeing the body laid out in its coffin seemed confirmation that his father was actually dead, but Jack had never really doubted that fact. Nevertheless, he had to suppress an urge to poke the corpse's stomach to make sure. They stood there, the three of them, in a silence that was as awkward as it was reverential. It was Georgina who finally stirred, who slipped her handkerchief into the sleeve of her cardigan and wearily said, "Let's go."

11

MAGIC

"Hello?"

"Gail?"

"Jack!"

"Gail, where have you been?"

"What do you mean, where have *I* been?"

"I've been trying to reach you, but you're never in, and both your answering machines have been off."

"What do you mean, *I'm* never in?" Gail said indignantly. "I've only been working and running round after you. I've tried to call you on your mobile several times, with no result—"

"No signal," said Jack, but she was still talking.

"—and when I *have* been in I've been like a cat on hot bricks, sitting with the phone next to me, waiting for it to ring."

"Did you go to my flat?"

"Yes I did. *And* I got your post."

"Didn't you hear my message?"

"Yes, and I rushed back, hoping you'd ring, but you didn't."

"Yes, I did, but there was no answer."

"You didn't."

"I *did*, Gail. You must have been out or asleep or something."

"What time did you ring?"

"I don't know—about half-ten."

"I was definitely in at half-ten, and I wasn't asleep. I was watching *Celebrity Wife Swap*."

"I thought you hated that programme?"

"I do, but I couldn't concentrate on anything else because I thought you were going to ring."

This discussion was going round in circles. Suddenly Jack grinned. It was great to hear Gail's voice, even if they (or rather he) had got the conversation off on the wrong foot.

"Gail," he said.

"What?" she snapped. For some reason Jack imagined her with hair newly washed, feet tucked under her on the settee, wearing her white towelling dressing gown, scowling.

"I love you," he said.

"Well, I don't love you. You're a pain in the arse."

"I know, I'm sorry. I've been wanting to speak to you, that's all, and it's so bloody frustrating when no one answers the phone."

"Well, that's not my fault, is it? You must have been dialing the wrong number or something."

Jack's initial irritation had fully evaporated now. He was prepared to concede anything. "Yeah," he said. "That must have been it. Let's not talk about it any more. It doesn't really matter."

"Say sorry," murmured Gail.

"What for?"

"For being a pig."

"But I've already said sorry once."

"Say it again."

Jack concealed a sigh. "Okay, I'm sorry. I humbly beg your apologies. Can we be friends now?"

"S'pose so."

"Good," he said. "Do you love me again now?"

"S'pose so."

"Good. So what have you been doing?"

"I told you—working and running round after you. Why didn't you leave your number when you left your message? Then I could have rung you back."

"I was in a pub."

"But you still could have left the number of where you're staying."

"Yes, I suppose I could. I didn't think."

"You never do."

"True. So how's London?"

"Same as ever. Dirty, smelly, noisy, crowded."

"I thought you liked London."

"I like it better when you're here."

"Shucks, thanks. I'm really missing you."

"You only saw me yesterday morning."

"I know, but time goes about ten times slower here. It's already Friday."

"So how's it been so far? As bad as you thought it was going to be?"

"Worse. I've been chased by a motorbike gang led by none other than Patty Bates' daughter, and I think I'm being haunted by my father's ghost."

"His ghost? What do you mean, Jack? Is that a joke?"

"I wish it was. The truth is, I don't know what to be more worried about: getting my head mashed in by the bikers, or the fact that my phantom father might pop up again at any moment."

"Oh, Jack. I wish I was there with you. I'd protect you from the hooded claw."

"Thanks," he said, smiling.

"Where are you staying?" she asked. "In that hotel you were on about?"

"No, it was full. I'm actually staying at the house."

"Your father's house?"

"Yeah."

"But isn't that in the middle of nowhere?"

"Yeah, sort of."

"Oh, Jack," Gail said again and gave a big sigh. "Shit, I'm really worried now. I wish you hadn't told me all these things."

"Sorry. But look, it'll be okay. I've only got to brazen it out for a couple more days."

She sighed again. "So what happened with this motor-bike gang? They didn't hurt you, did they?"

He told her all that had happened in Beckford, from the moment he first pulled up in front of his aunt's house to seeing his father laid out in his coffin that afternoon.

"Oh, Jack," she said softly. It was becoming her stock phrase.

"Yeah," he said ruefully. He half-wished now that he hadn't told her anything. She would only fret and there wasn't exactly a great deal she could do.

"I wish I was there with you," she said again. "I'm thinking of you, you know."

"Yeah, I know. I'm thinking of you, too. All the time."

A small silence fell between them. The phone line hissed. Jack had never been a great fan of the telephone as a means of communication. It was useful for exchanging information quickly over long distances, but when it came to the conveyance of emotion, it was grossly inadequate. In times like these you needed to touch, to kiss, you needed small silences, but what would have been intimate in the flesh was reduced to awkwardness when squeezed through the medium of the telephone.

"Anyway," Jack said eventually, making his voice bright,

"how's school been this week? And have I had any good post?"

They exchanged trivialities for a few minutes, each having little left to say but reluctant to let the other go. At last Gail said, "Ah well, I'd better make myself something to eat. If anything else happens, though, Jack, you ring me straight away. I'll be in all night."

"Yeah, I will."

"Promise?"

"Yeah, course."

"Okay then. Bye."

"Sweet dreams."

"You too."

"Bye."

"Bye."

There was a click and the line went dead. Jack sighed and replaced the receiver. Well, that's my socialising over for the evening, he thought. He could always have gone to a pub (though definitely not the Seven Stars), but after last night he didn't fancy it. No, he'd grab himself something to eat and do some work. Maybe have a whiskey or two later to help him sleep. He wondered if that was how his father had started; perhaps drinking had been the only way he'd been able to find sleep after Jack's mother's death. The parallel discomforted him. Maybe he'd do without the whiskey. Perhaps straining his brain over his novel for a few hours would be enough to tire him out.

He made himself some tuna sandwiches and carried them through to the sitting room. A fire was blazing in the grate. The curtains were drawn despite the fact that blades of daylight in the twilight sky were thinning only slowly. He put on his CD of didgeridoo music, decided it was too creepy and replaced it with Ennio Morricone. He read through his notes on the settee as he ate his sandwiches, then relocated to the laptop. He smoked as he paused between sentences; most of the time the cigarettes burned themselves slowly out in the ashtray. Normally when writing, Jack was aware of what time it was and how many words he'd written, he became distracted by the slightest sound, he jumped up and roamed around the room, as though searching for inspiration. But on this occasion he became completely, utterly engrossed. A hole opened in the page and he fell through it, right into his make-believe world.

Eventually the words petered out, broke up like a dream, and he came to, yawning and stretching. The house was silent, the music having finished long ago. The fire was barely flickering in the grate. Shadows clustered in niches like clumps of the greater darkness outside. Jack stood up, walked across the room and switched on the second lamp. He goaded the fire into grumpy life and fed it with fresh coal. He flipped through his CDs until he found U2's *The Joshua Tree* and put that on, nodding in satisfaction as the music obliterated a wind whose voice had sounded to Jack as if it were trying to form words. He looked at his watch—11:22. God, was it really that time? When he scrolled back through what he'd written he was astonished to discover he'd completed seven pages, around eighteen hundred words.

He decided to go to bed; he certainly felt tired enough to sleep. He placed the guard over the fire, switched off his CD player and exited the room. He was normally meticulous, even a little obsessive, when it came to switching things off and pulling out plugs, but he left the twin lamps on as a guard not only against the darkness but whatever walked in it.

He felt nervous as he ascended the stairs, the memory of last night still clear in his mind. However, the house was silent apart from the low moaning of the wind outside. He crossed the floor of his bedroom quickly and jerked the curtains closed. No sense allowing a bush or a tree, or the shadow of one, to set his imagination racing.

Into the bathroom, brush teeth, take a pee. He hurried out of the bathroom, pulling the light cord as he went. The click of the light preceded a sound that made him catch his breath, caused his heart to pause, and then quicken.

It came from above his head, from the attic, and sounded like mice scurrying across a wooden floor or perhaps the frenziedly beating wings of a trapped bird. Jack swallowed, stared up at the square wooden panel in the ceiling. That's all it is, he tried to assure himself. Just mice, nothing to worry about. He considered ignoring it, going to bed, and then he remembered his vow that morning in the woods. Hadn't he resolved to confront whatever sights and sounds he might encounter? And this wasn't half as bad as the slow march of footsteps above his head, the rasping voice on the phone. The scurrying came again, more agitated this time. "Bloody hell," he muttered. He clumped downstairs, deliberately making as much noise as he could, and stomped into the kitchen.

He pulled on the light and opened the pantry door, making the ancient hinges crunch. The pantry smelled good, like fresh warm peaches, though there wasn't a peach in sight. At the back was a stepladder. Jack dragged it out and hauled it upstairs, breathing hard with effort. He set the ladder beneath the attic entrance. "Right," he said, "here I come, ready or not."

He climbed the stepladder and reached with both hands to lift the square of wood up and over to the side. He paused for one brief, tottering moment; a scene from a film had crept unbidden into his mind. A girl follows the sound of a cat upstairs to the attic. She lifts the attic entrance as Jack is about to do, sticks her head through the gap, turns . . . and opens her mouth to scream as the psycho who is waiting for her swings a huge hook down on a chain. Before her scream can emerge the hook pierces her throat and continues its momentum along the chain, whipping the girl up through the attic entrance like a rag doll.

Jack closed his eyes and let out a quick breath, like a weight lifter preparing to lift. The scuttling sounds were continuing, like a lure. Bracing himself, he lifted the square of wood. Dust sifted down on to his face, pricking his eyes.

The noise stopped suddenly, as though switched off. Jack lifted the square of wood over to the side and released it, gritting his teeth as it scraped and thudded, the sound generating a dry echo of itself. He rubbed the dust out of his eyes and suppressed an urge to sneeze. Beneath him the stepladder creaked ominously. Gripping both sides of the attic entrance, Jack hauled himself up. The hook swung down . . .

But only in his imagination.

The reality was far more mundane. Gloom, dust motes that drifted through musty air like silt through pond water, mouse droppings, a few sticks of furniture, cobwebs, an old chest.

Puffing with effort, he dragged himself over the lip of the entrance so that his feet dangled out of the gap in the landing ceiling. He sneezed once, twice, and then a third time. His eyes itched, his throat felt sore. Above him lengths of timber formed an arch: the roof's skeleton. He looked around, squinting, but there was nothing else to see, no indication of what had made the sounds he had heard. Perhaps it had been something actually on the roof; maybe there was a nest up there. He saw a spider that would have filled his palm scaling one of the joists like an eight-legged mountaineer. Insects couldn't make that much noise, could they? He shook his head. Not unless they were wearing hob-nailed boots or had grown to the size of cats.

The chest intrigued Jack. He couldn't remember ever having seen it before. He felt a sudden delicious thrill of anticipation, which reminded him oddly of the joy he had gleaned from books as a child. That joy had been absolute, like losing himself in the best possible magic. It had been a reaction against the misery of the rest of his childhood, which was why he found it difficult to recapture that emotion now, except transitorily. He wondered what was in the chest. It looked like the sort of thing that would contain gold doubloons, pirate's treasure. And where had it come from? It was so old it seemed made from age, from the dry, sad substance of the passing years, from memories long perished, forgotten dreams.

Jack pulled in his legs and scrambled over to the chest, trying not to rouse too much of the thick dust to life. The dust on top of the chest was like grey sticky wool, though there were clear smudged spaces around the locks, indicating that though the chest had obviously stood here for some considerable time—perhaps for years—it had been opened and closed frequently. He touched the metal locks almost with reverence. They were cold and freckled with rust. He wanted to see what was inside, but at the same time was reluctant to do so for fear of breaking some spell. He smiled, took a deep breath, and then, heart quickening, pushed the catches aside with his thumbs.

The locks clicked up like small blades. Jack slid his fingers under the rim of the lid and heaved the chest open. More dust flurried, causing him to squint. He saw the gleam of glass.

Pictures. Paintings. There was a layer of them inside the chest laid frame to frame, and more underneath. Jack's initial feeling was one of disappointment: was this *all*? He lifted a couple of the paintings and held them up, catching what little light there was on the glass. They were rugged Yorkshire landscapes, watercolours, lots of greens and browns and greys. They were nice but uninspired. He peered at the black scrawled signature in the bottom right-hand corner of one of them: Alice Stone. He almost dropped the painting, shocked. This was his mother's! His mother had painted this! Jack had no idea she had been keen on art. As though realising it for the first time, Jack felt suddenly dismayed that he knew next to nothing about her.

He gazed at the painting anew, as if trying to read some message to himself in it, or perhaps to glean some inkling of the personality behind the brush strokes. Not even his aunt had spoken very much about his mother, her sister. Perhaps it was painful for her, or she thought it would be so for him. A pebble formed in his throat. Jack lifted out the paintings one by one and examined each of them minutely before laying them aside. Beneath the paintings was a layer of cloth, a sheet. With nervous fingers Jack lifted it to see what was underneath.

This time there were books, encased in plastic dustcovers. Jack didn't have to look at the books too closely. He'd seen them numerous times before. He lifted out hardback and paperback editions of his own novels, followed by American editions and some from the Continent. There was even a Japanese paperback of *Consummation* and a limited edition of *Splinter Kiss,* which was bound in leather and slipcased. Jack knew the price for the limited edition had been £150; it was now worth two or three times that amount. He was stunned by the find. He couldn't have been more astonished had he discovered the original manuscript of an unpublished novel by H. P. Lovecraft. He stacked the books next to his mother's pictures and turned back to the chest. One more layer, again concealed beneath a white sheet.

Jack's initial thought after removing the sheet was that he was looking at paper that had perhaps been used for packing, but when he lifted some out he realised his mistake. These were notebooks, perhaps diaries. He opened the cover of the first one and saw a blue looping scrawl that he recognised as his father's handwriting. At the top of the page was a title, twice underlined: *Red Summer.* What was this? He began to read.

Time passed. Seconds into minutes into hours. Jack for-

got about the dust and the dark, he forgot about his discomfort, hunched forward on a hard floor, brow furrowed
as he deciphered his father's untidy longhand. These were
stories. And not only that, they were good and varied stories. There was horror here, and science-fiction, and
crime, and plenty that did not fit into any particular cate-
gory. Depending on the subject matter they were funny or
scary, poetic or colloquial, entrancing or hard-bitten, trivial or profound. The writing was good, the characters
were people you cared about, the ideas were innovative,
the plots clever and original. Each of the stories con-
cluded with the words: *THE END by Terence Stone,* and
then these words would be followed by a date. Jack
flipped through the stories and counted them. There were
one hundred and seventy-nine. The first was dated
9/9/89, the last 3/5/04. His father must have started writing a few weeks after Jack's departure and had written his
final story less than two weeks ago. Jack thought of his father, old and bitter and sad, sitting down with a pen and a
notebook (and probably a bottle of whiskey) and creating
these stories, these beautiful things. It was such a tragic
image, full of loneliness and desperation and a kind of nobility, that, suddenly overcome, he gathered up as many of
the stories as he could, hugged them to his chest, bowed
his head, and wept.

12

Jewel

Someone shone a torch full into his face. Jack squinted at it, raised a hand feebly, wishing to push aside the light and go back to sleep. It had been warm and comfortable, this sleep, deep and long and without dreams. He felt loath to relinquish it. But the light jabbed beneath the lids of his eyes and prised them apart.

It was the sunshine, not a torch. There was a gap at the top of the curtains, a tiny isosceles triangle, and the sun had found it. Jack rolled onto his back to evade the probing beam. He groaned loudly as he did so, though only because he felt so well rested. Light filled the room like a promise. Birds gossiped, cows lowed in the distance. Jack would never have believed it possible here, but he actually felt calm, almost content. He propped himself on his elbows and looked across the room to where his father's notepads were heaped beside the bookcase.

They were like the expectations of a life never fulfilled and the sight of them saddened him. But by the same token Jack felt they would finally enable him to exorcise the

ghost of his father, for here was the man's soul laid bare.
Jack's lifelong fear had hinged on the image he had of his
father. He had seen him as rage, hate, violence personi-
fied. Beneath this Jack had envisioned an emptiness, or at
best a love that had grown black and stinking as a cancer
with his mother's death.

But no. These stories now gave lie to that assumption.
There was love in the man, there was tenderness. And
Jack intended to savour it all—the humour, the sensitivity,
the compassion that his father had restrained between the
bland blue covers of some four dozen notepads. It was as
though someone had said: *Your father is dead but here are
his thoughts. Sift through them and take what you will.* It
was as though Jack's yearning voice, his cry for help, had
finally been acknowledged.

He got out of bed, belly not quite bulging over the band
of his blue-and-white boxer shorts, and plodded to the
window. He threw the curtains wide, allowing the sunlight to stream over him and into the room. The smell of
grass and bark and soil and water, and perhaps even of the
sunshine itself, was so rich, so exuberant, it made him
giddy. Jack closed his eyes and felt the warmth of the sun
lap at the delicate skin of his eyelids.

His anxiety, his trepidation, he found, was almost gone,
or at the very least dormant; last night's discoveries had
knocked his emotions sideways. He felt buffeted by revelation, felt as though parts of his mind, tight as buds for
so many years, had now opened spectacularly, trumpets of
blossom, of piercing unexpected colour that hurt his eyes.
Born-again Christians must feel something like this, he
thought. He looked out at the spring morning, at the tangled conjunction of blue sky and dark, intricately limbed
trees, and he felt that he wanted to sing. He grinned at the
image of someone walking past and surprising him while
he stood there in his underwear, belting out, *Oh What A
Beautiful Morning.*

He went running. In lieu of a tracksuit, he dragged on the clothes he'd been wearing yesterday, laced up his trainers, and headed off into the woods. He was unwashed, tousle-haired and sour-breathed; he would never have set foot outside his home in London in such a state, but to do so here felt liberating.

The woods welcomed him as before. Sunlight danced in rhythm with his quick breath, the smell of foliage was like a lotion that eased the fire in his lungs. The ground seemed to cushion his footsteps, to protect his bones from jarring. Jack felt wonderful, his spirit unshackled as the wind.

He ran for twenty minutes, half an hour, forty minutes. Time slipped by as though it did not apply to him. Jack felt fresh and vibrant; he felt he could run forever. Undergrowth, stirred by his passing, fell back into place behind him as though covering his tracks.

Back at the house he took a long hot shower, shaved thoroughly, brushed his teeth and ate a large breakfast. He had carried his father's notepads downstairs and placed them on the floor in front of the television. He stared at them as he chewed toast spread with blackcurrant jam. Everything he had done so far this morning felt almost ritualistic, a preparation for what the entirety of the notebooks would reveal. After breakfast, he rang his aunt and asked her if she knew where his father had kept his legal documents. She told him that everything she had found that looked official she had put in the left-hand drawer of the sideboard in the sitting room. Jack looked in there and found every single item the solicitor had asked for; it seemed like a good omen. He put it all into a large brown envelope, which he sealed and addressed, then he curled up on the settee and began to work his way chronologically through his father's stories.

By lunchtime he had read sixteen of them, and each time he came to *THE END by Terence Stone,* Jack found his perception of his father had changed, had evolved, a little more. He began to think of his father's soul as a multifaceted jewel concealed by many doors. One story was the combination to a single door. At the end of each story the tumblers fell into place and that door swung open, revealing one more facet of the jewel.

Jack found that having his father's soul unveiled before him piece by piece was an experience both rewarding and traumatic. He felt exhilarated, enlightened, saddened, betrayed, exhausted. For lunch he ate cheese sandwiches and fruit, still reading. He would have liked to have remained in the house, reading his father's stories until he was finished, but the intensity of his emotions were becoming too much. He decided it would be a good idea to take a break, get away completely, give his mind time to assimilate the information. When he stepped out of the house the sun pierced his eyes and sparked the dull threat of a headache into life behind his temples. Squinting, Jack crossed to his car and got in. He put on his sunglasses, hoping to dampen the pain, and headed out of town.

He posted the letter to his father's solicitor, and then, using his *Skoob* as a guide, toured around some of the villages and small towns in the vicinity, hunting for secondhand bookshops. He often did this when his work was going badly and he never failed to find it therapeutic. Jack covered perhaps fifty or sixty miles, though he was never more than twenty miles from Beckford. The countryside was spectacular, the villages picturesque. Of the eleven bookshops he discovered, three had succumbed to halfday closing, four specialised only in antiquarian books, and one had been converted into a delicatessen. However, the remaining three were gems: by the time he headed back to Beckford, Jack was the owner of fourteen "new" books, among them a John D. MacDonald novel and a Charles Beaumont anthology, both of which he'd been looking for for ages.

He arrived back in Beckford just before five, and decided to call in at Taylor's for some provisions. Though he had vague plans to eat out tonight, he nevertheless needed a few bits and pieces—milk, matches, mineral water. In truth, he had had ample opportunity to buy these things already today, but he wanted to get them from Taylor's. He supposed what he really wanted was to see if the place had changed at all. Jack hadn't thought of Taylor's in years, had forgotten about it until yesterday when he had driven past it on his way back from the undertaker's. From the outside the place looked exactly the same. It had a blue, white and gold handpainted sign, which for some reason always reminded Jack of the corner shops in World War Two dramas.

Taylor's, however, was no mere corner shop—it was an all-purpose store, which he was delighted to see had survived the emergence of supermarkets, hypermarkets and shopping complexes. Jack had sometimes stopped for sweets here on his way home from school (when his aunt gave him the money for them, that was), and now and again, when he was really plush, he'd bought magazines and the odd paperback from the revolving book display.

Jack smiled at the memory. The contraption had been so ramshackle that if you pushed it round too fast it squealed like an injured mouse, and shed its books as a tree sheds autumn leaves. There was nothing, as far as Jack was concerned, that Taylor's didn't sell. The tightly packed shelves of the long, low, dingy room held everything from bicycle clips to baking powder, sherbet to shampoo.

When he pushed open the door he was delighted to hear the familiar *ting-a-ling* of the bell. He looked up. It even looked like the same bell, old and tarnished but still doing its job. The place smelled the same, too—a warm, unique mix of shoe polish and fresh bread and strawberries and a million other things. At the end of the room, standing behind a long counter, was a rosy-faced woman in her thirties wearing a floral apron. Jack smiled at her and she returned his silent greeting with a nod. He supposed it had been too much to hope that Mr. and Mrs. Taylor would still be running the shop. They had been old when Jack was a child; if they were still alive, they must be ancient now.

Though he knew what he wanted, he took his time, browsing amongst the shelves and racks and displays. The place really hadn't changed all that much, though obviously some things were different. Taylor's now sold CDs and DVDs, plastic *Star Wars* figures, squeaky dog-chews that were busts of Tony Blair and George Bush, Bart Simpson lunch boxes and computer games. One thing that did disappoint Jack was that the old revolving book display had been replaced with a newer, more streamlined model that neither creaked nor shuddered. As he slowly turned the display, lifting out the odd paperback and reading the blurb on the back cover, he heard the *ting-a-ling* of the doorbell behind him.

He glanced around casually, and then straightened, suddenly tense. Patty Bates, wearing a baggy tracksuit top and the same jeans he'd had on in the pub on Monday night, turned to close the door behind him. Jack turned back to the book display. If he ignored Bates, the guy probably wouldn't even notice him. He heard heavy footsteps behind him, the slightly laboured breathing of someone who was rapidly running to seed. A voice said almost directly into his ear, "You won't find any of yours on there."

Jack turned to face Bates, forcing a smile onto his face. "I'm sorry?" he said, pretending not to recognise the bully (ex-bully?).

Bates snorted a disdainful laugh. "You will be, pal."

Jack's smile faded, but he refused to be intimidated. He looked directly into Bates' stone-grey eyes, and said, "I'm afraid I don't know what you mean."

Bates leaned closer, and now Jack could smell the stale tobacco on his breath. "You'll find out," he said.

Jack shrugged, tried to look casual, even half-turned back to the book display as though dismissing Bates. "I really don't know what you're on about," he said.

The publican grabbed Jack's arm just above the elbow and yanked him back. "Don't pretend you don't fucking know me. I saw you in my pub the other night, chatting up my daughter. I don't want to see you in there ever again. Do you understand?"

Anger and fear fought for supremacy in Jack's mind. At the moment it was about fifty-fifty, but Jack felt as though the anger was slowly gaining the upper hand, and he was both glad of it and alarmed by it.

"Don't worry," he snapped back. "The beer was shit anyway." He yanked his arm out of Bates' grip. "Now get your fucking hands off me!"

Bates looked momentarily surprised by Jack's defiance, then he laughed again, harsh and throaty. Jack felt Bates' spittle fleck his cheek.

"You made a big mistake coming back here, pal," said Bates. "A fucking big mistake."

"Really?" said Jack, trying to sound bored.

"Yeah, really," snarled Bates. "You're gonna fucking regret it."

Jack felt an urge to laugh scornfully, or to punch Bates right in the centre of his stupid ugly face, and yet he also wanted to be out of this, to get some fresh air to calm his churning stomach.

"Oh grow up," he said, trying to instill as much contempt as he could into his voice.

Jack saw the violence swirling in Bates' eyes, barely suppressed. Would the bully start something here? Maybe back when they were boys he would have—or he would at least have waited outside and beaten Jack up in the street—but now he wasn't so sure. Now there were other things to consider—how would the brewery react to one of their landlords brawling in public, for instance?

Bates took a step back. He looked like a rottweiler, frustrated by the order not to attack. If he had been a rottweiler, he would have been snarling now, showing his teeth. He raised a stubby finger and pointed it at Jack's face, almost jabbing his nose. "Your days are numbered, pal. I'm coming for you."

"Are you really?" said Jack airily. "Or will you be hiding behind your little army of thugs again? Keeping out of the way?"

That comment got to Patty. Jack saw his face flush, a wave of crimson starting below his ears, sweeping across his cheeks and forehead. Jack swallowed with an effort; his mouth was very dry. Any moment he expected Bates to lash out at him. He felt nervous, almost flighty, with the expectation of it. And yet the outrage was still there, a voice inside him screaming: How dare this . . . this *nobody* threaten me!

Jack wanted to belittle Bates, to tear him apart with rapier wit, show him how pathetic he was being. But the sad reality was that a mere verbal assault would be lost on someone like Patty. Jack did not consider himself brave. Violence appalled him, the prospect of it being inflicted upon his own body even more so. And yet he refused to be pushed around by someone with the intellectual capacity of a plastic bucket.

These thoughts raced through his head in an instant, adrenaline-charged. Patty was saying, "Don't you fucking worry, pal. When it comes down to it, it'll just be you and me."

Jack wanted to ask why, what was the point, what was it that made Patty hate him, or anyone, for no reason? But he knew there was no answer, or none that he wanted to hear from Bates, anyway. Smiling tightly, he said, "Lovely, I'll look forward to it. And now if you'll excuse me . . ."

He squeezed quickly out of the gap between Bates and the book display and walked rapidly towards the open-fronted cooler that held milk, mineral water and various soft drinks.

If Patty follows me now, he thought, bending to lift a two pint carton of milk, I'll turn and smash this right into his face. But Patty did not follow him. Jack heard the bully's heavy footsteps approaching the door. Before leaving, Bates threw a parting shot: "You're a dead man, Stone."

Keeping his back turned, Jack waved and said, "So nice to see you again, too. Just like old times."

It was only when he heard the door of the shop slam behind Bates that Jack realised how rigidly he'd been holding himself. The instant he allowed himself to relax, his legs began to tremble and he felt a sudden urge to go to the toilet. He smiled at the woman behind the counter who was totting up his purchases on the till. "I love Beckford," he told her. "Such friendly people."

Despite his attempt to put it from his mind, Jack's encounter with Patty left a nasty taste in his mouth, and he decided to redress the balance by calling on his aunt before heading back to the house. It was just after six when he arrived. She was watching the news whilst eating her evening meal from a tray on her lap. She was pleased to see him, but said she wished he'd given her notice. She could have bought another piece of fish and made tea for both of them.

"That's okay," he said. "I'm not hungry yet. I'll get something later."

"Are you sure? I can do you some nice bacon and eggs. It won't take a minute."

"No," said Jack firmly. "You sit down. I only popped round to say hello on my way back."

She sat down and began eating again, taking small delicate mouthfuls like a bird. The smell of cheese sauce

turned Jack's stomach. He was annoyed that a no-hoper
like Bates could make him feel like this, but it wasn't just
Bates *per se*. It was pointless hostility, violence for its own
sake, that dismayed him. He smiled at his aunt, trying to
shake the feeling. Using her remote control, she turned
the volume down on the TV. "So what have you been doing today?" she asked.

He felt an instinctive reluctance to share both the discovery of his father's notebooks and his encounter in Taylor's. He told her about his afternoon exploring
secondhand bookshops and immediately she raised her
fork in the air. "That reminds me, I've got some books
for you."

"Oh?"

"Yes, they're in the wardrobe in my bedroom in a cardboard box. I'll go and get them."

"No, no, you stay there," he said. "I'll get them." He did
so. The box had once contained Persil washing powder. It
was sealed with a thick brown strip of packing tape.

"I've been meaning to mention it since you got here,"
Georgina said. "They've been up there for years. Your father brought them round one day and asked if I'd keep
them for you."

Jack's stomach began churning again, but this time
with anticipation as he scratched up an edge of the tape
with his fingernail and peeled it back. He had a good idea
what these books would be. The television showed a
building on fire, the night sky above it brown as sludge.
Jack tried to compose his face for his aunt's benefit, but
couldn't prevent himself from murmuring, "Wow," when
he folded back the flaps of cardboard that comprised the
lid of the box.

Rupert Bear, Korky the Cat, Jennings, William, The Famous Five. All his childhood was here, precious reminders of a happiness that was both desperate and total,
contained among yellowing dog-eared pages, between

covers whose colours were still bright despite the passage of time.

As Jack lifted out each book and hefted it in his hand, his head filled with memories, as though messages were flowing from the books themselves. Here was Ray Bradbury's *Something Wicked This Way Comes;* he'd read most of this sitting on a deckchair in his aunt's garden, wafting at wasps and sipping lemonade. And here was the *Fifth Pan Book of Horror Stories,* read one night in bed with a torch under the covers when snow was lying thick on the ground. And look here: *The Last Battle,* by C.S. Lewis; his father had threatened to throw this on the fire once when Jack had accidentally left it on the dining table. And there were so many more, all of them old, dear friends. *Charlie and the Chocolate Factory, Salem's Lot, Charlotte's Web, Five Children and It, The Secret Seven* . . . If his aunt had not been here, Jack might well have kissed some of the covers of these books, remembering how they had saved him from despair.

And near the bottom of the box, after removing a copy of Graham Greene's *Brighton Rock,* Jack glimpsed a portion of the cover of a larger book that made his heart leap with excitement. He could see the blue of a pond, the green of a lily pad with a frog crouched on it. He removed the scattering of books that concealed this larger one, and now he saw the title: *The Bumper Book of Fairy Tales.*

"Oh, wow," he breathed and lifted the book out. It was as hefty as he remembered it; picking it up as a small child had made his biceps ache. The back cover illustration was identical to the front. There was a large dent in the back of the book, completely mashing the princess' head. Jack touched the dent, knowing it was the mark his father had made with the golf club. He examined the book, half-fearing it would be smeared with long-dried blood. It wasn't, of course. He expelled a long slow breath and looked at his aunt. "This is amazing," he said. "I thought my dad had thrown all these away."

Georgina shook her head and smiled. "You used to love reading when you were younger, didn't you?"

"Still do," said Jack.

"That's how I remember you, curled up somewhere with a book in your hands."

The fairy tale book creaked when Jack opened it, like a door into a magical land that hadn't been used for centuries. He began to turn the pages, remembering their layouts so immediately that it felt he was preempting them. The dragon with the gaping mouth dribbling smoke; the trees with gnarled human features; the troll skulking under the bridge, ready to pounce on the unsuspecting merchant; the witch brandishing the poisoned apple as bats swooped around her head.

By the time Jack arrived at the story of *Jack and the Beanstalk,* he felt as if his memories were so strong that they were reproducing themselves in print. The title was entwined with green vines just as he remembered it, the cow was a comically lugubrious animal with a swaying udder and shoulder blades so prominent they resembled stubs of wings. Here was Jack exchanging the cow for a handful of multicoloured beans, and here was Jack's mother tossing the beans angrily out of the window. Over the page was a picture of the beanstalk disappearing into the clouds with Jack and his mother gazing up at it in awe, and in the next illustration Jack was nearing the summit of the beanstalk, where a craggy mountain peaked by a huge black castle rose impossibly from a swathe of thick grey mist.

Jack paused here, because he knew that on the next page was the ogre. He remembered his recent dream—he had turned the page and instead of the illustration he'd been expecting was an empty black rectangle. But that was before; everything was different now. His father no

longer *was* the ogre. He was (had been) simply an an-
guished old man, poisoned by grief, unable to find a way
to draw the humanity out of himself until it was too late.
Jack cleared his throat. On the TV a weather girl was
showing him large cartoon suns on a map of Britain. Jack
twitched his aunt a smile and flipped over the page.

And there was the ogre, ugly and snarling, crouched
over his coins.

Jack stared at the illustration for a few moments, breath
held as if afraid it might pull itself to life from the page,
break its boundaries. But the power of the picture seemed
actually to fade as he gazed at it, until it was no longer
threatening, impotent as make-believe.

Before he could stop himself, he smiled and said, "It's
okay."

"What is?" asked Georgina.

He looked up, and felt himself blushing. "Oh . . . er . . .
nothing," he said. "It doesn't matter. It's just something
that . . . no, it's okay. It's too complicated to explain."

He hoped she wouldn't press the matter. Explaining
what the ogre had meant to him would diminish its po-
tency, thus undermining his fear. And besides, that fear no
longer seemed appropriate. To deflect further questions
he skimmed through the rest of the book until he reached
the story of *Dick Whittington and His Cat.* "This is one of
the reasons I went to London," he said.

His aunt looked puzzled. "This story?"

"This illustration," he said, tapping his finger on the
page. "Streets paved with gold and all that."

Georgina shook her head. "You didn't really think it
was like that, did you?"

"Well, it was, wasn't it?" Jack retorted. "For me at least.
Going to London was the best decision I ever made."

She made no comment, merely set her face and drew
back her shoulders. Jack knew she was hurt. Whenever he
mentioned London, and how happy he was there, she

seemed to take it as a personal snub. Most of it, of course, was loneliness. If she wasn't so proud, he knew she would be begging him to stay. Lord knows, he owed her more than he could ever repay.

Seeing her sitting there, lips pursed, knobbly hands folded primly in her lap, Jack felt a fierce, protective love. He crossed to her chair and hugged her before she realised what he was doing. She stiffened, then relaxed. "What was that for?" she asked when he broke the embrace.

"Nothing," Jack said. "Everything. Can't I hug my favourite aunt without having to have a reason?"

"Get on with you, you daft bugger," she said. But Jack could see that she was touched.

He put the books into the box, stayed for a little while longer and then left. He wondered whether to get some food from the Top Wok, but the same gang of kids as before were hanging around outside it so he drove on. Ten miles outside Beckford was a village called Surley, which Jack hoped did not describe the nature of the inhabitants. He found an Italian restaurant called Da Mario's, where he ate excellent garlic bread and disappointingly tasteless lasagna. The place was bright and the young staff unnecessarily noisy, as if in the belief it would mask the mediocrity of the food. A couple sat at the next table with three uncontrollable children. He spent the meal devising inventive ways of silencing them for good.

Darkness was seeping from the horizon, blurring the lines of dry-stone walls, when he arrived back at the house. He parked the car, eager to get inside and reacquaint himself with his father's stories. Before he did that, though, he wanted to ring Gail and fill up the bookshelves in his bedroom. When he opened the door of the car and stepped out onto Daisy Lane, he was suddenly overcome by a sense of well-being. The encounter with Bates seemed distant now, insignificant. Jack grinned into the fading sun, drew a deep breath into his lungs, and simply stood there, savouring the moment. He had come here and done what he'd thought would be impossible. He had exorcised his ghosts, reconciled himself with his father—or at least with his own memories of him. Tomorrow he could head back to London, content in the knowledge that his life would become all the happier for having returned to Beckford.

As he stood there another idea jolted him, as if he hadn't been in the position to consider it until now: when he got back to London, when he saw Gail, the first thing he would do would be to ask her to marry him.

He laughed out loud at the sheer wonder of the idea and punched the air with both hands. "Yes!" he shouted. *"Yes!"* His voice bounced away over the darkening landscape, conveying his glee to the world.

He carried his books into the house and arranged them lovingly on his bookcase. When he had done, he ran his hands over the smooth spines, his fingers jolting over the ridges between them. This was a ritual he could have performed only by himself. Gail loved books too, but even she would have regarded his actions as somewhat fetishistic. Jack did not know if he could have conveyed how much having all these books back on this bookcase meant to him. It had a significance beyond words. Even the arrangement of the brightly coloured spines seemed to form a pattern that was almost mystical.

He felt eager as he dialed Gail's number, anxious to share his good mood. Her phone rang four times . . . five. Jack had resigned himself to the fact that she was not there, was waiting for her answering machine to cut in, or for the phone to go on ringing as it had before, when there was a click and she said, "Hello?"

"Hi, Gail, it's me!" he cried gleefully into the receiver.

"Jack, hi!" Then abruptly her voice adopted a note of concern. "Are you okay?"

"Yes, course. Why do you ask?"

"Well, with everything that's been happening to you . . ."

"Oh, that." He waved a hand in the air, as though batting away a fly. "No, that's all under control now."

"Are you sure?"

"What do you mean?"

"You're not just saying that to make me feel better? I've been worried about you, Jack."

He thought of Patty Bates again. Should he tell her about this afternoon? Deciding against it, he said, "No, I'm fine, Gail, really. In fact, I'm better than fine. I'm happy. Coming back here has been really good for me, like you said it would be. I think I've finally laid my ghosts."

She was silent for a long moment, as though taken aback, then said, "What do you mean?"

"I mean my father doesn't bother me anymore. I've found things out about him."

"What things?"

"Last night," Jack began, and told her everything, wanting her to share his elation. "It's almost like he left his soul behind. I feel like I'm really beginning to get to know him, to understand him. I only wish we could have been friends when he was alive. In some ways it's tragic, I suppose; such a waste."

He heard his own voice cracking, and took a deep breath, cleared his throat, wanting to carry on, to explain and share the depth of his emotion.

A few moments later, he said, "I don't know. I find it so hard to describe. But it's like . . . like I've found myself at last." He pulled a face into the receiver. "Do you know what I mean? I guess that sounds pretty corny, doesn't it?"

"No," said Gail, "it doesn't sound corny. It sounds . . . it sounds great. I know how you felt about your father before. I'm delighted that it's working out for you. I told you it would, didn't I? Oh, I wish we could be together."

"We will be," Jack said. "This time tomorrow, with any luck."

"I know."

But she sounded so wistful that he asked, "What's the matter? Don't you think I'm going to come back?"

"Yes, of course."

"So what's wrong?"

"Oh . . . nothing. I'm just being silly. Ignore me."

Jack sighed. "Gail," he said firmly, knowing she had something on her mind.

"What?"

"Spit it out."

"Spit what out?"

"Whatever's sticking in your throat."

She made a small sound, an ironic *hmph*. "You know me too well, Jack Stone."

"True," he said, refusing to be sidetracked.

She allowed a few more seconds of hissing silence to pass, and then said, "I just hope it is how you say it is, that's all. I hope you're not getting carried away with the situation."

"What do you mean?"

"Well . . . you suddenly seem to have put on a pair of rose-tinted spectacles, forgotten all the bad stuff, the violence and all that. I hope you're not going to come down to earth with a bump."

He thought for a moment and then said, "No . . . no, I don't think so. The violence was . . . was bad, there's no denying that. It was a wrong move my father made, a terrible mistake, as was the drinking and all the rest of it. But I think he's finally . . . apologising for all that, acknowledging it."

"By writing stories?"

"They're not *just* stories, Gail. They're more than that. They're a legacy. I'm sure he left them for me. He wanted me to find them."

"How do you know?"

He felt suddenly exasperated. Why did she have to

question what he knew to be right? "I know, that's all. I just know. You haven't been here, you don't understand."

She remained silent. Jack pictured her face, furrowed with worry, and his anger eased a little.

"Look," he said gently, "I know this all sounds a bit . . . I don't know . . . strange, maybe even slightly crazy. But this . . . this experience, Gail, it's a positive thing, and that can't be bad, can it? I'll still be the same person when I come back."

"Only happier," she said.

"That's right. Only happier."

She sighed, as if conceding defeat. "I love you, Jack."

"And I love you, too. More than anything. I'll see you tomorrow. And try not to worry."

"Okay."

"Promise?"

"Yeah."

"Bye then."

"Bye."

"I love you, petal," said Jack.

"We've done all this."

"I know. We must be in a time warp. See you tomorrow."

"Yeah, bye."

Jack put the phone down, feeling a little deflated. He had wanted to convey how significant he found the discovery of his father's notebooks, but sometimes the words were simply not there.

He considered calling Gail straight back, trying again, but what could he say to convince her that he hadn't already said? Sighing, he tramped to the kitchen. He spent the next ten minutes commuting between kitchen and sitting room, making tea, building a fire.

He closed the curtains, turned on the lamps and put on the Ennio Morricone CD he'd been playing yesterday with the volume down low. The music was nothing more than a murmur in the room. Occasionally the fire spat as it collapsed into itself in slow motion. Jack looked across at his laptop and felt a pang of guilt. He really ought to do some work before he lost himself in his father's thoughts, just a few hundred words to keep the wheels greased and moving. But the blue notebooks beckoned him. He'd been waiting all his life for their insight; they had to take priority. He poured himself a mug of tea and balanced it on the settee arm, then dragged the notebooks onto the cushion beside him. He opened the notebook to a story called *Floating*, which was dated 5/1/92 and almost immediately lost himself in its weave.

Only once, hours later, when an owl hooted outside, did Jack raise his head. Immediately, the warmth of the fire seemed to lay a hot film across his eyes, making them smart; a jabbing pain in his back made him realise how long his body had been locked in the same position. He groaned and stretched. His mouth tasted stale, his saliva thick as curd. The room around him seemed not quite there, like a faded painting or a movie vanishing in sunlight. Jack rolled his neck on his shoulders, wincing as his vertebrae crackled like paper. He switched off one of the lamps in the hope that it would ease his stinging eyes, then lay back on the settee, his feet dangling over the side, and continued reading.

Some time later he started awake. He turned his head slightly, stared at the brittle, blackened coldness of what had been the fire with complete incomprehension. What was he doing here? What time was it? What *day* was it, for God's sake? Jack always hated the feeling of disorientation upon waking up in a strange place. He often thought this was what it must be like to be senile, stumbling around blindly in your own head, unable to connect with anything.

He was cold, though he only discovered that when he tried to rise. And then he began shivering, as if someone had opened the front door, allowing freezing air to come rushing into the house. His arm had somehow got stuck beneath him and was jittery with pins and needles. One of his father's blue notebooks was standing on its end on the floor, the strip of paper used as a bookmark lying beside it. Jack's thoughts were still scurrying around like the Keystone Kops, trying to arrange themselves into some semblance of order. He leaned over the side of the settee and picked up the book. Turning it over, he blinked at the scrawled handwriting, feeling that if he could focus on something his confusion would pass more quickly. When he heard the door to the sitting room open behind him a sensation of extreme cold, like a blanket of snow, seemed to sweep over the settee and spread across his back.

For several long moments he literally didn't know what to do. He felt so bewildered, so out of it, that his brain seemed to stick, to refuse to make a decision. The door had opened slowly, as though the intruder were relishing the fact that he needn't rush. A thought suddenly came to him, strong and clear: Patty Bates that afternoon, pointing a finger and saying, "When it comes down to it, it'll just be you and me." Jack slid forward off the settee and onto the floor, tucking in his head to make himself less of a target. Even as he rolled over, closer to the hearth, and reached out for the poker, he became aware that the light was beginning to dim in the room.

But it was not until his fingers closed around the poker that he realised that was impossible. The lamps did not have a dimmer switch; there was on and there was off, nothing in between. Jack finished rolling and jumped lithely to his feet, brandishing the poker, half-expecting to see Patty Bates standing there with a baseball bat. The sitting-room door was wide open, the hallway black, indistinct. But there was nobody there. Unless . . . unless he was crouching behind the settee.

Before he was even aware of the thought, Jack pistoned his right leg out at the settee, jarring it backwards. The light in the room was very dim now, and reddish, as if someone had draped a thick cloth over the lamp. The bulk of the settee met with no resistance. Had the intruder already left? Jack's clearing but still befuddled mind groped for an explanation: a burglar who'd thought the house was empty, no stomach for violence, getting the shock of his life to find Jack in the house, maybe legging it up Daisy Lane by now.

But what about the lamp? A faulty bulb?

And then he heard footsteps.

They were loud, steady, and they were approaching along the hallway. Jack's belly became a flock of birds seeking release. He hefted the poker in his hand, crouched behind the makeshift barrier of the settee. The owner of the footsteps stepped into the open doorway.

And there was no one there.

He gaped; surely he hadn't misheard? The footsteps had marched right up to the open door. There should be a figure filling that doorway now but there was no one. Jack was reminded of a poem that had always made him shiver as a child:

> As I was walking up the stairs
> I met a man who wasn't there
> He wasn't there again today
> I wish that man would go away

And then a voice whispered, "Jack."

His hand spasmed around the poker. Not for the first time that day the saliva drained from his mouth. He swallowed, desperate to speak, gulped air that tasted coppery, almost electric. Around a tongue that felt fat and useless he managed to say, "Dad?"

There was no reply, but he sensed a presence in the room with him. The dim light flickered, causing shadows to balloon up the walls or to crouch like trolls in the corners. A tapping sound started up; it took Jack a moment to realise it was a resumption of the footsteps. They were getting closer—but how? This room was carpeted, and the footsteps sounded as if they were approaching across a hard surface. A splash of shadow appeared on the wall beside the door, and then another identical splash above it. Then a third . . . and a fourth. Jack made a sound, a kind of gasp, for all at once he realised what the splashes were.

They were footprints, and they were approaching not across the floor but up the walls, and now across the ceiling. Jack stared at them, openmouthed. They formed slowly, steadily, black as tar and yet insubstantial as shadow. They marched across the ceiling towards him and came to a halt immediately above his head. Jack murmured, "Dad? Is that you?" Receiving no reply, he stumbled on, "I've been reading your stories, Dad. They're good. Really good. Thank you for . . . for leaving them for me. I'm going to take some of Mum's pictures back to London, if that's okay. I . . . I wish we could talk. I wish you'd have told me about your writing. Maybe if you had, things would have been different. Maybe we could even have been friends."

The footprints began, slowly at first, to fade. Jack jumped to his feet and cried, "No, Dad, don't go. Why won't you talk to me? Why won't you show yourself properly? I don't hate you any more, Dad. I don't hate you any more."

The footsteps broke up, dispersed, like sand in the wind. The lamp brightened until its light was as strong as before. The door to the sitting room wavered a little, as if touched by a breeze. Jack ran to the door and into the hallway.

"Dad, come back," he shouted. "Come back!" But the house was hollow and silent as a tomb. Shivering, Jack re-entered the sitting room and closed the door. He lay down on the settee, hoping his father would return, but eventually his eyes slid closed and sleep claimed him until dawn.

13

CAR TROUBLE

The funeral car came to pick Jack up at eleven twenty-five the next morning. Because it would not have been able to turn round in the narrow lane, he had arranged to meet it at the top of Daisy Lane where it joined the main road.

He wished he hadn't. It was a miserable day, thin grey drizzle weeping from clouds the colour of oily rocks. A cold wind slithered around him, nipping and probing his exposed skin, numbing his ears, making his forehead ache. Jack had woken up in a foul mood, his shoulders and spine almost pulsing with pain. Why had his father not made full contact last night? He had done it before when Jack had not been ready, but now that he would have welcomed it the old man was choosing to be enigmatic.

Jack swore at the wind as it grabbed his tie and flailed it at his face. He tucked it back into his jacket and smoothed it down, flipping up his lapels to keep the wind from gnawing at his neck. It seemed strange to be about to attend the funeral of a man who, for him, had only just come alive. He stepped into the arch of trees at the top of

Daisy Lane, and paused for a moment, thankful for the shelter.

Just a couple of days ago he had found this place sinister, but now it reminded him of a cathedral, its muted colours seeming to radiate peace, blocking out all but a murmur of the wind. Jack palmed moisture from his face and tried to rake his hair into some semblance of tidiness. He took his cigarettes and matches from the hip pocket of his jacket and lit up as he strolled through the trees, enjoying the sound of water dripping from leaf to leaf, the mulchy squelch of his footsteps. "I'm going home today," he told the trees. "I'm going back to London to see Gail, and I'm going to ask her to marry me." The idea still seemed strange and delightful to him. He laughed and shook his head, shredding a sinuous curve of grey-blue smoke.

When the two cars eased into view at the bottom of the hill, Jack was still smiling. He smoothed his hair with his hands again, dropped his cigarette into the dirt and adopted a suitably sombre expression. The first car, driven by Jeremy Coombs, contained his father's coffin, on which three modest-sized wreaths had been laid. The car behind, driven by a hamster-like man with a tightly trimmed ginger beard, contained his Aunt Georgina.

She was dressed in a dark grey suit and looked pensive. Jack wanted to wave to her but decided not to; the gesture might be construed as flippant. Both cars indicated and cruised to a halt beside him. Beads of water shimmered on their waxed bonnets. From his glancing, distorted reflections in the cars' spotless side windows, Jack could see that he looked bedraggled. He stepped forward to open the second car's door, but as he was reaching for the handle, the driver threw open his door, catapulted from his seat and came bustling towards him. "Allow me, sir."

"Thanks." Jack ducked into the car, which rocked a little as the door slammed behind him. There was enough space inside for him to lie down if he'd wanted. His aunt was sitting upright, back rigid, handbag perched on her lap like a pet. She gave a tight smile, her face pale. As he sat down she grasped his hand and squeezed it. "Are you okay?" he asked. She nodded, but her eyes told him otherwise.

The drive to the church was brief, but Jack's inability to think of anything comforting to say protracted the minutes. He had never been to a burial before. The thought of it discomfitted him—the dark and the airlessness, the worms and the weight of all that earth above you. The fact that you were dead, or supposed to be, didn't matter. Even the fact that he'd had evidence that the human soul could transcend death, that the body was simply a casing, a machine that eventually broke down, could not alter his opinion. He shuddered and tried to tell himself this was what came of reading Poe at too early an age.

The ancient church was fettered with ivy. Jack could see four men in black suits—the coffin bearers, presumably—leaning in the open arched doorway, chatting and smoking. Beyond them was the vicar, inclining his head toward one of only half a dozen mourners. The other five mourners were gazing into space.

As the two cars pulled into the churchyard, people began to straighten up, adjust clothing, guiltily discard cigarettes and adopt looks of expectation, or, in one or two cases, practised sympathy. Jack couldn't help thinking that the mourners were here not because they wished to pay their respects, but simply out of a sense of propriety. Or perhaps it was less than that—he toyed with the idea that they had been hired by Coombs or the vicar to swell the ranks a little, pay him and his aunt lip service. As the two cars cruised to a halt, Jack stifled an urge to produce a stately wave, like an arriving royal.

Throughout the service his aunt clung to his arm. Jack stared at the coffin in front of the altar and felt nothing but the unease he always felt when faced with reminders of mortality. The vicar's voice was a drone, his words occasionally blurred by their own echoes. When Jack looked around, the other mourners, none of whom he recognised, were gazing at the floor or into space, as if lost in their own thoughts.

Outside, as the coffin was lowered into the ground and the words of committal were said, Georgina cried a few silent tears, which Jack acknowledged by briefly squeezing her hand. When it was over and they were back in the car heading towards his aunt's house, he found himself thinking—as he had in the registrar's office—is that all it is then, all that a life amounts to? A wooden box, a bored vicar who doesn't know you from Adam, and a meagre cluster of mourners whose only thought is to get out of the cold and back to their own lives? It seemed so pointless, so inauspicious, and, thought Jack, so English. Dying in this country was almost an embarrassment, something to be frowned upon, to be despatched as quickly and quietly as possible. When I die, he thought, I want a pink Cadillac, and I want everyone to wear bright colours, and I want them to play *No More Heroes* by the Stranglers at the funeral service.

They were almost at his aunt's house when they nearly had an accident. Jack was so lost in his own thoughts that the first he was aware of it was when the driver shouted, "Bloody hell!" and yanked the steering wheel to the left. He looked up to see flashes of gleaming silver and black streak past the windows, then together with his aunt he jerked forward as the driver stamped on the brakes. He recovered and raised his head just in time to see the passing of the last motorbike in the formation. The guy riding it had wraparound plastic shades, long greasy hair that streamed out from beneath the rim of his helmet, and facial fungus reminiscent of Motörhead's Lemmy. Sitting behind the Lemmy lookalike was Tracey Bates, clad in her usual jeans and leather jacket. Jack swivelled to watch the bike's progress through the back window. He saw Tracey twist, her stunning blonde hair streaming out behind her. She unwrapped her right arm from around the Lemmy lookalike's midriff and very deliberately stuck two fingers up in the air.

Fuck you, too, Jack thought coldly. He wondered whether Tracey had known this was his father's funeral procession and decided that she must have done.

"Are you okay?" Jack asked his aunt. Like him, she had shot forward when the car had braked and had ended up sprawling in the space between front seat and back, a jumble of arms and legs.

"Yes," she said weakly, "just a bit shaken." He saw her wince and rub her arm as she clambered back onto her seat and he felt a bright juicy hatred for Tracey Bates and her friends fill his mouth.

"Whatever happened?" Georgina asked a moment later, blinking at him. "Did we hit something?"

The driver turned, displaying his teeth in a grimace of excruciating apology. "Sir, Madam," he said, "I'm terribly sorry."

"Don't worry," said Jack, "it wasn't your fault. Half of those morons were on the wrong side of the road."

The driver nodded gratefully and turned back.

"Jack, what happened?" Georgina said again.

"Kids on motorbikes," Jack said. "They were riding two and three abreast, hogging the road."

Georgina tutted. "Ought to ban those things. They're nothing but death traps. I was only reading in the paper yesterday about a lad from Emley, eighteen he was, went out of control on a motorbike, ended up going through a wire fence and having his head lopped off."

Jack nodded, only half-listening. He was filled with a rage so acute that bottling it up made his temples feel tight, created a hard knotted ache in his stomach. That was twice now that Tracey Bates had nearly killed him.

She was a bloody psycho, just like her father. Jack had decided not to tell the police about his previous run-ins with the Bates family because he hadn't wanted to be detained in Beckford longer than was necessary. However, if he had not been heading back to London within the next couple of hours, he would have been straight on the phone to report this latest incident.

He tried to stem his anger as he nibbled dry salmon sandwiches and sipped tea at his aunt's house. Four of the mourners came back, as did Jeremy Coombs and their driver, who, Jack discovered, was Coombs' brother-in-law. Jack didn't much like any of the people he talked to. Perhaps it was the situation, but they all seemed edgy, taciturn. When a decent interval had passed, he crossed to his aunt, who was alone on the sofa drinking the latest of numerous cups of tea.

"How are you?" he asked.

"Tired," she replied without hesitation. "When are all these people going to go home?"

"Soon, I should think. How's your arm?"

"A bit sore." She smiled sadly. "I'll live."

Jack nodded and leaned back, waiting for the right moment to tell her the next thing, trying to formulate the words. At last he cleared his throat and said, "I'd better be thinking of getting back soon. I wanted to reach London before the rush hour."

His aunt turned to look at him, and despite himself Jack felt guilty. "You're going home today?"

"You know I am," Jack replied. "I told you." He placed his hand over hers. "I have to get back. I've got things to do. You know I can't stay here forever."

Georgina looked as if she were about to argue, then turned her head away. "Of course," she said tightly.

Jack felt bad, as if he were abandoning her, though he knew there was no reason to feel this way. "I'll come back to visit you soon," he said. "I'll bring Gail. It's been really lovely to see you again, Aunty. I have to admit, I didn't want to come back to Beckford, but now I'm glad that I did."

For a moment he thought his aunt was not going to grace him with an answer, then her expression softened and she turned to look at him once more.

"It's been lovely to see you, too," she said. "You might have turned into a bit of a city tyke, Jack Stone, but you haven't changed all that much. He would have been proud of you, you know, your father, whatever you may think of him."

Jack felt a lump rising in his throat and smiled it away. "Yeah," he said. "I know."

There was silence between them for a moment, then Georgina leaned forward, grasped his hand and kissed him on the cheek. "Go on," she said gently. "Off you go. Back to your smoke and pollution."

Jack chuckled. "It's a good life, you know."

She smiled. "I'm sure it is."

He stood up, palming the creases from his suit, then turned, leaned forward and hugged her tightly. "See you soon," he said. "I'll phone you when I get back."

Did he detect a glint of tears in her eyes? If so, they were rapidly blinked away. "Good-bye, Jack," she said.

He raised a hand and abruptly turned away. "Bye, everyone," he called at the door, and slipped out before they had time to acknowledge him.

He shivered and huddled into himself as he began the walk back to his father's house. It was cold, but at least the rain had stopped. The sky was the colour of old newspapers; a garden shed gleamed like raw liver. A Collie shook itself dry on the opposite side of the street, creating a fine halo of spray around itself.

Jack felt happy. The funeral was over, social niceties out of the way, affairs sorted and farewells made. All he had to do now was get his stuff together, load up the car and go home. He hugged himself, hunching up his shoulders, partly for warmth, partly in anticipation of the glorious moment when he could take Gail in his arms. It was almost one-thirty; depending on the traffic he should be home by six. Where can we go tonight? he thought. Poons? No, somewhere posher. How about Maxi's? He became aware that he was grinning like a love-struck schoolboy, but he didn't care. Life was so good. He could almost taste the prawn crackers, the fried seaweed, the sweet and sour chicken. He shuddered in delight. When should he ask her to marry him? As soon as he got home, during the meal, or later in bed?

When he turned onto Daisy Lane, the sun was struggling to show itself. Jack grinned, feeling as though it were making the effort solely for him. He squelched between the trees and out the other side, bracing himself against the pouncing wind. The fields looked green and lush as jungle vegetation, the distant woods a single varnished sculpture. The dry-stone walls gleamed like ebony. The air smelt of fresh clean earth, of renewal. The path had turned muddy, spattering his shoes, but Jack couldn't care less. This was one of those rare times when he felt as though his life were spread gloriously before him, a box of delights, full of wonders, of joy, of opportunity.

Reality hit him like a brick when he saw his car.

At first he didn't notice. He was gazing absently at the house, intent on his own thoughts. The house's black spiky chimneys bobbed into view first, then the shiny slate roof, then the rest of the place, the aftermath of the drizzle clinging to it like a pall.

He was perhaps forty yards away when he registered that the tomato red block of his car did not look quite as it was supposed to. Frowning, he turned and focused upon it and saw that the bonnet was yawning open. And when he looked down Jack noticed for the first time the imprints in the mud, leading up to the car and away from it. They were doubtless the impressions of motorcycle tires. They overlapped and then veered away from each other like the fraying twines of a rope.

"Shit!" he shouted, and ran towards his car, a clawed hand taking hold of his intestines and squeezing. When he got closer he saw the debris in the dirt—twisted bits of metal and plastic, shreds of his engine's guts.

"Bastards," he breathed when he crossed in front of his car and saw what was left of his engine. It looked as though someone had been at it with a sledgehammer. Jack knew next to nothing about cars, but he did know that he was looking at an awful lot of damage. Things were cracked and dented and mangled and ripped out. Though his mind was buzzing with shock, a small calculating part of it wondered whether the damage was reparable or whether he'd have to buy a completely new engine. If so, how much would that cost? Hundreds? Thousands?

"You fucking bastards," he snarled again. He spun round and shouted, "I'll kill you, you bastards!" But the landscape remained the same, stoically unimpressed. One thing was certain: Jack would not be leaving Beckford today.

Turning furiously from the wreckage, he stormed into the house.

INTERLUDE TWO

1997

If grudges were plants, Patty Bates would be a fine gardener indeed. He had always nurtured them lovingly, never allowing them to wither and die. Prize bloom in his garden of seething thoughts and dark resentments was the score he would one day settle with Terry Stone. Though it had happened fourteen years ago, Patty had never forgotten the humiliation of that day, and the hatred, the desire for revenge, was as strong now as it had ever been.

The reason why Bates had not already settled the score could be put down to one simple word. He would never have admitted it to anyone, did not even allow the word to form in his mind. But it was there nevertheless, a dull, throbbing, constant pain. The word was *fear*. Patty Bates was *afraid* of Terry Stone. In Stone he had seen a madness, a rage, that eclipsed his own. He had no desire to reawaken that . . . and yet he *would* get his revenge.

There were other ways. Methods in which he could exact retribution without encountering the man himself. Terry Stone, as Patty knew only too well, had a son. When they were kids, even before the incident at the garage, Patty had used Jack Stone as his occasional punching bag. Once, the best time, he had taken him into the woods and made him eat raw eggs. After the episode at the garage, Patty had laid low for a while, nursing his resentment, licking his wounds. Whenever he had seen Jack Stone at school, a dark, sickening fury had come over him, a desire to mash the little fucker's face to a sloppy pulp. But the memory of Jack's father, of the sheer insanity of the man, had held him back. No, Patty would bide his time. There would eventually come a day when he would be old enough and strong enough, and Terry Stone would be too old and too weak.

But when that day finally came, as indeed it did, Jack Stone was gone. According to local gossip, he had left for London after a row with his father and was not coming back. Patty was enraged. He felt cheated out of what was rightfully his. He considered going out to the Stone place, blowing Terry away with his father's shotgun and burning the fucking dump to the ground.

The fantasy gave him succour in his frustration, but that was all it was: a fantasy. In truth, there was no way that Patty would ever confront Terry Stone again. It had been 1989 when Jack had left Beckford. Patty was twenty-one and at the peak of his physical prowess, whereas Terry Stone was rapidly running to seed, ravaged by too much booze and tobacco. He was ravaged, too, by the rage that had been his strength back in '83, but which was now devouring him like a cancer. And yet for all this, despite the fact that Patty *knew* he could now tie Terry Stone in knots like so many pipe cleaners, he still stayed away from Daisy Lane. It was like an animal instinct, a primitive thing: once bitten, twice shy. In some ways it was an almost superstitious fear, as though Terry was some shaman, some dark diabolist, possessed of frightening powers.

Later, after his father had pulled some strings and secured Patty the tenancy of the Seven Stars, he would see Terry regularly, propping up the bar or sitting around a table in the snug with the rest of the old codgers. Terry didn't seem to recognise him, or if he did he didn't say anything. The old sod's brain was probably so alcohol-sodden that he couldn't remember the previous day, never mind fourteen years ago. Sometimes he even smiled and handed Patty his glass and said, "Put another spot o' bitter in there, would you, son?" On these occasions Patty would grit his teeth and resist the urge to wrap his itching fingers round the old bugger's neck. He often considered barring Terry Stone, but on what pretext? The old man nearly always got drunk, but instead of getting rowdy he just slipped into melancholia. It was not his scruples that prevented Patty from barring Stone without a bona fide reason, for Patty didn't really have any scruples. No, it was all part of that superstitious fear, that feeling that if he didn't have a reason, the old sod might well put a curse on him or something.

And so he waited. And he seethed. And he waited. And then one night . . .

Terry Stone bounded into the snug of the Seven Stars, making the old men stir. They were not used to sudden movement, and the breeze created by Terry's unusually buoyant entrance unsettled them. In the centre of the room the pool table stood idle, as it did most nights (Tracey Bates' friends, the bikers who would one day claim this territory as their own, were as yet barely in their teens). Roger Woodnutt, a shapeless Toby Jugg of a man who was never seen without his hat and pipe, raised his weathered face toward the newcomer. "Now then, Terry," he said in his gravel-throated drawl, "what's up wi' thee? Got ants in your pants?"

Terry Stone had been known to squeeze out the occasional laconic smile in the course of an evening's conver-

sation, but he rarely grinned as he was doing now. Both
Alf Dixon and George Blackburn were strangely unsettled
by the grin, as they were by the fact that Terry had not
only shaved his jowls pink, but was also wearing a tie, albeit a frayed and badly knotted one.

"I'm celebrating," he said, grinning his yellow-toothed
grin through a cloud of Roger's pipe-smoke.

George was instantly suspicious. "Why? Who's died?"

"Nobody's died," said Terry. "Come on, what're you all
drinking? My shout."

Alf, who saw more than he was given credit for, noticed
that Patty Bates, the landlord, was watching the group
with a scowl on his face. It was not the first time Alf had
noticed that expression, and it was not the first time, either, that he found himself wishing Billy Watson, the old
landlord, was still at the helm. Billy had had to pack it in
because of his heart. Like many people, Alf had been astonished and disgusted when Bates had got the tenancy.
Everyone in the village knew what a bad lot he was, but
Joe Bates must have put pressure on Billy to convince the
brewery that the sun shone out of Patty's arse. It was apparently because of some favour that Billy owed Joe that
Patty had been given a job first as barman, and then as bar
manager. Of course, like everyone else, Alf refrained from
voicing his objections. He simply kept his head down and
supped his ale. Crossing the Bates's was never a good
idea, principles or no.

Terry returned from the bar with a tin tray laden with
drinks. He distributed them among his compatriots and
sat down. "Cheers," said Roger and took a long draw on
his pint, the froth sticking to his upper lip. At last he lowered his glass, released a loud sigh of pleasure, and said,
"Now then, Terry. What's all this about?"

"I'll show you," said Terry. His eyes were alive in a way
the old men had never seen before; he looked like a little
boy with a secret. He reached into his inside coat pocket

and drew out a rectangular parcel in a brown paper bag. Almost reverently he unfolded the bag and pulled out what was inside. "Take a look for yourself," he said.

It was a book. One of them expensive hardbacks with the shiny covers. Alf found himself reaching for it instinctively, and the book was placed into his hands.

"Careful," said Terry. "Don't crease the cover. And don't get mucky fingerprints all over it."

Alf held the book as if it were something fragile and expensive. He looked at the picture on the front—a dove with a smear of blood on its breast superimposed over a woman's face. He read the title—*Bleeding Hearts*—and the author's name: Jack Stone.

He looked up at Terry. "This isn't . . ."

"Aye," said Terry proudly. "It's our Jackie. He's had a book published."

The old men around the table exchanged glances. *Our Jackie?* Terry had never referred to his son in such affectionate terms before. If truth be told, he barely referred to him at all. Alf nodded, "Aye, very nice," and passed the book to George. George gave it a cursory glance and passed it to Roger.

Roger placed his pipe in the glass ashtray in the centre of the table and examined the book closely. He opened the cover and read the blurb on the front flap. "One of these here science-fiction things, is it?" he said when he had done. He turned the book over and examined the photograph on the back.

Alf noticed that Patty Bates was leaning heavily on the bar and surreptitiously examining the photograph, too. Bates caught his eye, scowled and turned away. Alf shivered and gulped at his pint. Bates' curiosity would have been understandable if that was all it was. But there had been more than curiosity on his face. There had been . . . Alf tried to think of an appropriate word. Was *hatred* too strong to apply to that expression? Alf glanced at the landlord, who was now talking to Livvy Taylor. No, he reckoned hatred was just about right.

That night, Alf observed, seemed to mark a turning point in Terry Stone's life, or at least in his attitude to it. Suddenly he was talking about "Our Jackie" as if he and his estranged son were the best of buddies. It was, "Our Jackie was on telly last night," or, "Our Jackie's new one is in the top twenty bestsellers this week." No outsider would have guessed that Terry Stone was talking about a son whom he used to beat up regularly, and who had run away to London the best part of a decade ago after leaving his father unconscious with a broken nose.

Unbeknownst to Alf, that night marked a kind of turning point in Patty Bates' life, too. Seeing Jack Stone's book, and particularly the photograph on the back, seemed to give Patty a new impetus, a new direction. Alf Dixon had been right; it *had* been hatred that he had seen on Patty's face. The sight of Jack Stone looking fresh and eager, smiling smugly from the book jacket, awakened a rage in Patty that was like a cog of freezing steel churning in his stomach, twisting his guts. The next day he had driven to Leeds and had bought his own copy of *Bleeding Hearts.* He had to fight an urge to rip the novel to shreds, to slice open Jack Stone's supercilious smile with a razor blade. But Patty resisted his impulses; he had other, more constructive plans. As soon as he arrived back at the pub, he ascended the stairs to the living quarters and strolled along the landing to his ten year old daughter's bedroom, his sweating palm creating an arc of condensation on the laminated book jacket, a patina of mist on Jack Stone's celluloid face.

From beyond the door he could hear the theme tune of *Scooby Doo.* He gave a perfunctory knock and entered. Tracey was sprawled on her bed, staring blankly at the too-loud television, which he and Louise had given her on

her eighth birthday. She turned to her father and smiled.
"Hello, Daddy."

Patty was no aesthete, but there were times when his
daughter's beauty took his breath away. Now was one of
those times. The sun was shining on her golden waist-
length hair and the side of her face. She looked almost
ethereally perfect; at that moment his nickname for her
seemed especially apt. "Hello, Angel," he said, and sat
heavily on the end of her bed.

Tracey sat up, crossing her coltish legs Buddha-fashion.
She was only ten but already he had seen boys of fourteen
and fifteen mooning over her. He had seen, too, how she
played them along, twisted them around her little finger.
Sometimes he delighted in her powers of manipulation,
sometimes it reminded him depressingly of how Louise
behaved.

"Are you watching this?" he asked, nodding at the TV.

"Nah, it's boring."

"Do you mind if I turn it off then?"

She shrugged, uncoiled her legs, bounded from the bed
and turned the TV off herself, her movements fluid, ath-
letic. She pounced back onto the bed and sat beside her
father. "Are we going to have a talk?" she said. "Is it about
Mummy?"

Louise had finally walked out three months ago after
threatening to do so for years. The break up didn't seem
to have unduly affected Tracey; she had become a little
more withdrawn than usual, perhaps, but that was all as
far as Patty could tell.

"No," he said, "I want to show you something." He
passed the book to her.

She took it without hesitation. It looked big and heavy
in her small, slender hands. Unlike many children her age,
Tracey didn't ask too many questions. She was sharp and
shrewd, she knew when information was forthcoming.

She never wasted her breath on irrelevancies. One or two of the regulars called her the "little ice maiden," though not when Patty was within earshot.

She looked at the cover of the book, flipped through the pages, turned it over and looked at the photograph on the back. Then she placed the book on her lap and looked expectantly at her father.

Patty found he was breathing hard, rage simmering inside him. He jabbed at the photograph, fingernail leaving a small dent on Jack Stone's forehead, between the eyes. Trying to keep his voice steady, he said, "I want you to look at this man, Tracey. I want you to memorise his face. He's a bad man. Once he did something to me, and one day I'm going to get him back for it. He doesn't live here anymore, he lives in London. But he's going to have to come back sometime—I know he is. And when he does, I'm going to get him. I'm going to pay him back for the terrible thing he did to me. And I want you to help me, Tracey. You will help me, won't you?"

Tracey Bates looked up into her father's sweating, wild-eyed face. Her own face was coldly serene. She placed a dainty hand over her father's clenched red fist.

"Of course I will, Daddy," she said.

PART THREE

SLIPPING BETWEEN THE CRACKS

14

LOVE AND FURY

The police came first, a red-cheeked boy who couldn't pronounce his r's and an older, more world-weary colleague. They did not inspire confidence in Jack. They shook their heads, tutted a great deal at the mess made of the car, cursorily examined the tire tracks, and listened to his accusations without comment. By the time they went away, Jack was fighting an almost overwhelming urge to deliver a hefty kick to their shiny blue arses. They recommended a garage and promised Jack they would keep him informed of any developments. Sighing, he phoned the garage; despite all the evidence, he was almost certain that there would *be* no further developments. Maybe the leader of the bikers was the superintendent's son or something. Or perhaps the police simply regarded Jack as an outsider who had more money than he knew what to do with and probably deserved all he got.

The man from the garage was called David Rookham. He arrived half an hour after the police had left, driving a battered yellow pickup truck. He told Jack that when he had started out at the garage after leaving school, Jack's father, Terry, had shown him the ropes. "I owe him a lot, your dad," Rookham said. "I were right sorry to 'ear that he'd died."

Jack thanked him, though his first reaction was one of alarm. He'd completely forgotten that the only garage in Beckford belonged to Joe Bates, Patty's father and Tracey's grandfather.

"Do the Bates family still own the garage?" Jack asked, too casually.

Rookham tapped his chest proudly. "No, it's mine now. Old Joe retired about five or six years ago, and Patty weren't bothered about the place, so Joe sold it to me."

At least partly relieved, Jack nodded at the car. "How much will it cost to fix, do you think?"

Rookham scratched his head. "Hard to say, Mr. Stone. I'll do you t' best price I can, but it's still going t' be a pretty packet."

"Over a thousand?" Jack ventured.

"Oh, aye, I should think so. You need a completely new engine from t' looks of it. I'll ring round a few people I know this afternoon and get back to you later."

"And how long do you think it will take to fix? I could do with heading back to London."

Rookham pursed his lips. "Not much chance of that this weekend, I'm afraid. I'd say Monday at the earliest, though probably more like Tuesday or Wednesday."

"Is there no way of getting it done sooner?"

"I'm sorry, Mr. Stone, but not with it being Friday to-morrow. I'm quite happy to work over t' weekend, but other people aren't, you see."

Jack sighed. "Okay. Well . . . just do your best."

"Oh, I'll do that for you, Mr. Stone. You can bank on it. Your dad were a good mate o' mine, and he were right proud o' you with your books 'n that. I'll have this little beauty running good as new for you before long."

Like the funeral car, the yellow pickup truck was too

long a vehicle to turn round in the narrow lane, but Rookham remedied this by opening a gate further down the track and reversing into a field. Jack watched the pickup jounce away over the uneven surface, laden down with the weight of his damaged Mini. Then he went back into the house, took two paracetamol, and lay on the settee with his hand covering his eyes.

He tried not to think about the fact that he could be quarter of the way home by now. Just an hour before he'd been at peace with himself and the world, but now he felt tense and confused once again. Why were the Bates's out to get him? All he wanted to do was leave Beckford and go home. The fact that his car had been disabled seemed to suggest that they wanted to keep him here—an ominous development to say the least. Jack had a good mind to ring up Patty Bates and tell him exactly what he thought of him, but that might only worsen the situation. No, the best thing was simply to keep his head down and be careful. After all, he was on his own here and Bates had his entourage of bikers to call on. Even the police seemed to be of little use; he thought that this kind of victimisation was perhaps a bit beyond them. They were probably only used to lost cats and the occasional drunken driver. Jack was not aware he had fallen asleep until he woke up with the feeling he had forgotten something vital.

Of course: Gail. Shit, what time was it? She'd be wondering where he was. He tried to blink the blur from his eyes and concentrate on the watch that he was holding up to his face. For a few seconds his thoughts were like clouds, insubstantial and out of reach, and then they came together like the film of an explosion run backwards. Four twenty-five. Was she at work today or would she be at his flat now, eagerly awaiting his arrival? He got up, staggered into the hall and picked up the telephone. He gazed at the wall until his number came to him and dialed.

The answering machine replied. Jack left a message and

tried Gail's number, but she was not home. He stood in the hall for a minute, wondering what to do. He could throw his things together, call a taxi and take the train back to London for the weekend, come back Tuesday or Wednesday for his car. Or he could stay here until his car was fixed, and put up with whatever else the Bates's devised to antagonise him in the meantime.

He chewed his lip as he considered the options. He didn't feel like travelling on public transport tonight. And he couldn't believe the Bates's would try anything else after this afternoon's little stunt—at least not for a day or two.

No, he'd stay in Beckford tonight and then head back to London tomorrow morning. Matter resolved, he went into the kitchen and made himself some dinner. He was eating an orange and watching an Australian soap when the telephone rang. He scampered into the hall and picked up the phone with sticky fingers.

"Hello? Jack? Is that you?"

"Of course it's me. Hi, Gail. How are you?"

"Jack, what's happened? Why aren't you coming home?"

"I explained on the answering machine, didn't I?"

"You just said something was wrong with the car and you wouldn't be able to come back yet."

"Yeah, that's right. The engine's . . . er . . . broken."

"What do you mean, broken?"

"It's, er, packed in." He didn't want to tell her that it had been vandalised. She would only worry.

"Well . . . what exactly's wrong with it?"

"I don't know. I came back from the funeral and it wouldn't start. It's just . . . knackered. The garage have got it now."

"Maybe it's the starter motor."

"Yeah, maybe. I don't know anything about cars. You're the mechanical one."

"Did they say how long it would be?"

"Monday at the earliest. Could be as late as Wednesday."

"You're joking."

" 'Fraid not."

"So what are you going to do?"

"I thought I'd come home on the train tomorrow, then pop back and fetch the car next week."

"*Pop back and fetch it?* But it's a mammoth train journey."

"Yeah, but there's not much alternative, is there?"

"Couldn't you get the RAC to bring the car back to London?"

"Not really. I haven't got round to renewing my membership yet," Jack admitted sheepishly.

"Oh, Jack, you prize klutz!" Gail exclaimed. "How many times have I reminded you about that?"

"I'd say . . . fifty million."

"At least." She sighed, was silent for a moment. Then she said, "I've got a suggestion."

"What's that?"

"Why don't I come and spend the weekend with you?"

Jack felt a twinge of alarm, thinking of the potential threat from the Bates's and their cronies, and his reluctance for her to be involved. "I dunno," he said. "It's not very exciting here."

"What, with all those ghosts and bikers?" she tried to joke. Then she went on quickly, as though afraid she was giving him reasons for putting her off, "I'm not bothered about that. I just want to see you."

"We-ell," he prevaricated.

"Oh, come on, Jack, you know it makes sense. I'm not working next week, so I could stay until the car's fixed and then we could drive back together."

Jack thought of Patty Bates again, and almost immediately felt a surge of indignation. Gail's suggestion was a sensible one. Why should the possibility of what Bates might do even be an issue? "Okay," he conceded, "you ring me later and let me know what train you'll be getting and I'll meet you at the station. But you've got to let me pay for your fare."

"We'll sort that out later. I'm teaching in the morning, but I should be finished around twelve. I'll get a train as soon after that as I can."

"Okay. God, I can't wait to see you."

"Me too."

Now that she'd put forward the idea of visiting Beckford, Jack found he was quickly warming to it. He was surprised to discover that he was actually looking forward to showing her the house and the woods, that he felt a kind of pride in them. "I can read you some of my dad's stories," he said.

"Yeah," replied Gail noncommittally, and then, "By the way, how did the funeral go?"

"Oh . . . it was okay. You know what these things are like. Morbid. Depressing. Not many people came."

"I'm sorry."

"It doesn't matter. Tell me how your day's been. And what's been happening in the world? I haven't seen a paper since I got here and I've only caught snatches of the news."

They chatted for a while. Gail told Jack that she might take herself along to the NFT later if she didn't feel too tired. They were showing Resnais' *Last Year in Marienbad,* a film she adored and had already seen three times.

"So what are you doing tonight?" she asked him.

"Oh, I don't know. Read some more of my dad's stories. Watch TV. Do some work. Play some music."

"Sounds nice."

"It'd be nicer if you were here."

"Goes without saying."

Jack made a sound of acknowledgement in his throat, then sighed. "Oh well," he said, "better go."

"Don't want to keep Sandra waiting," said Gail.

"Who's Sandra?"

"Your fancy woman."

Jack grinned. "No, no, it was Sandra last night. It's Betty tonight."

"Is she as nice as me?"

"Nowhere near."

"Good job. 'Cos if she was I'd come round there right now and duff her in."

Jack laughed. "You're such a violent person." He puffed out air in another loud sigh. "You know, I'd really psyched myself up for Maxi's tonight."

"Maxi's, eh? Never mind, sweetie, it'll be something to look forward to."

"Yeah, suppose so. You'll ring me later then?"

"Yeah, when I've found out the train times."

Jack waited until Gail had put the phone down, then put it down himself. The hallway was gloomy and cold. He went back into the sitting room, massaging his ear where he'd pressed the receiver too hard against it. He ought to build a fire, but he was still wearing his suit from the funeral. It was already crumpled, but that was no reason to get coal dust all over it as well. He switched on the lamps, put on an Elvis Costello CD, then went upstairs and changed into his jeans and sweater. If he was going to be here all weekend he'd have to wash some of his clothes, but he couldn't be bothered to do it now; it could wait until the morning. He went back downstairs to make a fire and paused in the hallway by the telephone, realising his aunt didn't know he was still here. He ought to tell her before she heard it on the village grapevine and thought he was avoiding her. He picked up the phone and rang her. She expressed concern and sympathy when he told her about the car, but secretly Jack thought she was pleased he would be staying longer, especially when he told her that Gail would be arriving tomorrow.

As he put the phone down he wondered how the meeting between Gail and his aunt would go. It was only now, as he tried to picture the confrontation, that he realised they were similar in many ways. "Wow, Jack, Oedipus complex," he muttered to himself. Though Georgina was not his mother, she had been a surrogate mother to him, the woman he had looked to in his childhood. And now he had fallen for a woman who, like her, was independent, broached no nonsense and yet was infinitely caring. Jack wondered, not for the first time, what his own mother had been like. He thought of her paintings, pictured her working on them quietly and contentedly, and he felt a lump rise to his throat.

He made a fire, poured himself a whiskey and lit a cigarette. He was torn between reading his father's stories and doing some work. He knew he ought to work, but he was drawn to the blue notebooks by an instinctive and voracious desire. He drew on his cigarette as he struggled with his conscience, then he reached down and picked up one of the notebooks. He had a long evening ahead of him. There was no reason why he couldn't read first and then work later.

Because that afternoon's events had unsettled him, he thought he might have to concentrate a little harder than usual, but this was not the case; he slipped into the first of his father's stories quickly and effortlessly. He hadn't known this since childhood, this utter absorption in written fiction. It was akin to falling under the influence of a hypnotist. His surroundings dissolved, and even the physical act of reading—holding the book, his eyes travelling across and down the lines of his father's scrawl—became subliminal. Time became meaningless, his body's cravings subsided as in sleep. Jack became a willing slave to The Story; he would serve it for as long as it required him. Just as Jack had an inexorable hunger to read, The Story had an inexorable hunger to be read. It was almost akin to a physical need that worked both ways, a mutual parasitism. Jack felt all this subconsciously, and yet he also felt that the act was a positive one. Like sex, it was purging, loving, shattering, fulfilling.

Three hours after he had begun, Jack looked up and

blinked as if someone had clicked their fingers in front of his face. He scanned back and saw that he had read fourteen more of the stories. The last, entitled *Sitting on the Stairs,* was dated 8/8/94. A piece of coal shifted in the grate, drawing Jack's attention. He hauled himself up from the settee and tormented the fire back to life with the poker, then added more coal. His mind felt clear, sharp as a razor. Reading the stories had pepped him up, roused his imagination, made him eager to work. He would make some coffee and then write until he became tired. The idea excited him. He would only go to bed when he felt like it; he would not be constrained by the conventions of time, or even by darkness and light. He went out of the sitting room, rolling his head from side to side, aware of the crackle of his bones, and finding it a pleasurable experience. Jack had once toyed with the idea of taking up karate, but in the end had decided he did not have the necessary commitment, the required predilection for self-discipline. What had attracted him to the idea had not been the self-defence aspect, but the prospect of being vitally aware and in control of his own mental and physical being. He felt that way now; it was as if the separate components that made up Jack Stone had slipped into perfect alignment, creating an incredible harmony, a perfect pattern within which it might just be possible to glimpse some unbelievable truth.

He was filling the kettle at the sink when there came a loud, steady knocking—five beats—on the front door. Jack was so startled that, as he turned, he pulled the kettle round with him and water from the tap battered off the curving metal side and drenched him. "Bloody hell!" he shouted. He put the kettle down, turned off the tap and mopped himself with a tea towel. The knocking came again. "Just a minute," he muttered. He balled up the tea towel and dumped it on the kitchen table, then crept through the hall to the front door and pressed his ear to the wood.

He could hear nothing, but what did he expect? "Who is it?" he called and was pleased at the strength in his voice.

The sound of a female voice surprised him. "Mr. Stone? Jack? It's me, Tracey."

Tracey? Tracey Bates? Jack was astounded. How could she possibly have the gall to come here? "What do you want?" he demanded.

"I wondered if I could talk to you for a minute."

"What about?"

"It's about what's been going on. I just wanted to explain."

"What the bloody hell is there to explain?"

"If you'll open the door, I'll tell you."

Jack's fingers rested on the door handle, but did not turn it. The prospect of an explanation intrigued him, for how could she possibly justify her actions? Yet on the other hand this might be a ploy for her and her cronies to gain entry. He imagined Tracey Bates standing at the head of half a dozen bikers who were holding their breaths to keep quiet, trying not to giggle. The one who looked like Lemmy would be there, hefting the sledgehammer he had used to disable Jack's car. The others would be clasping pieces of wood or oily chains. Jack imagined the chains swaying and catching the moonlight.

"Do you really think I'm that stupid?" Jack said.

"What?"

"Opening the door to you and your friends? If you don't fuck off now I'm calling the police."

"For God's sake, I'm on my own. I walked here."

"Sure you did."

"I did! Honestly! Look, if we wanted to get to you, we would. We could drive a motorbike through the front door or smash all the windows without anyone hearing a thing."

What she had said was true, but Jack still thought that opening the door was a bad idea. "Look," he said, "I think you're in enough trouble as it is. The police already know what you did to my car, and if you don't leave I'll tell them about the other night as well, when you tried to kill me."

"We didn't try to kill you, it was only—"

"A bit of fun? Sure. What do you do for an encore? Set fire to people's houses when they're asleep?"

Tracey's reply was sulky. "How were we to know you'd overreact?"

"*Overreact?* Jeez, I don't believe this. How do you think *you'd* react, given the circumstances?"

He heard her sigh, as if he were being tiresome. "Look," she said, "are you going to let me in or not?"

"Not," said Jack.

"Oh, for Christ's sake, it's bloody cold out here."

"My heart bleeds for you."

She sighed again, deeper this time. Jack was enjoying her exasperation.

"Please, Jack," she wheedled. "Can't we let bygones be bygones? I only wanted to say I was sorry."

"So now you've said it. Good-bye."

He leapt back as something slammed against the door, making it vibrate. Here it comes, he thought, Lemmy's sledgehammer. But the sound was not repeated. Instead he heard a sliding sound and then, from knee-level, sobbing.

He waited, trying to decide whether this was all part of the ploy. If he opened the door would she lunge for him, grabbing him round the knees and knocking him off balance? Would her friends swarm over him and into the house, stinking of booze and leather and dirt? How could Jack find out if she really was alone? And then all at once he realised. He turned and raced up the stairs as nimbly and silently as he could.

He sped along the landing, bypassing his bedroom and the bathroom. He paused only for a second outside the door to his father's room, expelling a quick breath like a runner, before opening the door and stepping inside. Moonlight glowed on the other side of the drawn curtains, a dull lemony sheen. The texture of the darkness inside the room was grainy, rough, like black tweed.

Jack felt as though the darkness were wisping across his face and the backs of his hands as he stepped to the window. He took an edge of curtain between the index finger and thumb of his right hand and twitched it back. There was enough moonlight to see that the front garden, Daisy Lane and the surrounding fields were empty. Unless all the bikers, like Tracey, were crammed against the front door or hiding around the sides of the house, she was telling the truth.

Gritting his teeth against the sound of its squealing hinges, Jack pushed open the narrow window at the left-hand side, which would be directly above Tracey Bates' head. He leaned over the sill and peered out. She had been telling the truth about the cold, too; the wind which pressed against his cheeks and forehead was so icy it would make his skull ache before long. Tracey was sitting on the stoop, head resting against the door. Her blonde hair fanned out like a golden cone, obscuring most of her face. She looked to be sleeping or exhausted. Jack ducked back in, pulling the window closed, and ran across the room, along the landing and down the stairs, taking them two at a time. He unlocked the front door as quietly as he could, then took the handle in his hand, twisted it and tugged it open. Tracey cried out, her hands slapping the floor as she sprawled across the threshold. "Come in then," said Jack. When she gaped up at him, tearful and confused, he added gruffly, "Hurry up or I'm shutting this door again."

She got the message and pulled herself, crab-like, into the hallway. The charge from behind her, which Jack had been half-anticipating, did not come; nevertheless, he slammed the door shut and turned the key in the lock so fiercely that he hurt his hand.

"Right then," he said, "what is it you wanted to say?"

She looked at him with wide eyes and then got slowly to her feet. "I'm cold," she said, drawing the word out, making it shudder. She crossed her arms tightly across her chest and rubbed her shoulders. "Can I sit by the fire?"

Jack did not reply at once. He was very wary; he felt there was an ulterior motive in everything she said and did. At last he replied grudgingly, "Okay. Go on."

He followed her into the sitting room, keeping a little distance between them in case she should suddenly snatch something from her jacket, or even an ornament from the table, and threaten him with it. She released a moan of pleasure at the warmth of the room, crossed immediately to the fire and crouched before it, holding out her hands.

"That's better," she said. "I'm freezing."

"It's not that cold," replied Jack.

"It is when you've walked two miles. The wind that blows down that lane is evil."

"You should wear warmer clothes," he said reprovingly.

She smiled at that and turned back to the fire. Jack understood that smile perfectly. It would have translated as: Warmer clothes? You must be joking. I'd rather freeze to death than be seen in a scarf and woolly mitts.

What depressed him was the fact that fifteen years ago that was his attitude, too. For the second time in Tracey's company, he thought how staid, how horribly mature he had become.

He skirted around the edge of the settee and perched himself on the arm, a couple of feet behind Tracey. Her hair shimmered, catching the light. Jack was close enough now to smell her fabulous smell. Despite himself, he breathed it in deeply, relishing it. He wondered whether to offer her coffee, but decided not to because he wanted to keep her within sight at all times, wanted to control the situation. Even now, he wasn't sure if he had the upper hand; he felt nervous and awkward despite his anger.

"Look," he said in a dry, almost weary voice, "could we get this over with? You're interrupting my work."

She turned, wiping the last of her (crocodile?) tears

from her eyes, leaving smudges of mascara. "Were you writing?"

"Yes."

"What is it you're working on?"

"A new book. I told you."

"Oh, yeah. Is it going well?"

"Well enough," he said, "but never mind that. You said you'd come here to explain."

She rolled her eyes and tutted. "My, my, we are uptight, aren't we?"

"Hardly surprising, is it?" he snapped. "I've been victimised for no reason, my car's been wrecked—"

"Oh, come on," Tracey protested, "it wasn't wrecked."

Jack stared at her openmouthed; for a few seconds he was literally struck dumb by her audacity. Then a strangled sound lurched from his throat, releasing his words. "I don't believe you just said that. Do you know how much money that fucking damage you idiots did is going to cost me?"

Tracey looked sullen. "No."

"About fifteen hundred pounds! And for what? So that you and your dirty, brainless, fucking . . . gits of friends could have a laugh at my expense."

His heart was beating so hard it was making his head throb. Jack felt hot, almost dizzy with rage. Tracey was still staring at him, but he thought he now saw caution in her eyes. "I'm sorry for what happened," she said evenly. "It was never meant to go that far."

"Then why did it?" Jack said. "What have I ever done to you?"

"Nothing," said Tracey. She shrugged. "You made Boxer jealous."

"I did what? Who the fuck's Boxer?"

"He's my boyfriend. It was him who smashed up your car. Well . . . him and a couple of the other lads. He was really pissed off when he found out it had stopped you leaving today."

Jack's anger was beginning to ebb a little, leaving a backwash of exhaustion, depression, confusion. He brought a hand up to his forehead, tried unsuccessfully to massage the throbbing ache out of it. "I don't understand," he said. "Why the hell would he be jealous of me?"

Tracey was silent for a moment. She turned and looked into the fire, the movement releasing a faint waft of her delicious scent. When she spoke her voice was both apologetic and defiant. "Because I told him I loved you," she said.

"You did what?" Jack's heart, which had been slowing to its normal rhythm, began to thud again. He felt anger, alarm, disbelief at her words.

"I told him I loved you," she repeated, and there was more than defiance in her voice this time. She swung round, her jacket jangling, and fixed him with those glorious blue eyes. There was a pinpoint of light, like a golden stud, in the centre of each pupil. "And it's true, Jack. I do love you."

Despite himself, he felt his cheeks getting hot and knew that he was flushing. This couldn't be true; of course it couldn't. This was another of Tracey Bates' vicious games. And yet her statement had thrown him off balance, was enabling her to manipulate the situation once again. He struggled to organise his thoughts, to defuse her outrageous statement before it enabled her to tighten her control.

"Don't be ridiculous. You don't even know me," was all he could think of to say.

"I *do*," she insisted as though she had anticipated his reaction. She leaned towards him, her face earnest. "I've read all your books, Jack, and I feel I know you intimately, that I've been party to your innermost thoughts."

Jack tried to laugh; it had a hollow ring. "My books aren't about me," he said. "They're just words on paper, made-up stories."

Tracey smiled sweetly, indulgently, at him. "Oh, come on, Jack, you can't fool me. I know you too well."

She reached out for him. Her hand would have closed

over his thigh if he hadn't jumped up. He swung his leg over the arm of the settee and away from her, almost falling in his haste. "Stop this!" he shouted, as if at a dog. "This is crap. Just piss off, leave me alone."

Tracey stood up languorously, taking her time, removing her leather jacket with a single shrug. It slithered to the floor with a soft, metallic sound. Beneath the jacket she was wearing a white blouse of very thin material, through which could clearly be seen the soft pink of her skin, the outline of her white bra.

"What's the matter, Jack?" she said teasingly. "Don't you find me attractive?"

He was sweating, backpedalling, on the defensive. He knew this was nonsense and that he had to put a stop to it. "That isn't the point," he said. "Look, just stop this now, or I'll . . . I'll—"

"You'll what?" she purred.

"I'll make you leave."

She laughed. "Oh, I'm sure you don't want that. Do you? Not really?"

"Yes," said Jack, "I do. You've no right to come here and behave like this."

"But I love you, Jack," she crooned, still smiling, still moving slowly toward him.

The dining table shuddered as Jack backed into it. "No, you don't. You're just making fun of me, playing games. I don't have to take this."

"I'm *not* playing games, Jack. I love you." She halted in the middle of the floor, sighed, seemed to come to a decision. Then to Jack's horror—and shameful desire—she began to unbutton her blouse.

"Stop that!" he shouted. "What the hell do you think you're doing?"

"I'm all yours, Jack. I want you to know that. I want to give myself to you, to prove my love."

She took off her blouse and dropped it on the floor. Jack

was sweating heavily now, wondering whether he should grab her, propel her bodily from the house. But although his libido had turned traitor, was sending blood rushing to his penis, he felt loath to actually touch her flesh.

He held up both hands, showing her his palms in a halting gesture. "Put that back on," he said firmly. "This has gone too far. You're making a fool of yourself."

Her only response was to lift up each leg in turn in order to remove her high-heeled boots, then to unbutton and unzip her jeans. "Oh shit," he said as she peeled her jeans down her long legs and kicked them off. She was standing now in white bra, white ankle socks and a skimpy pair of white panties with tiny orange spots.

Jack couldn't think what to do. Should he leave the room, call someone? It wasn't as if he could force her to get dressed again; she wasn't a child. He cleared his throat, a staccato sound in the warm room. "Look," he said in the calmest tone he could muster, "this is getting out of hand. I think you should put your clothes on and go."

She smiled, reached behind her and took off her bra.

"No!" Jack cried and stepped toward her, holding out his hand. He halted, confused. What could he do? What *could* he do? The girl's nakedness should have made her vulnerable, reduced her power, but conversely it seemed to have put her into a position of strength. Jack didn't know where to look. Tracey was so stunning, so desirable, that he wanted to feast his eyes on her, but to have done that would have been to pander to her wishes, to fall under her spell. He looked desperately into her eyes, trying not to allow his gaze to fall to her breasts, but even that threatened to be too much. All her love, her adoration—authentic or not—was there. She smiled at him in an almost soporific way, parted her lips, revealing small white teeth, and prodded a tongue that was delicate and pink and gleaming with spittle between them.

Jack was at the door now, but he did not want to leave

the room, to leave her alone. She stepped forward, pulled a chair from beneath the dining table, removed her panties and sat down.

"Oh God," he said, looking up at the ceiling. This was agony. She spoke for the first time in what seemed like minutes, her soft purr lapping his ears, filling the room.

"Why resist me, Jack? I'm beautiful, aren't I?"

"Yes." He felt choked by his own self-denial. "Yes, you're beautiful, but . . . this isn't right."

"But I love you," she said with inexorable logic.

Jack swiped sweat from his face. "But *I* don't love *you*," he said. "I love someone else."

"Your other girlfriend?"

"My *only* girlfriend. Yes."

"But you've got me now. You don't need her anymore. There's no need to feel guilty about that. We'll tell her together if you like."

"What?" Jack felt as though this entire argument was slipping away from him. "What do you mean? Tell her what?"

"That we're together now, that she's no longer needed."

Jack glanced at her sharply and then wished he hadn't. His libido flared.

"Look," he said quietly, firmly, "we're not together. You know that and I know that. We both know also that this is just a game, it isn't real. I have a girlfriend who I love very much and who I'm going to marry. Now what I want you to do is put your clothes on and leave my house. Whatever you're doing this for, it won't work. Do you understand?"

There was no immediate answer, no sound of any kind, and for one absurd moment Jack thought Tracey had seen sense and taken his advice, had got dressed and left, all in the twinkling of an eye. He risked a look to his right, to where he knew she'd been sitting. The twin forks of passion and alarm jabbed hard at him again when he saw that she was still sitting there, still naked but for her white ankle socks. Now, however, there was a peculiar expression on her face, an expression that Jack did not like at all. It made him think of an approaching storm, of black clouds massing on the horizon. Her eyes were hooded, jaw tight, lips pursed. At last, in an icy voice, she said, "Getting married."

A big red danger signal began flashing in Jack's head. "What?" he said, trying to make his voice strong, authoritative.

She glanced at him so sharply that her breasts wobbled, causing Jack a further pang of longing. "Getting married," she repeated. "You said you were getting married."

"That's right," Jack said, "to my girlfriend." He didn't point out that he hadn't actually *asked* Gail yet. Maybe the information would be enough to bring Tracey to her senses, make her realise how foolish she had been. His optimism was short-lived. Tracey curled her lips into a snarl and shouted:

"No!"

Jack was so taken aback that he stepped straight into the half-open door, bumping his head. "Pardon?" he exclaimed.

"You can't marry that bitch. You *can't!*" She rose from the chair, the muscles of her body taut now, standing out like an athlete's. Jack would not have believed it possible, but her fury was making her ugly.

"Tell me you won't!" she screamed. Before Jack could even begin to reply, she repeated, shrieking, *"Tell me!"*

"Shit," Jack muttered. He held up his hands as if pushing a car. "Look," he said soothingly, "just calm down, okay? You're getting overexcited."

He wasn't sure if it was his tone that placated her, but Tracey stopped yelling. However, her voice, when she next spoke, was low and dangerous, which wasn't much better.

"Just tell me," she said. "You can't marry that woman, Jack. Tell me you won't."

She was glaring at him, her expression a horrifying paradox of intensity and emptiness. It was the look of a fanatic, of one whose mind careered along a single track, out of control.

Jack had no idea how to respond. Weakly he said, "Why?"

She jerked her head, flashed her teeth, as if tearing at the word as it emerged. *"Why?"* she repeated scornfully. "What do you mean, *why?* Why do you think? Are you fucking stupid or something?"

"No, I don't think so," said Jack.

"Then why ask why? It's fucking obvious, isn't it? It's bloody fucking obvious. Because I *love* you, Jack. If you marry that other woman you'll be making a big mistake. We were made to be together. You don't think I get naked for just anybody, do you?"

He flapped a hand. "But I don't *want* this. Don't you understand. I don't . . ." His throat closed over his voice, choked it. What was the use? The girl would not understand. Her mind discarded logic. It refused to stick to conventional rules of thought and conduct.

"We'll get married, Jack," she told him, her voice suddenly, shockingly, gentle once more. She spoke as if this would reassure him, as if it were the blindingly obvious answer to all their problems. "I'll love you and I'll make you happy and I'll do anything you want me to."

She padded towards him, balletic, cat-like. Jack slid along the wall, away from her.

"No," he ordered. "Listen to me, Tracey. I don't love you. I'm not going to marry you. I'm going to marry my girlfriend, Gail. I want you to put on your clothes and leave this house and don't come back. If you do that, we'll forget everything that's happened. Okay?"

Abruptly her face changed, and it was terrifying. Jack suddenly understood that Tracey's behaviour thus far had been restrained, her anger no more than the tip of the iceberg. He floundered backwards as she howled like an animal, sprinted the few steps between them, and leaped at him.

"No!" he heard her screech. *"It's not okay!"* The rest of her words, of which there were many, were swamped by the incoherence of her rage, by Jack's own cries, by the chaos of their struggle.

Jack caught a glimpse of hooked talons tipped with red swooping at him and he twisted away. Searing pain raked the side of his face, whilst more pain—like a deflected punch—smeared across his nose and lip. Tracey's naked body hit him hard, slamming the breath from him, sending him staggering back until he became the sandwich filling between girl and wall. Immediately her limbs began to flail at him, her nails to scratch, her teeth to bite. Jack spun and bucked in an effort to shake her from him, groped for her wrists to prevent her clawing out his eyes. He bent low, hunched his shoulders to protect himself, cupped a hand over his genitals, as something—probably her knee—whacked into his thigh, too close for comfort. He was receiving a beating from this slip of a girl, the violence coming so fast that he could do little to prevent it. His free hand groped at empty air, only occasionally encountering smooth hot flesh that slithered from his grasp like a snake before he could fasten onto it. He was shouting at her to stop, but he knew it was futile. She was like a wild animal; she might as well have been one for all the notice she took. The room spun around him, interspersed with glimpses of white flesh, the whirl of golden hair, a screeching, gnashing face. All at once his heel caught on something that was not fastened down. It skidded from under his foot, toppling him onto his back. His head hit something that was hard but padded, most likely an item of furniture. The threat of unconsciousness—white sparks dying in blackness—fizzed in his mind's eye. Jack tried to breathe and a weight landed heavily on his stomach, knocking the wind from him. When his vision cleared he saw Tracey sitting on his midriff, her back to him. Panic clutched him when he realised she was pawing at his genitals, trying to undo his trousers.

"Hey!" he shouted and began to struggle. "Hey! What are you doing? Get off me!"

She clenched her knees tight against his hips, pressing painfully on the bone. At the same time, she leaned forward to spread her weight, raising her buttocks in the air, giving him a candid view of her anus and vagina.

"Get off me!" he yelled again. "Get off me!" He pushed at the backs of her thighs, trying to heave her off him, but she was lithe and incredibly strong. He felt looseness around his hips as his jeans slackened, heard the metallic rip of his fly. His erection—to his undying shame, aching and full—sprang upright as it was released from his boxer shorts, which were being pushed roughly down to his knees. I'm being raped, Jack thought with a sense of wonderment, I'm being raped by a girl half my age and size.

It was a ridiculous, unbelievable situation, and yet it was happening. Jack cried out, not entirely without pleasure, as something warm and wet closed over his penis. Gripping both of Tracey's thighs hard just beneath her buttocks, he braced himself, then heaved again with all his might, trying to raise himself into a sitting position.

She struggled but Jack shoved relentlessly, and gradually began to gain the upper hand. His temples ached with the effort; sweat pimpled his body. He shouted in pain, but only increased his grip, when he felt her teeth biting down, scraping over his penis. But suddenly his penis came free, sliding from her mouth and springing back against his belly.

"You fucking bastard," he heard her snarl. She swung an arm round, clubbing the side of his head, making his ear ring and sparks leap across his vision. Jack lunged forward and bit her hard on the right buttock. She yelped, the shock causing her to lose some of her strength, enabling him to push her up and to one side like a heavy rock.

As she sprawled across the floor, limbs splayed, Jack leaped to his feet, dragging up his jeans and boxer shorts. One of the dining chairs had been knocked over in their struggle, the settee barged out of position, presumably by his falling body. He was now beginning to feel the results of his battering. His left shin, left bicep and ribs seemed to have taken the brunt of her violence. He was panting hard. As she struggled to her feet he swung the settee between them like a shield, castors squealing. She glared at him, hair hanging in front of her face. She looked more animal than human.

"That's enough," Jack gasped. Considering the circumstances, the comment was almost risible. Tracey's panties were lying on the floor less than two feet away from him. He bent down quickly, scooped them up and tossed them to her. "Get dressed," he ordered. The panties landed on her left foot. Tracey did not acknowledge them, merely continued to glare at him. Jack almost leaped out of his skin when the telephone began to ring. That'll be Gail, he thought, but he made no move to answer the phone and eventually it stopped.

The stalemate lasted for perhaps thirty seconds. Just when Jack was beginning to wonder what the next move would be, Tracey spoke. Her voice was low, her tone vicious. She said, "You won't get away with this, you bastard."

Despite himself, he was again taken aback by the comment. He didn't realise how dry his throat was until he croaked, "Get away with *what?*"

"Don't pretend you don't know. You've cheated me. Well, I'll fucking get you yet. Just you wait and see."

Jack felt suddenly furious. He wanted to hit out at something—the wall, anything—but he managed to restrain himself. Heart thudding uncomfortably, he snapped, "Oh? And what do you propose to do?"

She smiled slowly, craftily. "I'll tell them you raped me.

I'll tell them you got me pregnant. Then they'll make you marry me."

Jack barked a hard, scornful laugh. "Don't be stupid. Nobody would believe you. There's no evidence."

She spun round, looking back over her shoulder through a screen of hair. "Oh, no? What's this then?" She pointed at the purpling crescent of teeth marks on her bottom.

"That doesn't prove anything," said Jack. Nevertheless, he felt feelers of uncertainty impinging on his rage. It certainly didn't prove that he'd raped her, but what if she said he'd assaulted her, attempted to rape her? That kind of wound would prove pretty damn hard to explain away.

"It's a start," she told him. "I don't think I'd have much trouble making people believe what I wanted them to."

"You just try it," said Jack, "see how far you get." But he was worried now, could feel anxiety churning in the pit of his stomach. Had Tracey and Patty planned this all along? And if so, in which direction did they now intend to take it? If they took it to the police, Jack could be in trouble, particularly if the Bates's saw fit to concoct more evidence against him. All Tracey had to do was get someone to rough her up a bit, tear her clothes. If, on the other hand, the Bates's decided to take matters into their own hands, to play on public outrage, then Jack could be in even worse trouble. He watched her getting dressed, his mind racing. He considered pleading with her, appealing to her better nature, even threatening her, but doing that would be like admitting he was in the wrong, and so he remained silent. Besides, he didn't want to give the Bates's the satisfaction of thinking they had him over a barrel. No, the best thing was simply to say nothing and hope that Tracey's threat was no more than that, and that the whole thing would blow over. In any event, Jack decided, tomorrow he would revert to his original plan. He would ring Gail and tell her he was coming back to London.

Tracey watched Jack as she dressed slowly, a mocking

smile on her face. The silence between them was weighted and unpleasant, but neither seemed inclined to break it. Jack had no qualms now about looking at Tracey's body. Despite her beauty, despite his treacherous erection, she now repulsed him. She tucked her white blouse into the waistband of her jeans, pulled her boots towards her, sat on the floor and tugged them on. Then she picked up her leather jacket, swung it arrogantly over her shoulder and sauntered to the door.

Jack followed at a safe distance. Her heels clacked on the wooden floor, perfect bottom swaying from side to side. At the front door she turned the key in the lock and placed her hand on the handle, but before pulling the door open she half-turned and regarded him.

"I'm going now, but I'll be back," she said. "You'll never be rid of me, Jack Stone, Mr. Famous Writer." She blew him a mocking, poisonous kiss. Then she opened the door, stepped out and walked away.

The instant she was out of the house, Jack ran to the door, slammed it behind her and locked it. Immediately, a huge surge of relief swept through his body, but it took his strength and self-control with it. He began to shake, his legs buckled and he sank slowly to the floor. Ice cubes jitterbugged in his belly; he felt an urge to scrub himself clean. He leaned against the door, listening, shuddering, for a long time.

15

ARRIVALS

At first light Jack set off into the woods, hoping a walk would ease his mind. Already a pale sun was glimmering in the sky, birds were singing, a cool fragrant wind gently ruffling his tousled hair, whispering messages of wordless comfort.

He had been unable to sleep last night, had sat up fretting over the possible consequences of his encounter with Tracey. At times he had felt almost hopeful, had half-managed to convince himself that she wouldn't dare say anything. But there had been low spots, too, times when he had castigated himself for his inability to handle the situation. He should never have allowed things to get so out of hand. The moment she had started coming out with all that "love" crap he should have nipped the situation in the bud, ejected her from the house, physically if necessary. And why, oh why, had he bitten her? It was like leaving fingerprints at a crime scene. What was worse was that he had been unable to get through to Gail; until he did that he was effectively stuck in Beckford. There had been no reply at her flat last night or again this morning, and when he had called her mobile he had been diverted to her voice mail. She must have gone to see the film with a friend and then stayed over so she wouldn't have to go home alone, must have switched off her mobile last night and not turned it on again.

Jack had never met any of Gail's friends; like him, she had become so entrenched in their couple mentality that her platonic relationships had suffered. If he continued to be unable to reach her on her mobile, Jack knew that his only hope was to call the Education Department, find out where she was teaching and get a message to her. And if *that* failed, he guessed he would have to hang around here until she arrived. Perhaps they could spend a long weekend in Leeds or York—if the police didn't pick him up in the meantime and charge him with attempted rape.

He trudged between the trees, stepping over roots, weighed down with worry. If Tracey did manage to make the accusation stick, what would it do to his career, his relationship with Gail? Even if the case went to court and he was found not guilty, there would always be a stigma attached to him, a suspicion. He pictured himself trying to explain away the bite mark to a packed courtroom.

"Yes, milord, I know I'm twice the size of the girl, but biting her arse was the only way I could escape. She had me down on the floor and was trying to rape me."

The thought of it made Jack cringe. He had never realised before how easy it was to become so horribly trapped by circumstances.

Sighing, he came to a grassy bank where the dew was glittering in the sunshine and sat down. A few feet in front of him trees lined the edge of a valley, which cut a swathe through the earth for perhaps half a mile. In some places the incline was gentle; in others—like here—the drop was steep and sudden. Jack could hear water burbling somewhere, watched a ladybug manfully struggling to the sum-

mit of a grass stem. Fifty yards to his left, partly obscured
by trees, the main path through the woods—of dusty
packed earth, blotched with tufts of grass like green
mould—meandered across a bridge over the valley, which
was so old and crumbling and overgrown with foliage that
it seemed a natural part of the landscape.

The dew was soaking into his clothes, but Jack didn't
care. He lay back in the long grass and immediately felt as
if the soft ground were rising up to envelop him. Yesterday
at the funeral, the thought of burial had made the earth
seem cold and black, repellent, but today Jack thought
how wonderful it would be to lie here forever, bereft of responsibilities, gradually becoming part of nature like the
bridge. He closed his eyes. The sunlight, filtering through
his eyelids, turned his world a deep soothing orange.
Something tickled his top lip—an insect or a wind-blown
seed; Jack felt too indolent to brush it away.

If he couldn't get through to Gail, then presumably she
would call him to let him know what time her train was
due to arrive. On the other hand, she might simply turn up
and make her own way to the house—she had the address.
Jack wanted to contact her before anything happened. He
wanted to tell her the truth about last night before her
mind became poisoned with lies. The worst scenario
would be her turning up in Beckford only to find he was
being held in custody, charged with indecent assault.

Jack was so deep in thought that he lost all sense of
time and place. When a shadow passed over him, cool and
dark, he frowned and shivered. A second later, however,
the sun was back, a warm red sea washing across his
closed eyelids. Jack grunted and snuggled down, half-
thinking he was snoozing in bed.

"Jack."

The word, quietly spoken, oozed languorously into his
consciousness, like a rock sinking through treacle. Long
seconds passed before the implications of that word pene-

trated his mind, and then it was as though an electric probe had been thrust into his nerve endings. Jack jerked upright so suddenly that his neck cricked. He opened gritty eyes and immediately light gushed into them, blinding him. He threw up an arm, squinting at his bleached surroundings. Through a painful explosion of sunlight he half-saw a figure standing ten yards away, facing him. He could not see the figure's face, and even its silhouette was unclear, but Jack got the impression he was looking at an old man, thin and slightly stooped. All at once a smell touched his nostrils—freshly turned dirt. The smell caused his stomach and bowels to contract with nervous excitement. Before he could think to say or do anything the figure turned and walked away.

For a moment Jack stared stupidly after it, dismayed by its departure. Then he opened his mouth and croaked, "Hey! Wait a minute." He pushed himself awkwardly to his feet, limbs stiff with last night's bruises. The strength of the sunlight was diminishing by degrees as his eyes adapted to it. The figure was some distance ahead, its dark bulk flitting between the trees that lined the lip of the valley. Jack felt disorientated. He rubbed his face as though it would clear his head and began to stumble after the figure.

He was getting used to the feeling of shock, of reaction, that sapped the strength from his limbs, but familiarity did not make the sensation any less unpleasant. His bruises throbbed like tiny hearts, his belly juddered like a motor. Despite the warmth, his fingers and the inside of his mouth were icy. He called after the figure as he ran but it didn't stop, and neither, to his annoyance, did it get any closer. It was always some distance ahead, just visible as a dark shape. It seemed to move effortlessly, drifting through the undergrowth like smoke.

Rounding a bend, Jack emerged into a small clearing. The trees to his left, marching down to meet the valley floor, were thin here, little more than stumps and saplings.

To his right was a bank that sloped up to a fence entangled with some kind of furzy bush. The trees petered out altogether on this side, displaying a vast sky populated by a battalion of albino-white clouds.

Jack looked right and left, but the figure was nowhere to be seen. He took his spectacles from the inside pocket of his leather jacket and put them on, wondering whether the figure was standing motionless against a tree some distance away, blurred into the landscape by his myopia. He peered at his surroundings anew, but all he saw were the woods. The only movement was caused by an occasional breeze stirring the grass, coaxing trees to bob their outermost shoots.

And then, at the top of the slope against a backdrop of sky, the figure appeared. It rose from the undergrowth as though it had been crouching behind it. Jack registered it as a peripheral blot of movement. When he swivelled to look at it more closely it was already turning away, hiding its face from view.

"Hey!" he shouted and began to lope up the bank toward it. He winced at the toll this took on his pummelled muscles, reached down to clutch fistfuls of grass with which to haul himself up. He reached the top of the slope, gasping. Beyond the fence was a field that contained a rusting bath in one of its muddy corners and perhaps a dozen grazing cows. The old man was already halfway across the field, moving away from him, the speed at which he progressed seeming at odds with his slowly shuffling feet. "Why do you run away from me all the time?" Jack shouted. The figure did not respond. Cursing, taking care not to snag himself, Jack climbed over the fence and dropped into the field.

A few cows regarded him stolidly before returning to their meal. Jack plodded after the old man. It was heavy going; the ground was soft beneath his feet and he was soon dripping with sweat. He wondered why his father was being so evasive. If he didn't want Jack to catch him, why show up at all? There was a truth to be learnt somewhere; Jack was certain. He had only to be dogged and insistent, to follow without question, to trust, and he would find it.

The tiny figure of the old man led him across four fields—another containing cows, one containing sheep that had either lambed or were just about to, and one that was ploughed and planted with a crop that looked to Jack like dock leaves. By now he had no idea where he was. He had never had much of a sense of direction. He was not even sure whether his father had led him in a straight line, a gentle curve or a complete circle. He was therefore startled when he came to the top of a small rise and saw his father's house below him.

He thought at first it was some malicious joke. He'd been led on a wild goose chase for no apparent reason. But looking behind him, and thinking about it, he quickly surmised that perhaps this wasn't the case. Considering how deeply he'd progressed into the woods, this was perhaps the most direct route back to the house. For some reason his father had wanted him to return here as quickly as possible. But why? There was no sign of the old man now.

Wearily Jack began to trudge down the hill toward the house. A cool breeze ruffled his hair and the grass. A band of sunlight swept silently across the land and over him, then onwards toward the house. The sunlight alighted greedily on the shiny places of the house—the slates and the windows—making them gleam briefly before passing on. But as shadow settled darkly on the stone once more, one window remained alight as if the sunlight had left a scrap of itself behind. Jack's eye was drawn to this window; it was the one—his father's bedroom. Before the glare of light faded, Jack saw the dark silhouette of the old man beckoning to him. Shakily he began to run.

Bursting in through the front door, Jack was confronted

by gloom and silence. He stood for a moment, bent almost double, rasping breath scorching his lungs, sweat bathing his body. He pulled off his jacket and tossed it over the carved wooden acorn at the foot of the stairs. Sucking in a deep breath he yelled, "Dad, I'm here!" The instant his foot touched the first step the phone began to ring.

"Hello?" Jack gasped into the receiver. "Is that you, Dad?"

The voice snarled only six words at him: "I'm coming for you, you bastard," before the connection was abruptly broken.

Despite the brevity of the message, Jack recognised the voice immediately. So Tracey Bates and her father had decided to play out this idiotic game to its bitter end, and it didn't look as though they were going to rely on the police to make their final moves for them. Jack replaced the receiver gently, went through to the kitchen and poured himself a glass of water. His hand shook as he drank it. He leaned on the sink and looked out at the cobbled backyard, trying to get his head together.

Obviously his father had wanted him to know of Bates' intentions, which was why he'd led him back to the house. Jack decided he mustn't let the advantage slip. He must work out the course of action that would ensure him the best chance of impunity. If he went to the police he'd have to explain about last night, which might backfire on him, especially if Tracey Bates contested his version of events. No, the best thing to do, especially since it looked as though the Bates's were interested only in their own brand of vigilante justice, was to get in touch with Gail and then get the hell out of Beckford as quickly as possible.

He went back into the hall and picked up the phone, praying that he would be able to get through to her. Fifteen minutes later he put the phone down for the sixth or seventh time, his options exhausted, his prayers unanswered. After trying her flat again on the off chance, and then leaving a message on his own answering machine in case she happened by, he had attempted to track her down via various education channels, all without success. He knew she was teaching in Lewisham, but the people he spoke to either couldn't or wouldn't help him. Jack suspected that after finishing work she would make straight for the station. Frustration flaring into anger, he punched the wall, denting it, bruising his hand. "Thank you, God," he muttered savagely. "Thank you so bloody much."

So that was it then. He had no choice. He had to stay in Beckford until Gail arrived. The only option now was to meet her off the train and then get straight on to another one going to, say, Leeds or Bradford. Picking up the receiver again, he dialed the number for travel information.

Five minutes later he was beginning to feel as though there were a conspiracy against him. If Gail was teaching until noon, there was only one train she could catch to Beckford, and that was the connecting train from Wakefield, which arrived at 6:52 P.M. That was all very well, but the last train *from* Beckford, going in the opposite direction, departed at eleven minutes past six.

"You're joking," Jack said upon hearing this information.

"Nope," replied the voice at the other end, almost smugly. "18:11 to Leeds, calling at—"

"Aren't there any local trains?"

Acidly, nonplussed at being interrupted, the voice said, "No, there aren't, I've told you. You'll have to leave a bit earlier, that's all."

"I can't," said Jack through gritted teeth. "I'm meeting someone off the 18:52 from London."

"Looks like you're stuck there then, doesn't it?" the voice said with not inconsiderable satisfaction.

"Hang on," said Jack. "What about that train, the 18:52? Surely that goes on somewhere?"

The voice sighed, then said, "18:52, Beckford to Manchester-Piccadilly. Arriving in Manchester at 20:08."

That was it then. When Gail arrived he would jump on the train and they would spend the night in Manchester. There were good hotels there, good restaurants. They could leave Patty Bates and his poisonous daughter far behind.

Throughout the rest of the afternoon he felt on edge, flying to the window each time he heard the slightest sound from outside. He washed some clothes by hand in the kitchen sink, not trusting the battered, rust-streaked washing machine in the corner of the kitchen. He kept the carving knife from the kitchen drawer and the poker from beside the fireplace close to hand at all times. If Patty Bates and his chums came to call he wanted to be as ready for them as he could be.

He was only able to gain peace of mind from reading more of his father's stories. He read six of them over a ninety minute period; the experience was like communing with some greater force and thus being calmed by it. However, the instant he put the notebooks aside his nerves began jangling again. Although it was after six, time to go and meet Gail's train, he felt an urge to pick the notebooks up again immediately, lose himself in them afresh. He made himself pile the notebooks up beside the settee, put on his jacket, walk out of the room and then out of the house. He had thrown some overnight things in a bag earlier and he carried this with him. As soon as Gail stepped off the train, Jack intended to usher her straight back onto it again.

Walking the streets was nerve-racking; at every turn, Jack expected to meet Patty Bates heading a lynch mob. However, at first everything was quiet. The shops were closed, and there were only a few people around, walking dogs or strolling home from work. Jack was opposite a butcher's shop, a red-and-white plastic sign boasting of MEAT AT ITS BEST, when he heard the sound of engines.

Dread rising in him, he looked for somewhere to hide. Between the butcher's shop and the haberdashery next door was a narrow alley, red brick walls sliding into an envelope of shadow. Jack plunged down it, realising that if he'd been spotted he'd effectively stepped into a trap of his own making. He flattened himself against the wall, looking out at the strip of road as the sound of the bikes grew louder.

Just before it reached a crescendo, Jack was almost overcome by claustrophobia. He felt certain that the bikers *had* seen him, that they would surround the alley entrance if he didn't run, and he was bracing himself to do so when he realised he was too late. The section of street he could see was predominantly pale grey, almost milky with sunshine. Jack was taking a step toward it when all at once it became flooded with roaring metal and scuffed black leather. Pressing himself back into the shadows, Jack watched as the bikes thundered past like a herd of buffalo. To his relief they didn't stop, but what was disturbing was the fact that there were an awful lot more of them than usual.

There were dozens of them, in fact, riding in a convoy that seemed to go on forever. A posse, Jack thought. It's a fucking posse! He waited in the alley, time dribbling away, as the bikes sped past, heading in the direction of— among other places, admittedly—the Seven Stars.

By the time he emerged from the alley he had lost almost ten minutes. He had previously had almost quarter of an hour to undertake what would ordinarily have been a six or seven minute walk. Now, glancing at his watch, he saw that Gail's train was due in four minutes.

He began to run, looking this way and that, ears straining for the faint sound of engines. Adrenaline was rushing through him; he was not merely agitated now, he was downright scared. But could all those bikers really be there solely for him? What were they going to do? Take the law into their own hands? String him up on some spurious charge?

It was exactly 16:52 when he turned left onto the hundred-yard incline that led to the train station. He hurried across the tiny lot, which had room for no more than thirty cars, hoping that Gail's train would be late, thankful that he hadn't yet heard it approaching. He was sweating profusely and his stomach felt hard and tight with tension. His arm was aching from holding his overnight bag away from his body as he ran.

The station building was squat and flat-roofed, built of local stone. A pair of begrimed glass doors constituted the only entrance. As Jack ran toward them they opened and a figure stepped out, carrying a carpet bag. Jack's stomach turned over.

"Jack!" Gail yelled, grinning, eyes sparkling. "Hi!"

The strength drained out of him. He raised a hand in weary greeting and trudged across to her.

She saw the look on his face and her grin lost its lustre. "Jack, what's wrong?"

"We've got to get out of here," he said.

16

ENGINES

An hour later, despite their efforts, they were back at the house, drinking coffee. Leaving Beckford had proved to be far more difficult than Jack had imagined. First of all, there were no taxis, which, considering the size of the village, was neither surprising nor particularly ominous. What *was* ominous, however, was that neither of them could get so much as the glimmer of a signal on their mobiles ("All these hills," Gail said) and every single phone box that the two of them came across had been vandalised. Jack did not think he was being paranoid in assuming that the damage had been caused by Patty Bates' biker friends. The thought that Patty was going to such lengths to keep him here, was actually planning his moves like a combat tactician, was not a comforting one. A number of alternatives occured to Jack: he could go to the police and tell them everything, he could phone for a taxi from his aunt's house, he could phone for a taxi from a pub. As he still did not fancy explaining the situation to the police, nor did he want his aunt involved, he decided

on the pub option. He led Gail along back alleys and side
streets, avoiding the main roads, pleased with his ability
to remember his way around. Gail was scared and bewildered and more than a little bad-tempered, but for the
moment she had stopped firing questions at him.

They quickly found that all the pubs had been covered,
bikes cruising up and down outside or parked on the fore-
courts. Desperate, Jack decided to go to the police after all,
but there were bikes outside Beckford's small station, too,
and no sign of a policeman anywhere. By this time, though
he was trying not to show it, Jack was really scared. It reminded him of that John Carpenter film, *Assault on
Precinct 13*. He smiled at Gail and said, "Thwarted again,"
hoping his voice did not betray the extent of his anxiety.

In truth, his thoughts felt shredded. He tried to draw
them together, to think. Only by remaining calm could he
hope to outmanoeuvre Bates and his army. Would all the
bikers know what he looked like? Presumably. His face
had been on enough book jackets.

He could think of only one option and it was a very
risky one indeed. They could go back to the house, call a
taxi from there. If the place was already being guarded,
they would have to try and find a way to sneak in via the
woods at the back. At the moment, the bikers were simply
covering his retreats, cutting off his options. Jack had to
make use of this time, this hiatus, as best he could.

For a while everything went well, and he actually began
to feel a little more optimistic. They arrived back at the
house safely to find it quiet and unoccupied. They phoned
for a taxi from outside Beckford (Jack was relieved to hear
the dial tone when he picked up the receiver; he was
afraid the lines might have been cut), and were told that it
would be with them within the next half-hour or so. There
was nothing to do then but sit tight and wait. Jack made
coffee, and as he and Gail drank it he told her everything.
Afterwards she had been quiet for a while, gazing out

the window at the approaching twilight. Jack felt tense, as though awaiting her verdict on a crime he had committed. Finally she had stirred, turned to him and murmured, "It's okay, Jack. Don't worry, we'll be all right." She had held out her arms to him and they had embraced. Over Gail's shoulder Jack could see the kitchen clock, counting out the seconds. He urged it to go faster, faster.

"I love you," he said, mouth against her neck, and then, "I'm sorry."

She pulled back from him so she could look into his face. "What are you sorry for?"

He waved a hand vaguely. "For . . . all this. This mess. For dragging you into it."

She leaned forward and kissed him softly on the forehead. Gently, she said, "None of this is your fault, Jack. It's this place, isn't it? Beckford."

"What do you mean?" he said, surprised.

"I mean . . . it's a bad place for you, isn't it? There's still a lot of poison here, a lot of stuff that has to come out."

Jack was surprised by her perception; it was as though she had verbalised something of which, until now, he had been unaware. "Well . . . yeah," he said, "I suppose you're right. I thought when I found my dad's stories, when I had finally made my peace with that side of things, that everything would be okay, that it would all settle down. But it hasn't. It's only stirred things up more, made the hate and the anger blossom somewhere else." He wrinkled his nose. "Does that make any sense to you?"

Gail nodded. "It makes more sense than you think."

They were silent for a few minutes. Jack finished his coffee and glanced up again at the rapidly darkening sky outside the window.

"These last few days have been . . . strange," he said. "You know, I'm almost beginning to wonder whether this whole business with my father has just taken place in my imagination. I mean . . . ghosts? Hauntings? There are times when I accept it as completely natural, and then at other times I find that I'm looking for reasonable explanations. It's like . . . like there are two separate trains of thought both trying to occupy the same track. I don't think I've been thinking quite straight since I've been here; my thought processes have kind of . . . gone off at funny angles. Take my father's stories for example. Reading them has been like . . . like an epiphany almost for me." He shook his head. "I don't know. Even now I'm not making much sense. It's like my thoughts are all jumbled up, as if they're rattling around loose and need putting back into their proper compartments."

He sighed, shaking his head. Gail stood up, circled the table and squeezed herself onto his lap. "Poor Jack," she murmured, putting her arms around him. "It's been quite a year for you. You've had to learn a lot about yourself."

"Have I?"

"Wouldn't you say so?"

Jack thought about it for a moment. "I suppose so, yes."

"You don't sound too sure."

"No, it's just . . . I hadn't really thought about it before, but I suppose . . . yes, I suppose you're right."

"What would you say you've learnt then?"

"Is this a test?"

"If you like."

He was silent for a little while. Finally, he said, "I'd never really loved anyone before I met you. That's been hard for me . . . opening up, learning to trust you."

"And do you trust me now?"

"Yes. Implicitly."

"And what about your father?"

Jack frowned. "What do you mean?"

"Do you trust him, too?"

"He's dead."

"I know that." Gail looked at him as if he were being tiresome. "But do you trust him?"

"I . . . yes. Yes, I do."

"And do you love him?"

"Yes," Jack said, surprising himself. "I've found a way to love him, and I think he loves me, too." He grinned and squeezed her. "Thank you," he said.

"For what?"

"For teaching me how."

Gail smiled and squeezed him back. She lowered her face to his and they kissed, the first proper kiss since she'd stepped off the train.

At last she broke away from him gently and sighed.

"What's the matter?"

"Nothing," she said, but she was staring at him as though trying to memorise his features, a strange expression on her face.

"Why are you looking at me like that?"

She ran a hand through her short dark hair, flattening spikes which sprang back after her fingers had passed over them. "Do you remember the first time we met?" she said. "In Alfred's? It was a year ago on Sunday. Did you know that?"

"Yeah. So?"

She sighed, touched the back of his hand with one fingertip. "Such a lot has happened since then," she said.

She sounded wistful. Jack linked his fingers with hers. "You sound sad. Why's that?"

She shook her head as if it were not important.

"Gail," he said firmly. "Communication. Trust. Remember?"

"It's just . . ." She waved her free hand in a vague circle. Then all at once she stiffened and raised her head, reminding Jack of a vixen catching a scent on the air. "Listen," she hissed.

Jack listened, but could hear nothing. When he began to say so, Gail flapped a hand at him. *Shhh.*

They sat in silence for a few moments, perfectly still, as

though posing for photographs. Jack wondered whether this was a ploy by Gail to deflect his question. He was about to speak again when he heard it: a persistent growling sound, so soft and low it was almost inaudible.

"What is it?" he murmured.

Gail looked at him, eyes wide. "I'd say it was the sound of engines, wouldn't you?"

Jack's stomach did a quick flip. "Motorbikes," he whispered. When she nodded, he said, "Maybe it's the taxi," but he knew it wasn't. He could tell by the sound.

Gail jumped up and ran to the door that led out into the hall.

"Where are you going?" said Jack.

"To call the police."

Less than a minute later she was back, face taut. "Now the phone's dead," she said.

"Oh shit!" Jack placed a hand on his heart, as though afraid it was going to smash its way out of his chest. "What are we going to do?"

Calmly, Gail held out her hand. "Come with me."

Jack looked up at her, ignoring the offer, as an idea struck him. "We could hide in the attic."

"They'd find us, Jack." She straightened her hand and her arm, emphasising the fact that he should take it. "Come with me," she repeated.

Instinctively Jack took her hand, responding to the authority in her voice. She gave a slight tug and he stood up. "Where are we going?"

"No questions. Just trust me."

"But you don't—"

"Trust me, okay?" she said firmly.

Jack felt as though he should be the one taking charge. It was his problem, his territory. However, he nodded. "Okay."

"Come on then." Gail pulled him to the back door and opened it. Immediately the snarls of myriad engines, though still distant, became louder.

Jack felt an instinctive desire to tug her back into the house, slam and lock the door, but he knew the house was a trap, even though he felt exposed without its solid walls around him. He remembered sleeping under his bed as a child, curled up like a foetus, eyes squeezed tightly shut. He used to believe that if you closed your eyes at night and lay completely still it made you invisible to monsters, impervious to harm.

Hand in hand, he and Gail slithered over the cobbles of the backyard, ducked beneath a line of damp washing, and then they were leaving the shadow of the house behind and heading towards the darker shadows of the woods.

The flesh between Jack's shoulder blades itched as the two of them plunged over the open ground that lay between Beckford Woods and the back of the house. Somewhere behind him and off to his right the motorbikes were roaring like wild animals. The sky was darkening rapidly now, clouds like silent grey sharks sliding through a sapphire ocean. Yet there was still enough light for Jack to feel acutely vulnerable. The roaring of engines became louder still, and now, underlying it, Jack thought he could hear the sound of raised voices. Unable to resist it, he glanced back. The sight caused his stomach to convulse with shock.

There must have been forty or fifty motorbikes roaring up Daisy Lane towards his father's house. At their head was a battered pickup truck with perhaps a dozen men sitting in the back, holding what looked like thin poles.

Surely, Jack thought, such hatred, such antagonism, could not be solely directed at him? There must have been a hundred people down there, all of whom it appeared wanted a little piece of Jack Stone. The procession, lit by blazing headlamps, made him think of the villagers marching on the Baron's castle in *Frankenstein*.

"Why are they doing this?" Jack shouted, his voice ragged.

"Because they're ignorant," answered Gail. "They don't really know *what* they're doing."

"I don't understand. I haven't done anything to harm them."

"Save your breath. *Come on.*"

They stumbled on, Jack's breath catching in his throat like shards of metal. His feet slithered over the mud and grass, and he remained upright only because Gail's footing was sure as a gazelle's, her hand tight around his. Behind them the roaring died little by little as engines were switched off and were superseded by whoops, expletives, the banter of hunting men out for a night's sport.

Jack heard the smashing of glass, cheering and laughter, and then the sound of more glass breaking. "Come out, Stone, you fucking rapist," someone shouted.

"We're gonna chop your dick off, boy," someone else yelled heartily, and his words were greeted with cackles of approval.

All at once a voice shouted, "Hey, what's that?"

Jack heard Gail say, "Oh, shit," and saw weak light meandering across the ground in front of him, picking out little green daggers of grass.

"It's him!" someone shouted. "It's the rapist."

"And he's got a lass with him."

"Come on!"

"They've seen us, Jack," Gail murmured, half-turning, and increased her speed, tightening her grip on his hand.

Jack didn't reply. Adrenaline was flooding his body, spurring him on. Torchlight beams were probing the area around him, fluttering over his skin. The edge of the woods was only a dozen yards away, trees picked out in powdery yellow light, bark the colour of parchment. The trees were like portals to some unknown place; between them was a lumpy shapeless landscape, dark on dark.

A sharp crack reverberated through the air, making Jack flinch, his ears hurt. He thought of when he'd been ten and a paving stone had buckled and snapped right in front of him, expanded by the summer heat. To his astonishment a chunk of bark flew from the tree five yards away, spitting splinters. He didn't realise he was being shot at until he heard a second bang, saw more foliage fly.

He was so shocked by the fact they were actually trying to hit him that he almost stopped dead. Gail wrenched on his arm. "Come on!" she urged. "Keep going!" Jack ran with her, head spinning. He found it difficult to equate what was happening with reality; it seemed fanciful as a scene from a film.

They plunged into the woods, putting a wall of tree trunks between themselves and their pursuers. Jack was running blindly, disorientated by the occasional slitherings of torchlight, the sky flickering between the charcoal scrawls of branches overhead. Once or twice he thought he was going to fall on the uneven ground, but Gail's surefootedness kept him upright and moving. He heard someone shouting behind him and recognised the voice as Patty Bates'.

"Mickey, you take your lot over that way. Stan, you cover the other side. Me n' Ernie and the rest'll go straight through the middle. And be careful with them guns. Don't use 'em unless you're sure, all right?"

There were growls of acknowledgement, and then Jack heard the soft sounds of movement expanding, becoming diffuse somewhere behind him. It was like a single vast creature infiltrating the woodland, flexing its dozens of tentacles, reaching out along many paths, wheedling out its prey.

A little further on Jack's foot caught on a root or a tangle of bush and this time he did fall, his wrist twisting as he clung to Gail's hand, sending a bolt of pain through the bone. He went down heavily, crying out. Even before his senses had stabilised, Gail was by his side, tugging him to his feet.

"Come on," she said, "they'll have heard us."

Jack scrambled upright. "Where are we going?"

"You'll know when you get there."

"But how do you—"

"*Shh.*" She placed a hand lightly over his mouth and drew him gently behind the trunk of a tree.

They stood there, hugging the shadows, faces pressed to the bark, trying not to breathe too loudly. Jack felt a pulsing against his chest. It seemed to come from the tree rather than himself.

Voices approached, footsteps rustling in the undergrowth. Jack tensed, but Gail's hand on his arm was warning him not to move. The beams of torches danced like fireflies. "It was around here," someone said.

The sound of footsteps crunched closer. Another voice, sandpaper-rough, a little slurred through drink, said, "Hey, Beano, look here."

The footsteps came to a halt on the other side of the tree, perhaps five yards from their hiding place. Jack heard one of the men clearing his throat, and he clenched his teeth, sweat dribbling down his face and chest, tickling between his shoulder blades. If he made the slightest sound now, if his stomach rumbled or his bowels decided to void a little gas, then he and Gail would be discovered. Beside him Gail was statue-still; Jack could not even hear her breathing.

"Looks like one of them slipped or something," the first voice said.

"Maybe they're injured," gruff-voice replied. "I hope we'll be the ones to find 'em." He made a quiet gunshot sound with his mouth and chuckled.

His friend laughed along with him. "Hey, maybe they're hiding in the bushes or something, listening to us this very moment."

"Yeah," said gruff-voice, and then in a warbling drunken falsetto, "Coo-ee, fuck-face, we're coming to get youuu."

The two men snorted phlegmy laughter. "Come on,"

said the first, "we'd better push on while the trail's hot."

"While we can smell the shit of their fear," gruff-voice added with relish.

There was a shuffle of movement, which resolved into footsteps. Walk away, Jack willed, walk away. Torchlight suddenly slithered around the trunk of the tree and across Jack's sleeve. He snatched his arm back just as the two men came level with their hiding place and saw him.

In the split-second that followed, every detail of the men's appearance imprinted itself on Jack's mind. Both wore scuffed and filthy leather jackets and ragged jeans. The first man was thin, perhaps Jack's age, with short, sparse hair and hollow pock-marked cheeks. The man behind him was taller, more bloated. He had a straggly dark beard, wild eyes, a black-and-red bandanna around his head. If he hadn't been wearing a Harley-Davidson T-shirt and a denim waistcoat over his leather jacket he would have looked like a pirate. Both men carried rifles. The bearded one was just starting to grin, revealing a marked lack of front teeth, when Gail flew from behind Jack like a wildcat and slammed into them.

She moved so fast she was almost a blur. Jack saw her hands lash out at the thin man's face, rake down his cheeks, leaving stripes of blood. He cried out and lurched back to escape her, colliding with his companion. Before either of them could recover, Gail pushed the thin man hard in the chest and the two men went down in a heap. Jack felt bewildered at the speed of her attack, amazed by her strength, ashamed of his own lassitude. He saw that she was snatching up one of the rifles the men had dropped and was flinging it into the undergrowth, and he moved forward to do the same.

The two men were clambering to their feet, shouting obscenities, as Jack and Gail fled once more into the woods. It was almost full night now, the black branches above them merging with the starless sky, pockets of darkness, of ever-deepening shadow, filling in the gaps between the trees. Jack's heart was pumping with reaction, his mouth paper-dry. He was terrified of crashing into a tree or plunging into a crevasse masked by darkness, and wondered how Gail could be so confident. She seemed to be leading him some-where definite, but how could that be? As far as he was aware she had never even been to Beckford before today.

They ran on through the darkness, occasionally stop-ping when they heard footsteps or voices close by. It was like a deadly game of hide and seek; once, at the sound of a gunshot, Jack flung himself to the ground, dragging Gail with him. For the next few minutes they heard voices raised in anger, remonstrations. Someone shouted, "You fucking idiot, watch what you're doing. You could have killed me there." Most of the time, however, it was quiet, though that was almost as bad because it made Jack think of ambush, of stumbling into the unseen sights of rifles, blundering into concealed pits with wooden spikes point-ing upwards to impale them. He quickly lost all sense of time and place. The darkness was a black canvas upon which his imagination scribbled like an overactive child.

A number of times he asked Gail where they were go-ing, but she sidestepped the question, telling him to shush or simply muttering, "You'll see." This evasiveness did not help Jack's peace of mind. He began to suspect that she didn't really *know* where they were going. His faith in her was beginning to wane, and he was just about to yank her to a halt, when her steps slowed, then stopped and she murmured, "We're here."

Jack looked around, but could see only the same shape-less darkness they had been fumbling through for what seemed like hours. "Where?" he said grumpily.

Gail turned to look at him. Her face was a vague pale oval, blots for eyes. "Don't you recognise this place?" she asked.

Jack felt anger increasing the volume of his voice and

struggled to contain it. "How can I?" he said. "I can't bloody *see* anything."

"We need light."

"It *would* help."

Jack felt her hand touch his cheek tenderly and a little of his rising anger dissipated.

"Things are going to happen here, Jack," she said.

"What things?"

She ignored the question. "Don't be annoyed, and try not to be scared—"

"Scared? Why should I be scared? There's only a few dozen loonies out there, hunting for us with shotguns."

"—and please don't be sad."

This last request surprised him. "Sad? What do you mean? Why should I be sad?" He shook his head almost wearily. "Gail, what's going on?"

"Shh," she soothed. "Shh, my love. Everything will be fine. Trust me. You'll get your answers, I promise."

"But . . . but where *are* we?"

"You tell me." Before he could protest, she said, "When the light comes, you'll know."

"When the light comes? You mean, in the morning?"

"No, not the morning. Look."

Jack didn't know what he was supposed to be looking at. He was aware of Gail raising an arm, and he squinted in the direction of what he guessed would be her pointing finger. The night was a black swirling soup without form. He gazed dutifully into its depths for a minute or so, but his perception remained unchanged. Sighing, he was about to point this out to her, when all at once he realised that . . . yes, perhaps he *was* actually beginning to differentiate between shapes. Certainly this gradation of shadow now seemed separate to that, and wasn't there a certain suggestion of outline, of definite form, rising through the murk?

He looked at Gail. She seemed clearer, too, her features more in focus. Was this simply because his eyes were becoming accustomed to the darkness? But if that were the case, why hadn't they done so before? He looked up at the sky, as if seeking answers. Through a tangle of branches he saw clouds edged with silver luminescence. Even as he watched, the clouds shredded as though pulled apart, revealing the fat white face of the moon.

Moonlight seemed to lance down, a shimmering blue-white corridor, reminding Jack of a laser beam in an old science-fiction film. Considering the presence of the hunters all around them, he should have felt alarmed at being pinpointed so candidly, but instead he felt calm, even awed, as though the light contained a balm, a drug, that nullified his anxiety. He looked again at Gail. She had her eyes closed and a serene smile on her lips; her face was raised to the moon as if she were bathing in its icy splendour. She had spoken of light, but how could she have known? Was this a natural phenomenon or a coincidence? The idea that she had instigated all this was unacceptable.

"Gail—" he began.

Without looking at him she said, "Shh. Tell me what you see."

Jack looked away from her, let his gaze wander over their surroundings. They were standing at the edge of a clearing, which the light had transformed into an ice sculpture. Dominating the clearing, some twenty yards away, was a vast oak tree, raising its limbs to the sky. The tree was suffused with moonlight, the intricate whorls in its trunk picked out as though studded with diamonds. Smaller trees and bushes circled it, though at a respectful distance, like bondsmen. In places the tree's roots had forced their way up through the earth and then plunged back in again. The area was scattered with acorns.

Jack drew in a sharp breath, which felt as though he had sucked ice-blue moonlight into his lungs. He felt suddenly cold inside; pain blossomed at the base of his sternum, momentarily stabbing, almost doubling him over. He knew this place. A memory rose like bile: the sensation of an egg bursting in his mouth, releasing something salty, viscous, with feeble life. He tore his gaze from the glittering oak, turned accusingly to Gail. "Why have you brought me here?"

"You know this place," she said. A simple statement, not a question.

"Of course I do. You know I do. How could you have brought me here? I thought you loved me. I trusted you."

"I *do* love you, Jack," she insisted.

"How can you say that? You wouldn't do this to me if you loved me."

"Jack, listen to me. There's a reason for bringing you here."

"What reason? What fucking reason?" He heard his own voice becoming shrill with fury. Gail reached out a hand to touch him, but he recoiled from her as if she were diseased.

She sighed and said, "Exorcism."

Jack opened and closed his mouth like a goldfish before managing to blurt out, *"What?"*

"Exorcism," she repeated. "Laying ghosts, remember? Finding love. It's all here."

"What are you talking about?"

She was becoming angry now. "If you'll just listen a moment and not be so pigheaded—"

"I am listening. I just asked you a question, didn't I?"

"You're flying off the handle."

"Well, what do you expect? We're likely to get our fucking heads blown off at any second and you're doing a Sigmund Freud on me."

"Jack," Gail said, and her voice was now controlled, conciliatory. She reached out a hand. He stepped back again but she grabbed him by the sleeve.

"What?" he snapped.

She paused a moment, as if absorbing his anger, killing it. "Take my hand," she murmured.

"Why?"

"Because I want you to. Trust me."

He glared at her sullenly. Her face was alabaster, eyes silver.

"Take my hand," she repeated.

He yanked his arm from her grip. "No, I won't."

She was suddenly furious. *"Take it,"* she ordered.

Jack stepped back, mouth dropping open, eyes widening in shock. The voice that had emerged from her lips was not her own. It was a man's voice, deeper, older.

It was his father's voice.

He stood frozen, staring at her, unable to say or do anything. She looked back at him, her face calm, almost bland. There was no indication of what had just occurred, and Jack found himself wondering whether in fact anything had, whether perhaps it had been no more than a quirky aberration of his own stressed mind. For a long moment the woods were absolutely silent; silent as a vacuum, silent as death.

Then a voice from behind him said, "Jack."

Jack turned slowly, as if the word were a hand on his shoulder or a hook in his flesh. Moonlight still filled the clearing, bleaching the trees and bushes and undergrowth a uniform white. The figure, standing before the oak tree, silhouetted against its massive trunk, seemed to deflect this light, however, to be wrapped in charcoal shadow. Despite this, it radiated peace, serenity. In a quiet, clear voice it spoke three more words: "Come here, Jack."

He felt a strange blend of emotions swirling inside him—fear, peace, excitement, awe. He looked to Gail as though for guidance and saw that she was smiling, her face radiant. "It's okay," she whispered. "Please take my hand."

She held it out and this time Jack grasped it without hesitation. Together the two of them began to walk towards the dark figure standing before the oak tree.

Each step was a journey in itself, and each journey a regression. Jack felt his life unravelling, slipping through his hands and his mind. It was a life full of pain, of anger, of bitterness, resentment, fear. Occasionally slivers of love, of happiness, flared like matches in a darkened room, only to die when Jack reached out his hands to warm them.

He looked up at the figure and felt waves of sorrow, regret emanating from it, substantial as cold and heat. He understood that the figure was trying to atone for the darkness that had tainted Jack's early life, was somehow holding itself responsible. The closer Jack got to the figure the more he felt himself dwindling. But the sensation was neither unpleasant nor enervating; indeed, it was cathartic. Now he was close to the figure and it seemed to loom over him like a giant, beckoning him with its silence. Jack looked across at Gail for reassurance, and was surprised to find he was holding the hand of a young girl perhaps ten years old. He looked down and saw that he, too, had reverted to childhood. He clenched Gail's hand tighter; she seemed not quite there, ethereal, suffused with a faint golden aura that blurred her outline. They came to a halt a few feet from the figure. It bent toward them, craning into the light. With a sound like rustling silk the darkness fled from it, revealing its face.

"Jack," said the man again and held out his arms. Jack realised now that he had never seen his father without the grief and the pain and the anger. He was a handsome man, even a beautiful one. It was serenity, Jack decided, that made him so.

Releasing Gail's hand, Jack held out his arms, aping his father's gesture, and he was younger still now, eight years old, or seven. He felt himself swept up, swung round; he couldn't help but shriek with the joy of it.

"Come on, Jack, up you go," said his father. It seemed to him as though his father had said this many times before. Certainly Jack knew instinctively what to do. Aided by his father's strong hands, he scrambled up on to his shoulders, until his own feet were on either side of the man's neck, resting on his chest. Jack's hands were around his father's forehead, his chin touching his father's hair.

Jack squinted up into the sunny sky. Though he had faith in his father, he found all at once that he was confused, that his thoughts had fled. "Where are we going, Daddy?" he asked as his father began to walk.

"We're going to see Mummy and Gail," his father said. "Don't you remember?"

Mummy and Gail. Jack knew that the names were so familiar they were part of him, but strangely, he could conjure up no faces to accompany them. He put the thought from his mind for the time being and concentrated instead on holding tight to Daddy's forehead so that he wouldn't slip from his shoulders. It was an awful long way to the ground. Being up here was scary, but it was exciting, too. "I'm the king of the castle, you're a dirty rascal," he sang as they jolted along.

Then they were standing at the entrance to a churchyard. It was a sudden transition, like a cut in a film, or as if Jack had fallen asleep for a while and only now woken up. Except that he couldn't have been asleep because he was standing beside his Daddy, holding his hand, unless of course he'd been sleepwalking. In his other hand he was holding a bunch of flowers, some yellow ones which he knew as daffydills and some pink ones which were roses (he vaguely remembered Daddy telling him to "be careful of the thorns, they're sharp"). Daddy crouched beside him and Jack turned to him expectantly. "Okay, Champ?" Daddy said.

"Yes," said Jack quietly, reacting to the solemn tenderness in Daddy's voice.

"Face clean for Mummy?"

"Yes. And my hands, too."

Daddy smiled. "Come on, then."

He pushed open the creaky black gate and the two of

them turned left to walk up the gravelly path that snaked between the tombstones. Jack liked the church with its nooks and crannies, its beard of ivy; it seemed a nice peaceful place. The graveyard was peaceful, too. Tall grasses swayed in the wind, wild flowers bobbed their pretty heads. To reach Mummy and Gail you had to go over the grass, past some very old stones, all crooked and crumbling, and there they were. The plot was always nice and neat. Daddy took last week's flowers, which were beginning to wither, out of the metal thing with the holes in it and Jack put in the new ones. Then they stood and looked at the stone for a bit; sometimes when they were doing this, Daddy knelt down and bowed his head, and sometimes he cried and Jack did, too, because Daddy said it was all right to cry. Jack was only four and could only read little words, but he knew what the words on the tombstone said:

IN LOVING MEMORY OF ALICE STONE
BORN 15TH JULY 1938–DIED 10TH OCTOBER 1970
AND GAIL STONE
BORN AND DIED 10TH OCTOBER 1970
MOTHER AND DAUGHTER, AT PEACE TOGETHER
LOVED AND MISSED FOREVER, NEVER FORGOTTEN

Daddy turned to Jack and said, "You understand what this means, son, don't you?"

Jack shrugged. "Yes," he said, but he was not sure that he did.

Suddenly Daddy reached for him and hugged him tight. Jack knew Daddy wouldn't hurt him, but he felt a little frightened all the same. His face was pressed into Daddy's chest. Daddy began to make sobbing noises. Through the sobbing noises he said, "I'm sorry, son. I'm sorry. This is how it should have been. This is how I wanted it to be. I'm sorry."

Jack didn't like it when Daddy was sad, which he was

sometimes. He closed his eyes and pressed his face even harder into Daddy's shirt. He liked Daddy's smell; it was warm and comforting. He liked the steady boom of Daddy's heartbeat, too; it made him feel safe.

He felt the heartbeat growing louder, stronger, spreading out and enveloping him. Daddy's voice faded beneath it, and Jack felt himself sinking, going back, as if he were crawling into the centre of the heartbeat itself. External sensation—the rough-heavy feel of Daddy's hand tenderly stroking his hair, the material of Daddy's shirt on his face, the long grass tickling his legs—dimmed, merged and finally dissolved into a warm soft limbo where Jack floated, carefree and serene. His senses felt like one sense, unfragmented; his thoughts felt like one thought, uncluttered, pure.

He felt a presence beside him and knew instinctively that it was the complement to himself: yin and yang. Somehow he knew that he was poised, on the verge, but as yet he felt no anxiety, no fear, no excitement. His emotions were a single vital emotion, indefinable, flawless. Together, he and his twin were entire, immaculate.

When the pain came, splitting them, only he was ready.

As soon as the light rushed in he knew that it meant him harm. It was voracious, mindless. It had only its hunger, its desire for destruction, to maintain it. The twins were sundered. The weaker died. The stronger lived, but only just. As he crashed out into a screeching world of light and pain and terrible fear he felt the heartbeat that had sustained him lurch and die, lurch again . . .

And finally whisper its last.

Silence for a time, and then, faint at first, a new beat. Gradually it grew louder, stronger. It was harsh, ugly, and it tore its way out from inside him with increasing violence. With it, all knowledge came rushing back. The years were heaped onto his shoulders once more. The beat was a single word, "No . . . No . . . No . . . ," repeated over and over. Realising his eyes were squeezed tightly closed, Jack opened them.

He found himself standing alone in the clearing, howling his denial at the moon.

Falling to his knees he began to sob. He was crying for chances lost, relationships unformed. He grieved for the sister he had never known, the mother who had died so that he could live. He cried for his father, too, who had not had the strength to resist the outstretched arms of his devils and who had sought redemption only when it was too late. Though he felt wretched, they were cleansing tears. When they were done, the ache he felt was one of pity and love and loss. A cloud was sidling across the moon now, dimming its light. Jack wiped a hand over his face and climbed shakily to his feet.

"You pathetic bastard," said Patty Bates.

Jack turned unsteadily. Bates was standing at the edge of the clearing, between two trees. He was mostly in shadow, though Jack could see that his face was creased in rage and disgust, and that he cradled a shotgun in the crook of his arm. Oddly, Jack was not afraid; he merely felt tired and empty. Behind and all around Bates, circling the clearing to ensure Jack would not escape, were Bates' army—mindless, faceless and silent. Jack could smell their expectation, their desire to see blood spilled. Bates had a bandanna around his head. He looked ridiculous. Despite himself, Jack sniggered.

Bates took two more strides forward, posturing and arrogant. "You fucking worm," he sneered. "Haven't changed much, have you?"

There was a ripple of laughter from around the clearing. Jack sighed. Quietly he replied, "What do you know about anything, Bates? You haven't changed much, either. You've still got the intelligence of a plank."

Bates looked almost comically surprised. He clearly hadn't expected such defiance. He recovered himself quickly, however, all too aware of his audience. Taking a quick glance around, he lurched forward, roaring, "I know you raped my daughter, you scum!"

He was clearly encouraged by the growls of acknowledgement from around the clearing. Jack, however, stood his ground. He even threw back his head and laughed.

"Oh, for God's sake," he said, "you know that's not true. It's just a bloody excuse, isn't it? Why don't you give me a break?"

He was treading on very dangerous ground and he knew it, but he didn't much care anymore. After what he had just experienced the threat from Bates seemed puerile, insignificant.

Bates, however, clearly didn't regard it as such. Incensed almost to apoplexy, he screamed, "I'll give you a break, all right, you fucking bastard! Your fucking arms and legs!"

"Repartee," Jack said. "Very witty. Do you write all your own material?"

In some less reckless part of his mind warning lights were flashing. Jack knew that goading a maniac with a gun was not the wisest move he had ever made. But he couldn't deny that he felt a savage glee in the situation, a sense of almost suicidal power. He was spoiling Bates' party and it felt mighty good. Crimson-faced, Bates' only retort was to raise his gun and point it at Jack's stomach.

Jack lowered his gaze momentarily to glance at the deadly black muzzle of the rifle, then he reestablished eye contact with Bates. In a voice so calm and reasonable he might have been commenting on the weather, he said, "Aren't you now supposed to say, 'Go ahead, make my day,' or 'Eat lead, punk,' or something equally melodramatic?"

Bates' face turned an even deeper shade of scarlet. He hissed, "Shut up, you twat, shut up," as if Jack were spoiling a carefully prepared script.

"You're not looking too well, Patty," Jack said in mock concern. "Are you sure you wouldn't like me to call you a doctor?"

Bates' lips curled back from his teeth like those of a mad dog. His body went rigid, then his hand seemed to jerk on the trigger of the rifle.

Jack didn't immediately realise he'd been shot. He was deafened by the roar of the gun, which was like having someone slap both his ears at the same time as a bolt of lightning streaked through his head. He felt no pain whatsoever, and was certain Bates had missed him. It was only when he tried to raise his hands to cover his ears that he realised something was wrong. His body would not respond as he wanted it to. His arms felt heavy and woolly, his legs were suddenly weak, beginning to buckle beneath him. Bewildered, he looked down at himself, and saw that the left side of his stomach was a spreading ooze of slick crimson darkness.

Then he fell down.

He lay looking up at the sky. The sensation was not unlike being horribly drunk and knowing you were going to be sick, and being unable to do a damn thing about it. The focus of his eyes was wildly erratic; one second everything would be blurred and begin fading to black, the next it would surge into such breathtaking clarity that Jack felt he could almost distinguish the intricate patterns of the molecules and atoms of which everything was made. A pain, numb and yet simultaneously more deep-rooted and excruciating than anything he had ever known before, began to blossom in his midriff, quickly spread to encompass his hips, his legs, his chest, his arms. Jack felt as though he should have been terrified, but he was not. He thought quite lucidly that the enormity of what was happening was being shielded from him, that his body was anaesthetising him against it and yet even this knowledge failed to breach his defences.

Though sounds were muzzy, and becoming muzzier, Jack got the impression that something was moving toward him (this didn't seem quite the right way to phrase it, but his thoughts were breaking up, becoming muddled, too). His instinct was confirmed when something moved into his field of vision. A fumble through the perishing index file of his brain identified the something as a face. A further rummage gave the face a name: Patty Bates.

Jack grinned, or tried to; what expression he actually managed to produce was anyone's guess. "Hello," he thought he said. His lips felt huge and wet and uncontrollable. There was a gurgly copper taste in the back of his throat.

Patty Bates' words were only slightly distorted and not particularly inspired. He pointed the rifle at Jack's face and said, "Time to die, wanker."

Jack's grin grew wider. Something wet oozed out of the side of his mouth, ran down his face and into his ear. What he tried to make himself say, what he hoped he'd said, was, "Go on then. I don't care."

Time seemed to stop then, and Jack wondered momentarily if he was dead, if his final image—that of Patty Bates standing over him with a gun pointing at his face—had simply been frozen on to his retina. He expected the image to crumble and darken at any second, to dwindle eventually into black.

Then a breeze passed over his face and he realised he was not dead, after all. Not yet, anyway.

If he concentrated very hard, Jack could see that the gun barrel was trembling in Bates' hand, the great black O of its muzzle fluttering as weakly and erratically as Jack's heart. He could see Bates' teeth clenched tight, gleaming with spittle, sweat darkening the bandanna around his head, trickling down his crimson cheeks, tracing the line of his throat. Though his thoughts were vague and fragmentary, Jack knew that Bates was not at all happy with this situation. Bates had wanted Jack to crawl and squirm and plead—he hated weakness, fed on it, was enraged by it—and the fact that Jack had not con-

formed to his expectations tormented him greatly. Jack
would have laughed at this if he had had the strength.
Bates might have killed him, but the ultimate victory was
Jack's. With a supreme effort, he curled his lips around
words that felt almost impossible to form. Hoping that
Bates could hear the words, and hoping they were suffi-
ciently taunting, he said, "Well, come on them. I'm
ready."

Bates' face twisted as if in pain; he actually seemed to
grind his teeth together. He raised the gun once more, took
aim . . . and then with a sound that was very like a sob, he
lowered the rifle and allowed it to droop by his side.

"Whassamarrer?" Jack slurred, his eyelids drifting
closed, then opening again, his focus blurring and sharpening like an old TV set. "Loss yer boddle?"

Patty Bates' face expanded, filled his vision, a malevo-
lent moon falling to Earth. His voice was a choked whine,
almost a plea. "Shut up, you bastard. Shut up, just shut
up. I hate you. I hate you, you fucking bastard!"

Jack closed his eyes, smiling in satisfaction as if he'd
been paid the highest compliment. When he opened them
again an indeterminate time later, all was quiet and Bates'
sweating moon-face was gone.

Jack lay gazing up at the night sky, his being reduced to
a tiny buzzing core of consciousness. He felt no pain now,
no sensation of cold or heat. He felt divorced from his
body, from his senses; even his vision seemed to come
from somewhere other than his eyes. He didn't know if he
was dead yet, or still alive, or hovering somewhere in between, and he found that he didn't much care. Reduced to
this, all the Big Questions—life and death, order and
chaos, science and faith—seemed redundant, inconse-
quential, layer upon layer of tissue paper lies with which
to envelop and stifle the integral, ultimate truth. He *was*,
that was all, and *what* he was didn't matter, and *why* he
was mattered even less. Though he had no notion of doing

so, he closed his eyes again. When he opened them some time later, he found himself encased in golden light.

Jack mused vaguely that if this was what he aspired to, then existence was worthwhile. The light glittered, shimmered, formed myriad breathtaking patterns that suffused him, filled him, *became* him. In the midst of this light a shape formed. A face. The most beautiful face Jack had ever seen. It was Gail's face, though without human imperfection. Gail was the other part of him, the completion of the circle. Somehow, without words, they communicated.

And then Jack was observing himself, looking down on his own body. It was sprawled in the undergrowth at the base of the oak tree, head back, mouth open, eyes closed. His flesh, blue-tinged, looked clammy. There was a great deal of blood and mess.

Jack knew he should have felt distressed, shocked, but he merely accepted what he was seeing, believing it to be somehow . . . *right*. He couldn't explain it any other way. It felt right, and that was all. There was a movement in the air, a bloom of golden light, and then Gail was beside him, beside the body.

She crouched down, stretching out an ethereal limb toward his wound. The instant she touched it, the light that surrounded her flared like a dying sun, and she dissolved, rushing into his wound like a genie into a bottle, filling it with light. For an instant Jack understood exactly what damage had been caused by the bullet that had entered him, and the chain of events that had been activated inside his body as a result. He closed his eyes, and when he opened them again, he was gazing into a night sky full of ice-chip stars, and there was pain, far too much of it.

"Gail," he whispered, "Gail," but the whisper was no more than a thought and even that hurt. *I don't want this, I don't want this, I don't want this, I don't want this, I don't—*

He closed his eyes.

Epilogue

2005

It was August 16th, and the remix of *Love Me Tender* was riding high on the charts to commemorate the umpteenth anniversary of Elvis' death. London was wilting in a heat wave. It had taken less than three weeks for the general joie de vivre to degenerate into frayed tempers, sunstroke and heat rashes. Office workers around the capital grumbled about the lack of air-conditioning in their places of employment; local government employees in Tooting went on strike when a colleague was sacked for refusing to wear a jacket and tie. A hosepipe ban was implemented across the whole of Southern England and stern warnings issued about the "abuse" of water. In the boiling cauldron of the Underground people were dropping like flies.

The big event at Cormorant Books that summer was the release in paperback of Jack Stone's fourth novel, *Splinter Kiss*. Initially scheduled for March, circumstances had dictated that the book be held back until the beginning of July. Widely regarded as Jack Stone's big breakthrough novel, the inevitable decision to delay the book's release

had initially been met in Cormorant's publicity department with despair. A bold and expensive marketing cam-
paign had been meticulously planned, dates finalised,
money spent. It was, someone had said, like building a
palace only to have it destroyed by an earthquake and
having to start all over again. That same person also offered the gloomy forecast that seventeen months between
hardback and paperback release was far too long a gap.
Public interest would wane, he said, and the book would
die an ignominious death in the marketplace.

Thankfully, his pessimism was misplaced. If anything,
the delay in the paperback release of *Splinter Kiss* worked
mightily in the book's favour, to the extent that it almost
became a marketing ploy in itself.

By the time *Splinter Kiss* finally did hit the shelves, the
reading public were ravenous for it. It leapt straight onto
the bestsellers list at number five, and for over a month
had been vying for number one. It was outselling new re-
leases from some of the biggest names in the world. There
was a rumour that one of Hollywood's most famous directors was anxious to direct the film.

Sitting on the tube, white cotton shirt clinging to him
like a second skin, leather jacket draped over his lap like a
dead dog, Jack found it difficult to equate all this excitement with himself. The fifteen months since his return to
Beckford had been tough for him. He had been through a
lot of pain and trauma, both physical and mental. All the
furore surrounding *Splinter Kiss,* and the even greater
furore that was predicted to surround his forthcoming
novel, *The Laughter,* had been both a curse and a bless-
ing. At times it had been exhilarating, a more than welcome distraction. Alternatively, on bad days, it had
seemed shallow, exhausting, stiflingly overwhelming. On
these occasions he had simply had to grit his teeth and get
on with it, snatch whatever solitude, whatever thinking
time, he could and nurture it.

He drew in his knees a little as even more people piled onto the tube at Euston. As he did so, he heard the letter crackle in his pocket. He eased it out, taking care not to nudge the fat woman with the bad wig who was sitting beside him. Really he should have left the letter at home, forgot about it until after his lunch with the "film people" whom his agent was introducing him to. He didn't want to seem vague or uninterested in what they would undoubtedly offer him. But forgetting about the letter's contents was easier said than done. Selling his father's house was a big step for Jack, important in a way that only he could understand. He slid the letter from the envelope, unfolded it and read it for the sixth or seventh time.

His Aunt Georgina, who was conducting the sale for him, informed him in her small, neat script that a young couple, Mr. and Mrs. Geoffrey Thomas, had offered £177,500 for the property. It was £7,500 less than the asking price, but Georgina had decided to accept their offer. She knew how eager Jack was to get rid of the house and how little the money mattered to him. He stared at the letter, reread it, as if afraid he had overlooked some vital loophole. Not for the first time, he found himself drifting back, reliving the aftermath of that fateful night.

Throughout his convalescence, Jack had constantly been informed of just how lucky he was to be alive. He had lain in the clearing, losing blood, for over six hours, and it was amazing, he was told, that he had managed to survive for so long. What was also amazing was that the man who had found him, a butcher called Dennis Barber, had only done so through sheer fortune. Not normally an insomniac, Barber had been unable to sleep on this particular May night. After tossing and turning for what seemed an age, he had finally got out of bed, leaving his wife sleeping soundly, when the first glimmerings of dawn had begun to streak the sky. He decided to go for a walk, was almost out of the door when it struck him that he ought to take the dog with him, a red setter called Suzy. Why he hadn't simply crossed to the local park, less than five minutes' walk away, and wandered around there for half an hour or so he couldn't say. Instead, on an impulse he had got the Landrover out of the garage and driven it four miles to Beckford Woods.

Once in the woods, instead of sticking to the main path, he had decided to follow a secondary route, which was both circuitous and largely overgrown. Suzy had bounded joyfully into the undergrowth, deliriously excited by the plethora of new sounds and smells that assailed her senses. Dennis was enjoying his walk—the crisp air, the sweet virgin light of a new day. He had been walking along this secondary route for perhaps twenty minutes when Suzy had started barking.

There had been something about the bark. It was not simply the exuberance of an overexcited dog. There had been a note of alarm in it, a sense of determination, of purpose. Dennis tried calling her, but Suzy did not come. Something told him that she was barking to attract his attention, to lead him to her, and he had begun to jog, and then to run, through the foliage, occasionally jumping over tree roots and hummocky sods of grass like green punk wigs.

He was not used to running, had not run since his college days over twenty years earlier when he had been a prop forward, and by the time he reached the clearing his lungs were on fire and his heart felt as if it were ready to burst in his chest. Part of him rejected this entire scenario. Suzy was not bloody Lassie, after all. He would probably find her venting her frustration at a rabbit hole.

And yet, Dennis Barber later told Jack whilst sitting at his bedside in Leeds General Infirmary, he had not been entirely surprised when he had found his dog standing over the body of a man who looked to have been killed in a shoot-out. At the time, he had thought Jack was dead.

What made him realise he was not was when Suzy dipped her head and daintily licked Jack's face, whereupon the "corpse" had feebly raised a hand, either to pet the dog or push it away.

"You must be the luckiest man alive," Barber had said, grinning wildly, and Jack, returning his grin, had nodded. But oddly, Jack did not *feel* lucky. He felt empty, bereft. He wished earnestly that Barber had not found him, that he had simply been left to die.

It had taken him a long time to get over this feeling, and even now there were days when it took hold of him like a pit bull terrier and would not let go. But, on the whole, he was getting better. There were more bright days than dark. He was beginning to enjoy life again.

He had spent eighteen days at the hospital, during which time he had surgery twice, and afterwards he returned to London. For a time his best friend, Frank Dawson, looked after him. Jack found to his frustration that overexertion (which could mean something as innocuous as a trip to Sainsbury's) would make him sick as a dog and weak as a kitten. His physical convalescence was a long and boring process. For three months he felt like a prisoner in his own home. He had little appetite and lost eleven pounds, which ironically brought him down to his ideal weight. He filled in the time by working on *The Laughter,* reading the rest of his father's stories, watching TV, listening to music, and having long emotional phone calls with his Aunt Georgina.

It had taken a while for her to open up, but eventually, due to Jack's persistence, she had told him everything. The other baby, his twin, a girl who was to have been called Gail, had only been discovered during his mother's autopsy.

Appalled, even furious, Jack had asked, "How could anyone miss something like that? Didn't they realize—"

"It was 1970," Georgina interrupted gently. "They

didn't have the technology they have now. Mistakes were far more common in those days." She hesitated a moment and then went on, "Besides, Gail was a wee scrap of a thing. It would have been touch and go whether she'd have survived even if she'd been born."

"Still," he said, "it was a disgraceful mistake to make."

"It was a tragedy," Georgina replied, "and it happened a long time ago."

"But not for me," he insisted. "For me, it's only just happened. Why wasn't I ever told?"

"Things were bad enough, Jack. You had plenty to contend with without this extra burden. Your father couldn't accept that part of it. He attended the funeral, but he never talked about the little girl. I even had to have the wording on the stone amended to include her name. I think it was because of this that your father never visited the grave. If he had, you might have found out sooner." Her voice sounded strained, and Jack suddenly realised that this was hard for her, too. He felt a little ashamed for being so insistent, so accusatory.

"So you thought it best to let sleeping dogs lie," he said wearily, and immediately realised how inappropriate the phrase sounded.

"Yes," said Georgina. "It seemed the right thing to do at the time. Maybe I was wrong."

He expelled an almighty sigh. "No," he said, "you weren't wrong. I guess it would only have caused more misery. It would have given my father one more thing to blame me for."

There was a short silence on the phone, and then Georgina said tentatively, "I wish you didn't hate your father so much, Jack. I realise how he treated you, but it was—"

"But I *don't* hate him!" he blurted, surprised that she should think so. "Not any more. I know now he was sorry for what he did to me."

Now it was Georgina's turn to sound surprised. "Yes," she said. "Yes, I think he was too."

"It's just the situation I hate," Jack said. "The whole mess. And what's so frustrating is that there's no focus for that hatred. Except maybe God, and that seems pointless to me."

There had been other phone calls, other questions. Jack's emotions had veered from one extreme to the other during the course of his recovery, but Georgina had always been there to listen and respond. Throughout, he never told anyone what had really happened that last night in Beckford, not even his aunt. When the police asked him if he had known his assailant, or if he knew of anyone who might have had a grudge against him, he said no. He wondered at first why he didn't just drop Patty Bates in it, but even as he questioned himself he knew the answer. He wanted there to be an end to it, had no wish to resurrect what he finally considered to be dead and buried. Of course the police had their suspicions, and there must have been enough evidence at the house and in the woods to suggest that some sort of manhunt had taken place. But no one was ever charged with anything, and eventually the police visits tailed off.

Gail's mobile number yielded nothing but a failed connection, the number to her flat likewise. Even so, Jack tried this latter number again and again. For a while it became an obsession with him. Though he was met each time by the faint ticking of an attempted connection and then the dull hum of a nonexistent line, he would think, as his fingers punched out the digits, *This time. This time she'll pick up the phone and say hello.* Yet each time there would be that crushing sense of defeat, which would dwindle into black depression, and then deeper, into grief.

Jack knew in his heart he would never speak to her again. Part of him wondered whether he had *ever* spoken to her. But he remembered the taste of her, the softness of her kisses, their bodies together, loving. Had that been right, considering the circumstances? Could conventional morality even be applied here? His mind turned the matter over and over, digging up the same old ground, sifting through the same dark soil. When he asked Frank Dawson what he remembered of Gail, he was astonished to discover that Frank had never met her.

"What do you mean?" Jack said. "Of *course* you met her."

"No." Frank shook his head adamantly. "Never did. And neither did Nick and Julie, or Andre and Becca, or Wendy, or Kev, or James, or anyone. We used to joke about it, how you kept her to yourself, like a kid with a toy he didn't want to share. I think there were one or two occasions when she was *going* to come out with us—like when we went to Fino's for Becca's birthday—but for some reason she never made it; she was ill or you were away or something. I thought maybe you were just ashamed of us all. Or perhaps worried she'd be unable to resist my charm, sophistication and good looks."

"But . . . I can't believe this!" Jack said. "Are you *sure* you never met her?"

"Positive," Frank said. Seeing his friend's obvious distress, he patted his shoulder in an awkward gesture of consolation. As far as Frank was aware, Gail had finished with Jack out of the blue and had left town, making the break while he was in Beckford sorting out his dad's affairs. Apparently she hadn't even got in touch while Jack was fighting for his life in the hospital. In Frank's book that made her a complete cow. He didn't know the full story, but he felt sure Jack was the injured party and it upset him to see his friend torturing himself like this. "Forget her, Jack," he advised. "She's not worth all this hassle. You're well rid, mate, believe me."

It was obvious over the next few months that Jack could not forget her, and Frank was shrewd enough to realise he had to let the matter run its course. Only Jack could sort it out. Frank could be there, to listen and offer advice, but when it came to the crunch Jack would be on his own.

For his part, Jack racked his brains to think of somebody he knew who had met Gail. It took him a while, but at last he came up with a name: Tamsin Reynolds, the publicity manager at Cormorant. The three of them had gone out for lunch after his signing at Strange Worlds some months earlier. Jack was not sure exactly what it would achieve, but he phoned Cormorant at once, hands shaking with nerves, stomach in a flutter.

He was put through to the publicity department and after a few moments a female voice said, "Hello?"

"Tamsin, hi, it's Jack Stone. I wanted to ask you—"

"Oh . . . um . . . hang on. This isn't Tamsin. It's Liz Peacock."

"Oh. Er . . . hi, Liz. It's Jack Stone here. Is Tamsin there?"

"No, Jack, she isn't. I'm afraid she's left."

"*Left?*" he exclaimed.

"Yeah, a couple of weeks ago. Didn't you know?"

"No, I didn't."

"Oh. Well, it's been in the cards for a while now. You've been . . . er . . . away though, haven't you?"

"Yeah," said Jack. "Look, Liz, is there any way I can contact Tamsin?"

"Well, I can give you her address in Sydney if it's urgent."

Jack wasn't sure he'd heard right. "Did you say Sydney? Sydney, Australia?"

"Yes. She and her boyfriend have emigrated there."

"You're joking!"

"No. He got offered a really good job, so she went with him."

"Bloody hell, I don't believe this."

"I know," said Liz cheerfully. "Jammy what-not. All that lovely sunshine. Listen, Jack, we're a bit upside down just now with Tamsin redistributing her workload, but if there's anything I can help you with . . ."

"Er . . . no. It's Tamsin I have to speak to. Could you give me her address and phone number?"

"I can give you an address, but I don't have a phone number for her. Hang on a minute."

Jack wrote down the address and thanked her. That afternoon he wrote Tamsin a letter, and then, over the course of the next few months, three more.

She never wrote back.

These things have a way of sealing themselves, he thought, of covering their tracks, of blocking every available exit. He supposed that was the way it had to be, the only way that equilibrium could be maintained. And yet that didn't stop him from trying to find answers, hunting for the keys to unlock the succession of doors that had been slammed in his face. As soon as he felt well enough, he got on the tube and travelled from Archway to Seven Sisters. He felt exhausted when he reached the building where Gail had had her flat, as if he'd run a marathon, but the sight of the building excited him. It looked exactly as he remembered it. He trudged up the stairs, heart crashing with fatigue and expectation, and knocked on the so-familiar door. He waited, and at the sound of approaching footsteps a pulse began to thump quickly at the base of his throat, his tongue seemed to shrivel and curl like old leather.

The door opened.

A girl stood there—young, dark-haired, attractive.

But it wasn't Gail.

She smiled at Jack, though there was caution in her eyes. She kept the door three-quarters closed, shielding her body, prepared to slam it in his face if need be.

"Hello?" she said.

"Oh . . . er . . . hi. I was looking for Gail Reeves." (Jack had found out from his Aunt Georgina that Reeves had been his great grandmother's maiden name.) "I thought she lived here."

The girl shrugged and smiled apologetically. She still looked cautious. She pushed the door a little further closed. " 'Fraid not. Sorry."

Jack had to resist an urge to thrust out an arm to stop the door from closing fully. Hoping he didn't sound and look as desperate as he felt, he said, "Do you know if she *used* to live here?"

The girl shrugged again, evidently eager to end this conversation. "I've no idea. I don't think so. As far as I know, I'm the first owner."

"How long have *you* lived here?" Jack asked, trying to keep his voice steady.

The girl frowned. Caution was turning rapidly to suspicion. "I don't really think that's any business of yours."

"Is it longer than four months?"

"I'm sorry. I don't think I can help you. Good-bye."

The door closed in his face. Jack raised a furious fist, intending to pound on it until the girl opened up again. His hand hovered for a moment, knuckles turning white, and then fell limply, defeatedly, to his side. His stomach roiled, his chest felt tight, frustration squeezed his throat with cruel fingers. He turned and stumbled downstairs, sure he was about to be sick. However, as soon as he was out of the building and felt the air on his face, the feeling subsided.

He wondered whether to write the girl in the flat a letter, explain everything, but he never did. For a long time afterwards he felt a frequent urge to return to the flat, to stand on the opposite side of the road and look up at the lighted window in the desperate hope of seeing Gail pass across it. He knew what the implications of such an urge could lead to and so managed, not without a struggle, to resist. Soon after this he had a nervous breakdown, the effects of which lasted for almost four months, and returned to the hospital.

It was because of this that the release of *Splinter Kiss* in paperback was postponed from the spring to the summer.

He had returned to Beckford only once, in March, vowing it would be the last visit he would ever make there. Frank Dawson had driven him down, unannounced. He had paid a call on his Aunt Georgina, who had been so astonished and delighted to see him that she had uncharacteristically burst into tears. Knowing that his aunt had kept things ticking over with David Rookham, Jack had been to fetch his car and then had told Frank that he would be okay from there, that his friend should return to London. Frank had been reluctant, but Jack had insisted. "Okay," Frank said at last, "but you take care. Don't do anything daft." Jack assured him he wouldn't. He watched Frank drive away, then got into his Mini Cooper and drove to the church, parking outside its black iron gates.

It had been a cold windy day, the sky alternating between dark clouds and pale sunshine. Jack had pushed open the creaking black gate and turned left to walk along the path between the tombstones. The earliest of the stones, now so weathered and discoloured that they seemed a natural part of the landscape, dated from the 1860s. In contrast to this were black marble monuments, meticulously maintained, or grey-white stones so clean and new they seemed unreal.

Jack halted by his father's grave and looked down at it, suddenly wishing he'd thought to bring flowers. "Hi, Dad," he said. "I just came to say good-bye properly. I won't be coming back again."

He looked round as if to ensure no one had heard him. Tall grasses waved in the breeze; a tree rustled its leaves and Jack shivered, tugging the collar of his jacket up around his face. He strolled on along a path falling prey to weeds, allowing his instincts to lead him. It was an eerie sensation, like unearthing a route revealed in a dream, or a sustained and acute feeling of deja vu. He was almost surprised when he came to a halt before a stone half-concealed by undergrowth. He parted the damp grass and the dandelions to reveal carved letters clogged with moss and dirt. He stamped on the grass around the stone to flatten it, then crouched down and began gouging out the moss, revealing the message.

It was as he had expected, though he nevertheless began to shudder even more violently, as if the temperature had suddenly dropped like a stone. He heard whispering behind him, then he actually felt a shadow pass over his back like a blanket before it crawled up the stone, darkening its message. Startled, he spun round . . . but the shadow was simply a dark cloud bruising the sky, the whispering merely the sound of wind in the thin dry grass. He turned back to the stone, heart hammering. Where the moss had been, the stone was pale, like flesh. He murmured the inscribed words to himself, giving voice to the epitaph.

"In loving memory of Alice Stone. Born fifteenth July nineteen thirty-eight. Died tenth October nineteen seventy. And . . . and Gail Stone. Born and died tenth October nineteen seventy." His voice faltered, became a fractured whisper. "Mother and daughter, at peace together. Loved and missed forever, never forgotten."

His eyes blurred with tears. He swiped them away with his sleeve, sniffed, cleared his throat. He reached out with both hands to touch the stone, as if to ensure it was solid. He remained in that position for perhaps a minute, then he expelled a huge sigh and stood up, brushing grass seeds from the legs of his jeans. Abruptly, he turned and walked away, resisting the urge—even at the gate—to look back. He got into his car, started the engine and drove off. Less than four hours later he was back in London.

As the train slowed on its approach to Leicester Square, Jack stuffed the letter back into his pocket and stood up. He eased himself through the crush of hot damp bodies to get to the doors, grimacing at the reek of stale flesh comingled with various aftershaves and perfumes. Staring out at the rushing walls of the tunnel, he surreptitiously slipped two fingers between the buttons of his shirt and fingered the tender spot on his stomach, which was an angry crisscrossing mass of scar tissue. Touching his healing wounds reassured him in an odd way, for it seemed to parallel his inner wounds, to indicate that they too were healing.

The train hurtled into brightness and clamour, its brakes screeching. A sea of faces, most of them blurs, impressions, flowed by, becoming more distinct as the train dwindled to a halt. The doors opened and Jack tumbled out onto the platform, barely managing to keep his balance. Somewhere, underlying the din of the busy station, he heard the haunting primal sound of a didgeridoo. He began to walk, passing a large poster on the wall advertising the paperback release of *Splinter Kiss* with barely a glance. Raising his head to sniff the faint draught of cool air from above, he headed toward the light.

GRAVE
INTENT
DEBORAH LEBLANC

In all their years at the funeral home, Janet and Michael Savoy have never seen anything like the viewing for nineteen-year-old Thalia Stevenson. That's because they have never seen a Gypsy funeral before, complete with rituals, incantations and a very special gold coin placed beneath the dead girl's hands....

When that coin is stolen, a horror is unleashed. If the Savoys don't find the coin and return it to Thalia's grave before the rising of the second sun, someone in their family—perhaps their little daughter—will die a merciless death. The ticking away of each hour brings the Savoy family closer to a gruesome, inescapable nightmare. Only one thing is certain—Gypsies always have their revenge...even the dead ones.

- -